# PRAISE FOR WEN



## The Tale of Halcyon Crane

MINNESOTA BOOK AWARD, 2011, AND INDIE NEXT PICK

"Webb offers an engaging modern gothic tale with a strong female protagonist and well-done suspense. Fans of Mary Higgins Clark and Barbara Michaels and readers who like supernatural elements in their fiction will enjoy this debut."

—*Library Journal*



"Debut novelist Wendy Webb gives both Bram Stoker and Stephen King a run for their travel budget, inventing an island in the Great Lakes that can't be matched for pristine natural beauty, richness of history, touristic amenities . . . and sheer supernatural terror. . . . The novel . . . gives a more generous account of how the spirit of a beautiful place can complexly affect a human being, for both good and ill. Wendy Webb is a professional journalist, first and foremost. Like those journalistic masters Dickens and Twain before her, she knows that to write good travel prose, you must give a vivid account of both the demons you find along the way and the demons you bring along with you."

—Michael Alec Rose, *BookPage*

"This thrilling, modern ghost story will keep you reading straight through to the surprising end!"

—Midwest Independent Booksellers Association

"Entertaining to say the least. Sensational . . . Webb's page-turner is a guilty pleasure best suited for a lakeside cabin's bedstand."

—Megan Doll, *The Minneapolis Star Tribune*

"Booksellers are loving *Halcyon Crane*, which has been selected by three Independent Booksellers' associations—national and Midwestern—as worthy of special promotion. . . . Webb includes all the classic ghostly elements in her novel, but she gives the book a contemporary spin with a strong female protagonist."

—Mary Ann Grossman, *St. Paul Pioneer Press*

"This is what reading is supposed to be like: A story that comes across so well, so seamlessly that it is like a brain movie, that reminds you of the first books that kidnapped your attention. Webb has crazy chops as a storyteller, and plays this one exactly right. And there are scenes that are so, so visual that it is like someone is reading the book to you while you lie there with your eyes closed. This is one of my favorites this year."

—Minnesota Reads

"Although not usually a fan of ghost stories, I immensely enjoyed *'The Tale of Halcyon Crane.'* With intriguing characters, a vivid setting and gripping storytelling, this novel contains the ideal blend of sinister and charm."

—*Cityview*, Iowa's Independent Weekly

"I love a good, spooky ghost story that carries you deep into the darkest night and raises goose bumps and neck hair. First-time novelist Wendy Webb's book, *The Tale of Halcyon Crane*, does all those things with the seamless intricacy of a clockmaker and the silky smoothness of a baby's cheek. Webb hits every note just right. It's hard to read a story like this and not compare the author to Stephen King, so I'm not going to do much of that, other than to say Webb carries a lot of the same power in her words."

—*Seattle Post-Intelligencer*

"*The Tale of Halcyon Crane* is a wonderful gothic complete with ghosts and witches, graveyards and dreams. It whisks the reader up and into its magic from the first page. Captivating and haunting, this debut proves Wendy Webb is a very gifted storyteller."

—*New York Times* bestselling author MJ Rose

"Wendy Webb immediately captured my attention with her amazingly descriptive language. I could envision exactly what Hallie was seeing, experiencing, and even feeling. The description of the fog and the effect it had on Hallie was simply chilling and set the tone for the whole story to come."

—LibraryGirl Reads

"*The Tale of Halcyon Crane* throbs with the threat of menace; this is an atmospheric, gothic story reminiscent of *The Turn of the Screw* and had me racing to the finish late into the night to find out what happens next. Read this book."

—Misfit Salon

"Wendy Webb has created a wonderful gothic mystery in this novel, full of secrets and betrayals. It's definitely creepy—this is not a book I would want to read late at night, during a thunderstorm. I found it to be deliciously haunting with incredible atmosphere. I thoroughly enjoyed the process of reading this book, of watching this meticulously crafted tale unfold. I had to battle dueling impulses while reading—part of me wanted to rush through it, to get to the end, while the other wanted to savor every carefully drawn word. This is a book that you'll really want to experience. I'm very sad that it's over, and that Webb doesn't have an extensive gothic mystery backlist I can immediately devour. All I can say is I'll be watching Wendy Webb's future career with a lot of interest."

—S. Krishna's Books

## The Fate of Mercy Alban

Book-of-the-Month Club, IndieNext pick, five weeks on the Heartland Indie Bestseller List

"Webb has cooked up another confection filled with family secrets coming to light in the Midwest. . . . Magic and mystery intertwine in Webb's engaging Midwestern gothic."

—Kristine Huntley, *Booklist*

"If Stephen King and Sarah Waters had a love child, it would be Wendy Webb."

—*New York Times* bestselling author MJ Rose

"This second novel by Minnesota Book Award-winning writer Wendy Webb has all the elements of a downright haunting story—and it is. Be prepared to be scared—and entertained."

—*Minneapolis Star Tribune*

"If you're craving a good old-fashioned ghost story to scare you on these cold nights, this is it. There's a big house with secret passages (think Glensheen in Duluth), a body that may have left the crypt, a beautiful apparition dancing on the lakeshore in the moonlight, a hidden manuscript, a book of curses and an old relative who may be insane."

—*St. Paul Pioneer Press*

"I haven't picked up a thriller/horror novel this good in ages. This is the kind of book that gets your pulse racing as you frantically flip to the next chapter to find out what happens."

—No Map Provided

"Webb is amazing at writing a spooky, gothic atmosphere that will chill you to the bone. This is definitely a novel you don't want to read late at night while you're alone."

—S. Krishna's Books

"Ghosts, witchcraft, family secrets, money and power, and pure evil run through this book. I certainly enjoyed it! A fun read and sure to keep you turning the pages. And you just have to keep reading to find out who the heck Mercy Alban is—you'll be fascinated by the story this author weaves."

—Bookalicious Book Reviews

"This is a first by Wendy Webb for me, but if anything else she writes is even remotely like this book then she has a devoted reader and fan in me. I was hooked from the very first page and I refused to let go. Honestly, by the time I reached the final page I did not want it to be over. I felt like I hadn't explored every hidden passageway and secret tunnel that Alban House held, and I wanted to spend more time there. I honestly have not read a book that kept my attention like this in a long time."

—Dwell in Possibility Books

"I was spellbound. Webb's novel had me hooked from the get-go and I would not put it down until I had finished the last page."

—A Bookish Way of Life

"Webb has crafted a modern take on a classic genre—the Gothic ghost story. Family secrets, haunted houses, family curses with a little witchcraft thrown in as well. Webb's plotting is intricate and keeps us guessing with many red herrings and switchbacks on the way."

—A Bookworm's World

"Filled with multiple plot lines including a budding romance, family secrets, and a hint of the supernatural, it is hard to put this book down once you start reading. The ending to this tale almost leaves you to think there might be a sequel . . . and I would love that!!!"

—Always With a Book

"*The Fate of Mercy Alban* is a chilling, good read! This book just might make you glad you don't live in an old, haunted mansion."

—Cheryl's Book Nook

## The Vanishing

"Webb once again mines the secrets of an old mansion for an effective contemporary supernatural thriller."

—*Publishers Weekly*

"A brisk thriller tinged with gothic elements. . . . Careening through séances and ghostly encounters leaves the reader breathless."

—*Kirkus Reviews*

"Webb expertly builds suspense and offers a thought-provoking tease in the final pages."

—*Booklist*

"[The] opening line of Wendy Webb's contemporary Gothic thriller, *The Vanishing*, pays homage to du Maurier's classic [*Rebecca*]. But Webb infuses her narrator, Julia Bishop, with modern sensibilities, and manipulates the genre's melodrama skillfully."

—*Minneapolis Star Tribune*

"A deliciously complex blend of psychological suspense and ghost story, *The Vanishing* is pitch-perfect on every note, from its mansion setting in the pine-scented northern wilderness, to the secrets and specters lurking around every corner."

—Erin Hart, author of *The Book of Killowen*

"The haunting twists and turns of *The Vanishing* left me as breathless as the beautiful setting of Havenwood itself. Reminiscent of the classics *The Haunting of Hill House* and *Rebecca*, this novel grabbed me on the first page and didn't let go. A compelling, frightening, deeply satisfying tale that is as rich in setting as it is in storytelling."

—Suzanne Palmieri, author of *The Witch of Little Italy*

# THE END OF
# TEMPERANCE DARE

## OTHER TITLES BY WENDY WEBB

*The Tale of Halcyon Crane*

*The Fate of Mercy Alban*

*The Vanishing*

# THE END OF TEMPERANCE DARE

*A Novel*

WENDY WEBB

This is a work of fiction. Names, characters, organizations, places, events, and incidents are either products of the author's imagination or are used fictitiously.



Published by Lake Union Publishing, Seattle

www.apub.com



ISBN-13: 9781477824115
ISBN-10: 1477824111

Cover design by Emily Mahon

Printed in the United States of America

*For Joan Marie Maki Webb*
*I miss you every day, Mom.*

*Fear is pain arising from the anticipation of evil.*

—Aristotle

# PROLOGUE

## Cliffside Tuberculosis Sanatorium, 1952

They gave her the bed by the window, the one closest to the toy box. That was something, at least. But the very fact that she was there at all, away from home, away from her father, her sisters, her dolls, terrified the girl. Other children were there; she wasn't the only one. But this did little to soothe her.

Father didn't tell her he was leaving her here, that she'd be staying. She thought they were on an outing together, just the two of them, something rare and wonderful. But it wasn't an outing. He had brought her here to leave her in this place, with all of these sick and dying people. She'd clutched his hand as they walked through the foyer to the doctor's office, past patients with sunken eyes and ashen skin, their robes hanging loosely around them, living skeletons who had been nearly consumed by their illnesses. She watched as one man coughed into a handkerchief, staining it bright red with blood. She turned her face toward her father's trousers, not wanting to see any more. Death lived within these walls; she could feel it hanging in the air, as tangible as the fog outside.

As she sat on the table in the doctor's office, Father had explained to her that she had contracted a deadly disease, the disease this place was built to treat. As his daughter, she would receive the best care in the world here, he said, she shouldn't worry about that. She cried, telling him she wasn't sick at all, that she didn't belong here, begging him to take her home. But he wouldn't listen, convinced, no doubt, by the doctor and nurses that she had to remain.

She'd watched from her window as her father got into their black car and drove out of sight. She wondered if she'd ever see him again or if she was doomed to stay here, at Cliffside, for the rest of her life.

The coughing at night was among the worst of it. She'd awaken in an inky black room and hear the rustling of the other children in the ward, barking like seals and crying out for their mothers. She'd put her head under the covers and curl into a ball, trying to make those sounds go away. And when she set her mind to it, she could make them go away. She had learned this in her few short years on this earth.

It was there, in the dark under the covers, that she got an idea. If she didn't feel sick, maybe some of the other children didn't, either. She had stayed away from everyone when she first arrived, cowering by herself, not wanting contact with these terrible people and their sunken eyes. But now, after so many days of inactivity, being forced to lie on her bed for hours on end, she was bored and restless. Maybe she could get one or two of the other children to go outside to play. Maybe they could sneak, undetected, into the yard. She had spied a ball there earlier in the day, as she peered out from her window.

She reached out and poked the girl in the bed next to hers, one of the ones who wasn't coughing.

"Come on," she whispered to her. "Let's go outside."

The girl scowled. "But we're supposed to stay in bed."

"Do you do everything you're supposed to do?"

The girl shook her head.

"Then come with me and we'll go have a little fun. I'm bored silly and I'll bet you are, too. We won't get in trouble. My father owns this place."

The girl smiled and slipped out of bed.

Soon five children were stealing their way down the third-floor stairs, then through the hallway where the adults' rooms were, and then down the grand staircase to the main floor. It was dark, but the children could see the wall of windows leading out to the veranda and the lawn beyond. They crept toward it, not making a sound. They were almost there.

When she opened the door leading outside and got a faceful of the pure lake air, she knew this had been the right thing to do. They all ran into the grass, laughing quietly.

She took the hand of the girl next to her, who took another child's hand, and so on, and soon they had made a ring and were dancing.

"Ring around the rosy," they sang, bright smiles on their faces, their eyes lit up with the thrill of their illicit nighttime adventure, "pocket full of posy, ashes, ashes, we all fall down!"

And she smiled as they fell into the sweet-smelling grass. She lay there for a bit, looking up at the millions of stars in the sky. The moon was full and bright, shining down on her. Maybe this wouldn't be so bad after all.

But in a moment, when she scrambled to her feet, she saw that the others didn't get up with her. They just lay in the grass, lifeless as dolls, their limbs askew, their faces frozen. She nudged one of them with her foot. Nothing. She sighed. Not this again.

Oh, well. She'd find some new playmates tomorrow.

# CHAPTER 1

As we turned off the main highway and made our way down a meandering road lined with massive pines, the rain tapered off and fog crept in, enveloping the car so heavily that it nearly erased the trees from view. I could just make out a bough here and there, reaching toward me out of the whiteness.

"My goodness," I said to the driver, my voice wavering a bit. "This fog . . ."

"It's nothing to worry about, miss," he said, catching my eye in the rearview mirror. "We get a lot of it here on the shore. Makes the drive a bit tricky. Fog can send people right over the edge of the cliff, and has. But I've driven this road so many times, I could drive it blind. I'll deliver you there, safe and sound."

I rested my head against the back of the seat and exhaled, glad I couldn't see exactly how closely the road followed the shoreline, which, on this part of the lake, was a rocky cliff higher than I wanted to think about. I was in no danger here, I told myself. No danger at all.

I had been clutching my purse in my lap for the entire trip, and I opened it yet again to check for the letter. Yes, there it was.

I was in this car on this foggy road because I was headed to a new job. Director of Cliffside Manor, a Retreat for Artists and Writers, founded in the 1950s by local philanthropist and patron of the arts Chester Dare. Of all the things I ever imagined doing with my life, this was not one of them. Yet, here I was, taking the reins of this venerable institution because its longtime director, Penelope Dare, Chester's daughter, was retiring. I somehow managed to beat out hundreds of other applicants and land this job.

That may have had something to do with the fact that I'd had occasion to meet Penelope Dare twenty years ago, after the suspicious death of her father and sister. I was a journalist covering the crime beat at the time, and the case of Chester and Chamomile Dare was one of the first I'd worked on as a young reporter. I supposed Miss Penny, as she was known, was now nearing the age that her father had been all of those years ago.

Penelope Dare had inherited a massive fortune when her father and sister died, but according to local lore, had never again left the Cliffside property. She had spent the intervening years, between when I first met her and the day I was bumping along in the backseat of a chauffeur-driven car to see her again, devoting her life to carrying on her father's work of running a fellowship for artists and writers, a retreat where creative types could focus on their craft without any distractions from the outside world. Cliffside was nationally, even internationally, known, with artists and writers competing for the fellowships that would allow them to spend two or four weeks at Cliffside.

I had grown up in the area, knowing Cliffside's reputation, and had seen the Dare sisters and their father around town from time to time. They were an elegant family, the women so dignified in their beautiful clothes. I remember once running into one of the sisters on the street in front of the drugstore—I was about ten years old. She'd bent down and told me what a beautiful little girl I was. I never forgot that. It wasn't something I heard often. I had been abandoned as an infant, left in a local orphanage by a mother I never knew, and had grown up in a series of foster homes before being adopted when I was twelve. Suffice it to say there wasn't a lot of affection in my early life. As I rode along toward Cliffside, I still could scarcely grasp that the little girl without a home or a real family was going to be living in the most elegant and beautiful place in the county, carrying on the work of the Dares. I couldn't believe my luck.

Frankly, I needed a change. My nerves had been on edge for months, an indefinable sense of dread enveloping me as heavily as this fog. People said to trust one's instincts, and mine had always been spot on, but lately those instincts had been leading me astray. I had become skittish and fearful of, well, almost everything. I had been having horrible dreams, about death and danger. I attributed them to my job. I encountered horrible things almost every day—death, murder, unspeakable things—and it was seeping into my nightmares.

It had cost me my job at the newspaper, I'm ashamed to admit. Not that I blamed my boss. You can't have a scared rabbit as an investigative reporter, he said to me, and he was right. I had lost whatever it was that had made me good at my job, and I couldn't explain why.

The doctors told me it was a cumulative effect from all of the horrible stories I had covered over the years. Post-traumatic stress disorder, they said. Crime had been my beat, and as such, I had been deeply involved in all manner of horror and heartbreak in our corner of the world. School shootings. Teenage suicides. Domestic violence. A serial killer preying on young boys. I think a piece of me died every time I had to go to a crime scene while that monster was still on the loose.

I had seen too much death, and it was catching up with me. I felt, however irrational this may sound, that death was an entity unto itself, that there really was a Grim Reaper out there somewhere, and he was coming for me. It haunted me at night, made me wonder what manner of evil was lurking outside my windows. But, PTSD? I didn't agree with that diagnosis. That was for people who had been through real trauma themselves. Not for people reporting on the trauma.

What I did not know then, but do now, is that something wicked was indeed wending its way into my life, only I was too caught up in my own circumstances to notice.

I was busy looking for another job. Oh, I knew my former boss at the newspaper would give me a good recommendation and, with my experience and body of work behind me, I could land a job at just about any paper in the country. But I couldn't stomach the idea of doing that anymore. Chasing crime. Hunting down evil.

So, when I heard on the news about Miss Penny's decision to retire as the director of Cliffside, a possibility glistened on the horizon. Overseeing a place where writers and artists came for solitude and creativity seemed as far away from crime reporting as it was possible to get. I could feel my whole body relaxing at the thought of it.

It was strange—I had thought about that place often over the years. I'd catch myself daydreaming about the house and grounds on many occasions. I was oddly intrigued by the possibility of working there.

When I saw the notice that she was retiring, I wondered if Miss Penny had found her replacement or if she was still looking. So I picked up the phone and called her. She remembered me right away.

"How nice to hear from you after all these years," Penelope Dare said to me, her voice crackling with age. "I've followed your career, Eleanor—you've made quite a name for yourself. Your articles are riveting."

"That's very kind, thank you," I said, "but you may not have heard, I've left the paper."

"Oh?"

"It's true," I said. "And actually, that's the reason I'm calling. I'm wondering if you've already found a director to step in when you retire, or if the position is still open."

"Hundreds have applied," she said, clearing her throat. "I haven't made my decision yet. Are you calling to apply for the job?"

I winced. Hundreds. What were the chances she'd consider me? But I pressed on. "Well, yes," I said. "I am. I'd love the chance to talk with you about it."

She was silent for a moment and then said, "What a delightfully interesting idea."

And so, we talked. I asked her why she was retiring, and she told me age was taking its toll. She had devoted her life to this pursuit and now she was ready for a rest, it was as simple as that. She asked me why I was interested in being the director of Cliffside, and I told her I needed a change and the thought of working with artists and writers was appealing. More than that, Cliffside itself seemed to be pulling me toward it, I told her. I had been able to think of little else since I'd heard the news of her retirement.

As we were talking, Cliffside swam into my mind. It was a magnificent building sitting on forty acres of pristine forestland with hundreds of feet of Lake Superior shoreline. It had its own private system of trails through the woods and along the water. There was a boathouse with sailboats, kayaks, and a powerboat. From Cliffside's veranda overlooking the water, you could see up and down the shoreline for miles. It was quite spectacular.

Living in a beautiful place like Cliffside, hosting artists and writers—compared to what I'd been through recently—sounded like heaven.

We ended our conversation with her deciding to take some time to think about it and consider other candidates. I worried for days that she might not choose me. It was an awfully big responsibility, stepping into her shoes and running the institution her father had created.

But at the end of that week, I got the call. I was to be the new director of Cliffside Manor, starting in a month's time. The letter of agreement arrived in the mail the next day.

I remember hanging up the phone after that call and feeling a tingle of excitement sizzle through me. I was starting a whole new chapter of my life.

# CHAPTER 2

We rounded the last bend, and Cliffside came into view, materializing out of the fog. I had first seen it twenty years earlier, but I still gasped at the sight of it. It was an enormous, sprawling, white-stone structure with a red-tiled roof, its front dominated by a series of archways that ran the length of the building. It was three stories tall, and I noticed mullioned windows on the upper floors. I thought I detected movement in one of those windows but couldn't be sure. It might have been a curtain swaying in the breeze.

The place had a Mediterranean feel—the archways, the white stone, the tiled roof—and it reminded me, of all things, of a golf club where I had attended a wedding some years earlier.

Miss Penny was standing under one of the archways when we pulled up, and as we rolled to a stop, I was struck by how the years had aged her. The ramrod straight posture I remembered her possessing—even in the midst of her grief—had given way to the curvature of age. She seemed smaller now, diminished somehow. Her hair, pulled into a severe bun, had faded from mousey brown to gray. But her bright smile was warm and welcoming, in stark contrast to the gloom outside.

"You've arrived!" she called to me as I stepped out of the car. "Welcome! Welcome back to Cliffside."

The driver dealt with my bags as Miss Penny walked over to me.

"It's wonderful to see you again, Miss Harper," she said, extending her hand.

"It's lovely to see you, too," I said, taking her hand in mine, her skin paper-thin and brittle, as though it might disintegrate at the slightest touch. I noticed the lines surrounding her eyes, trails of the sadness and grief she had experienced. "It's been a long time."

"Twenty years and sixty-seven days since that horrible morning Father and Milly were taken from us," she said, smiling a sad smile.

My stomach did a quick flip as I remembered the scene of the accident, the car smashed to pieces at the bottom of the cliff, Chester Dare's eyes wide open, his hands still gripping the steering wheel, Chamomile thrown several yards away, her neck skewed at an odd angle. I shook my head to dissipate the vision.

"I'm sure they'd be very proud of what you've accomplished in their memory," I said. "This place, what you're doing for the arts. Carrying on your father's work."

"Father was a great patron of the arts, and Milly herself was a poet." She smiled. "I do what I can to keep their memory alive.

"But, no more talk of that now," she went on, waving her hand as if to sweep away the memories. "Today is a happy day." She gestured toward a set of massive double doors. "Let's go inside. I'll show you your new home."

We walked through the doors and into an enormous foyer, its pinkish marble floors gleaming. There stood a man and a woman, both dressed in black, waiting, it seemed, for me.

"I'd like you to meet Harriet and Mr. Baines," Miss Penny said to me. "They are in charge of the household here at Cliffside. The maids, the cooks, the gardeners, and the driver—all under their watchful eye. Generally, Harriet runs the inside of the house, and Mr. Baines runs the outside."

She turned to them. "Our new director, Eleanor Harper."

Harriet smiled warmly at me. "It's a pleasure, ma'am. Miss Penny has spoken so highly of you. Should you have need of anything, anything at all, please let me know."

Mr. Baines took a step forward and bowed slightly. "We're all very glad to have you at Cliffside, Miss Harper," he said. I noticed a slight accent buoying his words.

"I'm glad to be here," I said, my stomach tightening. "I hope you won't mind bearing with me while I learn the ropes."

"Not at all, ma'am," Harriet said. "I'm sure you'll do just fine."

They both stood there, expectant smiles on their faces. I wasn't sure what I was supposed to do or say next.

Miss Penny broke the silence. "I'm going to give our new director a tour and help her get settled," she said. "We'll have dinner at six thirty in the main dining room, with cocktails at five thirty."

"Very good, ma'am," Harriet said, and she and Mr. Baines shuffled off to points unknown.

Miss Penny took my arm, and we began our walk around the enormous house.

The foyer spilled down a couple of stairs to a sunken drawing room filled with sofas and overstuffed chairs arranged in groups. A piano sat in one corner, a fireplace in the other. Heavy Oriental rugs lay on the floors. Beyond the drawing room, there was a smaller salon, and on the opposite end of the building, I could see through the wall of floor-to-ceiling windows onto the veranda. A lawn stretched beyond that before disappearing into the fog.

"My father built Cliffside in 1925 as a sanatorium for TB patients," she said as we walked from room to room.

Tuberculosis. I remembered that. "He built it mainly for his employees, is that right?"

Miss Penny nodded. "He never came down with TB, but many of his employees did. It was a dreadful disease, just dreadful."

"We didn't talk about this back when I was first here—as you said, there were other things to cover—but now I'm curious. Why didn't they just send people to a hospital? Why build a special facility?"

"The treatment for TB consisted mainly of isolation, rest, and clean air," she explained. "They had to isolate the patients from the rest of the population because the disease was so infectious, and the treatment took months, if not years. TB was so rampant at the time that, if the patients simply went to a hospital, they'd be clogging up all of the beds for months and years, leaving no room for patients with other ills. It wasn't feasible."

"The treatment took months?"

"I can't imagine it, being away from one's family all of that time, in isolation," she said, a sad tone in her voice. "There wasn't a TB sanatorium in the region, so my father built one, thinking there was no place on earth with cleaner air and a more relaxing atmosphere than we have right here. It was something truly wonderful that he did. TB was a real plague in his time. The disease was a killer. Sanatoriums sprang up all across the country, but the cure rate wasn't very high. They used to call these places 'waiting rooms for death.'"

A shiver ran through me.

She pointed to a framed, black-and-white print hanging on the opposite wall. "During the renovation, we found some old photos that we've put up."

I walked over to get a better look. It was a shot of the Cliffside veranda lined with patients lying on chaise lounges, covered in white blankets.

I squinted. "There must be sixty people out there," I said.

"The facility could house twice that," she said. "The second floor had semi-private and private rooms, and the third floor was just one big, open space lined with beds, like a hospital ward. That's where the children were."

We crossed the room and went through a door leading outside to the veranda. "If it were a nicer day, you could see down the shoreline for miles from here. It really is quite spectacular. Apparently, it was one reason my father chose this location."

"I suppose he thought a nice view would alleviate the boredom," I said. I could almost see those patients from the photograph come to life here, lying on their chaises where we stood, nurses tending to them.

"If you're interested, Harriet could tell you some tales from when it was a sanatorium. My father kept Milly and me far away from the property in those days. Isolation of the patients was the whole point, and he had no intention of putting us in harm's way. But Harriet's mother was here. She has heard a lifetime of stories about Cliffside."

A possibility scratched at the back of my mind, the history of the place floating in the air around me like so many ghosts. An old TB sanatorium, turned into a beautiful retreat. It sounded like the stuff of a good feature article. I was giving up crime reporting, I told myself, but I didn't have to give up writing altogether. I decided to look into it and see what I could dig up.

"What happened to Cliffside when they cured TB?" I asked. "It wasn't a retreat right away, if I'm remembering correctly."

Miss Penny nodded. "The sanatorium closed in the early 1950s. After it had been thoroughly disinfected, my father sold our family home in town and we moved in here. That's when my father got the idea to turn it into a retreat for writers and artists. It became his life's passion. We were all so happy until—" She stopped short. Tears glistened in her eyes. "They were my life, you see," she said. "When they were gone, I had to do something. I had to find a purpose."

"So, you carried on your father's work," I said, getting the full picture now. An image of Penelope Dare floated through my mind, the way she had looked twenty years earlier. So stoic, so matter-of-fact, her grief never on display. But I knew it was always simmering just below the surface. And I could understand the need to throw oneself into a project, to channel that grief into something tangible and real.

We walked back through the doors and into the main drawing room, where we found Harriet holding a tray with a teapot and two cups.

"Some tea, ma'am?" she said. "I thought it would be just the thing on such a soggy day."

"Oh, thank you, Harriet," Miss Penny said. "I think we'll take it up in my office. We've got some matters to discuss, forms to fill out, that sort of thing."

She nodded, and then she was off with the tray, presumably heading upstairs to where I remember there being a study. Miss Penny and I lingered awhile, looking at photos hung on the walls in the main rooms, before walking up the long, wide circular staircase to the second floor, where she led me into a room lined with bookshelves. A heavy, antique desk sat facing a bay window with a built-in seat that overlooked the back lawn. A leather armchair and ottoman sat next to a fireplace that had been laid but not lit. Harriet's tea tray sat on the end table.

"This is the director's office," Miss Penny said, pouring tea into both of our cups and handing one to me. "Your office, now. A little better than the bullpen at the newspaper, I'll wager?"

"Slightly." I smiled and took a sip of the tea, remembering the chaos and noise of a crowded newsroom when deadlines neared. It was a stark contrast to this quiet haven.

We spent the next hour or so wrangling with paperwork—tax and insurance forms, an employment contract—but with that done, Miss Penny poured us both another cup of tea and sank into the armchair, crossing her legs.

"We should talk about the job itself," she said, taking a sip of her tea. "What you'll be doing day to day."

"I'm still not sure exactly what's required," I said. "I understand that the artists come for a month's time?"

"Two to four weeks," she said. "We do six sessions each year. Everyone arrives on the same day and leaves on the same day, generally. It's less confusing for us that way. The last group of fellows went home three weeks ago, and the new batch will arrive next Friday. I thought you could use some time to get acquainted with the place before the divas descend." She chuckled at this.

"Divas?"

"Oh, that's a bit of an exaggeration, of course. Most of the time, the guests are quite pleasant. Quiet, hardworking. Once in a while, though . . ." She chuckled again and shook her head.

"I get it," I said. "There's always one in every group, isn't there?"

"Especially when you're dealing with creative types. But here, they're the recipients of a fellowship. They're selected, in other words. Most of them are grateful. They're coming here for solitude, for the opportunity to focus on, as you said, nothing but their writing or their art. But they're also coming for the chance to meet other artists and writers."

"Why do you have two- and four-week sessions? Why not just choose one length of stay?"

"Many of the fellows have day jobs," she told me. "Not everyone can get away for four weeks, so we give them a choice."

It made sense.

"What's a typical day like?"

"There are no hard-and-fast rules," she said. "This is their time to focus solely on their artistic pursuits, and it's our job to make it as easy as possible for them to do that."

I nodded.

"We serve breakfast and lunch in the winter garden—"

"Winter garden?" I interrupted her. I wasn't sure what, exactly, a winter garden was.

She smiled, and I got the impression she not only understood the question but had heard it before. "Old, wealthy families of the past who lived in places where the snow flies would often include a winter garden in their grand homes," she explained. "A room made entirely of glass, even the ceiling."

"So they could have gardens in the winter."

"Exactly, my dear. You can see why Father wanted to include one at Cliffside. Patients were here year-round, of course, and while they could enjoy the outside gardens in the other months, winter would've been very bleak indeed without some greenery and blossoms to perk things up," she said. "Father believed the plants also helped purify the air in the house—he was ahead of his time on that one."

She took a sip of tea and continued. "Anyway, it's bright and sunny there most mornings. We serve breakfast from seven to nine thirty. Some of the fellows come, some don't. Whatever they want to do is fine. We keep coffee and light snacks available there all day, but Harriet will take care of that so you don't need to worry about it. Lunch is buffet style. Sandwiches, soups, that sort of thing. Harriet and her kitchen help will set it up for the fellows and for you, too. Again, nothing for you to worry about it."

It sounded easy enough.

"The day is theirs to do with what they will," she went on. "Work alone in their suites, explore the house and the grounds, take a dip in the pool. Whatever they'd like."

"Aren't they supposed to be working, though?" I asked. "Isn't that the whole idea?"

She nodded. "Yes, but in my experience, I've found that inspiration can come in a variety of ways, not only when one has pen and paper in hand. Walking through the forest to puzzle out plot points is working. Taking a dip to refresh the senses is working."

"I see."

"The one thing we do ask of them is to gather at the end of the day," she said. "We have it set up for five thirty. People assemble in the drawing room—artists and writers aren't the most punctual group, so we wait until everyone has arrived—and then, whoever wishes to join in will dine together in the dining room. One of the major benefits of Cliffside is the chance to commune with like-minded artists, sharing thoughts about their day's work, philosophies about art and writing. Even political discourse. There are some truly remarkable discussions to be had.

"You'll act as a sort of casual moderator for these gatherings," she went on. "All it really entails is getting the discussion going by asking people about the progress they've made that day, what they're working on, and so on."

I could do that.

"How do you select the people who get to come?" I asked. "I'm sure you're inundated with applications."

"When my father ran Cliffside, he made the selections," she explained. "During my tenure, I made them. Now that you have taken the helm as the third director of Cliffside, you will make the selections."

I winced. "I don't know if I'm qualified to do that," I said.

"Oh, but you will be," she said, taking a sip of her tea. "I've made the selections and notified the next four groups of fellows. That will take you to the end of the year and, after that, you'll have the experience of running those sessions. You'll see what works and what doesn't. We start taking applications for the next year's sessions in October. You'll have until Christmas to choose the fellows for the coming year and schedule them."

I ran a hand through my hair, imagining mountains of applications to sift through. How could I possibly choose?

As if reading my thoughts, Miss Penny reached over and patted my hand. "It's not as complicated as you might think. I've set up a file for you of all the applications of this year's fellows. When you read through them, you'll see they have a certain consistency. A seriousness. You'll begin to pick it up, to discern who is worthy and who is not. I have a hunch you're going to take to this right away. That it will come naturally to you. That's why I hired you, Eleanor."

I supposed she was right, but the idea of "worthiness" didn't sit all that well with me.

"So, now that you've heard everything," she said, folding her hands in her lap, "do you think you can handle it?"

I leaned against the back of my chair and exhaled. "After years on the crime beat, it sounds like heaven. I can't tell you how much I appreciate this opportunity."

Miss Penny leaned over and covered my hand with her own. "I'm the one who appreciates it. And I'm delighted to repay all of the kindness you showed to me when Father and Milly passed away. You worked very hard to get to the truth of what happened, even after the police had given up and ruled it an accident. I never properly thanked you. It's been eating at me all of these years."

There was an intensity in her eyes that I couldn't quite define—anger? Perhaps she harbored some resentment that I wasn't able to get to the bottom of the deaths of her father and sister. But, if that was the case, why would she have asked me to take over for her at Cliffside?

# CHAPTER 3

Miss Penny had shown me to my suite and then left me to my own devices. I spent the afternoon unpacking and settling in. She had encouraged me to explore the house and grounds, but the fog, the drizzle, and the cold that had descended along with it made venturing out less than desirable. Every time I opened my door and looked up and down the hallway, intent on familiarizing myself with the place, a veritable shiver ran through me, and I shut the door again. It must have been a good ten degrees colder in the hall outside my room. So, I busied myself hanging some of my clothes in the closet and folding others into the dresser drawers, lining my shoes into neat rows, and arranging my toiletries on the vanity in my bathroom.

My suite was made up of three rooms. Through the door from the hallway was a sitting room with a writing desk (antique, I suspected) and chair, along with a small, plush sofa, armchair, and ottoman. A thick Berber rug lay on the wood floor. On the wall across from the sofa hung a flat-screen television, and on another, French doors opened onto a balcony that overlooked the back lawn and, I had to imagine because of the fog, the lake itself. Through an archway was the bedroom, with its ornate, antique four-poster bed covered with a thick down comforter in deep red with a delicate floral pattern running along the edges. A fireplace stood on one wall, a bay window with a seat covered by a thick cushion on the other. There was an enormous walk-in closet for my clothes, and a dresser and mirror that looked to be the same vintage as the bed. Through a doorway, I found the bathroom, with its deep whirlpool tub, glassed-in shower, and marble vanity.

As I was closing the last of my suitcases and tucking them in the back of my closet, I heard a clattering of footsteps outside my door and voices talking in hushed tones. I turned my head to listen but couldn't quite make out what they were saying. Miss Penny had said there was a staff of maids, a cleaning crew, and others who were in the house. I hadn't met them yet but knew they were here. Still, something she had said earlier was echoing in my ears.

"Harriet and Mr. Baines—do they live here at Cliffside, too?" I had asked her as we drank our tea in the director's office.

"They do." She nodded and took a sip. "They have their own house on the grounds."

"So, they don't live in the building."

"No," she said.

"Does anybody?" I asked. "Apart from me, I mean?"

"Well, the fellows live in the building, of course, when they're here," she said. "Most of the household help live off-site, but there are quarters off the kitchen for the cooks. Three of them are living there now."

"And you? I hope you're not leaving Cliffside completely just because you've handed over the reins to me."

She smiled a rather sad smile. "I live on the third floor," she said. "In the same room I shared with my sister."

I swallowed. "Oh, I'm glad of that," I said, my voice wavering just a bit. "I was worried I'd be alone in this big, old place until the guests arrive."

Something about the way she looked at me then sent a shiver up my spine.

Now, as I snuggled into my armchair by the fireplace and drew up an afghan that had been draped across the footstool, I was thinking that, even if you excluded the rest of the house and the grounds, this suite of rooms alone was the nicest place I'd ever lived. My job at the newspaper had been so all-consuming for so many years, I'd had neither the time nor the inclination to decorate my one-bedroom apartment or even go as far as finding something more comfortable than the dingy building where I had been living.

After gazing into the flames for a while, I noticed I was fidgeting with my necklace and my feet were tapping against each other. Apparently, relaxation hadn't been on my to-do list for quite some time. I tried to reach back in my mind to a time when I'd had nothing to do, and I couldn't think of when that might have been. I had worked all the time, even weekends, when I was deeply into an absorbing case. But here at Cliffside, I had no case to solve, no crime to get to the bottom of, no victim to interview, no crime scene to steel myself against. I wasn't sure what I was supposed to do next.

Miss Penny had told me this job was going to be rather sedate when the fellows weren't in residence; apart from reading letters of application and keeping up with correspondence, there wasn't much else to do. I'd have to find things to occupy my time. I sighed and stared at the flat-screen television that hung above the fireplace, but I didn't feel like watching anything. So I pushed myself to my feet and headed toward the door.

Earlier in the day, Miss Penny had shown me dossiers on the five fellows who would be arriving at Cliffside the next week. I reasoned that I might as well read up on the people I'd be sharing this place with. I should be able to greet the fellows by name and know something about their work, Miss Penny had told me. *It's never too early to get a head start on that*, I said to myself as I turned the knob and pushed open the door.

A whisper of cold air slithered up the legs of my pants and down the collar of my shirt as I scurried down the hallway toward Miss Penny's office, which now, I knew, would be mine. I reached the door, stepped inside, and shut it behind me with a thud, my heart racing in my chest. *Get it together, Eleanor*, I said to myself.

But just then, a wave of nausea passed through me so powerful that it knocked me to my knees. My head began to pound, and I sat there for I don't know how long, with my face in my hands, waiting for whatever it was to pass. That would be all I'd need, to come down with some kind of illness now.

I looked up and noticed a pitcher of water on the table next to the window. I pushed myself up to my feet and padded across the room, then poured a glass with shaking hands. I drank it down and then another and then held the cool glass next to my face, which was heating up. Slowly, whatever it was that had hit me began to recede.

*Now, what did I come in here for?* Then I remembered. I crossed the room to my desk, where I found the thick leather notebook Miss Penny had shown me earlier. I pulled out the chair and had just sank down into it, opening the notebook's cover, when an intercom on the desk crackled and buzzed. The sound of it made me jump, my chair rolling back in the process.

"Excuse me, Miss Harper?"

It was Harriet, her voice scratchy and distant, as though she were calling from another era.

I reached for the ancient intercom—it looked to be at least fifty years old, and it suddenly struck me as odd, as everything else I had seen in the house was either a well-preserved antique or brand new—and held down the button that read, in fading print, *Reply*.

"Yes, Harriet?"

"It's nearly time for dinner, ma'am," she said.

I stole a glance at the clock. It was twenty minutes after five! I couldn't believe it. Last time I had checked, it was hours earlier. Here I thought the afternoon was dragging, and it was nearly over in a flash.

"Thanks for the reminder," I said into the machine, louder than, perhaps, was necessary.

"Please be in the drawing room at five thirty," Harriet said. "It'll just be you and Miss Penny tonight, of course."

"I'll be there," I said, pushing my chair back from the desk and grabbing the dossier folder.

I tucked the folder under my arm and slipped down the hallway to my suite. I wished I had left myself time for a shower, but it was too late for that now, so I changed into fresh slacks and a cotton shirt, ran a brush through my hair, and fixed my makeup. It would have to do. I pushed open the door of my suite into the hallway. The early summer light had not yet begun to fade, and the stained-glass windows that lined each end of the hall were catching the rays here and there, illuminating the hallway with color.

As I took the deep, circular staircase down to the first floor, my heart began to pound. There it was again, the indefinable sense of dread that had been plaguing me for months. I took a few deep breaths, trying to inhale calm and serenity into my lungs—a technique I had learned from my therapist. It was only mildly effective, but it was all I had. Maybe now that my life was no longer going to be a constant barrage of murder and mystery, death and destruction, these feelings would recede, just as the nausea had earlier. The worst I'd encounter here at Cliffside was a diva artist with unreasonable demands. And I knew I could handle that.

# CHAPTER 4

I waited for Miss Penny in the drawing room for nearly twenty minutes before using the intercom—the same antiquated model that was in the office—to summon Harriet. She pushed open the swinging door and stepped into the room, drying her hands on her apron.

"Yes?"

"Harriet, am I where I'm supposed to be?"

She frowned and shook her head. Had she not understood the question?

"It's just that Miss Penny isn't here yet, and she doesn't seem the type to be late."

Harriet looked around and furrowed her brow. "I don't think she has been late for dinner at Cliffside in twenty years," she said. "I'll just call up to her room."

She retreated to wherever it was she had come from but was gone only a moment before pushing her way through the door again, a worried look on her face.

"There's no answer," Harriet said. "She may be on her way down, but I'll nip up there, just in case, to check on her."

"Would you like me to go with you?" I asked her, but she was already halfway out of the room, headed toward the staircase.

"No need," she said to me over her shoulder. "You should be here to greet her if she arrives." With that, she was gone.

Moments later, I heard the scream.

I rushed up the grand stairs, past my second-floor suite, and down the hallway to the third-floor staircase. I hadn't been up to that floor yet and wasn't quite sure where I was going, but I followed the sound of Harriet's wails until I found her. I was wholly unprepared for what I was about to see.

Penelope Dare was lying on top of her still-made bed, her eyes wide open, her mouth contorted in what looked to be a smile. Her lips were painted bright red, haphazardly, and she had dark eyeliner ringing her eyes. She had taken her hair out of the severe bun she had been wearing, and it cascaded around her face, its streaks of gray framing her grotesque mask of death.

Her hands were clutching an envelope on top of her chest.

Harriet had crumpled to the floor by the bed and was sobbing, her head in her hands. I helped her to her feet and enveloped her in my arms, eyeing Miss Penny over her shoulder. "Oh my God," I whispered.

Harriet broke free of my grasp and lunged for Miss Penny, but I pulled her back. "Don't touch her," I said.

"But, shouldn't we do CPR?" she cried. "We need to resuscitate her! We need . . ."

Her words dissolved into a strangled sob as Harriet fully realized what I had known the moment I entered the room. Years of crime scenes had schooled me in the ways of death. There would be no CPR. She was gone.

Harriet turned to me, and I wrapped my arms around her in an effort to keep her from falling to the ground again.

"No, Penelope," Harriet wailed. "Not this. Not now . . ." Her words were swallowed by the grief that was settling in around her.

"We need to call the police," I said.

"The police? But—"

"Yes, Harriet," I broke in. "This is a police matter now. I'll contact them; you find Mr. Baines and let him know what's happened."

"Mr. Baines." She nodded. "Yes. He'll know what to do. Yes," she said again, wiping her eyes with a handkerchief she pulled from her sleeve. "And then there's the dinner to finish. Miss Penny likes her dinner promptly at six thirty." This was shock, I assumed, and I talked to her in as soothing a tone as I could muster, pushing my own bewilderment away, as I had done so many times before, at so many similar scenes.

"You head back downstairs now, Harriet," I said, my voice low and soft. "Go find Mr. Baines, ask him to let the rest of the staff know, and I'll deal with whatever comes next."

She nodded and backed out of the room, her eyes still on Miss Penny. "Mr. Baines," she said, more to herself than to me. "I'll find Mr. Baines."

I watched her until she disappeared down the hallway and then turned back to the body of Penelope Dare. Quick as a flash, I slipped the envelope out of her hands and stuffed it into my pocket. I needed to read what this letter said, and I knew that the police would confiscate it as evidence if they got to it before I did. This way, I could read it and give it to them when they arrived. No harm done.

I hurried down the hallway and the third-floor stairs to the director's office—my office—on the second floor, where I knew there was a phone on the desk. I picked up the handset but then thought better of it and sank into the office chair instead. I fished the letter out of my pocket, opened it, and found a single sheet of stationery inside. I unfolded it and began to read the words written in Miss Penny's spidery scrawl.

*Dear Officer Hanson,*

*I'm sorry to bring you out to Cliffside at this hour of the day when I'm sure you'd rather be home enjoying dinner with your family. I am assuming it is in the neighborhood of five thirty, perhaps closer to six, if my plan has come together as* it should. When I did not appear for cocktail hour, Harriet Baines surely came looking. Finding me must have been terribly shocking and frightening for her. Please apologize to her on my behalf. I hope my appearance wasn't too ghastly.

This is a suicide note, in case it's unclear to you. I, Penelope Dare, have chosen to take my own life today. There are two bottles of pills on my bedside table. Legal prescriptions, if you please. You'll find both bottles empty. I've ingested their entire contents along with several glasses of my father's prized Highland Scotch, which I have been saving for many years for just this occasion. I know enough to know that the combination of pills and alcohol will do the trick and I will swiftly leave this earth, bound, I do hope, for somewhere more pleasant.

I suppose you want an explanation, and the truth is, I am simply too tired to continue. Everyone I loved—my mother, my father, and my dear, dear sister—is gone. It is a burden to be the sole survivor, the last of the line. I am tired of carrying it.

And so, after finding a worthy successor in Eleanor Harper, I am able to put down my burden once and for all.

Do not for a moment think that anyone else had a hand in this decision. You know as well as I do that I am of sound mind. The decision was mine alone; the action was mine alone. Do not pester the staff, who will be grieving, with questions about this. They knew nothing.

My funeral arrangements have already been made and paid for. I wish only to be buried in our family plot, next to my sister Chamomile. Anyone who wishes to attend the committal at the cemetery may do so, but there is to be no service, no wake, nothing of the kind.

I sent two letters in this morning's mail—my obituary to the newspaper and a list of instructions for my lawyer. Please *tell the staff to expect compensation for all of their years of hard work when my will is read.*

*And, so, I take my leave for the last time. I feel my eyelids already getting heavy. I'll close them, and that will be that. My nightmare is over.*

*Yours very sincerely,*
*Penelope Dare*

I stared at the letter for a moment before I picked up the handset and dialed the police.

Twenty minutes later, the staff was assembled in the drawing room. Harriet, inconsolable, wept softly on the shoulder of her husband, whose face was ashen and drawn. The police had come. Miss Penny was already on a stretcher headed to the coroner's office. I knew from years of crime reporting that every death at home was investigated, but I also knew it was very clear this was a suicide.

A uniformed officer made his way down the stairs and entered the room.

"Who is in charge here?"

I looked to Harriet before I realized all eyes were on me. I cleared my throat. "I guess I am," I said, taking a step or two closer to the officer.

"And you are . . . ?"

"I'm Eleanor Harper," I said. "I'm . . ." I stumbled over the words, not quite believing what I was saying. "I'm the director of Cliffside."

"I thought Penelope Dare was the director here," he said.

"She was," I said, my voice wavering. "Until today. She handed the reins of Cliffside over to me"—I let out a sigh and shook my head—"today. I've been here only a few hours."

I fished the envelope out of my pocket and handed it to him. "I found this in Miss Penny's room," I said.

The officer took the envelope from me, opened it, and spent a few moments reading.

He looked up at me. "Is this Penelope Dare's handwriting?"

"I believe so, but I'm not certain. Harriet?"

Harriet crossed the room toward us and took the letter in shaking hands. She nodded her head, unable to form the words.

"Do you have examples of her handwriting so we can compare them?"

Harriet just looked at him. Mr. Baines crossed the room and put an arm around his wife. "Of course we have examples of her handwriting. Although I don't much like what you are insinuating."

"I'm not insinuating anything," the officer said. "We investigate all deaths at home, even if it's fairly clear it was suicide."

"*Fairly* clear?" Mr. Baines said, his face reddening.

The officer ignored this, turning to the assembled staff. "You all can have a seat. My partner and I are going to take some time to talk to each of you. But before we do that, I'll just ask—does anyone here know if Miss Dare was suicidal?"

Stunned silence. A few people shook their heads. Others dabbed at their eyes with tissues. Finally, Harriet found her voice.

"She was not suicidal," she said, the words seeming to shred into pieces in the air. "She was happier than ever, or so it seemed to me."

"Aye," her husband echoed. "That's right."

The officer nodded. "Okay, then." He turned to me. "I'll start with you."

I followed the policeman down the hallway to the dining room where we each took a seat at the table. I spent the next fifteen minutes or so telling him what he needed to know, that Penelope Dare had contacted me weeks ago about this job, that I had taken it, and that I had arrived just today. I took him through what had happened, step by step, from my arrival to the moment Harriet discovered the body.

He shook his head. "That's one hell of a first day on the job," he said.

I leaned back in my chair and sighed. "Tell me about it."

"What will you do now?" he wanted to know. "Will you stay on?"

In all of the commotion, my future was the last thing I was thinking about. He was right; I did have a choice. I could simply pack up and leave. But as soon as the thought floated through my mind, I knew it wasn't the right thing to do. Penelope Dare had entrusted me with continuing Cliffside's mission to foster and support the arts. I had agreed to take the job, given up my apartment, and moved here. That hadn't changed. I thought about why she was open to me applying for the job in the first place—my involvement in the deaths of her father and sister all of those years before. She was grateful for my efforts, she had told me.

"I feel like I owe it to her to do the job she hired me to do, at least for the time being," I said to him, finally.

He looked at me, a little too long, I thought. "Miss Dare's personal fortune keeps this place running," he said. "Now that you're director and she's gone, do you have access to those accounts?"

I held his gaze, determined not to look away. I had nothing to feel guilty about. "Not entirely," I said to him. "My name has been added to her accounts because, as director, I'll be writing the checks for Cliffside's monthly expenses. But Miss Penny's accountant is the one who sets the budget and oversees the finances. He has been with her family for decades."

He nodded and closed his notebook with an air of finality that caused me to exhale the breath I didn't know I was holding.

"Thank you, Miss Harper," he said. "I assume you'll be open to answering any other questions, should they come up."

"Of course," I said, pushing my chair back from the table. And that was that.

I walked back into the drawing room, where the staff was still assembled, waiting for their turns to talk to the police. I was the director of Cliffside now, and I might as well start acting like it. I took a deep breath and began to speak with an air of authority that I didn't really feel.

"Okay, everybody. Each one of you will be talking with the police, just as I've done. Tell them anything you think is important to mention. We've all had quite a shock today, and I know you're grieving." I looked around the room at their stricken faces. "Tomorrow is Friday—everybody take the day off."

This was greeted with murmurs from the staff and a scowl from Harriet.

"Monday is Memorial Day," I went on. "You'll have a nice, long weekend to yourselves to begin to come to terms with what's happened here today. We'll meet back here on Tuesday refreshed and ready to do what we need to do to prepare for the fellows, who will arrive a week from today, just as planned. It's up to us now to continue the work Penelope Dare dedicated her life to. We all owe it to her. I, for one, will not let her down, and I know you all feel the same way."

I looked around the room and saw tears and nods.

"Once you've finished talking with the police, you can go home," I said. "I hope you all have a relaxing, restful weekend, and I look forward to seeing everyone back here on Tuesday, ready for action."

That said, I wasn't sure what to do, so I turned and walked out of the room, Harriet at my heels.

"Mr. Baines and I will not be taking the day off," she said to me.

"Oh, Harriet," I said, taking her hands in mine. "You of all people need a break."

She shook her head. "Work is what we need. Continuing the business of the household. It's our life, Miss Harper. One doesn't take breaks from one's life. I'll be readying for the fellows, and Mr. Baines will be working in the garden this weekend, just as we had planned."

I squeezed her hands. "Very well," I said, understanding her need to keep the normal routine running. I had seen it before in victims' families. "But please, if you need time, promise me you'll take it."

She nodded. "Would you like your dinner in the dining room now, or would you prefer it up in your room?"

Dinner. It had been the last thing on my mind. All at once, I could feel the tide of exhaustion that would soon engulf me. "In my room would be lovely, Harriet. Unless you and Mr. Baines want to join me in the dining room."

"Join you? Oh, heavens no. We'll be eating in the kitchen when our work is done. I'll have Mary bring up a tray."

"Thank you, Harriet," I said, and she turned to go. She seemed smaller than she had this morning when I'd met her, and as she walked back into the drawing room, I wondered if grief and pain could actually diminish a person.

I made my way through the drawing room and spied a bottle of Chardonnay in an ice bucket on the sideboard. Harriet had opened it for Miss Penny and me, apparently. I poured a glass and took it upstairs.

As I settled into my suite and sank into the armchair with the glass of wine, something in Miss Penny's suicide note floated into my mind and stayed.

*My nightmare is over.* Whatever could she have meant by that?

# CHAPTER 5

Later, after I had finished the dinner Mary had brought to me, I decided to curl up in the armchair by the fire with a book. But, try as I might, I couldn't lose myself in its pages. I set the book in my lap and turned my gaze to the flames dancing in the fireplace.

*Long day* didn't begin to cover how I felt about what had happened to me in the past twelve hours.

My now-familiar sense of dread settled in around me like a scratchy wool blanket. Here I was, in this big, old building, nearly alone. I knew all of the staff had gone—I had watched out the window as they had gotten into their cars one by one after talking with the police. For all I knew, it was just Harriet, Mr. Baines, and me. All of those empty rooms. Those long, desolate hallways. Miss Penny's face, her grotesque smile, flashed through my mind, and I wondered if her spirit had found the peace in death that she hadn't found in life. Or was it wandering these halls still?

I shivered and pushed myself to my feet, crossing the room to check my door for the umpteenth time. Still locked.

Out the window, I could see some light hanging on in the western sky. The fog had lifted, and complete darkness hadn't fallen yet. I was glad of it. Maybe I could be asleep by that time. I pulled the shades on all of the windows and turned on the light next to my bed, the fire in the fireplace dancing merrily. Wasn't that nice, I asked myself, a cheerful fire? I took a couple of deep breaths, hoping I could inhale some calmness with it.

I changed into my pajamas, grabbed my book, and padded to the bed. I drew back the comforter, and that's when I saw it. An envelope had been slipped under my bedcovers.

*Eleanor Harper*, it said across the front, written in the same spidery scrawl as the note from Miss Penny I had read earlier in the day. I picked it up gingerly.

My dear Eleanor,

Well, this is a surprise, isn't it? I'm sorry to foist this upon you within hours of your arrival, but it had to be done, and done now. I wanted to leave you some time and space to acclimate to this new "state of affairs" before the fellows arrive at the end of next week. It's very important that they arrive on schedule and everything goes as planned. You understand that, don't you, Eleanor? I'm sure that you do. The work of Cliffside must continue, and you must be the one to continue it.

In case you are thinking of leaving on account of my death, please think again, dear. You signed an employment contract for a year's service earlier today, and it is on its way to my lawyer's office as you read this. What you might not have noticed in that contract is the severe financial penalty you will pay for leaving this job before your term is finished. I know you can't afford it, Miss Harper. I'm sorry for the manipulation you must be feeling at this moment, but it had to be done. I needed to know you'd be here, and now I can leave this earth in peace, knowing you are at Cliffside to stay, at least for the time being.

By now, you have discovered me. Police have been called. Tears have been shed. Poor Harriet and Mr. Baines. Please do all you can to comfort them. They have been loyal servants for more years than I can count and will be well taken care of, provided they stay on at Cliffside. That is in your, and Cliffside's, best interest, so I have stipulated it in my will. As far as the funds necessary to keep Cliffside running are concerned, don't worry about that. Aside from some stipends for the staff, I'm leaving my entire fortune to Cliffside.

And, by now, you have all read my suicide note. The substance of that note, Eleanor, is all anybody else needs to know. That's the information I want to be shared for public consumption, for police, for the staff, etc. But you need to know more.

The truth is, the time for me to join my father and my sister was long ago. Twenty years and sixty-seven days ago, to be exact. I know that now. I've known for some time. That I lived so long without them was an abomination. It is a tiring thing, carrying that burden.

But there is more to it than just that, I'm afraid.

Cliffside has been my home for nearly my whole life. I can scarcely remember a time when we lived anywhere else. Milly and I spent our youth running up and down these hallways, splashing in the pool, playing on the cliff, writing in our diaries before turning off the light at night. We grew up here. We were going to live the rest of our lives here together, she and I. Twenty years and sixty-seven days ago, all of that changed.

And now, you are the director of Cliffside. You are the next in line, my successor.

In my wake, I have left a puzzle for you to solve, Eleanor Harper. You, the would-be sleuth. You, of the curious mind. I know you will latch on to it, just as you latched on to the murders of my father and sister all those years ago. I trust you'll be more successful this time.

You see, that's why I chose you and brought you to Cliffside. Only you can work out all of the mysteries that are *swirling through these halls. You will be a quick study, I'm sure, and you'll soon learn all that you need to know.*

*Ah, I see the car pulling into the drive through the fog. You have arrived at Cliffside. It is time.*

*In closing, Eleanor Harper, about whom I have thought so much and so often over the past twenty years, I'll say this. The last line of my suicide note says that my nightmare is over. And, by now, it is. Yours, however, is just beginning.*

*Sweet dreams, Eleanor.*

I sat there for a moment, holding this letter in my hands. Then I dropped it as though it were on fire and hurried across the room to the intercom.

"Harriet?" I shouted into it, not sure if it would reach her or not. "Harriet!"

A few long moments later, I got a response.

"Yes, Miss Harper?" She coughed a few times. "What can I do for you?"

"Harriet, can you and Mr. Baines come up here to my suite?" I asked. "I'd come to you but I have no idea where you are. I'm sorry for the intrusion this late at night, but I have something that I really need to show you. It's urgent."

"Of course, Miss Harper," she said. "We'll be there in just a moment."

I could feel my heart beating, hard, in my chest as I waited for them to materialize. Would they never come? Finally, I heard footsteps in the hallway, but I waited for the knock and Harriet's "Miss Harper?" before opening the door.

"Oh, thank goodness," I said, holding out the envelope. "You have to see this. I don't know what to make of it, but it has scared me to death."

Both of them winced. Perhaps that wasn't the best choice of words. In any case, Harriet fished a pair of glasses out of her pocket, took the letter, and began reading. Her eyes grew wide. She handed the sheet to her husband without saying a word. After he had read it, the two of them exchanged glances. And I'd say they were charged glances.

"Do you have any idea what this is about?" I asked both of them. "To me, this sounds threatening. And it also sounds almost—I'm just going to say it—irrational. If you have anything to say about Miss Penny's state of mind, you need to say it now, or I'm leaving, contract or not."

After a moment, Harriet cleared her throat. "I wouldn't make too much of this, Miss Harper."

"Too much of this?" I shot back. "She has said my nightmare is just beginning. What is this all about? I'm certain that you two know more than you're saying."

"No," Harriet said, straightening her posture just a bit. "We know nothing of the kind."

"Oh, come on—" I began, but Mr. Baines jumped into the fray.

"My dear wife won't say anything against her employer, but I will," he said, smoothing his lapel. "We have noticed certain . . . incidents, I gather you'd call them, over the past few months."

I narrowed my eyes at him. "What sort of incidents?"

"I have to admit it—" Mr. Baines started.

"Oh no you don't," his wife broke in. "This is nothing we should speak of. Especially now. We do not speak ill of the dead. Especially in this house."

He looked at me in silence, his thought cut short.

"Harriet, Mr. Baines, please," I said, taking a few breaths, trying to calm myself. "I'll be honest with you. This letter frightened me. And without a good explanation, I'm leaving. Tonight."

Mr. Baines looked at his wife. "She'll leave," he said, his tone pleading. "Cliffside will close without a director. And then where will we be? After thirty years? Where do your loyalties lie, my love?"

Harriet sighed and took her husband's hand. "My loyalties lie with you, Mr. Baines." She turned to me, squared her shoulders, and cleared her throat. "The truth is, Miss Harper, we've been noticing a change in Miss Penny for some months now."

I could see her husband visibly exhaling.

"What kind of change?"

They caught each other's eyes again. Every word was a struggle for this loyal employee. "Her mental state, I'm afraid," Harriet said. "I can't rightly explain it, but something was happening, and we couldn't figure out exactly what."

Questions started forming in my journalist's mind, pushing the fear I felt to the sidelines. "Was it confined to her mental state? What I'm asking is, was this internal, or did something happen?"

Harriet shook her head. "We don't know. We couldn't find the words to talk about it with her—we are her employees, after all—and she didn't confide in us. All we know is that she was changed."

"That's why we were so happy she hired you," Mr. Baines piped up. "We thought that she realized she was losing the capacity to do the job. Maybe dementia was setting in. We believed she wanted somebody in place to carry on, somebody she could train, before she lost it all."

I took a deep breath. "So this bit about nightmares?"

"Miss Penny never had nightmares, not that I knew about," Harriet said. "I can't for the life of me think what she might mean by this."

"Perhaps the nightmare of running this place on one's own?" her husband offered. "The responsibility on one's shoulders? I can't think of what it would be, other than that."

I just looked at them, unconvinced.

"We were here with her every day, Miss Harper," Harriet tried again. "Believe me, if there were any nightmares, real or imagined, we'd have known about them."

"And you didn't," I said. "You have no idea what any of this in the letter might be about?"

Mr. Baines took a step forward. "No," he said. "Please, Miss Harper, chalk this up to the ramblings of a disturbed old woman on the day she took her life. It sounds a bit disloyal for me to talk so plainly about our former director, but I see that you are very upset by this and I feel that your needs, as director of Cliffside, must be our priority now."

"You're right, as ever, Mr. Baines," Harriet said. "Of course, Miss Harper's needs are our priority."

And they stood there, looking at me, blinking. I didn't know what else to say.

"If that's all, ma'am . . . ?" Harriet ventured.

I nodded. "That's all. Thank you both."

And they turned to leave. I noticed Mr. Baines put his hand on the small of his wife's back, gently guiding her. I watched them from my doorway as they walked down the dark hallway together. Neither said a word until they disappeared down the main staircase.

I closed my door and flipped the lock, shaking my head. That encounter hadn't told me much, except that Miss Penny might have been suffering from some form of dementia. Was that all there was to this? As Mr. Baines had said, the ramblings of an old woman on the day she took her life?

And yet, the woman who had greeted me earlier in the day certainly hadn't seemed in any way mentally impaired. There was no hint of any sort of dementia, or none that I could discern, anyway. It could very well be that the change Harriet and Mr. Baines noticed was caused by Miss Penny making the decision to end her life.

Still, something told me these two weren't telling me the whole truth. A career spent interviewing people had taught me a thing or two about when someone was lying or holding something back.

I crossed the room and pulled open my curtains just a bit with one finger and peered outside, hoping to watch Harriet and Mr. Baines cross the lawn to their house—the gardener's quarters, I've since learned—but I was greeted with a dense wall of fog obscuring everything beyond the windowpanes. I could see nothing but white, as though Cliffside were wrapped in cotton batting. I let the curtain drop.

My stomach was in knots at the thought of staying the night here, alone. *Breathe, Eleanor. Breathe.* Miss Penny and scores of fellows over the years had lived at Cliffside—I could too. I picked up my wineglass and sat on the edge of my bed. Only a sip or two remained, but maybe that would calm my nerves. As I took a sip, I told myself that it seemed silly, the whole thing. Nightmares. Last words. Miss Penny was gone, and whatever her motives for writing that letter, they died with her.

I curled into my bed and pulled the covers up around me, reaching toward the nightstand and grabbing the remote control for the television. I thought the sound of a sitcom or a nighttime talk show would help quiet the miasma that was swirling around in my brain. Thoughts had been screaming at me, but nothing congealed into a tangible possibility. In the end, as I settled in to watch a celebrity talk about his project du jour, I decided to chalk this letter, and its threatening tone, up to the strangeness of the day. Miss Penny had killed herself shortly after writing it. No telling what had been going through her mind. I'd probably never know. It had to be good enough.

Just as I was drifting off to sleep, something from the letter ran through my mind. What had she written about a puzzle?

I slipped out of bed and padded over to my closet, where I had stashed the letter in my suitcase. I pulled the sheet from the envelope and read it again.

> *In my wake, I have left a puzzle for you to solve, Eleanor Harper. You, the would-be sleuth. You, of the curious mind. I know you will latch on to it, just as you latched on to the murders of my father and sister all those years ago. I trust you'll be more successful this time.*

I didn't know what the puzzle was, but I certainly knew a threat when I heard it.

# CHAPTER 6

I didn't sleep much that night. I kept tossing and turning, drifting off only to be startled awake by my own racing heart. Each time, I'd look at the clock—eleven, twelve, one, two—and think to myself, *At least I can get a few good hours in, if I fall asleep soon.* And I'd snuggle down and close my eyes, willing sleep to come. At one point, I was sure I heard voices in the hallway, muffled voices. Coughing. I crept to the door to listen, but by the time I got there, they were gone.

It was a little before three o'clock when my eyelids began to get heavy and my body started to feel that light, swimmy feeling just before sleep. That's when I heard it—laughter. Children's laughter. My eyes popped open, and I sat straight up in bed. There it was again. I wasn't imagining it or dreaming. It was coming from outside, I was sure of it. I slipped out from under my covers and crept to the window, drawing back the curtain just a bit.

The fog had dissipated, and the moon was illuminating the lawn outside my window. And there, running back and forth and kicking a ball, was a group of children, all dressed in white. It was their laughter I'd heard, then. Who were they—children of staff members, maybe?—and what were they doing awake and outside at this hour? I watched them kick the ball back and forth for a moment, and just as I was about to open my window and tell them to go inside, a woman appeared from under the balcony. She was also dressed in white, or seemed to be, there in the moonlight. I didn't recognize her—I hadn't met her earlier in the day.

"Children!" she hissed.

They stopped abruptly when they caught sight of her. *Uh-oh,* I thought to myself, smiling. *Busted.*

"You know you're not supposed to be out here playing," she said, her tone muffled and distant. "Now get back inside to your rooms this instant. This instant, do you hear me?"

The children scurried off and out of my view. The woman turned, and just as I was about to let the curtain drop, she looked up at my window and locked eyes with me. I expected her to apologize for the noise the kids were making, but instead she gave me a look that chilled me to the bone, as though I were the one who had done something wrong.

I let the curtain fall closed and climbed back into bed, wondering what that was all about. It wasn't until I was drifting off to sleep that it hit me—had she been wearing a nurse's uniform?

The thought jarred me, and I was wide awake again. It couldn't have been a nurse's uniform, could it? And when I had asked Miss Penny about others at Cliffside, she hadn't mentioned any children. All at once I was ice cold.

I lay there, the covers pulled up to my neck, for hours. I remember seeing the first hints of light in the sky, but I must've drifted off shortly after that, because the next thing I knew, I was opening my eyes to a bright, clear morning.

I slipped from under the covers, drew back the curtains, pushed open the French doors, and walked out onto my balcony. The view made me take a quick breath in. I could see that my suite was directly above the veranda overlooking Cliffside's manicured lawn, which undulated in waves to the edge of the cliff itself. The bay shimmered in the morning sun. I could see the forest and the rocky cliff below it on the opposite shore and, down the shoreline a bit, the chain of islands floating in the lake beyond. One lonely sailboat drifted by, its colorful spinnaker standing out against the blue of the lake.

It was so beautiful, so peaceful, that, just for a moment, I forgot about the events of the previous day. A knock at my door pulled me back into my stark reality—Miss Penny, dead. Me, in charge.

"I thought you might enjoy your breakfast on the balcony today, Miss Harper," Harriet said, pushing her way through the door and carrying a tray. "I've brought it, your coffee, and the morning paper."

I held her gaze. "How are you this morning, Harriet?" I asked her. "Did you sleep at all?"

"Fit and ready as ever for the day," she said, carrying the tray to the table on my balcony and winding the umbrella into the upright position. All business, then. There was to be no talk of the previous day, I gathered.

She stood there, smoothing her apron, her face betraying the slightest hint of the grief I knew she was carrying with her. I wanted to reach out to her, to do something, but I got the distinct impression this approach was Harriet's way of carrying on.

"Thank you," I said at last. "I can really use the coffee this morning."

Harriet smiled. "I wagered you wouldn't have slept too well, first night in a new place. I brought the whole pot for you."

Harriet's eyes shifted to the window and she let out a deep sigh. But then she shook off whatever it was she was thinking. "I've much to do today to prepare for the fellows," she said quickly, "but anything you need, miss, please don't hesitate to ask."

"I suppose Mr. Baines will be working in the gardens?"

She nodded. "It brings him so much joy to tend the gardens Miss Penny loved," she said, her eyes glistening.

I took a sip of my coffee. "Harriet, who are those children on the property?" I asked her. "I didn't see them yesterday when I arrived, but they were playing outside my window last night."

She cocked her head to the side and furrowed her brow. "There are no children at Cliffside, Miss Harper," she said, slowly.

I put my cup down. "But I saw them, last night."

She shook her head. "You must be mistaken. There are no children here."

That same feeling of coldness slithered through me.

"Perhaps you were dreaming?" she offered.

I didn't think it was a dream. But I couldn't really be sure. It was so ridiculous, a group of children out on the lawn. Maybe she was right. "That must've been it. I'm sorry to have bothered you."

And then she turned to go, leaving me alone to wonder exactly what it was I had seen last night. The night had been bright and starlit—that was unusual after such a foggy, wet day. Wasn't it? I had tossed and turned for so long, maybe I did drift off and dream the whole thing. The alternative made my stomach seize up.

After devouring my omelet and sipping my coffee until the last of it had gone cold, I lingered on the balcony for a long time, too long. The view was simply entrancing, and it was difficult to tear myself away. But when I noticed Mr. Baines stump out to one of the flowerbeds with a bucketful of tools in tow, I couldn't justify my sloth any longer. He and Harriet were preparing Cliffside for the fellows' onslaught, and I might as well do the same. I clattered all of the dishes back onto the tray and carried it to my desk. I nearly pushed the button on the intercom to ask Harriet to pick it up but then decided against disturbing her. *Let her get on with her day.* I'd take the dishes downstairs with me when I went.

I looked around, wondering what to do next. Just as I was heading out of my room, I heard my cell phone ring in my purse. I fished it out and recognized the number on the display. Meg Roberts, a friend and colleague from my old job at the newspaper.

"Hey," I said.

"I just heard," she said. "Unbelievable. Are you okay?"

"I still can't quite believe it happened either, but yeah, I'm okay," I said.

"What are you going to do? Will you stay on?"

"For the time being—" I stopped talking when I heard the familiar click of a computer keyboard coming from her end of the line.

I could feel the heat rising to my face. "Is this an interview?" I asked her, my words coming out in staccato. "I thought it was just an old friend calling to see how I was doing after a horrible day."

Meg sighed. "A little of both, I guess. I'm sorry, Norrie."

"I don't have anything to say," I told her. "And I'm really busy today so—"

"Don't hang up," she broke in. "What's with you? You know we're going to be doing a story on this. It's what we do. It's what you used to do. When did you start thinking reporters were the bad guys?"

She was right, when did I? I had no idea why I was feeling so antagonistic toward her.

"I'm sorry," I said, "I'm just a little on edge." But, at that moment, I didn't really believe it. I realized that I was now on the other end of the countless phone calls that I myself used to make immediately after a tragedy, a murder, or an assault, to victims, to their families, to people who had witnessed crimes. All of a sudden I knew, firsthand, what an intrusion it was. I had a new respect for the people who had been kind and cooperative with me when I had asked those questions and I completely understood those who hadn't been.

Meg interrupted my thoughts. "So, can't you just give me a few quotes as the director of Cliffside?"

"Sure, I can do that," I acquiesced. "What would you like to know?"

And so, over the next fifteen minutes or so, I talked to my old friend about the events of the previous day, telling her just enough, doling out the information carefully.

"So you were there just a few hours before Miss Dare died?" Meg asked, clicking away in the background.

"Yes," I said, and left it at that.

"Do we know the cause of death? The police are being very tight-lipped about this with the media, but I figured you'd know."

She figured right. But that didn't mean I was going to tell her. All at once, I felt very protective of Miss Penny and Cliffside—more protective, perhaps, than I should have felt after less than twenty-four hours on the property. But this was my responsibility now, and I couldn't stomach the idea that her suicide, and the pain that had led up to it, would be splashed all over the front page of the newspaper. She had been such a great lady, who many in town had looked up to, including me.

"I don't know the exact cause of death," I said. It was mostly the truth. I knew she had taken the pills, but I didn't know which pills, specifically. Splitting hairs, I knew. And I also knew the truth would come out, but it didn't have to come from me.

"Come on, Norrie. Can't you tell me anything more?"

"I can tell you that she died in her bed," I said. "That's where we found her."

"So, you were the one who found her?" More clicking.

"No," I said. "It was a staff member, who then called me immediately. I was the one who called the police."

"Can you tell me the staff member's name?"

"I can," I said to her. "But I won't. The last thing this person needs is for you or another reporter to intrude right now."

"Fair enough," Meg said. "Anything else?"

"I want to assure people that the retreat for artists and writers here at Cliffside Manor will continue," I said, with an air of finality. "Our docket is full for the coming year, and those artists and writers need to know that nothing is going to change."

As I said the words, I realized what I needed to do with the rest of my day.

"Meg, I really have to go."

"Thanks, Norrie," she said, still clicking away. "I appreciate your time."

After we ended the call, I realized that she hadn't asked me too much about how I was handling this, how I was adjusting to my new life, or anything else a real friend would ask. She only wanted to get the story after all.

I crossed the room and pressed the buzzer for the intercom.

"Yes, Miss Harper?"

"Harriet, I have a feeling the news media is going to be calling here today and perhaps even stopping by," I said to her. "I just took a call from the newspaper."

"Aye," she said. "I suspected as much."

"Please let me do the talking about this," I said to her. "The last thing you need is to be answering a bunch of intrusive questions. That was my job for many years, what they're doing now, and I know just how to handle them."

"Of course, Miss Harper," she said. "I wouldn't presume to speak on behalf of Cliffside. That's your job now."

I supposed it was. "About that," I went on. "I made the decision not to tell the newspaper about the suicide. I told the reporter we found Miss Penny in her bed but didn't know the exact cause of death."

"I see," Harriet said, her voice cracking.

"If anybody corners you, that's our story. Okay?"

"I understand, Miss Harper," Harriet said. "And thank you. Thank you very much. I'll spread the word to the staff."

I wondered how many calls I'd be taking from the media in the coming days. But until they started coming, I had work to do, and it was best I get to it.

I had left the notebook containing the dossiers of the incoming fellows on the writing desk in my sitting room. I scooped it up and made my way back out to the balcony.

I settled onto one of the two chaises and opened the notebook, where I found a sheet on each one of the fellows, neatly typewritten on what must have been a manual typewriter, if the script was any indication.

Cassandra Abbott

Type of artist: Writer, nonfiction

Work in progress: A profile of TB sanatoriums in the Midwest, circa 1900

Reason for applying for the fellowship: Need for solitude.

Expected outcome of fellowship: Completion of the book.

Bio: Cassandra Abbott is the author of seventeen nonfiction books all dealing with aspects of United States history.

Richard Banks

Type of artist: Photographer

Work in progress: None

Reason for applying for the fellowship: Unrestricted access to the Cliffside grounds.

Expected outcome of fellowship: A series of black-and-white, atmospheric photographs of the Lake Superior shoreline.

Bio: After twenty years at *National Geographic* magazine, Richard Banks opened his own gallery, specializing in nature photography, in his home in Cornwall, England.

Henry Dalton

Type of artist: Painter, oils

Work in progress: None
Reason for applying for the fellowship: Unrestricted access to the Cliffside gardens.
Expected outcome of fellowship: A series of paintings of the gardens of Cliffside for an exhibit he intends to hold later this summer.
Bio: Henry Dalton is a successful artist, specializing in local landscapes.

Brynn Kendrick

Type of artist: Writer, fiction
Work in progress: A novel
Reason for applying for the fellowship: Miss Kendrick hopes to be inspired by the pristine natural beauty of Cliffside.
Expected outcome of fellowship: Forward progress on the novel.
Bio: Brynn Kendrick is a promising writer working on her first book.

Diana Cooper

Type of artist: Writer, poetry
Work in progress: A book of poems inspired by the concept of solitude.
Reason for applying for the fellowship: The isolation provided by the Cliffside setting.

```
Expected outcome of fellowship:
Completion of the book.
Bio: Diana Cooper is a professor of
poetry at the University of Wiscon-
sin-Madison.
```

So, starting in just a few days, these people would be my housemates for the coming month. This "dossier" certainly didn't tell me very much about them beyond the basics. I looked at the photographer's name again, Richard Banks, and a glimmer of recognition sizzled through my brain. Oh, yes, I remembered, we had done a profile of him in the newspaper a few years before. I don't think I even read it, but I recalled seeing his name splashed across the page above dramatic photographs shot, if I was remembering correctly, in Africa. Well, that was one I knew, anyway. The others I had never heard of.

*Something's missing, though.* Where were the essays each aspiring fellow had to write? I know Miss Penny had told me about those. The essay was one of the ways she decided who would come to Cliffside. I pushed myself out of my chaise. Maybe there was another folder in the director's office. My office.

I padded from my suite down the hallway and opened the door. The top of the desk was empty, save for an old, manual typewriter, the telephone, and a notepad and pen sitting beside it. The bookshelf was filled with books, but no files.

I sank into the chair and began opening drawers until I found what I was looking for—a drawer full of hanging files, each with a tab labeled for the coming sessions: *May/June, July/August, September/October, November/December, January/February, March/April.* This was it.

I saw that the *May/June* file was empty, having been filled, I assumed, with the notes I had read back in my room. I reached into the *July/August* file, pulled out a folder, and opened it onto my desk.

It contained notes just like the ones for the upcoming group of fellows, but it also included the essays.

*The opportunity to come to Cliffside is unparalleled . . .*

*Cliffside Retreat will provide me with . . .*

*As a writer, solitude . . .*

*No ringing telephone, no Internet distractions, no husband to make dinner for, no children to take to soccer practice . . .*

I smiled at that last one. But where were the essays for my upcoming group? I hunted around some more and came up with nothing. In the end, I said to myself, it really didn't matter. They had already been selected; their essays had done the trick. They were coming, whether I liked their essays or not. It was just that it might have been nice to know a bit more about the people in my first group before they arrived, but what I did know would have to do.

I did one last search of the desk and found something else that I needed. A file labeled: *Contact Information for the Fellows.* I smiled again. All of these paper files, organized just so, but paper nonetheless. I scanned the room and didn't see a computer anywhere, probably due to Miss Penny's age. I had my laptop with me, but I made a mental note to ask the accountant to authorize the purchase of a computer and Internet service to drag Cliffside into the modern age. That was one thing I could do with my time, at least.

I pulled out the contacts file, set it on the desk, and opened the drawer where I had seen stationery and envelopes a moment earlier. Everybody needed to be informed of Miss Penny's death before they arrived, and they'd need reassurance from me that it was going to be business as usual, that nothing had changed but the director. Now was the time to write those letters. I had everyone's email addresses and could have simply dashed off a group message if Cliffside had Internet service, but that just didn't feel right. No, a handwritten note to each of them was more appropriate. It would be a good opportunity to introduce myself to them as well. As I began writing, I hoped the fellows wouldn't be too disappointed that I, and not the storied Penelope Dare, was to be their hostess at Cliffside.

Thirty minutes later, my hand sore with writer's cramp—I hadn't put so many words on paper manually in a very long time—I had the letters written to the five incoming fellows. A brief explanation of Miss Penny's death with no mention of the suicide, a welcome from me, and that was that.

I stuck stamps I found in the top drawer onto the corners of each envelope and gathered them all up, intent on making my way downstairs to ask Harriet how we dealt with the mail here at Cliffside, when the telephone on the desk rang.

I groaned, thinking it was another media call or even Meg calling back. It wasn't.

"This is Cassandra Abbott," said the voice on the other end of the line—a rather harsh voice, I thought. "To whom am I speaking?"

"Eleanor Harper," I said. "I'm the director here at Cliffside. What can I do for you, Miss Abbott? I'm looking forward to your arrival next week."

"It's doctor," she said. "Doctor Abbott. I have my PhD." She cleared her throat. "Is it true?"

"Is what true?"

"You know very well what," she said, over-enunciating each word. "Is Penelope Dare dead?"

"I'm afraid it's true," I said. "I've just finished writing letters to each of the—"

"It can't be," she broke in. "It just can't be."

"I'm very sorry," I said to her, my tone gentle and low. "I know this must come as quite a shock to you, as it is to us. Did you know Miss Dare well?"

She let out an audible sigh. "Know her? I didn't know her at all. I'd never met the woman. But she was the whole point of me coming to Cliffside. I'm writing about TB sanatoriums—"

"I know what you're writing about, Miss—Doctor—Abbott." I was glad I had thought to read the dossiers.

"Well, then you know I won't be able to finish my project without talking to Penelope Dare. The wealth of personal information she had! What a waste. What an utter waste. All of the years I spent researching and waiting, completely down the drain."

I looked at the handset, my mouth agape. Did she really just say that? This was the diva behavior Miss Penny had warned me about. My tone went ice cold. "I'm so very sorry that Miss Penny's death has inconvenienced your highly important book project," I said, the sarcasm dripping from my words. "But we here at Cliffside, especially the longtime staff, are dealing with the grief of losing a great lady. Since her death has made your visit to Cliffside such a waste of time for you, I will happily take you off the roster for this session. There are literally hundreds of people who would be thrilled to come in your place. Goodbye, *Miss* Abbott."

As I was putting the handset back on the body of the phone, I heard her speak. "Wait! Wait! No!"

"Did you say something?"

"You can't take me off the roster."

"I most certainly can," I said to her.

"But I have my time already scheduled," she said. "My plans are made."

"I really don't care about your plans."

There was silence on the other end of the line. Finally, "I've offended you. Is that it?"

"Yes," I said. "That's it. How dare you call here, today of all days, in a snit because your research plans were disrupted by the death of a woman who was beloved here at Cliffside?"

"I'm sorry," she said, sighing. "I didn't think."

"That, Miss Abbott, is obvious. And I daresay that the hundreds of people who applied for your spot here wouldn't think it a waste to come to Cliffside."

"I'm sorry," she repeated. "I don't think it's a waste. It's just that I was planning to interview Penelope Dare about her experiences at Cliffside when it was a sanatorium. It was going to be the basis of my book."

"Apparently, death cares just as much about your plans as I do," I said to her.

She ignored this. "I really do want to come to Cliffside," she went on. "You don't understand—or maybe you do—I've applied for this fellowship seven times. That's how long I've been waiting to talk to Penelope Dare. And now, just when I get accepted . . ." She wisely didn't say any more.

My spine tingled. It really was bad luck; I had to admit that despite the bitter taste this woman left in my mouth. "No, Doctor Abbott, I didn't know you had applied seven times," I said. "I'm new here. I just started. Yesterday, as a matter of fact."

"Yesterday?" she parroted. "Oh, Lord. What an ordeal you've been through."

"My first day was quite interesting, I'll give you that," I said. "I'm expecting it to get easier from here." I sighed. "Please tell me the truth, Doctor Abbott. Is there still value for you to come to Cliffside, now that Miss Penny is gone? I really meant it about the hundreds of people who applied for your spot. If this isn't going to benefit you—"

"No!" she said. "I mean, yes. I'll have to shift gears in my focus, but it will still have enormous value for me to write on the grounds of a former sanatorium, especially Cliffside. The inspiration alone. Please. May I still come?"

I considered this for a moment. Denying her now as a punishment for her thoughtless remarks, after she had applied seven times, would simply be vindictive. "Very well," I said, finally. "It would likely be too late to invite someone else, anyway. But let me warn you not to say anything to the staff like you said to me. It would go over even worse with them."

"Duly noted," she said, her tone becoming much more pleasant. "Keep foot from mouth at all times. I'll remember. And thank you."

Something Miss Penny had said to me the day before rang in my ears. "You should know, also, that the mother of a member of our staff was a TB patient here when Cliffside was a sanatorium," I said. "Perhaps she'd agree to talk with you. She basically runs the show around here."

"Oh?" she said, her voice brightening. "I didn't know that. I would indeed like to talk with her."

"I'm not sure she'll be willing, but I'll be happy to ask her on your behalf."

"Thank you, thank you so much, Miss—Harper, was it?"

"Please, call me Eleanor," I said. "Miss Penny was very formal, but I'm a much more casual person. First names are fine with me."

"Then I'm Cassandra," she said. "I look forward to meeting you. I'm so sorry my thoughtlessness caused us to get off on the wrong foot."

"Think nothing more of it," I said. I was about to hang up, but something occurred to me then. "May I ask—why didn't you just interview Miss Penny by phone, or simply pay a visit to Cliffside, if her experiences were so important to your book? Why wait until you got a fellowship?"

"I tried, believe me," she said. "She wouldn't allow it. She said she'd only share her memories if I were a fellow at Cliffside. So I kept applying, and she kept turning me down. For seven years. I have to be honest, it started to feel personal."

"And now this."

"And now this."

After we hung up, I had to admit to myself that I could understand the reason for Cassandra Abbott's anger upon learning of Miss Penny's death, despite how off-putting it had been for me to hear. And I wondered why Miss Penny had turned her down time after time only to accept her into the first group of fellows she knew she wouldn't be around to greet.

# CHAPTER 7

After delivering the envelopes to Harriet and telling her about my encounter with Cassandra Abbott, I spent the rest of the day as I had predicted—dealing with the media firestorm that Miss Penny's death had caused. Call after call from local, and even national news organizations. *Smithsonian Magazine. Vanity Fair.* Even AARP. I was interviewed on-air for all of the local television stations. NBC sent a crew. ABC was coming the next day. Someone from the National Endowment for the Arts called to pay their respects. I had known that Cliffside Manor was an important arts organization in the area, but I hadn't known how revered it was nationally, now and even during Chester Dare's day.

By dinnertime, I was exhausted and retreated back to my suite.

"Miss Penny, where's that sedate, uncomplicated job you promised me?" I said into the air. I shuddered when a tendril of icy cold slithered up my spine in response.

I was stretched out on the chaise on my balcony, my eyes just fluttering closed, when Harriet poked her head around the French door.

"I've brought your supper, ma'am," she said. "With everything that you've handled today, I thought you'd prefer it in your room."

Until she mentioned supper, I hadn't realized how hungry I was. "Thank you," I said, my words coming out in one long sigh. "I don't want to seem antisocial, but I think my lack of sleep last night is catching up with me. It will be nice to just climb into my pajamas and curl up in front of the television. I want to see how the news treats this story."

"You're not antisocial one bit," she said. "The director of Cliffside has a lot to carry on her shoulders. Your first two days have been a walk through fire—we've all seen it—and you should know that the staff is very, very glad you're here with us. You've handled it all beautifully. But I'm sure you could use some solitude now. It's what Cliffside is famous for, after all."

She was right. I stretched and wondered how much effort it was going to take to get out of that chaise.

"I've set your dinner on the desk," she said. "And now, I'll take my leave. I have a dinner date with Mr. Baines in the kitchen, and then we'll be off. If you need anything, just ring."

"Goodnight, Harriet," I said. "I'm sure I won't need anything. I'll see you in the morning."

When she had gone, I pushed myself up from the chaise, slipped into my pj's, and settled into bed with my dinner of roast beef and vegetables—hey, people had breakfast in bed, I reasoned, why not dinner?—and clicked on the television news.

*"Patron of the arts Penelope Dare, the director of Cliffside Manor, died in her sleep last night at the age of seventy—"* the newsman said.

Seventy? Was she really only that old? It had to be a mistake. Robert Redford was older than that, for goodness' sake. Miss Penny looked ancient, and had seemed just as old twenty years earlier. I would have put her a decade older than that, maybe more. If she was seventy when she died, that meant she was just fifty when I first met her, when her sister and father died. I had young, vibrant friends from the newspaper who were older than that now, and yet, Miss Penny had seemed like such an elderly woman back then.

I took another bite of my roast beef and wondered what had aged her so terribly. Sure, grief ages a person, but when I met her, she hadn't been grieving, not for long, anyway.

I turned my attention back to the news report, with old photos of Miss Penny, her father, and her sister flashing on the screen as the reporter narrated.

*"Chester Dare, a patron saint for the tuberculosis patients of the day, turned patron of the arts—"*

I clicked from channel to channel, until I was stopped by my own face on the screen. How jarring it was to be the person on the news instead of being the person reporting it. I squinted at my image. Miss Penny wasn't the only one who looked a little rough. I made a mental note to put on some makeup and run a brush through my hair the next time cameras were rolling.

I finished my dinner, stacked my plates on the tray Harriet had left on my desk, and headed into the bathroom to brush my teeth and wash the day off my face. I eyed the tub and thought how wonderful a good, long soak would feel, but I was afraid my exhaustion might cause me to fall asleep in a warm bath. That's all Harriet would need—to find a second director dead in as many days. Instead, I slipped under my covers and settled in to watch an NBC special about Cliffside and the Dare family.

Before I knew it, my eyelids were feeling heavy. I really wanted to see this special, but I couldn't fight it anymore. I'd just close my eyes for the commercial break, I told myself. And then I began to dream.

I was walking around Cliffside's main floor, but it didn't look like it did today. It was more stark, more clinical, the furnishings dated, as though they were from another time.

I saw two men playing cards at a table by the fireplace in the drawing room, where several tables were set up, presumably for this purpose. A checkerboard game in progress sat on one. A chess set on the other. I went on to the winter garden to find people slumped in chairs. One woman was struggling to breathe; another man just looked at me, his eyes sunken, his skin gray. He put out a hand to me, but I backed away and then turned and ran, hurrying through the rooms until I got to the veranda.

I slipped out of the French doors and saw the veranda was full of people lying on chaises, covered with white blankets. It looked like a battlefield hospital, so many people lying side by side.

The sound of painful, deep coughing rang in my ears, and I watched as one man held a handkerchief to his mouth and then pulled it away, soaked red with blood. A nurse pushed past me toward another man lying on one of the chaises. The nurse took his pulse and shook her head as she covered his face with the sheet that was wrapped around him.

And then she looked at me. "Get back to your room with the others," she said. "You're on bed rest. You shouldn't be wandering around down here."

My eyes opened with a start, my heart racing.

The television was still on. I glanced at the clock. It was 3:45. I thought back to the last thing I remembered—the television special about Cliffside—and realized I had been asleep for nearly eight hours.

I tossed and turned for a bit, trying to will myself back to sleep, but it wasn't going to catch hold.

I slipped out of bed and poured a glass of water, finishing it in two big gulps. I couldn't get that dream out of my mind. Obviously, I had been dreaming about Cliffside's sanatorium days, influenced by the television special. I remembered seeing the photographs hanging on the walls downstairs—that's where the dream must've come from. Still. I couldn't shake the images of those patients, lying side by side on the chaises, just waiting. What had Miss Penny called sanatoriums? *Waiting rooms for death*, that was it. That's just what the veranda looked like—people lined up, waiting for their turn to slip to the other side.

Now I was wide awake, rested after a long night's sleep. Except it was still the middle of the night. What to do now? Part of me wanted to settle back into bed and watch some mindless TV until the sun came up, but I clicked off the television instead. What I really wanted was coffee. I could make some, bring it up to my balcony, and watch the dawn break through the darkness. Lovely. Just what I needed to shake off that dream. I hadn't seen the sun come up in some time.

But, if I wanted to be sipping coffee when it happened, that would mean a trek through the big, dark, empty house. I got goose bumps at the thought of it.

*Quit being such a scared rabbit, Eleanor.* I was fed up, already, with this skittishness, this fear that had plagued me and cost me my job. I was a strong woman, I had handled the events of the past two days beautifully, Harriet had said so. More than that, I had interviewed murderers, sociopaths, and pedophiles in the course of my work. Faced down all manner of monsters to get the story. I had solved crimes the police couldn't solve. People were in jail because of me. The woman who did that could damn well walk through the house to the kitchen to make some coffee.

I pulled on my robe and slid my feet into my slippers. There was nothing terrifying about coffee. I opened the door and peered around it into the darkness. All of those empty rooms to pass before getting to the stairs. Fortunately, all of the doors were closed, even the door to my office. Beside it, I knew there was a light switch that would illuminate the hallway and the stairs. I took a deep breath, hurried over to it, and switched it on. Let there be light. I wouldn't have done that if the fellows were here and asleep in their beds, but I was alone on this floor. If I wanted it to be bright as day at 3:45, it could be bright as day.

I could feel my heart pounding in my chest as I descended the stairs, beating harder with every step I took. My breath was coming fast and shallow now, and I could feel little beads of perspiration beginning to form on my forehead and on the back of my neck. *You're having a panic attack just because you want some coffee, Eleanor? Really?* I had let this feeling control me for too long, I told myself. I had lost too much because of it. I wanted some coffee, and I was going to get some coffee, by God.

"There is nobody lurking in this house," I said aloud as I hurried through the darkened foyer, wondering where the light switches were. I couldn't find any, so I switched on table lamps as I went. With each illumination, I took a deep breath.

"There is nobody hiding here," I said again, scurrying past the wall of windows leading out to the veranda. And then, louder, "If anyone is hiding, come out now and get it over with."

Nothing. Only the silence and stillness of an empty house. Just a house. But then another thought slithered into my mind. It was a house that had seen more than its share of death and suffering. Even as recently as yesterday. And what of those children . . . ?

But that was silly, I told myself. Miss Penny had lived here nearly her whole life. None of the fellows ever ran scared from Cliffside, that I knew of. If death and suffering had left an imprint here, it wasn't bothering them. I cut those thoughts off when I finally reached the kitchen door. I pushed it open, felt around for a light switch, and mercifully found one. The room lit up, bright as the afternoon sun.

The countertops were empty and sparkling clean, just like they must've been during the sanatorium's heyday, I thought to myself. In fact, the whole kitchen had a sterile look about it. Stainless steel sinks. Institution-grade refrigerator. Gleaming white tile. The walls were also white, and the floors were made up of that particular kind of speckled tile—light gray, a dash of red, a dash of blue, a dash of black—popular in the 1950s.

I muddled around, opening the cabinets and drawers, which I found to be metal, and finally unearthed the coffee (pre-ground, in a silver tin with a copper cover, labeled *Coffee*) and an old-fashioned coffee pot. An electric percolator of the 1950s variety. I had been looking for something a little more in keeping with the modern age—even a Mr. Coffee—but I really wasn't surprised to find this relic, given the manual typewriter on Miss Penny's desk and the drawer full of paper files. This was probably the same coffee pot her father had used.

Fortunately, I knew how to use one. I'd had a roommate, way back when, who loved vintage things like old percolators. So I filled up the internal basket with coffee, poured some water into the pot, plugged it in, and waited. While it was brewing, I found milk in the fridge—in a glass bottle, no less—and a porcelain mug in the cupboard. I wondered if anything had changed in this kitchen since the 1950s.

No matter, I thought. I knew people in this part of the country were very into not just vintage things, but sustainable everything. It was a movement of sorts, a complete deviation from the convenience products we had come to rely on in the modern age. Getting one's vegetables from sustainable, backyard gardens or local growers instead of at the grocery store. Eating only what is in season. Meat from local ranches. And milk, as I smiled at the glass bottle I had placed on the countertop, from local dairies. I had been too busy in my former job to really bother about all of that. A box of mac and cheese from the convenience store or a frozen pizza had been dinner too many nights of my life. Maybe all of that could change now. I felt healthier just thinking about it.

Funny, those simple, normal actions like making coffee in this old-fashioned pot and fishing milk out of the fridge did wonders for my mood. My heartbeat had settled back down, the tinny taste of bile that I always felt in my mouth during these panic episodes receded. As the intoxicating aroma of coffee filled the air in the kitchen, I took a deep breath. My first since I had left my suite. I was okay. This was okay. And the coffee was just about ready. A triumph over terror. Take that, scared rabbit.

I poured my first cup, splashed some milk into it, and walked back through the darkened rooms, bolder now. I thought of going back up to my suite, but trekking all that way with a hot cup of coffee wasn't too appealing at the moment. I decided to head out to the veranda instead. I told myself I was being bold and unafraid, but really, I wanted to make sure that awful row of patients wasn't somehow still there, coughing into their handkerchiefs, waiting to die.

I flipped on the outside light and peered out into the night. No patients. No coughing. I pulled open one of the French doors and settled onto a chaise. I noticed there were many of them in a row, many more than I had noticed yesterday. Mr. Baines's handiwork, no doubt, readying the place for the arrival of the fellows. Each of the chaises had a white afghan folded neatly at its foot. *A nice, crisp touch,* I thought, pulling the one on my chair up around me to ward off the cold night air.

I took my first sip of coffee and exhaled, gazing up into the starry sky. I couldn't remember the last time I had done that, just sat and looked up into the heavens on a starry night. Being away from the lights of the city really made a difference. The sky was filled with stars, so many that I could almost feel vertigo settling in. I understood why the ancient people the world over would look upward and create stories from the designs in the night sky. There was Orion. There was the Big Dipper. So many stories told, so many battles fought, so many loves lost and won, so many tales told by parents to children around small fires before bedtime.

I was rapt by the sight of it all, wondering what was up there, what was happening on each one of those stars. I wondered if there was somebody looking back at me.

A voice broke my reverie. "Look long enough and you'll see the northern lights."

I snapped my head around to see a man standing at the edge of the veranda. He was smiling and running a hand through his mop of sandy brown hair.

I wanted to run away but felt tied to the spot, as if making myself small and silent would send him away. I curled my legs up to my chest, spilling my coffee as my cup fell onto the cement and shattered.

"Oh, I'm so sorry," he said, walking toward me. "I've startled you. I certainly didn't mean to do that."

"Who are you?" I croaked, my tongue thick, my throat oddly dry. I could feel the blood racing through my veins at top speed. "What are you doing here?"

He stopped, his smile drooping slightly. "I could ask you the same question."

"I'm Eleanor Harper," I stuttered.

"And I'm Nathan Davidson," he said, inching closer and extending his hand. "Nate."

I didn't make any move to take his hand. "I thought I met the entire staff when I arrived."

He rubbed his hand on his pants rather than let it hang in the air. "Oh, there are a lot of us around here," he said, perching on a chaise next to mine. "You never know when somebody will turn up."

His manner was so easy, so casual. Sociopath? I had met my share.

He smiled again, a brilliant, movie-star smile that lit up his face. His eyes smiled, too, crinkling up at the edges and glistening. I had learned to look for that with sociopaths. Their eyes never smiled.

His gaze dropped to the coffee I had spilled on the ground.

"I'll get you another cup," he said, standing up and stretching. "It's only right for startling you like that. I think I'd like a cup myself. Cream?"

I was about to object when he strode off, through the French doors and into the house.

What had just happened here? I had certainly not met this man when I arrived at Cliffside, nor had I seen him the next day. I wondered if I should ring for Harriet, but I realized that I'd have to go back into the house to do it. And he was in there. The last thing I was going to do was put myself into a dark, empty house with a stranger.

I scanned the lawn. Where was Harriet's house? I had seen a map of the grounds in the information packet Miss Penny had given me on my first day at Cliffside, but I didn't study it as well as I should have. Past the light of the veranda, the lawn was pitch dark. If I ran, I could very well be running in the wrong direction, toward the cliff for all I knew. It was miles back to the main road. And I was in my pajamas and slippers. I could feel my heart beating so hard in my throat I thought it might choke me.

I was just trying to decide what to do—take off into the night? Hurry up to my room and lock the door? Get to an intercom to summon Harriet and Mr. Baines?—when the man came back, holding two mugs of coffee.

He handed one to me and I took it, gingerly.

"I thought I was the only one around here with insomnia," he said, taking a sip of his coffee before settling into a chaise, leaning back, and stretching out his legs, crossing them. He put an arm behind his head and smiled at me.

I curled into the corner of my chaise, as far away from him as I could get. My mind was racing with possible exit strategies—throw my coffee on him? Hit him with my cup?—but in the end, I did neither of those.

"I understand," he continued. "It's unsettling, your first days in a new place." So, he knew who I was, then. "I suppose neither of us should be out here at this hour," he said, grinning. "But I won't tell if you won't."

I wasn't quite sure what he meant by that, but I half smiled, going along with it.

"But truly, you don't have to be afraid of me," he went on. "You're looking at me like I'm going to murder you."

"Are you?"

At this, he laughed. "That's not on my agenda for the day, no," he said. "You know, had we met at four o'clock in the afternoon, I think you'd feel differently about me." He took another sip of his coffee. "I wouldn't be some strange guy showing up in the middle of the night."

"No," I said. "You'd be some strange guy showing up in the middle of the day."

He chuckled again. "I suppose you have a point," he said. "If you'd feel more comfortable, I'll go. You really do seem on edge."

I shook my head. I didn't want to lose sight of him. At least while I could see him, I knew he wasn't lurking in some corner, ready to strike.

"What do you do here at Cliffside?" I asked him, finally. "You live on the property, I'm assuming?"

"I live in the big white house just across the lawn from here," he said, gesturing. "One of the perks of the job."

I looked at him, and just for a second, was lost in his gaze. "Why didn't you get coffee in your own house?"

He turned his eyes to the stars. "And miss this view? It's best from here. No trees to obscure the show. I wasn't kidding about the northern lights, you know." He leaned his head onto the back of the chaise and took another sip of coffee. "Look."

I did look and saw what he was seeing. Streaks of red, deep green, and purple, shooting across the sky. Some seemed like a haze of fire on the horizon, hovering just above the tree line. Others stretched the whole length of the sky as far as I could see, tendrils of color blazing across the inky universe just above where we were sitting.

"Wow," I said, conscious of my own heartbeat. "That's amazing. I've never seen the northern lights before."

He didn't take his eyes off the skies. "Really?"

"Really," I said. "I've always lived in the city. You really can't see it there. All of those streetlights."

"Well, this is one of the benefits of living at Cliffside," he said. "Here's to your first aurora borealis."

He held his coffee cup out to me, his eyes still fixed on the show in the heavens above us. I quickly clinked his cup with mine and took a sip. Maybe this guy wasn't out to murder me after all.

I settled back into my chair and drew the blanket up around me, my fear receding a bit, my breath slowing. I was sitting there with a strange man in the middle of the night, nearly alone on a huge property.

But I had the sense that I was in no danger. Why I felt that way, I had no idea. Any sensible woman would have hurried away from there. My only explanation was that I had been fighting my feelings of fear for so long, trying so hard to break through all of that crippling anxiety to do something as benign as go downstairs to make coffee, that when I felt at ease, it was all too tempting just to go with it.

"Tomorrow, you really should take a walk on the path that goes down to the lake," Nathan said, after a bit. "I'd take you down there now but you'd be sure I'd jump you."

"You don't know," I said to him, a teasing tone in my voice. "Maybe I'd jump you. Maybe you're the one who should be afraid out here on this dark night."

He grinned and took a sip of his coffee. "Eleanor," he said, finally. "I once knew a beautiful girl named Eleanor. They called her Ellie. Is that what they call you?"

"Norrie," I said quickly, and then wished I could suck the words back into my mouth. I didn't want the staff knowing my nickname in such an oddly formal place.

"Norrie," he said. "It's nice. Do you mind if I call you that?"

I wasn't sure. In response to my scowl, he said, "You can call me Nate. Instead of Doctor Davidson."

"Doctor?"

He squinted at me, not quite understanding my question.

"It's just, I thought you were on the grounds crew."

Again, his easy laugh. "I do love gardening, but no," he said, pointing to his white coat, which I had noticed but not quite registered. Above his pocket, in cursive stitching, it read *Dr. Davidson.*

"I had no idea we had a resident doctor here," I said.

"With all of the people coming in and out of Cliffside, it makes sense to have a doctor living on the property," he explained. "Town is miles away."

I supposed it did make sense. Six groups of fellows each year. I'm sure Miss Penny didn't take medical histories from each of them—that just wasn't done in this age of healthcare privacy—but, all the same, what if something went wrong while they were here? It would be beneficial to have a physician on the property. It wouldn't be too hectic of a job, to be sure, but who was I to judge? My job as director would be just as sedate, once everything settled down to a normal rhythm.

"That's all the patients you have, the ones at Cliffside?"

"No," he said, stopping to take a sip of his coffee. "My practice is in town. I just live here on the grounds."

Something about what he was saying wasn't ringing true. Then I realized what it was. "Where were you when Miss Penny died? Why weren't you called immediately? Or barring that, why didn't you come and help?"

"I was at the hospital in town when it happened. I wish I had been here. But I think you know as well as I do . . ." His words trailed off into a shrug.

"You know about the suicide." I wondered if Harriet or Mr. Baines had talked to him. "Are you the one who prescribed her those pills?"

"I wouldn't have done that."

"Can you shed any more light on what happened?"

"Mr. Baines called me as soon as he heard the news," he said. "She was gone. Cliffside has seen its share of death over the years, but none of us were expecting that."

*A waiting room for death,* I thought, taking a sip of my coffee, which was now getting cold.

"And speaking of that, as a doctor, I have a duty to inform you that this night air is damp," he said, grinning. "You really should get back to your room before the day breaks. Shall I walk you up?"

I stretched, noticing the first tiny hint of light lapping at the edges of the night sky. All at once, despite the coffee, I felt like I could use a few more hours of sleep.

"No need," I said, sitting up. "I know the way."

"Let me take that cup from you," he said, reaching out. I handed the cup to him and our fingers touched, just for a moment. Electricity shot into my hand, up my arm, and sizzled through my whole body. I could feel my face start to redden.

As I was placing my feet on the cement patio, I noticed the shards from the cup I broke.

"Be careful not to step on those," he said. "I'll clean it up, don't worry."

"Thanks," I said, pulling my robe tighter around me.

"It was nice, sharing the middle of the night with you, Norrie," he said, and flashed that movie-star smile again.

"Same to you, Nate," I said. "Maybe we'll do it again sometime."

"I'll count on it," he said.

We walked through the French doors—any thought of him as a predator was long gone—and he gave me a smile as he headed off toward the kitchen with our two cups.

"See if you can get a few more hours of sleep before morning," he called to me as I made my way up the stairs.

Back in my suite, I padded over to the window and peered around the curtains, hoping to see Nate walking back to his house, but I only saw the lawn, the first hint of light illuminating the grass.

My eyelids felt heavy, and I let out an enormous yawn. The good doctor was right; maybe I could catch another hour or so. I deposited my slippers and robe next to my bed and curled under my covers, resting my head on the nest of pillows I had assembled earlier. *The good doctor,* I thought. Nate Davidson. I still wasn't sure quite what to think of him, but his name was the last thought on my mind before I drifted off to sleep.

# CHAPTER 8

The next few days were a flurry of activity. Harriet and Mr. Baines were constantly buzzing here and there, she readying the house and the rooms for the arrival of the fellows, he planting flowers and mowing the grass. The housekeeping staff, more people than I had ever seen at Cliffside, were in high gear as well, polishing the silver, dusting the chandeliers and topmost shelves, and polishing the woodwork on the stairs, banisters, and the tables until they gleamed.

Harriet was deeply entrenched in preparing the menus for each week, and at one point, she and I sat in the dining room talking about breakfasts, lunches, and dinners for four weeks, taking into account the food preferences of each of the fellows. Mushrooms were fine for some, disastrous for others. Spices needed to be rather mild to suit all tastes. Seafood was not a favorite of most, but Lake Superior whitefish would do just fine. Horseradish was a definite no. Harriet ticked items off her list rather hostilely, I thought.

One near crisis arose when she got word by letter just a few days before their arrival that one of the fellows was allergic to tomatoes. Harriet wailed, not being able to fathom enough recipes without tomatoes to get her through an entire month's worth of meals.

"Why not offer him a simple alternative to the regular meal you'll make?" I asked. "If you're making spaghetti for the crowd, offer him an Alfredo or pesto sauce instead."

This seemed to do the trick, and she scurried off, writing furiously in her notebook.

Food delivery trucks came and went, UPS and FedEx trucks dropped off packages. I could feel the atmosphere at Cliffside sizzle with anticipation—something was coming, and coming soon.

One thing we needed to take care of—and the thing everyone was dreading—before the fellows descended, we needed to have the committal ceremony. Miss Penny was to be buried next to her father and sister, per her wishes, and so we held the ceremony on a bright, sunny day two days before the fellows arrived.

Most of the staff assembled for the burial, and we all watched as Penelope Dare's casket was lowered into the ground, Harriet taking deep, throaty gulps of air to keep from breaking down. The minister said a few words, and it was done.

I knew what Miss Penny had said about no service and no wake, but all the same, I had asked Harriet and her kitchen help to make up a few trays of hors d'oeuvres and open the bar. I thought the staff might appreciate some time to reflect, to share stories, and to toast a life well lived. She protested initially but relented, agreeing that the staff might need some time together before the fellows arrived, to remember Miss Penny in their own way.

"Please join me in the main house now," I said to the staff after the committal, "and after that, don't worry about your duties for the rest of the day. You all have been doing an absolutely stellar job preparing for the fellows, and we're as ready as we'll ever be. Today, we'll gather in the house and raise a glass to Miss Penny and the wonderful work her family has done to foster a long line of artists and writers over the years. And, in two days' time, we'll be ready to welcome the next in that line together, just as she would have wanted us to do."

The words came easily, as though Miss Penny herself were whispering them into my ear.

I looked for Nate during the reception, hoping to share a glass of wine, but never did find him. So I circulated among the staff, talking about Miss Penny, letting people share their memories of her with me. I was the person there who knew her the least, it occurred to me, but even so, I enjoyed hearing their reminiscences. Obviously, she was well loved. I sipped my Chardonnay and stood alone while people who had worked together for many years shared memories and laughed at old times.

All at once, I felt very much like a third wheel. I topped off my glass and had decided to take it upstairs to my room when I noticed Nate outside, talking intently to Mr. Baines, grave looks on both of their faces. I watched them for a moment, and then Mr. Baines went on his way, giving Nate a nod and a handshake before he walked off, leaving Nate alone.

I grabbed a beer from the bar, pushed open the door, and walked across the veranda toward him.

"Hey there," I said, handing him the beer.

"What, no chilled glass?" he asked.

I crinkled my nose at him. "That's a little highfalutin, don't you think?"

"Doctors are like that," he said, taking a long sip from the bottle. "It's a class we take in medical school."

"You're not with the rest of the staff," I said.

He leaned one elbow on the wall behind him. "One could say the same of you."

I shrugged. "I'm the newest one here," I said. "Everybody else has memories of her. Shared experiences. I'm the outsider, and I really don't want to intrude."

"I can relate," he said. "I'm here on the grounds, but I'm not a part of the staff, not really. So many people come through here, it's hard to keep track of them all."

"You came to pay your respects, though," I said, taking a sip of wine.

"I owed that much to Penelope, and the whole Dare family, at the very least," he said. His eyes shifted and darkened. I could feel something—grief?—radiating off his skin.

"Did you know her well?"

He nodded. "We go way back."

"We can go inside if you'd like," I offered. "There are plenty of people to share memories with."

"No," he said, taking another sip. "Like I said, I don't really know the staff apart from Harriet and Mr. Baines. You organized this whole thing so *they* could have some closure. It was a nice thing to do. But I notice you ended up feeling lonely in the crowd."

I held his gaze, not sure of quite what to say. He was exactly right; I did feel lonely.

"Well, you're here now," I said. "My only friend on the playground."

He laughed at this. "I have an idea," he said, his eyes dancing. "You go back inside and grab another beer and wine, and I'll take you down to my favorite spot on the lakeshore. You haven't been down there yet, have you?"

"Oh, I see," I said to him. "You're the naughty friend on the playground." But I couldn't contain my grin.

"You've pegged me," he said, raising his eyebrows. "But it sounds like fun, doesn't it?"

I looked through the windows to the party inside, everyone laughing, talking, dabbing their eyes with handkerchiefs. I didn't belong in there, not really.

"I'll be back in two minutes," I said.

A short while later, I was back with a picnic basket. He shook his head and laughed. "Exactly how many beers do you have in there?"

"Two, for your information," I said to him. "Along with some cheese, crackers, salami, and wine. Courtesy of Harriet."

"Perfect," he said, taking the basket from me and starting off across the lawn. "Follow me."

I did as I was told. We headed toward the cliff, where I hadn't yet been. When we reached it, he led me down a path carved through the rock. It meandered back and forth and back and forth again in an effort to abate the steep grade. We ended up on a sandy beach, the lake gently lapping on the sand, an old, wooden boathouse perched on its shore. A boy poked his head out of the door.

"Hey, Doc," he called, lifting his hand in a wave.

"Hey, Eddie," Nate called back. "Going sailing today?"

"Too calm," the boy said, gesturing to the colorful wind sock lying deflated on its pole. "Maybe tomorrow."

Nate and I ambled down the shoreline a bit. We rounded a corner, and there I saw an enormous, flat rock, big enough for two. He climbed onto it, sat down, and placed the basket in front of him.

"Perfect," I said, and sank to my knees before sitting down on the smooth rock warmed by the midday sun.

He opened the wine and poured a glass, handed it to me, and laid the plate of cheese and crackers in front of the basket before opening his beer.

It really was a lovely spot. The cliff loomed large above us. I couldn't see beyond it to the house or the grounds, but I could see down the rocky, windswept shoreline for at least a couple of miles and across the bay to an island not far offshore.

I popped a piece of salami wrapped around a bit of cheese into my mouth.

"It seems like it should be colder here, right down on the lakeshore," I said, not knowing quite what else to say now that we were well and truly alone.

"You'll be surprised," he said. "Especially in winter, it's warmer by the lake."

We smiled at each other, both knowing we were doing that typical Midwestern trick of talking about the weather when awkward situations arose.

"So, how long have you been at Cliffside?" I asked him, taking a sip of wine.

"It seems like forever," he said, stretching his legs out in front of him. He picked up a small stone and, with a quick motion, skimmed it along the water. We watched it skip once, twice, three times before slipping beneath the surface.

"I've had jobs that seemed like that," I said.

"Chester Dare hired me," he continued. "Back in the day."

That had to have been at least twenty years ago, before Chester and Chamomile died. I sipped my wine and searched Nate's face for any hint of age—he seemed much too youthful to have held his position for that long. The man had to be in his mid-forties, but he looked about twenty-five. I thought about how age had not been kind to Miss Penny, but it was just the reverse with Nate. Almost as though she did the aging for both of them.

*In any case, good,* I thought. I had estimated myself to be at least a decade older than Nate, but now I knew we were more evenly matched. Not that I was entertaining any romantic feelings for him. This was only the second time we'd spoken, and I was still on my guard. I liked this man, but I didn't know quite what to make of him. All those years of crime reporting would do that to a person, I supposed; suspicion becomes a way of life. A hard shell forms around you as a barricade against all of the horror you confront on a daily basis. Makes it difficult for the joy to get in.

"I investigated their deaths, Chester's and Chamomile's," I said, giving voice to my thoughts. "For the newspaper. I was a reporter."

Nate nodded and smiled. "That's why you look familiar. You've been here before."

"I don't remember seeing you, though," I said. "Miss Penny didn't mention there was a doctor living on the grounds. At least I don't think she did. I'd have remembered that. Sought you out."

"She had a great deal on her mind back then," Nate said, staring out over the water. "Penelope Dare."

*Curious, this reaction.* I decided to push further.

"Miss Penny suspected it was murder, and so did I," I said, taking another sip of wine. "But the police dropped the case—too soon, if you ask me. I investigated much further than they did but didn't come up with much of anything. I think it wore on her, all of these years. Not knowing. I believe it was the reason—" I stopped myself before I said the words.

"Guilt is a powerful thing," he said. "It erodes something inside of you. A person can live with it only so long."

I narrowed my eyes at him. "You're implying she was guilty of something."

He leaned back onto his elbows and gave me a slight smile. "Aren't we all, Norrie Harper?"

My stomach flipped, and I smiled back. Charming as he was, I couldn't let it go. "It sounds like you know something you're not saying."

He reached up, took hold of a lock of my hair, and twirled it gently. "Oh, I know plenty I'm not saying."

We weren't talking about Miss Penny anymore. Were we? The air began to thicken between us. I noticed his broad shoulders beneath his shirt, the light in his eyes. I wanted to reach out and touch his cheek, to pull him close, and feel his arms around me. But—why? I had just met this guy and really didn't know much of anything about him. I shook those thoughts out of my head. I curled my legs up under me and busied myself pouring another glass of wine. I cleared my throat a couple of times and could feel the heat rising to my face.

"Norrie, Norrie," he said. "What am I going to do with you?"

"Well, you could continue with our picnic, for a start."

"That's a very good idea," he said, sitting up and cracking open another beer.

We made small talk after that. When we got to the obligatory "Where did you grow up?" question, his response made my palms tingle.

"I grew up here," he said. "At Cliffside. I've never lived anywhere else, other than during my years of medical school."

I squinted at him. "Are you a member of the Dare family?"

"No." He shook his head. "My father was the last physician on staff at the sanatorium. When it closed in the fifties, he stayed on as the family's personal physician, and later as the doctor on staff of the retreat, also seeing patients in town."

"And you took over his practice when he retired," I finished his thought.

"I did."

"He must've retired a very old man," I said, trying to calculate the years.

Nate chuckled. "I thought he'd never leave. I started to feel like Prince Charles waiting for Queen Elizabeth to step down already."

I shook my head and laughed.

"Seriously, the old man practiced until he was well into his nineties," Nate said, flashing that movie-star grin again. "I came on as his partner as soon as I finished with my residency, but his patients, especially his longtime patients in town, wanted old Doc Davidson to take care of them."

"How did you feel about that?"

"Oh, I was completely fine with it," he said, his eyes looking into the past. "He was the quintessential small-town country doctor. His patients idolized him. Births, deaths, and everything in between. I remember once attending a basketball game at the high school with him, and he told me he had delivered everyone on the court. Both teams."

I smiled at him sharing these memories with me. "You don't find many doctors like that anymore," I said.

"That's very true," he said. "But enough about me. What about you, Norrie? Where did you grow up?"

"Oh, there's not much to tell," I said, shrugging. I wish he hadn't asked, but he had no way of knowing I was ashamed of my upbringing. "I was in and out of foster homes until I was twelve. An elderly couple, Joe and Phyllis Harper, adopted me, and I finally found a soft place to fall. It was my first true home, the first place I felt wanted. They were everything to me." Tears stung the backs of my eyes.

"Were?"

I nodded. After all this time, it was still hard for me to get the words out. "They died when I was in college," I said, finally. "It was a robbery gone wrong. Dad took a bullet for Mom, and she died the next day. Of a broken heart, everyone said."

He reached up and touched my shoulder, running his hand down the length of my arm until it got to my hand, which he took in his. I felt the skin-on-skin touch all throughout my body.

"I'm so sorry you had to go through that," he said, his eyes filled with compassion. "You must miss them terribly."

"Their killer was never caught," I said, clearing my throat. "It's part of the reason I went into crime reporting. I knew police work wasn't for me, but I wanted to do what I could to help put the bad guys away."

"Why did you leave it? Why come here?"

I shook my head. "I got fired," I admitted. "For the past several months, I have been feeling—it's hard to explain. The doctors called it post-traumatic stress disorder. I began to feel afraid all the time. Wary. On edge. As if something was coming for me. It made it really hard to do the job. And when I heard about Miss Penny retiring . . ."

"You were drawn here?"

I looked into his eyes. "Exactly. I felt it was where I belonged."

I couldn't remember the last time I had been so honest and open with anyone. We sat there looking into each other's eyes for a long moment, my heart pounding. Something was building between us.

I knew this was the moment that a kiss might happen, and I sort of wanted it to, I imagined it, but my stomach tightened, and I pulled back.

"Don't be afraid, my dear," he whispered, raising his eyebrows. "I'm a doctor."

We both burst into laughter, then, and the moment was lost, but another one, just as pleasant, even more pleasant, slipped into its place. We laughed together for a bit as the feeling washed over me—I really liked this man.

Just then, a raindrop or two tickled my cheek. I looked up to see dark clouds hovering overhead; beyond, they were darker still. He gathered our plates and glasses into the basket, stood up, and extended a hand to me.

"We had better go before we get ourselves into trouble," he said, casting a glance skyward.

But as I looked at Nate Davidson, I knew trouble had already found me.

# CHAPTER 9

We hurried up the path, reaching the top of the cliff just as the sky opened. Nate held my hand as we ran together across the lawn toward the house, not stopping until we were on the veranda under my balcony.

"Why don't you come in?" I said to him, the rain pounding down just beyond the balcony. "We can get warm and dry by the fire."

He shook his head and handed me the basket. "I need to get back. Harriet will throttle me if I drip all over her clean floor. I'll see you soon, Norrie Harper." He took a few steps out into the rain and turned back to me—his hair soaking wet, his clothes sodden—and flashed me the brightest smile I think I have ever seen. "Thank you for being my only friend on the playground today," he said.

"Thank you for a lovely afternoon!" I called, but he was already on his way, loping across the lawn. I watched him go, his rain-soaked shirt sticking to his muscled frame, and I made a mental note to pay a visit to the good doctor's house sometime soon.

Inside, Harriet gave a slight shriek when she saw me, and scurried over to take the basket from my hands. "Whatever were you doing out there in this rain, Miss Harper? You're soaking wet! You'll catch your death!"

"I was down on the beach, and I guess I didn't notice the clouds coming in," I said, purposely omitting Nate from the explanation. I didn't know what, if anything, was happening between us, and the last thing I wanted was for gossip to start flying in the house.

"Why don't you go up to your suite and have a nice bath before dinner?" Harriet suggested. "Otherwise you'll be cold to the core."

What a delicious thought—an afternoon bath. "Thank you, Harriet, I think I will do just that," I said, kicking off my sodden shoes.

"You leave those down here and I'll get them dry by the fire," Harriet said, crinkling her nose up at my shoes. "Once you get out of those wet clothes, send them down the laundry chute and I'll have Mary see to them."

I was really beginning to love having someone like Harriet around to tend to my every need. What an utter indulgence. How did I get so lucky? I could feel the gratitude from the inside out.

"And where shall you have your dinner tonight, Miss Harper?"

"Why don't we do a dry run?" I suggested. "I'll come down at five thirty and have a glass of wine, and then we'll have dinner in the dining room, just as we'll do with the fellows when they arrive."

"Very good, ma'am," she said and was off to tend to whatever it was Harriet tended to.

I tiptoed across the floor, hoping I wasn't leaving too much slop trailing behind me. Once I reached the stairs, I hurried up to my suite.

I flipped on the tap over the tub and peeled off my clothes before dropping them down the laundry chute I spied on the wall of my bathroom. I had brought my favorite bath salts with me, and I sprinkled some into the water as the steam began to rise.

As I sank into the warm water, I thought of Nate, and the time we had just spent together. As wonderful as it was, a dark thought slithered into my mind. Here I was, the brand-new director, going on a picnic with a staff member—I know he said he wasn't really staff, but as Cliffside's doctor, he was, all the same—right out in the open where anyone might have seen us. Was it unseemly? It wasn't the wisest course of action, I thought, as I submerged my head and let the sound of the water rush into my ears.

As I floated there in the massive tub, my face just above the surface and my body totally submerged and weightless, it occurred to me that gossip among the staff was probably the reason Nate had declined to come into the main building with me. He was thinking ahead. I had never been the director of anything before, and I had never had to consider something like propriety. How things would look.

What an idiot I was, I thought as the warm water worked its magic on my muscles. Making a spectacle of myself, running through the rain with some guy I just met. I wondered if the staff had seen us through the windows and was whispering about us now. My stomach seized up at the very idea of it. What would Harriet and Mr. Baines think? What would the staff think?

*Discretion, Eleanor. Discretion.* That was going to be the name of the game from now on. What was done was done, but I was going to be much more careful in the future.

~

Two hours later, dressed, hair dried, makeup on, I was headed back downstairs to the drawing room for my dry run of the dinner ritual here at Cliffside. I poured a glass of wine for myself, sank down into an armchair, and stared into the flames crackling in the fireplace. It was just me, and I felt a little foolish, all dressed up for a solo dinner, so I tried to imagine how it would be when the fellows had assembled for their first gathering, nervously chatting about the house and grounds and their various projects.

Soon, Harriet appeared in the doorway and summoned me for dinner. I followed her into the main dining room where a place was set for me at the head of the table, which—I did a quick count—could seat twelve. A massive fireplace, with floor-to-ceiling stone, stood on one end of the room, its blazing fire illuminating the ornate, green wallpaper adorning the walls. An armoire made of deep, dark wood, carved with animal heads and decorated with inlaid gems, dominated one corner, a gleaming silver tea set on its exposed shelf.

"I'll always sit here at the head?" I asked her, slipping down into the chair.

She nodded, placing a bowl of soup in front of me. "Yes, ma'am. It was Mr. Chester's place, then Miss Penny's place after him, and now it's your place."

The sense of responsibility struck me, then. I was only the third director in Cliffside's history.

As I lifted the first spoonful of the thick lentil soup to my lips, I couldn't help wondering, again, why Miss Penny chose to take her own life nearly the moment I had arrived. It was inexplicable. My reporter's instincts took hold. She had indeed left me a mystery to solve—was this it? The reason she asked me here?

And now that she had been laid to rest, now that everything was set for the fellows' arrival, now that I was more comfortable with my new surroundings . . . now was the time to begin to look into it.

These thoughts swirled around in my brain as I finished my dinner of salad and roasted chicken, and all at once, I knew I wanted to take a look at my notes from the Chester and Chamomile Dare case, all those years ago. I kept meticulous records of all of my stories on my computer, which I had brought with me. I had heard about Cliffside all my life, but the only thing really connecting me to this place was their deaths and my work to try to solve what I believed were their murders. That was the place to start.

Harriet arrived with my dessert and coffee just as I was pushing my chair away from the table and dropping my napkin on my plate.

"Would you mind if I took this up to my suite?" I asked her. "I've just remembered some work I really should finish. I'd like to get started on it right away."

"Of course, ma'am," she said. "I'll just—"

"Don't worry about it, Harriet," I said, taking the delicate ramekin of crème brûlée and the coffee cup out of her hands. "I can manage."

I made my way upstairs, careful to not spill my coffee as I went. Back in my suite, I turned on the desk lamp—an old, beautiful thing with a rosy glass shade etched with a floral pattern—and settled down into the chair. I opened my laptop and took a few spoonfuls of the sinfully creamy dessert while the computer whirred to life. A quick search of my hard drive turned up what I was looking for: a folder labeled *Chester Dare, Chamomile Dare, Cliffside Manor, March 1991.*

I opened the file. I might as well start with the first story I had written about it. I clicked it and it popped up on the screen.

## Wharton: March 19, 1991 Chester Dare, Chamomile Dare, Dead in Apparent Accident

Chester Dare, local industrialist and patron of the arts, and his daughter, Chamomile "Milly" Dare, both died in the early morning hours of March 18 on the Cliffside Manor property, when the car Chester Dare was driving plunged off the cliff just south of Wharton. Chamomile, who had been a passenger, was not wearing a seat belt and was thrown from the car, apparently during the fall. Of the twenty-three staff members at Cliffside, none saw what happened, and none heard the accident. There is speculation that heavy fog in the very early morning hours played a contributing role.

I shuddered when I remembered the fog on the day I arrived at Cliffside.

Penelope Dare could not be reached for comment. Chester Dare founded Cliffside Sanatorium in 1925, first for tuberculosis victims in his own employ in the various businesses he owned in and around

> Wharton, treating most of them without payment. Later, it was opened up to TB patients in the general population. Now called Cliffside Manor, it is a retreat for artists and writers. Chester Dare was a lifelong patron of the arts.
>
> Funeral arrangements are forthcoming.

It seemed pretty straightforward—a windy, cliffside road, a foggy day, a terrible accident. Why had I been so sure it was murder?

I had covered hundreds of stories in the twenty years since then, and the details of countless individual cases floated through my memory, the boundaries between them blurring with the passage of time. I closed my eyes and let my mind wander back to that day, the first time I set foot on the Cliffside property. I could see myself here, all those years ago, in my jeans, black turtleneck, and blazer, clutching my notebook, my stomach in knots. It was my first big story. I was so determined to get it right.

After talking with the police about the specifics of the accident, I approached some members of the staff. They had all been very tight-lipped and grief-stricken, which wasn't surprising—they had all suffered a terrible loss. But, it was what they weren't saying that set off my radar. The looks on their faces. Their eyes, shifting. I detected an undercurrent, but what was it, exactly? Suspicion? Guilt? Remorse? Maybe a combination of the three?

I didn't remember Harriet specifically, but I knew there was a housekeeper who seemed to be the head of the operation, and everyone else deferred to her. It must have been Harriet. She had been at Cliffside for eons.

I clicked open another folder, this one labeled *Dare Case Notes*. I had a nightly habit of transcribing my scribbled notes into computer files—a trick shared with me by a veteran journalist on my first day on the job. It not only forced me to go over the details of any given case one more time, but it made for easy storage of those notes. I couldn't even imagine the amount of reporter's notebooks I had used when covering stories over the years. The sheer volume alone would've made it impossible to keep all of them. I was glad for that practice now that I was able, with a couple of clicks, to access my notes about that day:

*Fog*
*Drove off the cliff. Car found at bottom.*
*"Certain it was an accident," Officer Tom Johnson, Wharton police.*
*Chester Dare, father. Chamomile Dare, daughter. "Milly." Both dead.*
*Milly thrown from car. Not wearing seat belt.*
*Staff isn't talking. They know more than they're saying.*
*Penelope Dare—interview tomorrow.*
*Follow up with Harriet Baines. Lead housekeeper.*

So it was Harriet after all. Now that my memory was jogged a bit, I could see her back then. Jet-black hair pulled into a bun. All-business demeanor. Sensible shoes. I went back to my reading:

*Questions to answer:*
*Where were they going at that hour?*
*Why did they set out in the fog and not wait for it to lift? Train to catch? Plane?*
*Did Chester Dare have enemies?*
*What is the condition of the brakes in the car?*

I sighed. As I read through them again, I remembered my first conversation with Penelope Dare. It was the day after the accident, and I had driven back to Cliffside at her request. I was stunned to get the call because she had flatly refused to see anyone, even the police, on the day of the accident. I never quite understood why they acquiesced to that, actually, especially with all of the knowledge I had gained in the years since about how the police worked in situations like this. Back then, I chalked it up to the sometimes cozy relationships very rich families have with the police in small towns, and I still think that's right, considering how quickly they ruled it an accident, how the bodies were buried without autopsies per the family's request, and how fast the police moved on.

I remembered pulling up to Cliffside in the old, green Jeep Cherokee I was driving at the time and chuckling slightly at the sight of it parked next to the Dare family's two Bentleys.

A woman, who I now knew was Harriet, was standing outside to greet me.

"Miss Penny is on the veranda," she said, leading me through the door. "She will see you there."

As Harriet led me through the Cliffside entryway, I remembered gasping at the opulence around me. *This,* I remembered thinking, *is a retreat for artists and writers? Nice work, if you can get it.*

Harriet pushed open the French doors leading to the veranda, and I caught my first sight of Penelope Dare. She was standing, looking out onto the great inland sea, her posture ramrod straight. I don't know why I always remembered that—posture is a funny thing to note—but it said something to me about her character. Controlled, strict, rigid. When she turned to me, I saw that her eyes were red, a lone tear gliding down her cheek before she whisked it away.

"You are the journalist who was here yesterday," she said, crossing her arms.

"Yes," I said. "I'm Eleanor Harper. I'm so sorry for your loss."

She smiled slightly as her eyes filled with tears. "Are you?" she said to me. "Are you really?"

I shook my head, wondering why she had called me there. "Of course I am," I said to her.

"Well, I'm glad to hear that, Eleanor Harper," she said, motioning to a pair of chairs on one side of the veranda. "Please sit down."

I did as she asked, and she joined me. But before I had a chance to ask her any of my questions, she began to speak.

"The police think this was a simple accident," she said, eyeing me. "What do you think?"

My stomach knotted, wishing I'd had years of experience instead of only days. I didn't know what I was supposed to say or do in a situation like this, so I just followed my instincts.

"I think it's a little early to be making definitive conclusions about the deaths of two people," I said.

She nodded. "Exactly what I believe."

I took a deep breath and opened my notebook.

"What do you think happened to your father and sister?" I asked her.

"I don't know," she said, dabbing at her eyes with a handkerchief. "But I do know that my father had driven that road hundreds—thousands!—of times. He could drive it blind, he was fond of saying. Something had to have happened to make him drive off that cliff."

"Like what?"

She shook her head. "It could be something as innocent as a heart attack behind the wheel," she said. "Or . . ."

"Or, what?"

"I don't know," she said. "But they're gone, and I need to hold somebody, or something, responsible."

Was her grief leading to a need to blame? An accident was simply out of the question in her mind. But I had the same inklings in the pit of my stomach. I felt that there was more to this than an old man driving off the road.

"Where were they going at that hour of the morning?" I asked her. "Did they have a plane to catch?"

"No," she said, dabbing at her eyes again. "Chamomile would never have gone anywhere without telling me. We were as close as can be." I can still see the sad smile on her face, the tears filling her eyes.

"But, she did," I persisted. "She was in the car with your father. They were going someplace."

"I don't accept that."

"But—" I didn't know quite how to phrase my next statement. Their bodies were found with the car. Chester was still behind the wheel. Chamomile had been thrown. They *had* been in the car, going someplace.

"You don't understand," she said, her voice rising. "The police don't understand, either, but to your credit, at least you've come here to hear my side of the story. Milly and I went to sleep the night before as we always did. We talked about the day ahead. We had planned to take a long walk the next day. We had plans—do you see that, Miss Harper?"

"And you believe those plans preclude her getting in the car with your father early yesterday morning?"

She nodded, hard. "Yes, I do. She never did anything without telling me. We shared a room, Miss Harper, for our entire lives. She would never have risen early, not awakened me, and left. Never."

"And yet she was in that car."

"And therein lies our mystery," she said, sitting back.

I dove into the case after that, talking to everyone on the staff (with Miss Penny's blessing, they were a bit more forthcoming), but I never did find out the answers to any of those questions, not definitive answers, anyway. What were they doing? Where were they going? And, to me, most telling was the fact that Milly had left Cliffside without telling her sister. It told me there was more to this story than a simple accident.

But, in the end, I'd had other stories to cover that took my attention away. I moved on and left Cliffside behind. And now, here I was again, in the middle of a two-decade-old mystery that had gotten murkier with the addition of Miss Penny's suicide.

I fished the letter she had written me out of the drawer in my desk where I had left it. I opened it up and read it over again, hoping to find something in it that I had missed. But it was just the same enticement to solve a puzzle she had left behind and the same veiled threat. I sighed, wondering what to do next, when something in the letter grabbed my attention.

> *Milly and I spent our youth running up and down these hallways, splashing in the pool, playing on the cliff, writing in our diaries before turning off the light at night.*

Diaries. I quickly scanned my case notes and did a word search—no mention of a diary or diaries there. She hadn't told me back then that she and her sister regularly kept journals. My gaze drifted to the ceiling. Miss Penny and her sister had shared a room on the third floor of this house for nearly their whole lives. Could those diaries still be there?

# CHAPTER 10

It was nearly eight o'clock, but there was still plenty of sun in the sky. I figured that at this time of year, I had at least an hour before it started to fade. I was glad of that as I climbed the backstairs to the third floor.

I hadn't been up there since we'd found Miss Penny, and that day, I had rushed toward the sound of Harriet's screaming so quickly that I hadn't taken any time to look around. I wasn't sure what I'd find now, and as I reached the top of the stairs, my stomach tightened. I flipped the light switch and gasped.

Miss Penny had told me that the third floor had been an open ward for the children who were TB patients back in the day, and part of it was still that way. A wooden floor stretched to a wall of windows on one side, facing the driveway. A couple of the windows were open a bit, their sheer curtains fluttering. Light shone in, illuminating the dust particles floating here and there on the soft breeze. Boxes were stacked in one corner. I saw my suitcases near them, along with several large trunks. On the other side of the room, I saw a wall that had clearly been added to the big, open space to create a bedroom. Miss Penny's room. I remembered it from that horrible day when we had discovered her in it.

I was there to look through her room for her diary, but I got sidetracked by the trunks on the opposite wall. I wondered—could it be as simple as opening one and finding a stash of journals? So, I walked toward them, my footsteps echoing throughout the room so loudly that it startled me, as though the sound itself was an abomination in the silence in the room.

I pulled open the lid of one of the trunks and was hit in the face with a burst of cold air. Where had that come from? Not from the trunk, certainly. I glanced up at the windows, but the curtains were still fluttering softly. Had I really felt that cold air? I shook my head and thought about how I had doubted my own senses many times since coming to Cliffside.

The trunk, I found, did not contain any diaries. It was full of toys. Old toys. Dump trucks, their paint fading, old play telephones with knotted cords, balls losing their air. Sad relics of the past. I wondered if they were the toys of Miss Penny and Chamomile but then thought better of it. No, surely these were the toys of the children who had been sequestered in this place when it was a hospital. I could almost hear the same laughter I'd heard outside my window that night. Children, most of them dying, were the ones who'd played with these toys. I shivered again at the thought of it.

Just across from the trunks, I saw two doors with faded lettering on them—*Boys* and *Girls*. Bathrooms, obviously. I wasn't up there to investigate every nook and cranny, but for some reason, I really wanted to have a look so I walked over, trying to make softer footfalls this time, and pushed open the door labeled *Girls*.

I was taken aback by how large the room was—more like a school locker room than a bath in a household. The room was entirely white with octagonal tiles on the floor and larger subway tile on the walls leading up to small, rectangular windows that ran the full length of the room. It had to have been freshly cleaned; it was spotless and gleaming. Several stalls lined one wall, with sinks opposite them, fresh, white towels hanging nearby. Around a corner, I found four glassed-in shower stalls and, past them, behind a half wall, an enormous claw-foot tub. A collection of bath salts and lotions and a couple of candles were placed on a shelf near the tub. Ah, I thought. That's why the bathroom was so fresh and clean. This was the bathroom Miss Penny used, obviously.

Just then, I heard the sound of water running. I poked my head around the wall and saw it was coming from one of the sinks. A slight stream of water was trickling from one of the taps. Had it been on when I'd come into the room? I didn't think so. Had it somehow turned on by itself? A faulty gasket, maybe? I stared at the running water for a moment, not knowing quite what to make of it, then walked over and turned it off. As I did so, I glanced in the mirror above the sink. There, quick as a flash, I saw a face. And then it was gone.

I whirled around. "Harriet?" I croaked out, but I knew it wasn't Harriet. It was the face of a child, I was sure of it. Laughter floated through the air, low and scratchy, as though traveling from another time. I tried to listen, but then it dissipated. And I wasn't quite sure whether it had really been there or not.

All at once, I wanted very much to get out of that bathroom. I pushed my way through the door and hurried back into the main room, my pulse racing. Had I just seen—and heard—a ghost? I didn't know. I thought I was above all of that nonsense, but the coldness that now enveloped me was telling me that *something* had just occurred. I just didn't know quite what.

I stood there for a moment, looking around the empty room. Everything was just as I had left it. The curtains were still fluttering, the trunk's lid still standing open. But something had changed. I imagined this room as a hospital ward, beds lined up, one next to the other—I could almost see the image of the room in the past, hovering, just beyond what was really there. The sick children, taken away from their parents, probably afraid, wondering if they'd ever go home. I shivered when I realized that many of them hadn't. TB was a killer. This was indeed the waiting room for death Miss Penny had described.

Was that what I was seeing and feeling—the residue of the children's suffering and pain, somehow still here, hanging in the air, lurking in dark corners?

I eyed the stairway, my stomach in a tight knot, fear wrapping itself around me and squeezing, hard. I wanted to retreat back down those stairs to the familiar second floor, abandoning what I had come up here to do. But then, I thought: no. *Walk through the fear, Eleanor.*

Daylight was fading, and I really did want to have a look inside Miss Penny's room while there was still light in the sky. If I went downstairs now, I might never gather the courage to come back up.

So I cleared my throat and crossed the room to Miss Penny's door, turned the knob, and went inside.

In all of the commotion on the day we found her, I hadn't really registered what the room looked like. I don't remember seeing anything except her body and the letter. But now, I was able to take it all in.

The room was actually a suite of rooms with an archway separating them. In the main room, the bedroom, two twin beds sat on each side of a wooden bedside table with what looked to be a small Tiffany lamp on it. Both beds had cream-colored chenille bedspreads and several floral pillows in reds and yellows and blues, all arranged on the beds in exactly the same way. Windows spanned the length of the room with a cushioned window seat running under them, and books were stacked neatly beneath it.

Two identical dressers stood next to each other on one wall; a vanity with an enormous mirror and a long bench seat was positioned in the corner. Two sets of silver hairbrushes, combs, and mirrors waited on the vanity, as if their users might pick them up at any moment. An old-fashioned, round, glass container that I knew held powder foundation and a puff sat on a mirrored tray along with several lipsticks.

Through the archway, I found a study. Two desks sat side by side, with identical green lamps placed in the same left-hand corner on each one. A bookshelf dominated one wall; two wing chairs stood nearby with a shared ottoman between them.

Miss Penny had kept Chamomile's furniture in the room they had shared, all of these years. It wasn't unusual—I had heard of parents keeping their child's room just as he or she had left it, long after that child was buried in the ground, or wives who never could bring themselves to take their husbands' clothes out of the closet. The grandmother of a friend of mine kept her husband's pipe by his favorite chair for thirty years until she herself died. My heart ached for Miss Penny as I looked around her room, knowing she had been living with that kind of grief.

I sighed and scanned the room behind me, wondering where the diary might be. It wasn't on the bedside table. Where to look next?

On one wall in the study, I spied a small doorway, child-sized. The door was ajar, and I could see light coming through the opening. I walked over to it and bent down, creeping my way through. I was not prepared for what I found.

It was a playroom. The cracked and chipping faces of at least a dozen dolls—now antique, but surely purchased new when the girls were children—stared at me from a series of shelves on one wall where they sat, their dresses faded with decades of exposure to the afternoon sun, which was now illuminating them in the deep oranges and reds of sunset. A tea set was placed on a small table in the corner, two stuffed bears sitting on chairs around it, waiting to be served. A trunk was tucked in a corner under an eave, surely filled with more toys. But it was the enormous wooden dollhouse that drew me in. I stared at it for a few moments before I realized—it was an exact replica of Cliffside.

I sat down in front of it and peered inside. There was the drawing room on the main floor, complete with its marble entryway. Dolls were positioned in a group in the drawing room and more were seated at the table in the dining room. In the kitchen, a doll was standing at the stove. I gingerly reached into the room and picked it up. It wore the same kind of black dress and shoes as Harriet. I shuddered and put it back in its place.

On the second floor of the dollhouse, there were dolls in the bedrooms—one was painting, another was seated at a tiny typewriter, a third stretched out on a bed. The fellows of Cliffside, here on an artistic retreat. There was even the director's office with a doll seated at a desk. And there was my suite of rooms with a male doll nestled into a big armchair in front of the fireplace. Chester Dare?

On the third floor, a replica of the suite of rooms in which I was sitting, complete with two dolls in front of a tiny replica of the dollhouse itself. Penelope and Chamomile.

I shook my head, in awe of the painstaking detail work someone had undertaken to make a miniature version of Cliffside, so that two children could control the comings and goings of everyone within it. In a sense, it made young Penelope and Chamomile into gods, peering into the lives of everyone within those walls, manipulating their actions, calling all the shots.

All at once, a violent shudder passed through me, and I wanted very much to be out of there. The diary be damned. I scrambled to my feet, stooped, made my way through the little door, and was heading out of the bedroom when I noticed the painting.

It was hanging on the wall between the twin beds—I don't know why I didn't notice it when I came in, but there it was. A watercolor of three girls, each wearing colorful dresses, standing in a field of flowers. The Cliffside gardens? Two of the girls looked like Penelope and Chamomile. They stood together, arms entwined, wry expressions on their faces. Small smiles, laughing eyes. Behind them stood another girl. She was holding a flower, a gladiola, and wearing a lovely little yellow dress, but her expression was anything but lovely. She was staring directly at me, it seemed, her eyes intense and focused. She was not smiling. In fact, she seemed to look menacing and, dare I say it, even dangerous. I feared for the young Penelope and Chamomile with such an evil-looking playmate.

I wondered who the girl was and whatever would possess Chester Dare to commission that painting and hang it in his daughters' room.

And that was it. I couldn't spend one more moment in there. I pushed my way out the door, closing it behind me, crossed the empty room, and hurried down the stairs, feeling more relieved with each step.

Night was falling, and I was glad to be back in my room with the door locked before it became too dark. There would be no creeping around the house tonight for me. I was staying put. I poured a glass of water with shaking hands and sank down into the armchair next to the fireplace, shivering as I thought of how eerily similar my room looked to the one in the dollhouse upstairs.

# CHAPTER 11

I watched some mindless television until I had trouble keeping my eyes open. Time for bed. I changed into my pajamas and crawled under the covers, hoping sleep would come quickly. It did, because the next thing I knew, I was opening my eyes. Three thirty. I let out a groan. Not again. I hated waking up in the wee hours of the morning. It was rare that I could ever get back to sleep, and the grogginess would follow me throughout the day. Nonetheless, I was determined to try, so I snuggled back down and closed my eyes. They popped open again when I heard the noise that had, no doubt, awakened me in the first place. I sat up and listened.

Footsteps. Upstairs on the third floor. It sounded as if somebody was running, or walking quickly, back and forth. It wasn't a pounding noise, but a softer one, as though the person or persons running weren't very heavy. And then it hit me. Children. It sounded like children at play.

But that just couldn't be. Could it? I slid back down and drew the covers up around me, ticking off plausible explanations in my mind for what I was hearing. Miss Penny had mentioned that the cleaning crew oftentimes worked during the night so as to not disturb the fellows during their workdays—was that what this was? Maybe, but what kind of cleaning would take people back and forth across the floor so fast? You didn't exactly run with a mop or a broom.

Could it be animals? Maybe a couple of raccoons or squirrels had gotten inside somehow? I wasn't sure. But it was awfully loud to be small animals.

Was Harriet up there creeping about? I couldn't imagine what she would be doing, or why.

Slowly, the sound of the footsteps began to fade, and soon they stopped altogether. I lay there, now fully awake. Try as I might, I couldn't convince myself of any worldly reason someone should be up on the third floor at this hour walking back and forth across the floor.

There wasn't any other possibility. It was children at play, and I knew there weren't any living children anywhere at Cliffside. Was it the lost children of the TB ward? Perhaps. But then another thought hit me. Maybe it was Penelope and Chamomile. Together again in the room they once shared.

~

I didn't sleep for the rest of the night. When morning finally came, I made my way downstairs to breakfast to ask Harriet about what I had heard the night before.

I found the winter garden just off the kitchen. As Miss Penny had said, it was an enormous, octagonal room, completely glassed in, including the vaulted ceiling. Windows were open on all sides, and a massive ceiling fan slowly rotated. Plants were everywhere, many varieties I didn't recognize, though some, like ferns, were familiar. A fountain with seating running all the way around it stood in the center of the room, and I noticed goldfish swimming in its pool. Wicker and rattan chairs with cushions in greens, blacks, and whites sat in pairs here and there. The floor was a deep green and black tile, art deco style, it seemed to me, and a long, glass table ran along one side of the room, with ten chairs with black leather cushions around it. On the table, several newspapers were stacked in a row, and a place was set, presumably for me.

I wasn't sure if it was the trickling of the fountain or the sun streaming in through the glass and shining through the leaves, but I felt my blood pressure drop several points as I entered that room. *What a peaceful place to start the day,* I thought to myself. It almost made me forget what had happened the night before.

A silver pot of coffee, a chafing dish of scrambled eggs and another of sausage, and a plate of fresh scones were on the sideboard. I chuckled at the huge amount of food for just me, but I knew Harriet was doing another dry run. The fellows would arrive the next day, and I had heard her saying something about having a new girl in the kitchen that she was training.

I filled a plate and took a seat at the table, unfurled one of the newspapers, and was enjoying my first sip of coffee when a strange thought slithered into my mind. I had dreamed about being in the winter garden a few nights before. But I had only peeked into the room once or twice in the week I'd been there. I sipped my coffee and thought back. Maybe I had been in the winter garden when I was at Cliffside the first time, twenty years earlier. No . . . that couldn't have been it. I'd had no idea what a winter garden was when I arrived—Miss Penny'd had to explain it to me.

Harriet came through the swinging door, interrupting my thoughts.

"Good morning, ma'am," she said. "You slept well, I trust?"

"Well enough," I said, wincing a bit. "I woke up in the middle of the night. I heard something."

"What did you hear, ma'am?"

"It sounded like somebody was upstairs on the third floor," I said. "I know this is going to sound silly, but it really did sound like children playing."

She crossed her arms. "Everyone's been a bit on edge since Miss Penny's passing," she said. "And you, in a new place."

"Yes, but—" I started.

She cut me off. "Cliffside is a very old house, Miss Harper," she said, her voice soft, as though she were talking to a child. "Very old indeed. She has her moans and groans, especially during the change of seasons like it is now. You're not yet accustomed to the particularities of life here, not used to the sounds you might hear at night. There's nothing to be afraid of here, I assure you."

I took a sip of coffee, unconvinced.

"And no children," she said. "No children at all."

I decided to let the matter drop, for the time being at least. So I changed the subject.

"I remember Miss Penny saying that your mother was a patient here," I said. "She mentioned that you might be willing to tell me some stories about Cliffside in those days, stories of your mother."

Her face softened a bit. "Yes, Mother was here," Harriet said. "She always credited Mr. Dare and the doctors with saving her life. It's the main reason I wanted to come and work here, once tuberculosis was cured and they transformed this place into what it is today."

"Because Cliffside had saved your mother's life?'

"And in doing so, gave me life," Harriet said. "Cliffside is responsible for me being here at all. Had my mother died from TB, I'd never have been born. That's why I wanted to dedicate my life to serving Cliffside."

I nodded, letting that sink in. Talk about a loyal employee.

"Not all the people here were as fortunate as your mother, I understand."

"No, indeed," she said. "No, indeed."

"How long was your mother a patient here?" I asked her.

"Almost a year, ages six to seven," she said with a sigh.

She was getting ready to open up, but then I made a mistake.

"Harriet, will you join me and tell me some of her stories? I'd really love to hear them." I nearly bit my tongue as the words came out of my mouth. I knew better than to change the flow of a conversation once a tight-lipped source had started talking. I should have just let her talk.

She cleared her throat and straightened her apron. "I'd love to tell you all about it, ma'am, and I will. At some other time. The fellows arrive tomorrow, and I've really no time to be sitting and chatting. I need to get back to work, if that's all right with you."

I knew our conversation was at an end.

"Of course," I said, pushing my eggs around my plate. "I'll just finish up and get to work myself."

And she was gone. I'd have to hear about the children of Cliffside another day. I had hoped . . . well, I wasn't really sure what I had hoped. Perhaps that, by hearing the stories of the real children who had lived and died here, it would humanize whatever otherworldliness I was hearing and seeing. After all, if you have the names and know the stories of the people who might be haunting your house, they become more real. Or at least, less frightening.

I thought about a friend of mine who had recently purchased a very old, stately home. Soon after moving in, strange things began to happen. Lights would go on and off. Windows that my friend knew were closed would be open when she came into the room the next time. Doors would refuse to budge and then open by themselves. The backstairs had a deathly cold spot that even the family dog wouldn't walk through. And my friend herself would often feel her hair being pulled from behind, or feel a shove on her back.

She did some research and found that, a century earlier, a maid had committed suicide in the house. She even found the maid's name—Sarah. So, armed with that information, she simply began saying: "Sarah, knock it off," when otherworldly things would happen. And Sarah would knock it off.

"Oh, she's still around," I remember my friend saying. "She just doesn't push my buttons anymore."

She went from being afraid to being in control. I wondered if I could do the same.

# CHAPTER 12

I had organized the dossiers for the incoming fellows and checked on their rooms (everything was shining clean and in order), chosen my outfit for the next day (a black, jersey-knit dress and flats), and sent word to the staff via Harriet that I wanted to have a quick meeting just after breakfast the following day to get everyone's ducks in a row, for my benefit more so than theirs. I was set and ready for the fellows' arrival the next day, and it wasn't yet noon.

I wasn't sure what to do with myself for the rest of the day. I could go back up to the third floor and look for Miss Penny's diary, but after what had happened the day before, I really had no desire to do that. All was quiet up there now. Let sleeping ghosts lie.

Yes, the mystery was still scratching at the back of my mind, but frankly, I had the present day to worry about. Whatever had really happened to Chester and Chamomile Dare all those years ago and whatever reason Miss Penny had really killed herself on the eve of a new group of fellows coming to Cliffside, it didn't have anything to do with what was happening in the present, despite her cryptic letter filled with veiled threats.

I glanced out of the window and saw that the sun was shining brightly in a clear, blue sky. My eyes fell on the forest just beyond the yard, and I realized I hadn't been out there yet. I remembered Miss Penny telling me about Cliffside's extensive trail system. Why not go for a walk in the woods? A little jaunt in the fresh air would do me good. I had been itching to get some exercise since I had gotten here. I wasn't usually much for working out, but something about being here made me want to stretch my legs, to walk, even to run. I felt a vitality surging through me, and it made me want to move my body to its limits.

That was it, then. No more sitting around inside. I thought I had seen trail maps in the entryway, so I pulled on a pair of sneakers and trotted down the stairs to find one.

There was indeed a table with several brochures about the area in the entryway, so I grabbed a trail map and was about to head out the door, but then I remembered something. I wasn't familiar with the property and, even though I had a map, there were some forty acres of forest to get lost in. If that happened, I wanted somebody to know where I had gone. That was Wilderness 101, I knew, and even though Cliffside's grounds weren't exactly the last frontier, I still wanted to play it safe. I made a mental note to mention that to the fellows the next day.

Harriet was probably in the kitchen, I thought, so I crossed the foyer and made my way through the drawing room. But I stopped short as soon as I pushed through the kitchen door.

I saw an enormous stainless steel fridge on one wall and a restaurant-grade stove with three ovens on the other, stainless steel pots and pans hanging above it. Every high-tech, modern appliance known to man sat on the gleaming marble countertops. A long butcher-block table stood in the middle of the room with a great round of dough waiting to be kneaded, a rolling pin lying next to it.

I blinked and shook my head, not sure, exactly, what was going on.

A few nights previous, when I had first met Nate, I had come into this kitchen and been amused that it was such a relic of the past. I could've sworn it was an all-white, farm-style kitchen. Isn't that what I had seen? Milk in glass bottles? I made coffee in an old percolator . . . didn't I?

As I was standing there, mouth agape, Harriet came in carrying an armload of silver trays.

"Oh! Miss Harper! What can I do for you?"

I slowly shook my head. "I'm not sure."

She set the trays on the counter with a clatter. "Is something wrong, ma'am?" She put a hand on my arm. "Miss Harper? Are you all right? You seem a bit confused."

"Harriet, when was this kitchen renovated?' I asked her, not really wanting to hear the answer. I knew full well it hadn't happened within the past couple of days.

"It was 2011, I believe," she said. "Why?"

"And, what did it look like before?"

"Before this renovation? It was rather ghastly, but you didn't hear me say that." She chuckled under her breath. "Lots of green. Countertops, appliances. You know, that avocado color that was all the rage back in the seventies. Before that, it was more stark and industrial in keeping with the original purpose of Cliffside."

I just looked around, not quite believing what I was seeing or hearing.

"Why are you concerned with the kitchen, Miss Harper? Has anything been wrong with the food?"

This shook me out of my stupor. "No, no," I said. "It's nothing like that. The food has been superb, Harriet, it really has. It's just . . ." I had no idea how to go on. I wasn't about to tell her I had seen how this kitchen looked in the 1950s, just the other night.

"Well, then," she said, gathering the trays back into her arms, "these won't polish themselves, will they? I was just looking for Sylvia. Have you seen her?"

I wasn't even sure who she was, having met so many staff people. And then I remembered why I had come into the kitchen in the first place. "Harriet, I came to find you because I'm going to take a walk on the trails." I stopped, feeling a little guilty to be doing that while she was scurrying around, busy as a bee. I added, quickly, "I thought it would be a good thing to familiarize myself with the whole property before the fellows arrive, in case they have questions."

"Oh, yes," Harriet said, nodding. "Yes, indeed. You should do that, ma'am."

"I wanted you to know where I was going because, if I don't show up for dinner, that means I'm roaming around in the woods lost." I managed a chuckle.

She smiled. "I'll send out a search party if we don't see the whites of your eyes in the drawing room at five thirty."

I left her then, out the kitchen door to the backyard, trail map in hand, thinking that we really should have some sort of system in place to keep track of people's whereabouts. Not that I needed to know where they were at all times, but there were a lot of dangers here—the forest, with any manner of twists and turns, to get lost in; the lake, with all of its power; the cliff. I shuddered at the thought of it.

I loped across the lawn, savoring the feeling of stretching my legs. I had never been much of a runner before, but it felt fantastic to be getting some exercise, finally. At the edge of the woods, I stopped, spying a wooden sign: Penny Trail. I dug the map out of my pocket and checked it—yes, there was Penny Trail. It snaked through the woods, across a small creek, and ultimately to the lake, before circling back up to the lawn. The legend said it was three and a half miles long. Perfect. It went only one way, and if I didn't deviate from the trail, I'd wind up back where I started.

I saw there were other trails, too. Milly Trail followed the cliff and went up a series of hills, Chester Trail went the other way around the property and hooked up with another trail that led to town, some ten miles away, and Temperance Trail wound its way through it all, twisting and turning. I'd steer clear of that one for now. I hoped there were clear signs at the trail intersections to tell me which way to go.

Eyeing the map, I saw the trails were rated by difficulty based on hills and terrain (Penny was moderate) and they were also groomed for cross-country skiing in the winter. Just like a state park. It really was quite wonderful, having all of this right outside my door.

I stuffed the map back into my pocket and stepped out of the bright sunshine into the shady woods. The scent of the pines wafted through the air and immediately relaxed me. There was something about the scent of the Northwoods—a mixture of pine and earth and the cool, clean air of Lake Superior—that was like a healing balm to me. Not a sedative, exactly, because when I was in the woods I always felt a sizzle of energy running through me. It was more like a relaxant, a calming incense that made me feel all was right with the world. That's just how I felt as I walked, my feet crunching on pine needles that carpeted the path.

Enormous pines towered overhead, and I wondered if this area had ever been logged. I knew part of the history of the Northwoods involved logging around the turn of the century, but these trees seemed so ancient, so tall, it was hard to believe they had grown back in that time. I wondered who had seen these trees when they were young. Were they standing sentinel here when the Revolutionary War was being fought?

Around one bend, I came upon a massive poplar, its white bark gleaming in the sun and its crown of leaves quaking in the breeze. I remembered Miss Penny had said the property had always been in the Dare family, so perhaps Chester's father had indeed spared his corner of the woods from the lumber barons.

I walked on, trying to quiet the stream of chatter in my head. I breathed in and out, in and out, in time with my steps as a sort of meditation, and soon all of my distracted thoughts—the fellows, Miss Penny, even the history of the area melted away and I was just present in the moment, putting one foot in front of the other. The sun was poking its way through the pine boughs and maple leaves in delicate streams that illuminated the way before me. With its carpet of soft, green undergrowth, the woods seemed enchanted, as though I might encounter a fairy or an elf at any moment.

The trail took me down a hill, and I saw an old, wooden footbridge crossing a small creek. I stood in the center of it, watching the water bubble downstream, a leaf taking the journey now and then. I heard a soft rustling and looked up, just in time to see a doe and two spotted fawns stepping carefully down to the creek for a drink. The doe locked eyes with me—a careful mother with her young—and I held my breath, hoping I wouldn't scare them away. *I mean you no harm,* I said in my mind, and somehow, I think she understood. She and her fawns drank from the cool water and then made their way back into the woods again, disappearing as quietly as they had come.

That was my cue to continue my trek, so I crossed the bridge and walked on. The trail was steeper here, twisting and turning as it descended the cliff toward the lake. I scrambled to keep my balance in a few places, wishing I had worn proper hiking shoes instead of the sneakers I had on.

Soon, the trail opened up, leading me out of the woods and onto the rocky beach. I looked behind me, trying to get my bearings. I couldn't see Cliffside from here. This wasn't the same stretch of beach I had seen with Nate a few days ago, although I knew if I walked long enough along the shoreline, I'd find it. I just didn't know which way to go. No matter. The map told me Penny Trail picked up a quarter mile down the beach, and it would take me back to where I started.

The lake was glistening in the midday sun and lapping gently at the rocky shore. I settled onto a large piece of driftwood and stared at the water and the islands in the distance. Lake Superior had a sort of magic, a mythology and a power that was difficult to define, even by the people who lived along its shores. I always felt at peace when I was near this great inland sea, and I let that serenity wash over me, breathing it in on the cool, clear air. It was intoxicating, and I felt calmer than I had in, well, I couldn't remember how long.

I got the sense, there on the lakeshore, that all was right with the world and I was where I was supposed to be. I had a new job and was living in a beautiful place. The fellows were coming the next day and we were ready for them to arrive. Yes, there was more than a good bit of strangeness going on—the kitchen, the eerie third floor, the tragedy of Miss Penny, and the undercurrent of mystery that ran through it all—but somehow, as I sat gazing out onto this massive body of water, all of that seemed small and very far away.

I pushed myself back up to my feet and strolled down the shoreline a ways until I came to an old, wooden boathouse with a dock stretching out into the water. I had seen a boathouse the other day, but this wasn't the same one. I looked down the shoreline to see if I could spot the one I had seen, but I noticed I was in a cove, and I could only see the shore for another half mile or so before the cliff blocked the view.

I walked down the dock—the boathouse was closed up tight—and sat down on the end, my feet dangling down toward the crystal-clear water. I was watching the light dance across its surface when a voice startled me out of my daydream.

"Who's there?"

I turned around to see an old man poking his head around the boathouse door.

"Oh!" I said. "I didn't know anyone was here."

"You're the new director of Cliffside," he said, opening the door wider and taking a few steps toward me.

"That's me," I said, smiling at him. "Eleanor Harper." But my smile wasn't returned. His eyes were wary, his look stern.

"You shouldn't have come here," he said. His comment hit me like a cold wind, and I scrambled to my feet.

"I'm sorry," I said, quickly. "I was walking along the trails, and I thought this was still Cliffside property. I'm terribly sorry to intrude."

I wanted to leave and go back into my enchanted woods, away from this disagreeable old coot, but now he was standing in the middle of the dock between me and the shoreline. I didn't want to push past him, so I stayed where I was.

He crossed his arms. "Oh, it's Cliffside property, all right. You haven't been trespassing."

"Then, I'm not sure what you mean," I said, narrowing my eyes at him.

"You shouldn't have come here," he repeated. "To this place. To Cliffside." All at once, he seemed to be larger than he was. More imposing. I wondered if I'd have to jump off the dock to get away from him, but I knew the water was ice cold.

"Well, Penelope Dare asked me to come and hired me as the director, so I'm going to have to disagree with you, there," I said, my voice rising a bit. Where did he get off?

"And now, if you'll excuse me, I really have to get back to the house," I said, taking a few steps forward.

"That's what I meant, miss," he said, not moving to let me by. "The house. It's not a fit place for you to be living. It's not a fit place for any one. Those fellows shouldn't be coming here, neither."

I really wanted to get away from this man but was now glued to the spot by the intensity of his words.

"Why would you say that?" I croaked out.

He took me by the arm and looked into my eyes. "Because Death himself lives at Cliffside," he said. "He got Miss Penelope. And he'll get you, too."

I wrenched my arm from his grasp. "That's ridiculous," I spat back, but even as I said the words, I could feel an icy coldness wrapping itself around me.

"You know I speak the truth," he said, his milky blue eyes wide. "And you knew it before you came. You could feel him, reaching out for you."

I thought about the feeling of dread I'd been experiencing for months before coming to Cliffside. Could it be . . . ?

"This house has known nothing but death since it was built," he went on, speaking more quickly now, his voice low. "So much suffering. Many came, few left. The children, miss. Those innocent little children. He nearly took them all. That kind of thing changes a place. There was so much death here, he took up residence. He stayed when the patients had gone. When Death takes hold, he seeps into the very foundations."

I pushed my way past him. "I have to go," I said and hurried down the dock toward shore.

"Death took the Dares," he called after me.

At this, I stopped and looked back at him. "Yes, they died," I said, a bit louder than I had intended. "People do. There's nothing supernatural or strange about it. For Chester and Milly, it was an accident. For Miss Penny . . ." My words trailed off.

"You know it was no accident that took the Dares that day," he said. "And you know it was no suicide that took Miss Penny. It was Death, wanting them all to pay his price."

I backed away for a few steps and then turned to go. I had had enough of this old-timer. He obviously had dementia and might be dangerous.

"Why do you think they have a steady stream of people coming here?" he called after me. I began to run. "It's for him! He always takes somebody! He'll come for you, too, if you don't get out while you can!"

I bolted into the woods, my heart beating in my throat. *Who was that guy?* I wondered if Harriet knew him or if he was a stranger who just happened to be taking shelter in the boathouse.

That had to be it, I said to myself as I scrambled up the hill, glancing back now and then to make sure he wasn't following me. He was homeless and had dementia or some form of mental illness. He had taken refuge in the boathouse. I hurried up the trail toward the house. I'd alert Harriet and Mr. Baines to the situation, or call the police myself to get that man out of there and into a hospital where he belonged. I didn't want any of the fellows running into him. He'd scare them half to death with all of that nonsense, just as he had me.

After a mile or so of twisting and turning through the woods, I found my way back to where I had started. I took a deep breath. There was Cliffside, which had already come to seem like home to me. There was the beautiful lawn, undulating gently toward the cliff. And there, in the garden, was Mr. Baines. I was never so glad to see anyone in my life. I hurried over to him. When he saw me coming, he stood up and took off his gardening gloves.

"Hello, Miss Harper," he said, smiling a broad smile. "Is there something I can do for you?"

My heart was still pounding. I took another deep breath and bent low at the waist.

"What's the matter, miss?" Mr. Baines said, concern replacing his smile. "You look as if you've seen a ghost."

In that moment, I wasn't sure that I hadn't.

"I was walking on the trails," I began.

"Did you come upon the fawns down at the creek?"

I smiled, remembering. "I did see the fawns, and their mother," I said.

"Two of them this year," he said, wiping his brow with his glove. "I call them Bessie and Belle. I leave corn at the edge of the woods for the deer in the winter. There's no hunting on the property, you see, and they take refuge here."

Corn for the deer. It was such a sweet, ordinary thing, I suddenly felt silly bringing up my strange encounter with the old man. But I had no choice.

"I ended up at the boathouse in the cove, and I ran into the strangest old man."

He nodded, knowing just whom I was talking about. "You met old Pete."

So he wasn't some odd apparition, after all. "You know him? The old man in the boathouse?"

"He's a fisherman, local. His people have been fishing these waters for generations. Pete's father and his father before him. They had the old boathouse there even before Cliffside was built. Mr. Dare let them stay on after he developed the property. They've never given us any trouble, and in the old days, we'd get fresh fish, right out of the lake."

"He's not still fishing . . . ?"

"Oh, no, no, no," Mr. Baines said. "Not for many years now. He retired when his boys took over the business."

"So, he has family, then."

Mr. Baines shook his head. "Not any longer. His sons were killed on the water. The lake took them, God rest their souls. Good boys, they were. Pete's wife died shortly thereafter. Of a broken heart, or so everyone said."

And just like that, it became clear. How terrible, losing his whole family. No wonder the man thought Death himself resided here. I'd probably feel the same way, in his place.

"That explains at least some of it." I squinted at Mr. Baines. "But it seemed like he was . . . well—" I stumbled over my words. "Mr. Baines, is Pete . . . does he have some sort of mental illness?"

Mr. Baines chuckled. "I'll give you that he might be a bit peculiar," he said. "But he's all right in the head. Old Pete's harmless, Miss Harper."

I wasn't convinced. "Well, that's the thing," I pressed on. "I'm not so sure he's harmless. He was very threatening. He scared me just now, he really did."

"Threatening?" Mr. Baines put a hand on my arm. "What, exactly, did he say?"

"He told me I should never have come to Cliffside," I said, wincing as I repeated his words. "He said Death himself lives here."

Mr. Baines was silent for a moment, staring into my eyes. A flash of anger crossed his face, and then it melted into concern. "Death himself? Pete said that?"

"He did," I said. "And a whole lot of other nonsense about how Death came for Miss Penny and it would come for me, too."

He let out a long breath, shaking his head. "Oh, Lord."

"It made me think, I don't know, that he had dementia or something like it."

Mr. Baines nodded, gazing toward the woods.

"You said he doesn't have any family," I went on. "I'm wondering if we should call the authorities. It seems like he needs medical care. Like he should be in a nursing home."

He turned his eyes back toward me. "Oh, I don't know about that," he said. "It could be he's just having a particularly bad day. He gets that way around the anniversary of his boys' passing. I'll go down and speak to him, see for myself what's what."

"I wish you would," I said. "What he was saying was absolute nonsense, but he really seemed to believe it. The last thing I want is for him to come into contact with one of the fellows and start spouting off about how Death is a resident around here. That's all we'd need."

"I'll go down there straightaway and give him a talking-to," he said. "Don't worry, Miss Harper."

"Thank you," I said, placing a hand on his arm. "I really appreciate that. Even with the help of you, Harriet, and the rest of the staff, I still feel like I'm flying blind where this group of fellows is concerned because it's my first time hosting. I really want this to go off without a hitch, for Miss Penny. I want to live up to her trust in me."

That brought the broad smile back to Mr. Baines's face. "There's no doubt about that, Miss Harper. Everyone has the utmost confidence in you. We know you're just the person to run Cliffside, now that Miss Penny is gone."

I felt a weight drop off of my shoulders and fall to the ground. I wanted to hug him, but I didn't know if it was appropriate or not, so I squeezed his arm.

"Thanks for the vote of confidence," I said. "I'm going to head back up to the house. Will you let me know later if you were able to talk to Pete and get this straightened out?"

"Of course, ma'am," he said, clearing his throat. "I'll head down to the cove right now."

I turned and made my way across the lawn toward the veranda, the relief evident in my slowing pulse. Pete was just a sad, deluded old man, overcome with grief. That was all.

# CHAPTER 13

I awoke to pouring rain. As I lay there, watching it pound against my windowpanes, I groaned aloud. I usually loved the rain, but why today, of all days? The fellows would be here by noon, and I had planned on welcoming them with a small reception on the veranda. I slipped out of bed and padded over to the window. The cloud cover was thick and gray. This wasn't going to dissipate anytime soon.

Ah, well. We'd just have to move the reception indoors. The best laid plans, as they say.

An hour later, after showering and dressing for the day, I grabbed my notebook and made my way downstairs for breakfast, where I found Harriet's crew already in full swing. One of the girls was giving the carpets one last vacuum, another was wielding a feather duster, and a third was running a dust mop over the marble floors in the entryway. One last spit and polish before the troops arrived.

I was taking my first sips of coffee when Harriet walked in carrying a plate for me—scrambled eggs, sausage, and broiled tomatoes. "We're giving the chafing dishes one last scrub," she said, setting the plate in front of me.

I smiled up at her. "It's showtime, Harriet."

"It is indeed," she said, straightening her apron.

"I imagine we're as ready as we're ever going to be."

She gave me a quick nod. "Shall I move the welcome reception to the winter garden?" she asked.

"Just what I was thinking," I said, sighing and gazing out the window into the rain. "Why couldn't it have been a nice day?"

"Mr. Baines will have two of his men waiting under the archways with umbrellas," she said. "To usher them inside."

"Oh, perfect," I said, taking a sip of my coffee and opening my notebook, where I kept my schedule for the coming days. "I see that Charles is picking four of them up at the airport—Cassandra Abbott, Henry Dalton, Diana Cooper, and Brynn Kendrick. They'll be here at noon. Richard Banks, though, is driving himself."

"And he's arriving when?" Harriet asked.

"I'm not sure," I said, wincing at her. I knew her well enough to know she was not fond of ambiguity. The info packets Miss Penny had sent all of the fellows upon acceptance said they were expected at noon on the day of their arrival, but since this man was driving himself, we really had no idea when he'd show up.

"I probably should have reached out to him and asked," I said.

She raised her eyebrows. "Well . . ." She didn't have to finish that statement. I'd know better than to leave anything hanging next time.

"I'll welcome everyone when they arrive," I said, moving things along. "I'll be in the entryway about eleven forty-five, just to be sure."

Harriet blanched and gave me a look as though I had slapped her. "Oh, no, no, Miss Harper," she said. "That isn't done!"

I furrowed my brow. "What isn't done?"

"The director doesn't usher the fellows into Cliffside," she said. "That's for the staff to do. We'll greet them, show them to their rooms, deal with their luggage, all of that. You'll meet them at the welcome reception."

It seemed silly to me—I was the hostess, after all—but I knew Harriet was a stickler for tradition. Things were done a certain way at Cliffside. Richard Banks had already thrown a fly into the soup by driving himself; any other deviation might make Harriet's head explode.

"Of course," I said to her, figuring I could make any changes to the almighty routine when I had a few sessions of fellows under my belt, so to speak. I was still the newbie here. "Where should I be when they're arriving and getting settled, then?"

"Miss Penny always watched from the windows in the director's office, as did her father before her," Harriet said. "That way, you can observe them on their way in, get a bit of an impression before meeting them."

"Sounds good," I said, taking another sip of coffee. "I'll do that."

"I'll ring for you when they're assembled in the winter garden," she said.

"Got it."

"And I'll be leaving you to your breakfast now," Harriet said, turning on her heel. "I have things to take care of for the reception and the lunch."

I finished up my eggs and sausage, reading over the names of the fellows and their disciplines yet again. I had been doing it for days, familiarizing myself with who they were and what they did, wanting to cement that knowledge in my brain.

Cassandra Abbott I felt like I knew already because of our phone call the day after Miss Penny died. Henry Dalton, painter. Brynn Kendrick, fiction writer. Diana Cooper, poet. Richard Banks, photographer. My eyes lingered on his name, and my heart seemed to skip a beat at the thought that he'd be at Cliffside very soon.

But I shook the thought out of my head. What was I thinking? It was like I was anticipating the arrival of a long-lost friend, or a celebrity. But I had never met the man before and although I knew his work, I wasn't anything near starstruck.

I chalked it up to opening-day jitters and took a long sip of water before pushing my chair back from the table. I was as ready as I was ever going to be.

# CHAPTER 14

I stood at the window of the director's office, staring out into the rain. It hadn't lessened at all, and indeed seemed to have grown stronger as the day went on. As I watched it coming down in sheets, I fretted about the condition of the road leading to the property, remembering the narrow shoulder and the cliff below. I wondered, all of a sudden, why they hadn't put a guardrail up after the accident. I'd ask Mr. Baines. Maybe we could make that happen.

At the stroke of noon, the Bentley pulled into the drive and came to a stop in front of the door. Good old Charles, punctual to a fault. Harriet would, no doubt, be pleased.

Another car followed, an enormous SUV, and pulled in behind Charles.

I watched as one of Mr. Baines's men ran out from under the archway, a huge umbrella unfurled. Another two scurried to the second car and popped the back hatch. *Ah,* I thought. *One car for the fellows and another for their luggage and equipment. So that's how it works.*

The first man opened the back door of the Bentley, and out came the fellows. I couldn't get a good look at them because of the umbrella—I saw a flash of a blue shirt, a long leg ending in a high-heeled shoe, another in jeans. They disappeared under the archway, and, I assumed, were now inside. My stomach seized a bit—this was really happening. They were here.

Mr. Baines's other two men were busy with the luggage, hauling suitcases and trunks, computer bags, and what looked to be painting supplies—an easel and several canvases stretched over frames.

As I stood there watching the scene unfold from my perch on high, I understood why Miss Penny and her father had watched the fellows arrive rather than greet them. I was always one for questioning traditions, but I had to admit, sometimes things were done a certain way for a reason. Even though I didn't quite see everyone clearly as they arrived because of the umbrellas blocking my view, I did get a sense of . . . not power, exactly. Superiority? That was closer to it. I was here, watching them, making my first impressions. They couldn't see me and didn't know I was doing it.

The Bentley pulled away, and, as soon as the SUV was unloaded, it did the same, parking across the lot near the gardener's quarters. I watched as the drivers, Charles and another man, got out of their respective cars, shut the doors behind them, and loped off around the building.

I looked at my watch. Twelve fifteen. What was I going to do with myself for the next hour or so until it was time for the welcome reception? I heard a commotion on the stairs—voices and footsteps and laughter—and knew that Harriet was showing the fellows to their rooms on this floor. I shouldn't go to my suite. Harriet might have a stroke if I was seen by the fellows before the reception. No, my instructions had been clear. She was going to ring me on the intercom when it was time for my grand entrance.

So, I stayed where I was at the window and watched the rain pelting the two black cars, puddles pooling in the gravel drive.

A few minutes later, another car pulled in, a gray SUV of some kind. Richard Banks, no doubt. He was here! He parked next to the other two cars, and before Mr. Baines's man could get out to him with an umbrella, he opened the driver's side door and slid out, seemingly unconcerned by the downpour. Something about it made me smile. No arriving in a fancy Bentley for this man.

He flipped up the collar of his jacket and hurried to the back of the car, popping the hatch and drawing out a large duffle bag and another heavy-looking black bag—his cameras, no doubt—which he slung over his shoulder.

He looked familiar to me somehow, this man, his head full of dark hair, his broad shoulders. I leaned in to get a better look, my heart beating in my throat as though I were a teenage girl catching sight of a boy-bander. *Pull yourself together, Norrie.* Just then, he glanced up toward my windows. He saw me. So much for peering down from on high, unseen.

We locked eyes, and in that moment, a jolt of electricity sizzled through me so strongly that it might have been a lightning strike had I been outdoors. He broke into a wide grin, his face soaking wet from the rain, and raised one hand in greeting. I smiled and did the same, my own face reddening.

Just then, the man arrived with his umbrella, obscuring Richard Banks from my view. I watched as the blue umbrella came closer and closer to the house and then disappeared under the archway.

A few minutes later, I heard more voices in the hallway. Someone was showing him to his room. I listened until their footsteps faded.

Everyone had arrived. All of the fellows were at Cliffside.

~

One thirty came and went. I expected Harriet to buzz me on the dot, but apparently the fellows weren't as concerned with punctuality as Harriet was. I smiled at the thought of her waiting in the winter garden, hand on her hip, toe tapping.

I had checked my hair and makeup in the mirror over and over again, eyeing my black dress darkly. Now I wished I had chosen something a little less dour. I was contemplating dashing to my suite to change when the intercom crackled and buzzed.

"Miss Harper?" she said, the connection scratchy. "It's time."

All feelings of superiority that my window-watching had afforded me dissipated.

I pushed myself up from my chair, opened the door, and walked through it, very conscious of my own movements. *What am I doing here? This is Miss Penny's place, not mine.* I felt every inch the fraud as I descended the staircase. I had no business being the director of Cliffside, no business at all. *Please let me not screw this up.*

But as I walked through the foyer, my footsteps echoing on the marble tile, I tried to counter those thoughts, taking deep breaths in time with every fourth step. *In and out, Norrie. In and out.* These people weren't here to see me, I told myself. I didn't have anything to prove to them. I was simply their hostess. Just the person who was on hand to make sure things ran smoothly. And, really, I told myself, the person who would see to that was Harriet. I was just the figurehead. There was really nothing I could ruin, nothing I could get so horribly wrong as to mar somebody's experience here. There was nothing to fear. So why was I quaking?

I took one last deep breath and walked into the winter garden, trying to exude a confidence I wish I felt.

The women were seated at the round table; the men stood by the wall of windows. Harriet was positioned by the sideboard, ready to serve. They all looked at me as I entered.

On cue, three of Harriet's girls appeared carrying trays. One held glasses of red wine, another white, and the third, hors d'oeuvres. The girls circulated with the trays until everyone had a glass, including me.

"Hello, everyone," I said, my voice a bit too loud as I held my glass aloft. "Welcome to Cliffside!"

A weak chorus of hellos came in response. I didn't know quite what to do or say after that. I had prepared a welcome speech, but it flew out of my mind the moment I entered the room. Thankfully, Harriet came to my aid.

"This is Eleanor Harper," she said, her tone stern. "Miss Harper is the director of Cliffside, as you know."

Another man, who I assumed to be Henry Dalton, crossed the room and extended his hand. I judged him to be in his mid-fifties or early sixties, his shock of gray hair betraying his age, although his face was quite youthful. He wore khakis and a crisp, blue-striped shirt, and looked as though he'd be more at home at a polo club than in a studio. This was no starving artist.

"Hello, Mr. Dalton," I said to him, smiling as I took his hand. "I do hope you find inspiration for your wonderful paintings here in the gardens, although today isn't the best day for that."

He raised his eyebrows and smiled, lifting my hand to his lips and kissing it softly. I was very glad I had studied those dossiers.

"I'm sure I will, ma'am," he said, bowing his head, a slight Southern accent making music of his words. "The Cliffside gardens are legendary. Thank you so very much for this opportunity."

At this, the three women scrambled to their feet and joined us, all of them beaming. I didn't know who was who among them, so I was glad when they introduced themselves.

One of them, a petite woman in a cream-colored Chanel suit, her dark hair styled in a neat bob, grasped both of my hands. "We already know each other, but I'm afraid I didn't make a very good impression." She turned to the others. "I was quite rude to Miss Harper on the phone a few days ago, I must confess."

"Were you?" I smiled, squeezing her hand. "I had forgotten. Cassandra, I'm eager to hear all about your research into TB sanatoriums. We must sit down one day soon and talk about it."

"I'd like that very much," she said. "I'm just so thrilled to be here. I feel the inspiration already!"

"Yes, we heard all about it on the drive," said another of the women, drawing out the *all* as though it had several syllables.

I saw a twinge of something in Cassandra's eyes—hurt? Or was it anger? I squeezed her hands as we exchanged a look.

"I'm Brynn Kendrick," the woman said, pushing her long, blond hair behind her ear. She was a young woman, mid-twenties to early thirties at most, her slacks and tight-fitting top accentuating her slim figure.

"You're the novelist," I said, turning to her, managing a smile.

"Yes," she said. "As it happens, I'm writing about TB, too. Fiction. I'm setting my novel here at Cliffside. She didn't know that"—she glanced over to Cassandra and narrowed her eyes—"but I'm sure you do. It was in my letter of application, of course."

"Of course," I said, but I didn't know anything of the kind. Those letters of application weren't in the dossiers. It made me wonder, again, what Miss Penny had done with them.

I took a sip of my wine and turned to the third woman. Her long, dark hair was a mass of curls. She held it at bay with her glasses, pushed up on her head as a sort of headband.

"And you're Diana," I said. "Our professor."

She smiled a warm smile. "I, too, am very glad to be here," she said, glancing at Henry. "It's going to feel like such an indulgence, having nothing to do but focus on my poetry. No phone calls, no Internet. No students! I hope you all don't mind if I'm a bit antisocial, but that is why I've come. To be inspired by solitude."

I took the lead, then, filling them in about meals, the policies of the house, giving them the rules of the road, so to speak.

"Your time is your own to do with as you wish," I said, "but we do ask everyone to gather in the drawing room at five thirty. One of the many perks of being at Cliffside is the opportunity to talk with like-minded people about their work and yours. Miss Penny told me about the wonderful discussions people have had during that time. The fellows before you have all enjoyed this, and it is our hope that you will, too.

It's an important part of what we do. We'll have a drink, and then if you wish to have dinner with the group, it will be in the dining room. If not, you're welcome to take it in your room or elsewhere in the house.

"There is one other thing you should know," I said. "If you need anything, day or night, I'm here. My office is on the second floor, as is my suite of rooms. Please don't hesitate to seek me out if you need anything at all."

And then I raised my glass. "To your first day at Cliffside," I said to them. "May you find inspiration and creativity here, as so many have done before you." The words rolled off my tongue easily. I didn't know where they came from, but I was glad they did.

"To Cliffside," Henry said, the others repeating it.

They finished their drinks and filed out, each thanking me as they went. All but Richard Banks, who was leaning against a window frame grinning at me.

"Something I can do for you, Mr. Banks?"

He walked across the room and extended his hand. "I didn't get to introduce myself before you started in on your spiel," he said. "So very nice to meet you, Miss Harper."

I slipped my hand into his, and that same jolt of electricity flowed through me that I had felt when I first saw him get out of the car barely more than an hour earlier. I could feel the heat rising to my face, and I prayed I wasn't blushing. I fought to suppress a giggle. What was I, twelve?

"Nice to meet you, too, Mr. Banks," I said.

We stood there for a moment, not letting go of our handshake, until Harriet and her minions burst through the door, there to collect the trays and glasses, no doubt.

She narrowed her eyes at us, and I dropped his hand as if it had stung me.

"I'm wondering if you'd be so kind as to give me a tour of the house," he said, his accent—certainly not upper-crust British—sounding almost

Irish, even though I knew he was from Cornwall. "There's not much photography to be done outside on a day like this." He flashed Harriet a smile and winked at her. "Isn't that right, Mrs. Baines?"

"Yes, yes, I suppose," she stammered, and I swear I saw a flush come to her cheeks. He was a flirt, this one. After giving a few short orders to the girls, Harriet hurried out of the room.

I stifled a chuckle, but when she had gone, I caught his eye and let it out. "There aren't many people who can disarm Harriet, but I think you just did."

He grinned. "Now, how about that tour?"

# CHAPTER 15

As we strolled from room to room, I told him what I knew about the property, that it had been a sanatorium for TB patients back in the day before Chester Dare decided to make it a retreat for artists and writers.

"And why did he do that, do you suppose?" he asked, running a hand through his dark hair.

"I really don't know," I said. "She would have been the one to ask about that." We were in the drawing room now, and I gestured to a painting that hung above the fireplace. Chester, Chamomile, and Penelope. The girls looked to have been teenagers when it was painted.

"Ah, yes, the famous Penelope Dare," he said, staring at the portrait. "I was so sorry to learn of her passing. Both sisters gone, now."

"Thank you," I said, remembering the way she had looked when we discovered her on that horrible day. So grotesque compared to the beautiful girl in the painting. I shook my head, as if to shake that image away. "It was such a shock to everyone."

"And you had just arrived, isn't that right?"

"It was my first day. She had just hired me."

"It's a wonder you stayed on."

"Oh, no," I said to him. "Not at all. I made a promise to Miss Penny that I'd be the director of this place. Her death didn't change that. It made it more difficult, because I've had to muddle through without her, but it didn't change the promise I made to her."

"Well, I personally thank you for it," he said, leaning against the sofa. "For purely selfish reasons. I don't know what would have become of our session had you not stayed on."

"That's my point exactly," I said to him. "Life had to go on here at Cliffside. There's a whole staff of people dependent on Cliffside for their livelihoods, and an entire year of fellows, you included, who were counting on coming here. I had to make it work."

"You've had quite the trial by fire then," he said, reaching over and touching my arm. That small, caring gesture was enough to make tears sting at the backs of my eyes. I turned around and whisked them away. Trial by fire, indeed. He had no idea.

"I'm sorry," I said, turning back to him. "It's just that—" My words dissolved into a sigh.

"It's stressful, I know," he said, his deep voice and musical accent acting like a balm on my frayed nerves. I felt myself exhale. "Not to mention that everyone's still in a state of grief," he went on. "You've pulled it all together beautifully, if I may say."

I managed a smile. "I'm only the third director in Cliffside's history. First Chester Dare, then Penelope, and then me."

"Quite the responsibility, carrying on somebody's life's work," he said.

This man truly understood.

"I still can't get over it," he said, "her dying on the very day you came. She handed over the reins and then passed away. Almost like she planned it."

Almost, indeed. I nearly told him everything right then—it felt so good to have someone to talk to. But I kept quiet about Miss Penny's suicide. That she died was public knowledge. How she died was her own business.

"Maybe she knew she was dying and wanted to put a successor in place," he offered.

"Yes, I think that's probably right," I said. "We had known each other before, twenty years ago. I hadn't talked to her since. But I had just left my job right around the time she announced she was retiring, and everything seemed to fall into place for me to come to Cliffside."

"Interesting," he said. "That's how I came to be here, too."

I squinted at him. "How so?"

He shook his head. "I met the Dares"—he furrowed his brow—"it must be twenty years ago now. Chester had seen my work in *National Geographic* and wanted me to shoot Cliffside—the grounds, the shoreline, his daughters. I wasn't interested in that kind of portrait work, but then he mentioned how wild and untamed Lake Superior was, and I got interested."

"So, you did the shots?"

He shook his head. "I got a bit of shooting in, but not what they had asked for," he said. "I found myself on my own and was taking advantage of that to shoot some of the area, but a few hours later I was told to leave."

"Leave?"

"Yeah," he said. "It was so odd, I came all this way—on their dime, no less—and I had no more than just arrived when he cancelled the whole thing."

"That is odd," I said. "Did they say why?"

"Only that something had come up that made it impossible for me to be given access to the grounds," he said.

"And so you turned around and went home?"

"I did," he said. "But Lake Superior always called to me. I felt like I had really missed out on something, that I should have stayed and explored the lake with my camera. The shoreline reminds me a bit of the Cornish coast."

"Why didn't you come back? I mean, the Dares aren't the only ones with shoreline. There's plenty of access. It's a big lake."

He shrugged. “Penelope called several times, inviting me back. But life intervened. My career started taking off, and one thing led to another and soon twenty years had passed.”

I knew the feeling.

“And then Penelope rang out of the blue and asked me to come to Cliffside again,” he continued. “She wanted me to finish what I had started. I had another photo shoot scheduled for these two weeks, in Kenya actually, but it was cancelled a few days before she rang. I found myself free. And so I came.”

We stood there, looking at each other. He had a puzzled look on his face, and I was sure I did, too.

I had found myself out of a job just before Miss Penny announced her retirement. Richard had found himself out of a job just before she called with the offer for him to come and be a fellow. I also thought of Cassandra Abbott—she had applied, and was turned down, seven times before being accepted for this session.

*What were you up to, Miss Penny?*

All at once, a shiver ran through me. I thought of the dollhouse sitting in her room on the third floor, the perfect replica of Cliffside, all of those tiny people in it. I got the sense that she was up there even now, playing God, manipulating us all.

# CHAPTER 16

After Richard had gone to his room to settle in, I sat in the winter garden sipping tea, a file of applications for next year's round of fellows in my lap. I had read through about half of them when I took a break to watch the rain hit the windowpanes in bursts. The serenity here was quickly making it my favorite room in the house.

My mind wandered back to the mystery at hand. What could Penelope Dare have been up to, engineering things so Richard, Cassandra, and I were at Cliffside at the same time? Yes, I had sought out the job myself, but I had felt inextricably pulled toward it all the same. And now, it did feel like she had had a hand in it. But how?

I wondered about the manner in which the others in this group had come to Cliffside. Maybe they were marionettes in Miss Penny's puppet show as well, and that could be why their letters of application were missing.

But it didn't make sense. Why manipulate things so at least a few of us were at Cliffside at the same time, only to take her own life before she saw her little dollhouse drama played out?

I took another sip of tea and let my mind wander.

Cassandra was writing a history of sanatoriums like Cliffside. Richard was a photographer with no particular interest in the place, but rather in the lake where Cliffside stood. And me? I couldn't find a link connecting any of it to me, other than having been here twenty years ago.

I finished my tea and put the cup back down on its saucer with a note of finality. I couldn't figure anything out myself until I knew more, especially about how the others had come to Cliffside. If they were just ordinary fellows who had applied and been accepted, I was at a dead end. But if they, too, had strange circumstances that had brought them here, I'd have something to go on. I thought about asking them at dinner but then thought better of it. No, I'd ask each of them in private. Better to keep any of my questioning under wraps, for now.

Harriet poked her head around the doorway, interrupting my train of thought. "I buzzed your suite," she said. "And your office."

"Oh, I'm sorry you had to come looking for me, Harriet," I said. "I've been right here, going through next year's applications."

She pursed her lips and let out a *tsk*, and I got the distinct impression I had done something wrong.

"We try to remain as invisible as possible when the fellows are here," she said, scowling at me. "Miss Penny always remained in her suite or her office during the day. I'd have thought she would have told you that."

"No," I said, shaking my head. "She didn't."

She folded her arms across her chest and tried again. "That's how it's always been done. We don't want to disturb their creative process."

Was she serious? I was supposed to stay cloistered in my room for the entire time?

"That might have been how Miss Penny did things," I said, sounding more bold than I felt, "but I really don't think me drinking tea on a rainy afternoon in the winter garden is going to disturb anyone's creative process."

She huffed. I went on, "And, no, to answer your question, Miss Penny didn't tell me to stay in my suite or in my office. She said just the opposite, as a matter of fact. She told me my time was my own and to enjoy the house and grounds as I saw fit, but not to leave the property."

"Well, I—" She struggled to find the right words.

"Had she told me to sit in my suite all day, every day while the fellows were here, I wouldn't have taken the job," I said. "I suspect she knew that, despite what her routine had been. But trust me, Harriet. I know better than to disturb the fellows. I'll be quiet as a mouse."

"Yes, ma'am," she said, a sour look on her face. She definitely didn't like my answer.

"Now," I said, desperately wanting to get out of this line of conversation, "you said you were buzzing me. What's up?"

She cleared her throat. "I wondered if you were wanting to go over the dinner menu," she said. "I know we've already sketched it out, but Miss Penny always approved the menu again before dinner each night."

I pushed myself up to my feet and walked over to her, and took her hands in mine. "Harriet, you are much more capable than I am at the art of choosing wonderful menus and making the meals sing," I said to her. "Everything you've made for me since I've been here has been just delicious."

"So, you want me to—"

"Yes," I cut in. "I do. I have complete trust in your judgment. You're in charge of the menus from now on. I don't need to approve them."

"All right," she said, nodding her head, trying this enormous breach in tradition on for size. "Thank you, ma'am."

And she turned to go, leaving me wondering if giving her complete authority over the meals had pleased or angered her. She was, I was finding out, such a stickler for the old ways, for how things had been done in the past at Cliffside. Perhaps this freewheeling new world of directors roaming out of their rooms and autonomy over menus was going to be too much.

~

It was nearly five fifteen. After my encounter with Harriet, I had retreated to my suite, careful to not make noise in the hallway as I went. Freshly showered, wearing a long, purple dress, strands of silver beads, and my favorite silver earrings, I made my way back downstairs. I knew I was supposed to be in the drawing room to welcome the fellows to their daily gathering, and I didn't want to be late, irritating Harriet even more than I had earlier in the day.

I thought of apologizing to her, but then I thought, no. I didn't want to hurt her feelings or step on her toes, but the fact was, no matter how Harriet felt about it, Miss Penny had told me I was free to enjoy the house and the grounds while the fellows were in residence. And, further, I thought to myself as I descended the stairs, I was the director here, wasn't I? That meant I made the rules, didn't it? And Harriet, technically, was my employee. They all were. I didn't answer to anybody. I smiled to myself, gaining confidence with each step. Where was that scared rabbit now?

I entered the drawing room and saw two bottles of what I found to be Chardonnay and several local craft beers standing in the enormous ice bucket on the sideboard, with a couple of bottles of red—one merlot, one Cabernet—open next to it. Glasses stood in neat rows.

I wondered if I was to pour my own glass of wine, or if a bartender would materialize. No matter. With my newfound boldness, I picked up a glass and poured some Chardonnay into it, consequences be damned.

I took a sip, and before I knew it, Diana Cooper walked through the doorway. I noticed she had changed clothes as well. She was now wearing a flowing, blue cotton dress, decorated with moons and stars, and silver sandals.

"Professor Cooper," I said to her. "Good evening! Please, help yourself. We've got red and white wine and locally brewed craft beer."

"A glass of red sounds lovely," she said, moving over to the sideboard to pour it. She took a sip and sighed. "Heavenly. I can use it, after the day I've had."

"Oh?" I said. "Is everything all right?"

She sank down onto one of the sofas and crossed her legs. "More than all right," she said, smiling. "After our reception, I headed back up to my room and spent the next few hours writing. I can't remember having a more productive day!"

"That's wonderful," I said, sitting down beside her. "Good work, I trust?"

"Phenomenal," she said. "It just seemed to flow. But now"—she stopped to take a sip of her wine—"I'm exhausted. It happens like that, for me. I work in a frenzy and then I'm spent for the rest of the day."

Just then, Brynn and Henry joined us, entering the room arm in arm.

"Good evening, ladies," he said to us, bowing his head slightly.

Before we had a chance to respond, Brynn piped up, "Mr. Dalton is such a Southern gentleman. Offering his arm as we came down the stairs."

He nodded at her and moved across the room to the sideboard. "What's your pleasure, Miss Kendrick? Red or white?"

She wrinkled her nose at the collection of bottles. "No gin?" She turned to me, her eyes wide.

Ah, I was to see if we had any gin, that was it. So much for my hubris, thinking I had no one to answer to at Cliffside. Of course I did. I answered to the fellows.

"And tonic, I presume?" I asked her.

"Please," she said, smiling broadly. It reminded me of an animal baring its teeth. "And lime, if you have it."

I realized I had absolutely no idea where we kept the alcohol here at Cliffside, so I wandered through the house to the kitchen to find Harriet. She was at the kitchen table, eating her dinner with Mr. Baines. Whatever she had prepared, the kitchen smelled like heaven.

When I walked in, Mr. Baines dropped his fork and stood up. Harriet wiped the corners of her mouth with her napkin.

"Yes, Miss Harper?" she said. "What can we do for you?"

"I'm so sorry to interrupt your dinner," I said. "Please, Mr. Baines, sit back down. I'm only wondering if we have any gin, tonic, and lime. Brynn Kendrick's request."

Harriet pushed herself up from the table and crossed the room to the refrigerator, where she found a bottle of chilled tonic water and a lime. She handed them to me and shook her head. "It's always something with them," she said, and we shared a grin. So, she wasn't angry with me, then. Thank goodness.

"I'm finding that out," I said. "I'm wondering if someone will want champagne and caviar next."

This elicited a snort from Mr. Baines and a stifled grin from Harriet. "You wouldn't believe what some of them ask for," he said, shaking his head. "Do you remember the lobster, Mrs. Baines?"

They exchanged an amused glance. "Here we are on Lake Superior, and one wanted fresh lobster," Harriet said, her eyes looking a bit guilty, as though she was talking out of school. "Fresh salmon and whitefish we can do, but lobster? It's a freshwater lake!"

I laughed and took the tonic and lime from her. "Miss Penny said some of them can be divas," I said. "I guess this is what she was talking about."

"Indeed," she said, settling back down in her chair.

"And the whereabouts of the gin?"

"In the sideboard," she said. "You'll find all manner of alcohol there. Anything they should want, we have."

I thanked her and turned to go. "Enjoy your dinner, you two, and I'll see you in the dining room at six thirty."

Back in the drawing room, I found Richard and Cassandra had joined the party. The two of them were standing by the sideboard, and he was pouring red wine into a glass that she was holding. She had changed clothes as well, into a very low-cut black dress. The way she was looking into his eyes and smiling . . . it sent a rush of something through me, but I wasn't sure what. Anger? Jealousy? That was ridiculous. I had just met the man. I shook my head, as if to shake the feeling away. *Stop being such an idiot, Norrie.*

He turned to me. "There she is!" he said, flashing that devilish grin of his. "I was wondering where our lovely hostess was."

I smiled at him, hoping my face wouldn't betray me by blushing. "I was on a mission," I said, holding up the tonic and the lime. I set them down on the sideboard and opened its double doors, revealing a stash of bottles.

"Excellent," Brynn said and resumed her conversation with Henry, making no move to get up. I was to make her the drink, apparently.

Richard caught my eye and smiled. "Allow me," he said, filling a highball glass with ice. "I was a bartender, back in the day."

"Were you, now?" I said, smiling back at him.

"Bartender, taxi driver, waiter—you name it, I've done it," he said, delivering the drink to Brynn and taking a seat on the opposite sofa.

Everyone stopped talking then and looked at me. Apparently, I was supposed to say something—I just didn't know what.

Grasping, I said, "So, how was everyone's first day at Cliffside? Diana reports that she had a productive afternoon."

"I didn't get anything done." Brynn sniffed, taking a sip of her drink. "I just unpacked. What about you, Mr. Dalton?"

He leaned against the back of the sofa and crossed his legs. "I unpacked as well," he said. "My room has a lovely view of the gardens. Even in the rain, I could see how beautiful they are. I do hope we have better weather tomorrow. I can't wait to get started."

"Oh, I agree," said Cassandra, settling in next to Richard on the sofa. "I love my workspace. I've got all of my notes arranged and I'm ready to go. It's inspiring just to be here. I'm feeling like—I don't know . . ." Her words trailed off.

"What?" I asked.

"I just feel really at home here," she said. "I'm sure it's all the research I've done, but for me, the place has a really good vibe."

"Tell me more about your project, Cassandra," Henry Dalton said. "What is it that you're working on, specifically?"

And the evening began. I sat back and let the fellows talk about their work, occasionally offering a comment here and there, but generally staying out of it. This was how it was supposed to go, I thought to myself, artists of all types communing with each other. I didn't have much, if anything, to add. I could see how, with all of Chester Dare's experience, he would "hold court" as Miss Penny put it, telling stories about all of the famous people who had once been Cliffside fellows. But I didn't have any stories to tell. Not yet, anyway.

I was standing at the sideboard, lost in my own thoughts, not really a part of the group, not really listening to the conversation, when something Brynn said jolted me out of my reverie.

"It's a work of fiction, but I'm basing it on the scandal involving the third Dare sister, Temperance," she said.

I had just taken a sip of wine and gasped at the same time, sending the wine down the wrong pipe and me into a fit of coughing. Everyone turned and stared. Richard Banks rose from his seat on the sofa. "Are you all right?" he asked.

"I'm sorry," I choked out. I coughed again and then turned to Brynn. "Did you say there was another Dare sister?"

She looked at me as though I had just asked the most foolish question in the world.

"You didn't know?" she said.

"No," I said, remembering the painting in Miss Penny's room. So that was who the third girl was. "What was the scandal?"

Brynn's eyes lit up. "Murder, of course," she said, raising her eyebrows. "She was a TB patient right here at Cliffside."

I took another sip of my wine. "Well, TB was certainly a killer, but I wouldn't exactly call it a murderer," I said. There were chuckles all around, but not from Brynn. She narrowed her eyes at me.

"Temperance died here," she said. "But I don't think she had TB."

"How could you possibly know that?" I asked her.

"My grandmother was also a patient here at the time," she said. "She never talked to anyone in the family about her experiences, but when I was cleaning out her attic after she died I came upon a journal she kept while she was a patient here. I read it, and I was really surprised by some of the things she wrote."

"Like what?" Cassandra asked.

"She wrote about Temperance and how strange she was. Menacing, almost. 'Not right in the head.' My grandmother was a grown woman when she was at Cliffside, and yet she was actually afraid of this girl."

I thought about the expression of the girl in the painting in Penny's room and shivered.

"It seemed to my grandmother that Temperance wasn't sick at all," she went on. "This little girl led a gang of kids that apparently ran wild here, always out of their rooms when they weren't supposed to be, making noise and disturbing the other patients."

The children I had seen my first night here. The presence I had felt on the third floor. The footsteps running around at night.

"Why would Chester Dare put his own daughter in a TB facility if she wasn't ill?" Richard piped up. "That doesn't make sense to me. If she didn't have it, she'd certainly contract it in a hospital with other TB patients. It was very contagious, from what I understand."

Brynn took a sip of her drink, obviously enjoying being the center of attention. "I don't know for sure, and as I say, my book is a work of fiction, but I think that was the idea."

"What was the idea?" I asked. "To infect his own daughter with TB?"

"I think so," she said. "I think Chester Dare put Temperance in here to kill her."

"But why?" I asked, a wave of rage passing through me that I couldn't explain. "Why would he do that to his own daughter? By all accounts, he was a wonderful man and a great humanitarian. I don't believe it."

"He did it because she was evil," Brynn said, her eyes shining. "Rotten to the core. Think about it—my grandmother was frightened of this girl. Maybe he was, too. Maybe he put her in here to keep her away from his other two girls. What would a 'wonderful man and a great humanitarian' do with a little girl who had no soul?"

Richard joined me at the sideboard, rolled his eyes, and popped open a beer. "So, you're writing a horror novel, then," he said to her.

"Supernatural, yes," Brynn said.

I wondered if anything she said was true, or if she was simply extrapolating, inventing a narrative to go along with her grandmother's journal. "You said Temperance died here," I asked her. "How do you know that?"

"It was in the journal, and that's the part that made me want to write this novel," she said, grinning. "One day while she was here, Grandma Alice saw a nurse giving Temperance an injection and a short while later, the girl was dead."

"The nurse killed her?" It was Cassandra, jumping in.

"That's what my grandmother thought," Brynn said. "She packed up and left here the next morning, against doctor's orders."

"And did she survive, your grandmother?" Cassandra asked.

"She did." Brynn nodded, and then turned to me. "But, Miss Harper, you should know all of this. It was in my letter of application."

The applications that had conveniently disappeared.

"I haven't seen it, actually," I admitted. "But, frankly, I'm astonished that Penelope Dare would sanction you turning that story into a novel. Her sister, some sort of demon? Her own father, putting a healthy daughter in with a bunch of TB patients? She idolized that man. And the nurse intentionally killing the girl? The reputation of Cliffside would be ruined. If she knew what you were intending to write, she'd get a team of lawyers to stop you. And she never would have let you come here."

"That's the odd thing," Brynn said, swirling the ice in her glass. "I filled out the application as sort of a lark—I didn't think she'd allow me to come, either. But I really wanted to write the book—or at least start writing it—here, and I was also hoping to talk to her about Temperance. So, I told her everything in my application letter and sent it off. That was just three weeks ago."

"Are you sure about that?" I asked her. "The fellows are scheduled a year in advance."

"Not me," Brynn said. "She called me as soon as she got my application and said she was eager to talk with me. She asked if I could come to this session, so I dropped everything and came."

First, Richard. Now Brynn. The all-too-familiar sense of dread wrapped itself around me again, as I wondered exactly what Miss Penny had set the stage for.

# CHAPTER 17

"Brynn," Cassandra began, as we were nearly through with dessert, "did you say you brought that journal here with you?"

Brynn took a bite and nodded. "I did."

"Would you mind if I took a look at it, for my own research?" Cassandra asked. "I've read a couple of journals written by TB patients who were in various facilities around the country, but I've never read one from a patient right here at Cliffside. I think it would contain some valuable insights."

"I don't know . . ." Brynn said, scowling.

"I'd actually like to take a look at it, too," I said, jumping into the fray. "It would be a fascinating peek inside life here before it became a retreat."

Henry reached over and put a hand on Brynn's arm. "I think we're all interested," he said. "Why don't you run upstairs and get it, and you can read parts of it to us, the parts you're comfortable sharing, that is. You might not want other people touching it."

Brynn looked from one to the other of us, assessing.

"I think it's a great idea," Diana piped up. "I'd love to hear it, too. Please?"

Brynn wiped the corners of her mouth with a napkin. "Okay," she said, pushing her chair back from the table. "I was really taken with it, and maybe you will be, too. I'll be back down in a minute."

"Why don't we retreat to the winter garden with coffee after dinner?" I suggested. "That would be a great place to hear a story."

And so, after we had chatted over dinner, we were all sitting in the winter garden, rain trickling softly down the windows and the glass ceiling, and Brynn began to read from the journal her grandmother had written at Cliffside all those years ago:

*It is my first day at Cliffside Sanatorium, the first of many, many days I will spend here. My husband gave me this diary the day before I arrived, suggesting that writing my thoughts and experiences might do me some good. How sweet of him—he's always thinking of little things to do for me like that.*

*How did it all begin? It was on a Thursday when I suddenly coughed up a mouthful of blood. I had been tired for a while, but I thought it was simply due to the hectic days of a new mother and wife. But the blood—it frightened me. I phoned the doctor, who told me to go to bed immediately, and that he'd come by the house in an hour. But I had the baby to put down and dinner for my husband to cook—little did I know it would be the last meal I'd prepare for a long while.*

*An x-ray the following day proved the diagnosis of tuberculosis in my left lung. And that was it. I was to go to a sanatorium for six months to a year. Luckily, Mr. Dare had built one not far from our home, but all the same, the idea of being away from Jim and baby Lucy for all of that time made me weak in the knees. I'm going to miss it all—her first birthday. Her first steps. Will she remember me when (or if) I am allowed to come home? It's too much to even think about—I must steel myself to the reality of my situation and know that my time away will allow me to heal so I can be there for the other milestones. Her second birthday. The first time she learns to ride a bicycle. Her first day of school. Our fifth wedding anniversary. Even writing this now, from my chaise on the veranda, I can't hold back the tears. How will Jim cope on his own?*

Brynn stopped to take a sip of her tea and looked up at us. We were all rapt by these words, written in this very house so long ago.

"It's so sad," Cassandra said, leaning back in her chair. "I can't imagine it, a young mother being away from her baby for all of that time."

"And her husband," I added.

"Read some more, Brynn," Henry said. "Will you?"

"There's an interesting part in here about the rules—what it was like day to day," she said.

*It's my second day here and already I've become accustomed to the routine. The doctor and nurses have rules for me, of course, and I've set up rules of my own, to help me get through this confinement. I am determined to get well and go home. What are some of the rules?*

*Complete bed rest. I am allowed no movement, except to go to the bathroom. I am not to sit up in a chair, but instead recline on my bed or a chaise. I am to keep my strength up by eating well and breathing in the crisp, fresh air. I am allowed to write in this diary and write letters to friends and family for one hour per day. I may read or simply enjoy the beautiful scenery. I'm going to ask Jim, in my next letter, to send me some books. I'll need them to stave off the boredom. Talking to other patients is discouraged—talking takes effort and taxes the lungs—but it seems completely ridiculous to restrict all talking.*

*Others here are on different schedules, based on how ill they are. Some may only speak in a whisper. Some are flat on their backs in bed, no reading, no writing, so I'm lucky in that regard. Some may walk about the house and grounds for an hour each day. Others may lead a more normal, yet quiet, life. The point is to get people ready to re-enter the outside world, allowing them more and more activity until they are strong and healthy once again. That is the goal for all of us, but clearly there are some who do not improve.*

*Those are their rules. What are my rules for myself? I am not allowed one ounce of self-pity. Yes, I am here, away from my husband and baby. I miss them terribly already. But everyone else in this place is in the same boat, and some are far, far sicker than I. Oh, their sunken eyes. Their skeletal frames. Death is all around me here. It is a daily, sometimes hourly, occurrence. And that brings me to my other rule. I am not allowed to dwell on all of the death here at Cliffside, or feel afraid. It is easy to imagine oneself in similar circumstances, to fear the worst. I cannot have one moment of that thinking. I must focus on getting well and going home and never imagine the alternative. I will see Jim and Lucy again. I must and I will.*

Brynn's voice wavered as she read that last sentence and she stopped for a moment to brush a tear from her cheek.

"She sounds like she was a great lady," I said, reaching over to squeeze her hand.

Brynn nodded. "She was," she said. "We lost her a few years ago, and I still can't quite believe she's gone."

Henry took a sip of his tea. "You were close?"

"Oh, yes," Brynn said. "Grandma Alice lived with us when I was growing up. She was funny and warm—she doted on my sisters and me."

"And your mother," Henry said, "was she the baby Alice was writing about in this diary?"

"That's right," Brynn said.

Diana leaned forward in her chair. "So, what happened? I mean, we know Alice got out of here, got well, and went home. But how long was she here? And did Lucy remember her?"

"She was here for almost nine months," Brynn said. "But I only know that because of the diary. How my grandpa coped without her for all of that time, I don't know, but I do know they stayed married and had another child, my uncle. Grandpa Jim died in the eighties, and that's when my grandma came to live with us. My mom, of course, doesn't remember anything from that time—she was just an infant—and my grandma never talked about it. Never. We didn't even know she had TB until I found this diary."

Henry rubbed his chin. "I wonder why she never talked about it," he mused. "It's not like there was a stigma attached to TB."

"I think it had something to do with Temperance," Brynn said, raising her eyebrows. "Grandma was really afraid of her. Listen to this."

She turned several pages and began to read:

*It's the children that evoke the most pity from me and, I think, from everyone else here. I can't imagine how terrifying it must be for these poor little ones, some as young as five and six years old, to be away from their parents, their homes, and everything they know and love, and be here in this place, surrounded by all of these sick, dying people. The third floor is their ward—it's one big room, unlike ours—but I think that's good. At least they're not alone in their rooms; they have other children around them. The nurses have a hard time keeping them quiet! Some are allowed to play quietly with toys, but others must be confined to their beds. And here is the worst news: today Melody told me that Mr. Dare's own daughter Temperance is now a patient here! My heart bleeds for that poor man. All that he's done to help TB sufferers, and now his own child is among our sad, sorry ranks. I will be praying for her. And for him.*

Brynn flipped ahead a few pages.

*I can hardly write these words, but I must, before I burst. There is something wrong with that child. The Dare girl. And I don't mean TB. Several of us believe she's not sick at all, not with TB, that is. She's healthy and strong, and a little terror. She leads the other children on "raids" at night—they get up out of their beds and rampage through the place. They're so noisy and wild, they disturb everyone. She is impossible for the nurses to control, and poor Dr. Davidson is at his wits' end with her. Everybody's whispering about it. They've had to separate her from some of the children who are the sickest, because they don't get any rest when she's there. Four of them died yesterday—four in one day! I saw Dr. Davidson break down and weep when he learned they had passed. I heard the nurses say all four of them seemed to be on the mend. Dr. Davidson was so hopeful they'd go home.*

*But there's something more than just an unruly, disobedient child in this girl. It's the look in her eyes. They are completely devoid of any . . . how can I put this? It's like they're a doll's eyes. Not human. Or even alive. They're dark and dead and cold. She looks at you, and—I know this sounds crazy—but it seems as though she is wishing you dead. That's a terrible thing to say about a child, but I must say it. She is not right in the head, and I'm not the only one who thinks so. This also sounds crazy, but that little girl scares me. I had intended to do my small part to watch out for Mr. Dare's daughter, but I don't want her anywhere near me, and I'm not the only one. I'm going to go to one of the nurses and request she be kept separate from us.*

"There's a couple more entries that don't mention her, but here's the next one that does," Brynn said. Everyone was leaning forward in their chairs—you could have heard a pin drop.

*I am writing this from a café in town, having left Cliffside Sanatorium. A few others and I simply walked away during our exercise hour and were given a ride to town by a passing car. We have left our things behind—they can be retrieved later. The only thing I took was this diary. The lady who runs this café was good enough to let me use her telephone. I called Jim, and he is picking me up in a few hours, so I have some time to sit, have a meal, and gather my thoughts. I wanted to put this on paper so I'd have a record of it, should I ever need it. I will write it down, close this book, and never open it again, unless the need arises. Here is my story of the terrible events that took place today.*

*I happened to be passing through the drawing room when I saw Mr. Dare, Dr. Davidson, and one of the nurses huddled in a very serious conversation. Normally, I wouldn't stoop to eavesdropping, but I heard the name*

Temperance *and it stopped me. I wanted to hear what they were discussing because, earlier in the week, I had gone to the nurse to tell her I didn't want Temperance anywhere near me and relayed a message from several of us that something needed to be done about this girl. I don't know what the doctor and Mr. Dare and this nurse were talking about, I couldn't hear much more, but I did hear the words* today *and* morphine.

*A few hours later, it was the children's outside time. (Adults are inside at this time.) I was watching from the window in my room as that same nurse (I'm omitting her name for her own safety, and mine, I suppose) came to check on the children who were on the chaises on the veranda. Temperance was one of those. She was playing with a doll. I watched as the nurse gave her an injection, to much protest from the girl, but she gave it all the same, and I watched as Temperance leaned back and lay down on the chaise—the first time I had ever seen her quiet. I thought the nurse had given her something to help her nap. The nurse left very quickly—where she went, I have no idea. But a while later, Dr. Davidson came on the scene, checked Temperance's pulse, and listened to her heart. I thought she was sleeping.*

*Things got a bit hectic after that. Another nurse ushered the rest of the children into the house. Mr. Dare and his other two daughters were here, and he joined the doctor at Temperance's side. He patted Dr. Davidson on the back and thanked him before breaking down in tears and covering her body with the white blanket on the chair. He sobbed at her side for a long, long time. And I realized the little girl was dead!! I watched the whole thing unfold!*

*That's when I decided to leave Cliffside. I don't want to compromise my own health, but I am strong and getting stronger. I simply cannot stay in that place anymore after what I saw. I will never mention it to anyone, except to Jim, but I believe they killed that girl because she was a monster. I don't think she ever had TB. I think he put her in here to infect her, and when that didn't work, they took matters into their own hands. God help them all.*

# CHAPTER 18

It had stopped raining while Brynn was telling her tale, and after hearing it, I think everyone needed to clear their heads. So, Brynn, Richard, Henry, and Cassandra decided to walk around the grounds in the fading light. Diana retreated to her suite, exhausted, she said, from her flurry of productivity that day.

The group had asked me to walk with them, but I declined. After hearing what Brynn's grandmother had written about Temperance, I was unsettled and even angry. This sounded like a very credible eyewitness account of a murder, but as the director of Cliffside, I simply could not accept that Chester Dare had anything to do with it. It felt like an affront to me, more personal than I could explain.

I decided to seek out Harriet. Maybe she could shed some light on it. I didn't know whether to believe Brynn's tale or not—maybe her grandmother hadn't seen what she thought she had—but after hearing her story, I wanted to find out more.

I pushed through the door to the kitchen and found Harriet loading plates into the dishwasher.

"Something I can do for you, Miss Harper?"

I pulled out one of the kitchen chairs and sank down into it, not knowing quite how to ask what I wanted to.

"I just heard the strangest story from one of the fellows," I began. "It was about a third Dare sister. Temperance."

A dish fell out of Harriet's hand and shattered on the tile floor.

"Oh!" she cried. "How clumsy! I'll just clean it up." She reached down and began picking up the pieces. "Dash it all, it was one of the good dishes."

I noticed a broom standing in the corner and hopped up to get it. "Don't touch the shards," I said to her, sweeping them into a pile. "Do you have a dustpan?"

She crossed the room and opened a door revealing a cleaning closet with all manner of implements and grabbed a dustpan. I swept the shards into it while she held it.

"Well, that was uncalled for," she said, wrinkling her nose at the shards as she deposited them into the trash. "Those were antique dishes. They belonged to Mr. Dare's mother."

"I shouldn't have come in here to distract you," I said.

"Not your fault," she said. "I'm to blame. I'll let Mr. Baines know. Maybe he can find a replacement. He loves that eBay. You'd be surprised what you can find there."

She popped a cleaning packet into the dishwasher, pushed the door shut, and turned it on. "Now, if you don't need anything else, miss, I think I'll be off. Mr. Baines and I like to watch a police drama that's starting in a few minutes. I'm sure he'll be in his recliner waiting for me." She chuckled at the thought of it.

She hurried out the kitchen door and was halfway down the lawn before I realized she hadn't answered my question.

I stood in the empty kitchen listening to the dishwasher whir, wishing my mind would go into high gear, too. Now I had another piece of the puzzle—Harriet's avoidance of my question about Temperance Dare.

I went through the kitchen door and out onto the lawn. Maybe I could catch up with the group. I was in no mood to go back to my suite alone. I had been by myself here at Cliffside the whole while, and I had to admit that it was nice to have some conversation and company, even though I didn't really belong with them.

Since Henry was here to paint the garden, maybe that's where they were headed. But when I got there, they were nowhere in sight. Had they gone down to the lakeshore? I walked across the lawn to the path Nate and I had taken during Miss Penny's wake, and then it struck me that I hadn't seen him since then. I had been meaning to find my way to his house, but in the flurry of everything, I hadn't gotten around to it.

I turned on my heel and headed the opposite way. I'd find him now, if he was at home. Maybe he knew something about Temperance. According to the journal, his father was the doctor when she was at Cliffside as a patient. I wasn't sure how those timelines matched up, though. At the very least, maybe he could shed some light on this whole thing.

I walked for about ten minutes or so across the lawn, and there, just beyond a rise near the forest's edge, stood a large, white house with a porch running across its entire front. I had found it! And on the porch swing, there sat Nate Davidson, white coat and all. He waved.

I trotted across the lawn and up the steps. "Hi!" I said to him. "I have just committed a cardinal sin—the unauthorized stop-by."

He grinned. "The unauthorized stop-by," he said. "You have indeed committed it. In retaliation, I'm afraid I'm going to have to offer you a glass of wine."

"Do your worst," I said, settling into an Adirondack chair and crossing my legs. "I brought it on myself."

He disappeared into the house and returned in a minute with a glass of wine and a beer in a frosty mug.

"It's my policy to keep wine on hand, just in case a pretty woman stops by," he said, handing me the glass and taking a seat next to me.

I flushed at the compliment. "I think that's a fine policy," I said. "One might even call it a motto."

"Or a creed," he said, sipping his beer. "It helps if one knows a pretty woman's wine preference, which one does."

"It does help," I said, raising my glass. "This is a fine wine."

"And finer company," he said, lifting his glass to me in return. "I hereby authorize all of your future stop-bys."

"That's a bold action," I said.

"That's what they call me," he said. "Bold."

We sat, smiling at each other, for a bit.

"How are things?" he said, breaking the silence. "The fellows arrived."

"They did, indeed," I said. "And things are fine, if mysterious."

"Mysterious? How so?"

I took a deep breath and told him everything, from Miss Penny's secret playroom—an homage to the past—to my theories that she had brought some, if not all, of us to Cliffside for a reason, to Brynn's idea about Temperance, and finally to the most perplexing thing of all—why, if she had gone to so much trouble to bring at least some of us here, would she kill herself before she had a chance to carry out whatever it was she was planning? It didn't make any sense.

He didn't say anything for a few moments but seemed to be digesting what I had said.

"I don't mind telling you that the dollhouse business gives me the creeps," he said, finally.

"Me, too," I said. "What do you think, though? She said she had left me a puzzle to solve, and I feel like pieces are scattered all over the place. I was hoping you might be able to help me put some of them together."

"Ah," he said. "An ulterior-motive-filled unauthorized stop-by."

"Is there any other kind?"

"In that case, you might be forced to accept another glass of wine."

I looked down into my empty glass and shrugged. "If I must."

He pushed himself up, took my glass, and returned a moment later with it and another beer.

"I was just stalling for time," he said.

"I expected no less from you."

He laughed, settling back into his chair. "That's one formidable can of worms you've got on your hands."

I looked at him, hoping he would offer a quasi-plausible explanation for it all.

He seemed to sense what I was thinking. "You know, Norrie, I'm just a simple country doctor," he said. "I'm no Sam Spade. You're the reporter—what do you think?"

"I think you know a whole lot more than you're saying, Mr. Country Doctor."

"That's Doctor Country Doctor, if you please," he said, grinning.

"Seriously, though, you live here and have for your whole life," I said. "How does all of this strike you?"

He leaned back in his chair and was silent for a moment, choosing his words carefully. "Cliffside is a strange and mysterious place, Norrie," he said, finally. "It always has been. Things happen here that just don't happen elsewhere."

I thought about everything that had happened to me since I'd arrived and knew he was right.

"That said, though, I agree with you that all of these puzzle pieces don't fit together," he said. "Maybe that's because they're not supposed to. Maybe it's all just one big, random coincidence. Maybe it's just as her suicide note said, she was tired, and, having finally found a 'worthy successor,' she did what she had wanted to do since her father and sister died. She joined them."

"Had she always felt that way, do you know?"

He shook his head. "It's hard to say. But I do believe she carried a sense of guilt with her after they died. And she missed Milly terribly. It's amazing she had the strength to carry on after losing her. They were so close, they were almost like one person. You never saw one without the other."

I thought about Miss Penny's room, a shrine to their childhoods.

"It's hard to lose any family member," I said, "but losing a sister who was that close must have been devastating."

"It was," he said. "I'm surprised it took this long for her to swallow a bottle of pills."

"About the other sister," I said. "Temperance. What do you know of that? Is what Brynn said true?"

He sipped on his beer. "Well, I know there was a Temperance, and I know that, despite her name, she was a hell-raiser."

"Did Miss Penny tell you stories about her?"

He shook his head. "She never talked about her. Neither did Milly or their father."

"Then how do you know?"

"My dad," he said. "He had a lot of stories about her."

"Is it true about her being a patient at Cliffside?"

He nodded. "That's true, yes. Temperance was a patient here. But the bit about her not having TB—that's fiction. She was a very sick little girl." He stopped for a moment and then went on. "According to my dad."

"So, he was the doctor here when she was a patient?"

"He was," Nate said.

"And the part about Temperance being evil, Chester putting her in here to kill her, and a nurse finally finishing the job?"

Nate's eyes grew dark. "The nurses here were the finest around. Every one of them, world-class professionals. None would have ever done anything like that, even if Chester Dare himself ordered her to."

I didn't know what to say to that. His story didn't quite ring true for me. It felt like he knew more than he was telling me. But, then again, he had heard this story secondhand from his father, who would never admit his complicity in a murder to his son. Nobody would, unless it was a deathbed confession. But it didn't seem to be the case here.

Maybe Nate was right. Maybe this was all just one big, strange coincidence, fanned by my crime reporter's imagination. I had been missing my work, puzzling out mysteries. Maybe I had invented one for myself here. And the question of Temperance might be one I'd never answer.

He leaned forward in his chair and put a hand on my knee. "The thing is, Norrie, maybe Penelope did engineer it so you and all of the fellows in this session were here at the same time, for some reason known only to her. Whatever that reason was, it died with her. So, does it really matter anymore? What I mean is, it's not like she can carry out whatever it was that she was planning—if there was anything planned."

I exhaled. He was right, of course. Whatever little game Penelope Dare had been playing with us, it didn't matter anymore. She was gone.

# CHAPTER 19

Darkness had fallen by the time I walked from Nate's house back across the lawn toward Cliffside. He had offered to walk with me, but even though I would've liked his company, thoughts were swirling through my mind, and I felt like a good walk might help sort them out. There was something nagging at me about my conversation with Nate, but I couldn't put my finger on what, exactly, it was. An odd sense of unfinished business? A lingering question? I wasn't sure. I only knew there was something.

It wasn't until later, when I was upstairs in my suite getting ready for bed, that it hit me. The suicide note. How had he known she'd written about being tired and just wanting to join her father and sister, having found a "worthy successor"? The only people to read it were Harriet, the police, and me. As I washed my face and brushed my teeth, I reasoned that he must have talked to one of them. Still, it was odd that he knew the exact phrasing—"worthy successor." I made a mental note to ask him about it the next day and crawled into bed.

As I drifted off, I tried to think of more pleasant things. I really was pleased that everything had gone off without a hitch during the fellows' first day. Maybe this job wouldn't be so hard after all.

~

I awoke to the sound of screaming. Was I dreaming? But no, there it was again. My room was pitch black—the sky had evidently clouded up again, obscuring the stars and moon that usually illuminated my room at night. I quickly felt around for the light switch, threw on my robe, and flung my door open, hitting the switch in the hallway as I did so.

I saw Brynn hurrying down the hallway toward my room. Her face was ashen.

"Was that you screaming?" I asked her.

One by one, doors opened, and heads poked out into the hall. "What's the matter?" someone said. "What's going on?" said another.

Richard materialized—I hadn't noticed him coming down the hallway from his suite—and put a hand on Brynn's shoulder. "Are you all right?" he asked her.

She looked at me with wild, terror-filled eyes. "Somebody was in my room."

The group gathered around us. "What do you mean somebody was in your room?" Cassandra said, cinching the belt on her blue satin robe. "Didn't you have your door locked?"

"Of course I had it locked," Brynn snapped at her. She turned to me and took my hand, and I could feel that she was physically shaking. "Come and see."

She led me to her suite, the others following behind. The door was standing open, the light on. She pointed to the study. "In there," she whispered. "Look."

I started to cross the room toward the study, but Richard took my arm. "Let me go first," he said and then turned to the others. "You all stay here. Just in case."

He and I moved into the study, and both of us let out a gasp. On the desk, the old, weathered journal sat open, its pages ripped out and strewn all over the desktop, the chair, and the floor.

I turned to Brynn. By this time, Henry was standing with her, a protective arm around her shoulders. "You didn't do this yourself, obviously?"

"Obviously," she said. "Look closer. Look at the individual pages."

I picked one up and then dropped it again, as though it had burned my fingers. Scrawled across the journal entry on the page, in black ink, were the words: *Lies Lies Lies Lies.* And there it was on the other pages, written over and over again.

"Holy Jesus," Richard said, his voice low. "Who would do something like this?"

Brynn turned her face into Henry's chest rather than look at that scene any longer. I could see her shoulders shaking. He rubbed her back and cooed, "There, there, my dear. There, there."

"Okay, listen," I said, trying to take charge, my voice a bit louder than I had intended it to be. "Brynn, I need to know exactly what happened."

No response. "Brynn," I said, taking her arm. "Turn around and tell us what happened. You're safe now. We're all here."

She did as she was told, and I led her out of the study and into her bedroom. She crawled into her bed and sat propped against the pillows. As the others gathered around her, she took a tissue and dabbed at her eyes.

"There's not much to tell," she said. "I fell asleep right away when I went to bed, but I woke up in the middle of the night. After lying here tossing and turning for a bit, I thought I might as well just get up and start working. But when I got to the desk, I saw"—she flailed an arm toward the study—"that!" She let out a strangled cry. "Somebody was in my room while I was sleeping!"

I got a sick feeling in the pit of my stomach wondering who, or what, that "somebody" might have been. But I wasn't about to tell any of them what I had seen and heard and felt since coming to Cliffside.

I perched next to her on the edge of the bed. “Okay, this is a silly question, but I have to ask it. You’re sure it wasn’t like that when you went to bed? That would be a simpler explanation—somebody got in here while we were all downstairs at dinner, or afterward.”

She shook her head. “I don’t think so,” she said. “But it was dark, and I didn’t turn on the light in the study.”

“And what time was that, about?” I asked her. I hadn’t seen her at all after coming home from Nate’s.

She glanced quickly at Henry Dalton and then back at me. “It was after midnight,” she said.

Even in the midst of this, I had to stifle a grin. Miss Penny had warned me about fellows scurrying from room to room in the middle of the night. It certainly hadn’t taken them long.

I surveyed the other faces in the room, as I had learned to do during my years of crime reporting. Nobody looked guilty. “Did anybody hear anything between midnight and now?” I asked them. “Any movement in the hallway, someone coming or going?”

Diana and Henry shook their heads.

“The only thing I heard was the screaming,” Richard said, running a hand through his hair. “It woke me out of a dead sleep.”

“Cassandra?” I asked. “What about you?”

She winced. “I did hear something, but I hate to even mention it,” she said.

I stood up. “What was it?”

“I’m not sure if I was dreaming,” she said. “But I heard . . .” She sighed. “I know it’s going to sound crazy, but I thought I heard laughter out in the hallway.”

“When was this?” I asked.

“Earlier. Probably around eleven,” she said.

“Were any of you in the hallway then?” I asked the group.

Everyone shook their heads.

"Like I said, I'm not sure if I was dreaming or not," Cassandra went on. "It was one of those things where I wasn't entirely awake or asleep but sort of floating in between. I didn't think too much of it at the time, but now . . ."

"Now, what?" I asked her.

"I know it sounds crazy, but I could swear it was the sound of children laughing," she said.

My stomach seized up. I had heard that same thing, many times, since coming to Cliffside. But I wasn't about to admit it to all of these people.

"There are no children here, are there?" Henry piped up.

"No," I said. "You might have been dreaming, Cassandra, or you might have heard something outside that sounded like laughter. An animal. I don't know."

"Well, an animal didn't destroy my journal," Brynn said, her fear giving way to anger. "Aside from the creep factor of somebody being in here while I was asleep, it's a priceless family heirloom. Now it's ruined. I could sue you."

"Well—" I began, but Richard broke in.

"I suggest you calm down," he said, fixing a stern gaze at Brynn. "Eleanor has been nothing but helpful to you, and to all of us, since we arrived. We just need to focus on who did this, and why."

"We can answer that by you answering the question—who has keys to our rooms?" Brynn spat out at me.

"I do," I told her. "And Harriet does."

"Then, it was obviously one of you."

"That's ridiculous," I spat back at her. "We don't make a habit out of ruining the work of the fellows here at Cliffside. Just the opposite, as a matter of fact. But since I answered your question, you answer this one. Did you have the door latched?"

"Of course it was locked."

"I didn't ask if it was locked. A lock can be opened with a key. Did you have the door latched?" I strode over to the door and pointed to the oval attachment that, when mated with a bolt, prevented the door itself from opening, even if someone had a key.

She narrowed her eyes, as if thinking was painful. "It was latched," she said. "I had to open it to get out of the room just now."

I looked around the room. The others were shaking their heads and muttering. Cassandra threw up her hands. "For God's sake, nobody could've gotten in here," she said, her voice shrill.

"But—" Brynn tried, but Cassandra cut her off.

"They couldn't possibly have latched the door on the way out." She let out a sigh. "That means nobody was in here while you were sleeping. It happened before you turned in. I'm going back to bed. And if I'm too tired to work tomorrow, you are to blame."

She stomped out of the room with Diana slipping off behind her.

Brynn, a look of utter confusion on her face, was staring into the study. "I don't understand it," she whispered.

"We'll sort this all out in the morning," Henry said, rubbing her arm. "I'm going to retire as well. If you need anything, you knock on my door." He kissed her on the cheek and was gone.

I grabbed a couple of pages of the journal. "I just want to examine these a little closer," I said to Brynn, who had now turned her confused eyes to me.

"I don't understand this," she repeated. "What happened here?"

I patted her arm. "I don't know," I said to her as gently as I could. "But I do know that journal didn't tear itself up. We'll get to the bottom of it, I promise." I took a breath. "If you'd feel better about it, I can call the police right now. They'll have somebody here in no time."

She crossed her arms. "I don't know," she said. "It really scared me."

"I suggest you try to get some sleep," Richard broke in. "I'm just next door. You call out if anything else happens, and I'll be in here in a heartbeat."

She nodded, eyeing her study and the strewn papers.

"Tomorrow, if you want to call the police, we will," I said. "Make sure you latch the door after we go. There's no way anyone can get in here with the latch on."

Richard and I walked out into the hallway, and I pulled the door closed behind us. I could hear Brynn locking and latching it.

"Do you buy that?" he said, his voice low.

"Buy what?"

"This whole thing," he said.

I nodded my head toward my room. "Let's go in here," I whispered. "I don't want to disturb anybody."

He followed me into my room, and I shut the door. "Now," I said. "What do you mean?"

"Obviously nobody was in her room while she was sleeping," he said. "It's impossible, because of the latch. So, either somebody got in there while she was looking at Henry's etchings . . ." He raised his eyebrows.

I let out a chuckle. "You caught that, too?"

"Oh, yes." He grinned. "They weren't exactly discreet about it. So, either someone was ripping up the journal while she was with him and she just didn't notice it before going to sleep, or—nobody did it at all."

I squinted at him. "I don't follow you."

"Who benefits from her 'priceless family heirloom' being destroyed?"

"You sound like a police detective, Mr. Banks."

"And you, a reporter, Miss Harper." He smiled. "I think we're thinking the same thing."

"She did it herself."

"Either that or she had an accomplice," he said. "Did you notice, Diana didn't say a word. She seemed to be trying to make herself very small and unremarkable."

"I did notice that," I said. "But, I don't know, it could be Diana was just really tired. Tell me, how did you come upon your theory that Brynn herself did this?"

"At first, I thought she was truly terrified," he said. "Good actress, that one. But then, the 'Lies' rubbish." He rolled his eyes. "A little over-dramatic, don't you think? That made me suspicious, even more so when she mentioned the bit about suing you. It was too much. And the latch sealed it. So to speak."

"So, what should I do?" I asked him.

"Watch what she does tomorrow," he said. "If she persists with this lawsuit business, or even makes noises about contacting her insurance company for a payout, I think we'll have our answer."

I let out a groan. Miss Penny had warned me about diva-ish behavior but nothing like this.

The thought of Miss Penny's name made something click in the back of my mind, and all at once, I wanted Richard to go.

"Well," I said, with a note of finality, "thank you for your help tonight. We'll sort it all out tomorrow, and I think you're right. If she starts talking about insurance or suing us, we'll have our answer. Why don't you try to get some sleep before morning?"

He let out a yawn and ran a hand through his hair. "I think I'll do that. It was a tiring day. Travel always takes it out of me."

"Sleep as late as you can," I said. "There's always coffee and things to nibble on if you miss breakfast."

He put his hand on the doorknob. "Goodnight, Miss Harper."

"Call me Norrie," I said, smiling at him.

"Norrie," he repeated. "It suits you. Goodnight, then, Norrie. Sleep tight."

I shut the door behind him, latched it, and hurried to the study. I sat down at my desk, opened the drawer where I had stashed Miss Penny's suicide note, and pulled it out. I flipped on the lamp and set the page I had taken from Brynn's journal next to the letter.

My whole body went cold at the sight of it. The message written on the journal page, *Lies Lies Lies Lies*, was written in the same spidery scrawl as Miss Penny's suicide note.

# CHAPTER 20

There would be no more sleep for me that night. I lay in bed, my eyes open wide, my heart pounding in my chest. I had locked and latched the door, knowing it wouldn't do one bit of good if the perpetrator could simply float through it.

Brynn Kendrick might very well have ripped the pages from her journal, but she certainly didn't write those words. It wasn't possible. That was Miss Penny's handwriting. There was no mistaking her distinctive scrawl.

But, how could it be?

A cold, stark terror gripped me when I let myself think what I had been trying to convince myself wasn't true. Was she here, at Cliffside still, threatening us? Is that why she killed herself—to terrify us?

It sounded fantastic, even to me, alone and shivering in my bed that night, but what other explanation was there? I thought of all the strange things that had happened to me since I arrived at Cliffside—the voices and laughter in the hallways, the sight of those children outside my window, my ghoulish experience on the third floor. Even my encounter with that old man in the boathouse—what was his name? Pete? He had said Death himself resided at Cliffside. What if it wasn't Death but the three Dare sisters, finally together once again?

Just hours before, I was laughing with Nate. I had left his house convinced that my suspicions were just a product of my imagination running wild, that there was nothing going on at Cliffside, and that, whatever Miss Penny's reasons for bringing at least some of us here at the same time, they died with her.

But now, I suspected that just the opposite was true. It felt like something dark and dangerous was happening, and I had no idea what it was.

I sat up and poured a glass of water from the pitcher on my bedside table. I drank it down, holding it with shaking hands. I needed a plan. As the director of Cliffside, I needed to take control of this situation. But what should I do?

I looked at the clock. Four twenty-five. It would be a few hours before people were moving around.

I slid back down under the covers and made a list in my mind—that always helped me make sense out of the nonsensical. The first thing I'd do in the morning was talk with Henry and Diana. I wanted to know exactly how they had come to be at Cliffside. I'd also get the whole group together to brainstorm any connections we might have between us, to figure out a reason for this thing.

~

I must've drifted off, because I found myself opening my eyes to a bright, clear day. The sun was streaming into my room, warming me as I slept. I rubbed my eyes and glanced at the clock—it was after nine, already! I bolted out of bed, cursing myself. I had wanted to talk to everyone at breakfast.

I glanced out of the window toward the gardens and saw Henry set up there, his easel and paints in front of him. He had obviously been at work awhile. I wondered about the others. Where were they?

I didn't bother showering. I just threw on some clothes, brushed my hair, and started to make my way downstairs when I thought better of it. I turned around and headed to Brynn's suite. I knocked on the door, hoping she was all right.

A moment later she opened the door, scowling. "I thought we weren't supposed to be disturbed."

I couldn't believe what I was hearing. "I came to check on you," I said. "After last night. I wondered . . ." But my words trailed off. Her expression told me all I needed to know.

"You wondered what?" She stood there, one hip jutted out, arms crossed.

"I wanted to make sure you were okay," I said.

"You yourself said there's no way somebody could've gotten into my room while I was sleeping because the door was latched. So it had to have happened when I was . . ." She thought a moment. ". . . out of my room, and I just didn't notice it before I went to bed."

"But you said you turned off the light in the study and didn't see anything."

"Well, I was tired." She sniffed. "It had to be that I just didn't notice it."

"We mentioned the police last night," I said. "If you'd like me to, I can make the call right now."

She wrinkled her nose. "Waste of time," she said. "I think it's just somebody's idea of a practical joke."

"If that's a practical joke, it's a pretty nasty one."

"Malicious," she said. "Absolutely malicious. That odious Richard Banks made a crack about me writing a horror novel, and then a few hours later something out of a horror novel happens to me. Ripped out of the pages of a horror novel, to put a fine point on it."

"Are you saying you think Richard Banks did this?"

"Who else?"

"I don't know," I said. How could I possibly say that I thought it wasn't a practical joke, that the malevolent ghost of Miss Penny had destroyed her journal? In the light of day, it seemed like a ridiculous idea.

"Now, if you'll excuse me, I'm going to get back to writing." And with that, she shut the door in my face. *Temperamental divas* was right.

I found Cassandra and Diana at the table in the winter garden, finishing their breakfasts. I smiled, noticing that these two ladies couldn't have been more different. Cassandra's sleek, black hair was styled in a neat bob, not a strand out of place. She was wearing a blue, silk blouse, cream slacks, and heels, a strand of pearls wound around her neck. Diana, on the other hand, wore a purple cotton dress and flip-flops, her long hair a wild tangle, cat-eye glasses on a silver chain around her neck. So typical of their roles: the serious, nonfiction writer and the poet.

I poured a cup of coffee for myself, grabbed a croissant, and joined them at the table.

"Hi, ladies," I said. "I hope you got some sleep after the incident last night."

Diana pushed the eggs around her plate with a fork but didn't respond. I remembered what Richard had said about her the night before. She did look a little guilty, now that I thought about it.

"Well, I slept like a baby," Cassandra said, taking a last sip of her coffee. "I woke up early and got some work done. Now I'm going to go back upstairs and continue. I'm on a roll! This place has really got my creative juices flowing." She pushed her chair back from the table and dropped her napkin on her plate. "Shall I take this into the kitchen?"

"Not necessary," I said, "but, can you wait for a moment? I wanted to talk to you about something."

"In that case," she said, crossing the room to the sideboard with her coffee cup, "I'll have a little more of this. Diana, can I refill your cup?"

Diana shook her head. "I've got tea."

Coffee poured, Cassandra returned to her place at the table and settled back into her chair. "Now, Eleanor, what did you want to talk about?" she asked me.

"I wanted to take your pulse, so to speak"—I shot a look at Diana—"both of your pulses, actually, about how you're feeling after last night. I spoke with Brynn this morning, and she's convinced that someone—one of us—did this as a sort of practical joke because she's writing a horror novel."

Cassandra nodded her head. "She was down here at breakfast earlier, and she said the same thing to me. She thought someone was making a pun, so to speak, ripped from the pages of a horror story."

"Henry came up with that," Diana said. I was getting so accustomed to her silence that I was taken aback at the sound of her voice. "I heard them in the hallway as they came down to breakfast. She was still upset, and he was trying to calm her down."

"Calm who down?" It was Richard, padding into the room in his sweatpants and slippers.

My face felt hot at the sight of him, standing there, smiling at me. *Get it together, Norrie,* I thought. First Nate, now Richard. I hadn't had a date in two years, maybe longer, and suddenly I was blushing over every man I came into contact with? It was ridiculous. What was I, a teenager?

I shook it off. "Brynn."

"Is she still in a snit?"

"Brynn actually thought you did it," I said to Richard, "because of your crack about her writing a horror novel."

"Me?" Richard looked mildly amused. "But it wasn't a crack. She *is* writing a horror novel about something that took place in this very building."

Diana set her cup down on the table with a flourish. "You were thinking it was one of the spirits who live here," she said to me. "This house is full of ghosts. I've never been in a place that has had so many."

We all stopped and stared at her. She wiped the corners of her mouth and pushed her chair back from the table. "Most of them mean no harm."

"Oh, that's total rubbish," Richard huffed, taking a bite of eggs.

Cassandra caught my eye, a worried look on her face. "I really don't put any stock in things like that, but I guess I'll just ask. Is Cliffside haunted, Eleanor? It is a very old house."

What, exactly, was I going to say to that? "I don't know," I said, finally. "I'm new here myself." My heart was pounding in my throat. "But, Diana," I went on, "you think a spirit did this?"

"Who else? Listen, it's just like you said." Diana turned to Richard. "Brynn is writing about something very strange that went on here when that little girl—what was her name? Temperance?—died. Maybe she doesn't like it."

"Maybe who doesn't like it?" Richard asked, furrowing his brows.

"Temperance," Diana said. She turned on her heel and was about to go, but I held up a hand to stop her.

"You think Temperance is still here?" I croaked out.

"Oh, they're all still here," Diana said, as nonchalantly as if she were reciting a grocery list.

"What do you mean, 'all'?"

"There's just something about this place," Diana said, opening her arms wide. "When you die here, you stay."

"Oh, for the love of—" Richard mumbled into his coffee cup.

Diana went on. "Cliffside is full of spirits, yes, but the world is full of spirits. They're all around us, all the time. We pass them on the streets and sit next to them in restaurants, we chat with them in elevators and on trains, never knowing that they've passed over, and are just biding their time here on this earth."

Richard shot me a glance and winked. "That does it. No more talking to strangers in elevators. One of them might be the Grim Reaper."

"Why don't they go?" Cassandra asked her. I didn't know if it was a legitimate question or if she was just playing along.

"I don't know why they stay at Cliffside, specifically, but our world is the garden of earthly delights," Diana said. "Look around you. Would you want to leave this place for the unknown?"

She did have a point.

"But the ripping out of pages," I pressed on, bringing the subject back to last night. "Isn't that pretty angry?"

Diana smiled an indulgent smile. "Oh, Eleanor," she said. "Those words on the pages, and the fact that they were all ripped out of the book—it didn't seem threatening to me. It seemed juvenile. Like something a child would do."

"A naughty child," Richard said, with a huff.

"Yes, a naughty child," Diana said. "But a child nonetheless." She looked at each of us in turn. "You don't have any experience with spirits, do you?"

I shrugged. "I was a crime reporter for twenty years before I came to Cliffside, so I have a lot of experience with dead bodies. Their spirits? Not so much."

"Me neither," Cassandra said. "I deal in facts, remember?"

"And I think the whole thing is a load of shite," Richard said.

"Well," Diana said, "I'm here to tell you, ghosts are no more threatening dead than they were when they were alive. And the one that ripped up Brynn's journal is nothing more than a naughty, little child trying to scare us."

I wasn't so sure about that. But I was willing to let her have the last word. For now.

# CHAPTER 21

After Richard went upstairs to gather his camera gear for his first day of shooting and Cassandra returned to her writing desk, I made my way into the kitchen. I had just finished nibbling on a croissant, but I had a craving for something and I wondered if we had any on hand.

Harriet had her hands in a ball of dough.

"Do we have any olives?" I asked her.

She looked at me as though I had just asked if we had any human heads. Apparently, impromptu visits to the kitchen for snacks were not encouraged. I winced at yet another faux pas.

"Why?" she said, finally.

"I've been craving them for a couple of days now," I said. "It's weird, I don't mind them in a Greek salad, but I don't usually crave them. Maybe I'm low on sodium or something. Anyway, do we have any?"

She narrowed her eyes at me. "Green or black?"

I cringed. She was really not happy with me. "Black. But if it's too much trouble . . ."

She stopped me by pulling her hands out of the dough and washing them in the sink before crossing the room to the panty, where she found a can of black olives. She opened the can, dumped the olives into a bowl and handed it to me, all without saying a word.

I popped one into my mouth. The salty, briny taste was like heaven.

"Thanks!" I said. "I'll take this and put it on the sideboard in the winter garden. Let's leave it out in case anyone else wants some."

And then I hurried out of the kitchen, wishing I had never gone in there. But, at least I had my olives. I popped another into my mouth, and then a third before I went out into the gardens to find Henry.

"Beautiful," I said, looking over his shoulder at what was shaping up to be a landscape painting that, to my eye, was reminiscent of Monet. "I've never seen the gardens looking so lovely."

He turned to me and smiled. "It's getting there," he said.

"I'd love to be able to do what you do," I said to him, still entranced by the painting. "I've never been much of an artist."

"Oh, I don't know about that," he said, putting his brush on his easel and wiping his hands on his painter's shirt. "You organized this lovely gathering. And you were a writer for your whole career before this, at least that's what I've heard."

"That's right," I said, segueing into the reason I had sought him out. "I came to Cliffside quite unexpectedly. I was a journalist for twenty years, but I lost my job at the newspaper. It was right about the time Penelope Dare announced her retirement, and I thought I could use a change, so I applied for the job."

He gazed at me, a look of concern on his face. "Out of the frying pan," he said. "Isn't that what they say? I was so shocked to get your letter saying that Penelope Dare had died. You've had your hands full, I daresay."

"I have, indeed," I said. "So many things fell through the cracks after she passed. I've been muddling my way through."

"Beautifully, if I may say so."

I smiled. "Thank you. But I never did get to see your letters of application, for example. I'm supposed to know your backstories, but I really have no idea how you came to Cliffside. It's embarrassing, when people have brought it up, to have to admit that I don't know."

"Oh, nobody thinks anything of it," he said, brushing the gray hair from his eyes.

For a moment, I thought he wasn't going to take the bait and I'd have to ask him outright, but then, mercifully, he continued. "My story is a little unusual, actually," he said. "I've heard about Cliffside my whole life, since I was a little boy."

"Oh?" I said. "That *is* unusual. You're from the South—quite a ways away. I would think you hadn't heard of Cliffside's reputation down there."

"All of the stories came from my mother," he said, a sad smile crossing his face. "She's gone now, of course. Cancer. Ten years ago, already."

"I'm sorry," I said, putting a hand on his arm.

"She was a nurse here," he went on. "And if you want to know the truth—I suppose it doesn't hurt to say it, now that everyone concerned is gone—I was born seven months after she left Cliffside." He raised his eyebrows. "Yes," he said. "Apparently, I was conceived right here."

My mouth hung open for a moment until I realized I must have been staring at this poor man as though he had just confessed the original sin. "That's incredible" was all I could manage.

"I know," he said with a laugh. "That's how I felt, too. I never knew my dad, and she never divulged who he was, but I have a suspicion"—he leaned in and lowered his voice—"that it was either Chester Dare, whom she idolized, or the doctor working here at the time. Davidson was his name. Of course, he's long gone by now.

"Or, she could have fallen in love with one of the male patients and had an affair," he continued. "I'll never know for sure."

I knew one way to find out, I thought. Nate was the doctor's son. Their blood tests would reveal if they were siblings. But I didn't say it to him, not just then. I wanted to mention it to Nate first.

"Wow," I said. "That's some history with Cliffside. Did Penelope Dare know any of this when she accepted your application?"

"It's why she accepted it," he said. "I had been putting this off for a long time, always wanting to come, but too . . . I don't know if *afraid* is the right word, but reticent. Hesitant. Here was my past, my origins, waiting for me. But, somehow, I just couldn't put pen to paper to get it done."

"So, how did it happen, then?"

"My husband, Stephan, filled out the application, unbeknownst to me."

He had a husband? The look on my face must've betrayed my feelings, because he burst into laughter.

"Thirty years now," he said. "We were married just last year."

"But—" I couldn't help laughing myself. "You know everyone thinks you slept with Brynn last night."

"They don't!"

"They do!"

"Well, that would have been a first." Between bursts of laughter, he fished into his pocket for a handkerchief and dabbed at his eyes. "I can't wait to tell Stephan I was part of the first scandal of our session at Cliffside. I'm twice her age, for goodness' sake, and not to mention, that poor girl is not my type."

This sent us both into another fit of laughter. "Miss Penny told me there would be days like this," I managed to say.

And then, at the mention of her name, I remembered why I had come to talk to him. I cleared my throat and continued. "Say, about that. You said Stephan mentioned your connection to Cliffside, and that's one of the reasons your application was accepted."

"Yes, that's right," he said.

It might have been the laughter we had just shared, or it might have been something else, but at that moment, I trusted this man.

I sighed. "I'm finding out that Penelope Dare had personal reasons for wanting everybody at Cliffside this session. Including me."

He squinted at me for a few moments. "That's curious, isn't it? What sort of reasons?"

"I'm not sure, but everyone seems to have a personal connection to the place, beyond just their artistic endeavors," I said. "I haven't spoken to Diana yet, but it's true for the rest of you."

"Stephan did show me the application letter, after the fact," he admitted. "He definitely played up my connection to Cliffside. It took about a year, maybe a bit more, to hear back from her. She called me several weeks ago and asked me to come to this session."

"So you, too," I said, taking a deep breath in.

"When Brynn was reading out of her journal last night, I started to get a little—I don't know—uncomfortable," he said. "I didn't mention my mother being a nurse here because . . ." His words trailed off into a sigh.

"You didn't want anyone to suspect that she was the nurse who gave Temperance that injection."

"She would never have done anything like that," he said, his voice catching. "She was the most caring, wonderful person I've ever known."

I put a hand on his arm. "We don't even know if what's written in that journal is true," I said. "Brynn could've made up the whole thing, even the existence of the journal. She is a fiction writer, after all, and that's one hell of a hook to sell a story to a publisher."

It made me wonder if I might be overreacting to the whole thing, even though the handwriting on the torn-out pages was identical to Miss Penny's.

I left Henry to his painting and retreated inside to find Diana. I wanted to talk with her about how she had come to Cliffside, but in truth, I didn't need to know, not really. Everyone else was summoned by Miss Penny personally, and I would have been stunned to find that Diana was the exception.

I climbed the stairs to the second floor and knocked lightly on her door, cringing a bit because I knew she was here for the isolation and solitude. Well, I told myself, this wouldn't take long, and then I'd leave her to it.

She opened the door a crack and peeked around it. "Yes?"

"I'm so sorry to bother you, Diana, but may I come in for a minute? It won't take long, I promise."

She opened the door wide. "Of course," she said. "I can use a break. Do come in."

I found her room in complete disarray—clothes everywhere, stockings balled on the floor, her suitcase open in the middle of the room, a fluffy, white towel hanging over one of the bedposts. She had only been here one day, and already the room looked like a hurricane had passed through. I tried to suppress a grin. She saw my amusement and let out a laugh. "I can't help it," she said, opening her arms wide. "It just happens. I open my suitcase and things fly out."

"A place for everything and everything in its place, it is not." I smiled at her.

"How boring that would be," she said. "I never was a black-and-white sort of person. There always seems to be a wild tangle around me."

She perched on the edge of the bed and gestured to the wing chair. I moved the shirts that were hanging over the armrest and sank into the seat.

"Now, what can I do for you, Eleanor?" she asked. "Is this about our conversation at breakfast this morning?"

"Sort of," I said and dove right into it. "I'm wondering how you came to be at Cliffside during this particular session. You see, all of your letters of application are missing. Ordinarily, that wouldn't be a problem, but—" I stammered over my words. "Diana, I'm starting to believe that Penelope Dare wanted all of the fellows here together during this session for some particular reason. And me, too."

"And not just because we'd mesh artistically," she said, nodding.

"Exactly," I said.

She shook her head. "I hate to break up your matched set, but I'm the odd girl out, it seems," she said.

My heart sank. Maybe I wasn't onto the truth after all. "No special summons, then?"

"I'm afraid not," she said. "I was accepted back in December for this session."

I saw my theory collapsing and falling to the ground like a house of cards.

"Oh," I sighed. "Well, then."

"You look disappointed," she said, smiling at me.

I took a deep breath. "It's just that . . ." My words trailed off.

"Why would you be concerned about people getting special invitations to attend this session?" she asked, squinting at me. "I think there's more to this than you're saying."

"You might say that, yes," I began but didn't quite know how to continue.

"You said it had something, sort of, to do with our conversation at breakfast, and . . . let's see. We were talking about what happened in Brynn's room, and spirits at Cliffside," she pressed. "Now you've piqued my interest. What is this all about, Eleanor?"

I decided to be honest with her. What could it hurt? After all, she was the one who'd said Cliffside—and the world at large—was full of spirits. At least she wouldn't think I was crazy for what I was about to tell her. I was about to just blurt it all out when I had a better idea.

"Will you come with me to my suite?" I asked her. "It won't take long. I just want to show you something."

She hopped to her feet. "Why not?"

A few moments later we were sitting in my study, me at the desk, she in the armchair beside me.

I took a deep breath and began. "You know that Penelope Dare died shortly before you arrived, but you don't know the whole story." I opened the drawer, pulled out the letter and handed it to Diana.

As she read it, her eyes grew wide. She looked up at me and mouthed, "Suicide?"

"Nobody else knows," I told her. "Well, Harriet and the police know, obviously, but this isn't public knowledge."

She shook her head. "I don't understand," she said. "You thought she assembled all of us here for a purpose . . . but, why? She killed herself before any of us arrived."

"That's what I've been trying to figure out," I said. "But, now I'm not so sure there's anything to it. You didn't receive a special invitation."

She locked eyes with me. "I was thinking about that," she said. "Maybe I was the first one on deck, so to speak. I applied through the regular channels and was accepted for this session, and she then invited the others."

"That could be," I said, my mind whirring around that theory. "But what I still can't fathom, is why."

Diana turned her eyes back to the letter and read part of it aloud. *"In my wake, I have left a puzzle for you to solve, Eleanor Harper. You, the would-be sleuth. You, of the curious mind. I know you will latch on to it, just as you latched on to the murders of my father and sister all those years ago. I trust you'll be more successful this time."*

"She wants you to solve a mystery she's left for you," Diana said. "That's crystal clear. And you think last night is part of it."

"I do," I said, my stomach seizing up at the thought of it. "I had a conversation with a friend of mine, the doctor on staff here, actually, earlier yesterday and he had me convinced all of this was nothing more than my imagination. But then there was the incident in Brynn's room."

I opened the desk drawer and pulled out the journal page. "This is what I wanted to show you," I said. "Look at this." I held the page next to the letter she still had in her lap. "What do you make of it?"

She gasped. "Oh, Lord," she said, her voice dropping to a whisper. "This is the same handwriting."

"That's what I thought, too," I said.

"There's no doubt," she said, still looking from one page to the other.

"Richard is convinced Brynn did this herself for attention or drama or whatever it is that drives her, and I would tend to agree . . ." I said.

"If not for this handwriting," she finished my thought.

"Exactly. I thought it looked familiar, and she might have fabricated it somehow, but I took a page to compare it with the suicide note. When I saw them side by side, it scared me to death."

"It scares me, too," Diana said, reaching over and putting her hand on top of mine, her eyes wide. "This scrawl on Brynn's journal was written by Penelope Dare. And she's dead."

# CHAPTER 22

"This is what you really wanted to bring up at breakfast," Diana said, her hand still clutching mine.

"It is," I said. "I just couldn't find the words. It sounds crazy. I mean, if this is really true, then it implies—"

"That the dead at Cliffside are out for vengeance?"

It was a little dramatic, but basically true. "Something like that," I said. "There's no earthly way Penelope Dare could've ripped up Brynn's journal and written on it. But somehow, she did."

"So it would seem," Diana said, nodding. "But why would she do it?"

"That's one question we don't have to puzzle over," I said. "I was stunned when I found out what Brynn is writing. There is no possibility that Penelope would sanction that novel. No possibility at all. It would ruin the reputation of her adored father and tarnish, if not ruin, Cliffside's reputation as well. To see their names dragged through the mud with a scandalous book like the one Brynn is intending to write . . ." I let out a sigh. "I'm here to tell you, that's a motive for murder."

I could almost see the wheels turning in Diana's mind. She crossed her legs and leaned in toward me.

"Maybe," she said. "But maybe not. I still stand by what I said before. This seems juvenile to me. Childish. I say we wait and see what, if anything, happens next."

"And what if that's somebody winding up dead?"

She shook her head. "I really don't think it's going to come to that," she said. "I think the best thing to do is to get us all together and talk about this. Knowledge is power. You've already found out that everyone but me received special, last-minute invitations directly from Penelope Dare to come to Cliffside this session. That's a fact. We know she called us all here, but we don't know why. Maybe we can all brainstorm and figure that out."

I wished, in that moment, that I had never come to Cliffside. That sense of dread and fear I had been feeling for months had been starting to abate in recent days, but now it was awakened from wherever it had been lying dormant. I could feel it grow inside of me until I was shaking from deep in my core.

I felt Diana's hand rubbing my back. "Don't worry, Eleanor," she said. "It's all right."

I looked up at her. "How do you know?"

"Because," she said, smiling at me. "What people never seem to understand when dealing with the dead is this—we hold all the cards."

"I don't get it," I said, squinting at her.

"We're alive," she said. "We have all the power because we're supposed to be here on earth. She's not, not anymore. She has someplace else to go. And we can make her go there."

I nodded. It sounded reasonable. I wanted it to sound reasonable.

"It's what needs to be done," she said. "If we don't do it, who will?"

# CHAPTER 23

We made plans to talk with the group during dinner, and Diana went back to her suite to continue working. I was glad that I had confided in her. The fear that gripped me was slowly subsiding, trickling back to wherever it had come from. Diana had taken some of it away with her reasonable thinking, her steady voice. It felt good to have someone to talk to about this who didn't think I was a lunatic, and it felt even better to have a plan.

I had some work to do—I really needed to wade my way through those applications for next year and make some decisions about who to invite—but I was itching to get back outside and stretch my legs. It felt good to move, to be physical, to be out in the fresh air. I trotted down the stairs, made a side trip to grab a couple of olives, and headed out the door.

It was a beautiful, warm day, and I decided to take the path down to the lakeshore. I scrambled my way down and began to walk along the shoreline, picking up a rock here and there as I went. The lake was like glass. There aren't too many Lake Superior days when the great spirit, Gitche Gumee, which the ancient Native Americans in the area believed lived in the lake—and many Lake Superior residents still do—is this calm, this peaceful, and I stood for a moment and took it in, the beauty and wonder of the largest freshwater lake in the world, as still as a millpond.

That's when I noticed a kayak moving around the cliff, back toward me. *Richard?* I shielded my eyes from the sun to get a better look and, sure enough, I could see his shock of dark hair and a camera dangling from his neck. I watched as he paddled closer to shore, and I wished I was out there with him, kayaking side by side.

As I kept watching, I began to imagine us together, and not kayaking. But I shook that thought out of my head—I had only just met the man. Sure, I was intrigued, but . . . I truly didn't know what to make of my attraction to both him and Nate at the same time. If given a choice, whom would I choose? Both had good qualities, both had mysterious sides. A delicious thought entered my mind then. Maybe I didn't have to choose, not now, anyway. Maybe I could let all of this play out naturally. I couldn't believe my luck. Two great guys on my radar at the same time.

Richard caught sight of me and put a hand up in greeting. I did the same. And that's when it happened. I watched as Richard's kayak seemed to heave out of the water and overturn. He was underwater, as quickly as that.

I knew that water was ice cold, but I didn't care. I wasn't sure if he could swim, or how accomplished he was at freeing himself from an overturned kayak. I kicked off my shoes, ran into the lake, and swam toward him, pounding through the water with a force I didn't know I possessed. When I neared the kayak, I submerged myself in that freezing water and helped pull him out of the skirt that held him, using all my might. We surfaced together, him coughing up the water that had gotten into his lungs.

We both got on one side of the kayak and swam to shore, pushing it all the way.

"The skirt wouldn't release." He coughed as we dragged ourselves and the kayak up onto the beach. "I was trying to right the damn thing when I was upside down, but that hip action always eludes me. I've never been able to do it."

"What on earth happened?" I said.

He shook his head. "I'll be damned if I know," he said. "The lake was like glass. There wasn't so much as a ripple on the surface. A perfect day to shoot on the water. But that's one cold lake, I don't mind telling you."

"That's no joke, Richard—this time of year, people can get hypothermia in minutes out there," I said. "Ice was still on the lake a month ago. And you weren't wearing a wet suit! My God . . ." My words trailed off as the realization hit me. If it had happened in the middle of the lake, he could have been killed.

"I could say the same for you," he said as we hiked up the trail toward the house.

He was right. I hadn't thought a bit about that when I dove into the lake—I just knew I needed to help him.

A very bad feeling rumbled in the pit of my stomach. Was I to blame for this? There was a packet of info in each room about the area, common safety procedures and warnings about dangers like the ice-cold lake this time of year and the forest full of animals. But even so, I should have talked to everyone when they arrived, made sure they knew not to go kayaking without a wet suit, or not to trudge into the forest without letting someone know where they were going. There were real dangers here. My carelessness might have cost Richard his life, had I not been right there to help.

"This is my fault," I said to him, my teeth beginning to chatter. "I should have made sure to tell you to wear a wet suit."

"And what's your excuse?" he said, managing a grin with lips that were turning blue. "I didn't think they made wet suits out of denim these days."

"I saw you go over," I said. "I had to help if I could."

He grabbed my hand. "I thank you for that, Norrie Harper," he said.

I shook my head. "It was nothing."

"No," he said. "You plunged into icy-cold water and helped me out of that skirt. I was having real trouble. Had you not been there . . ."

I smiled, warmed by his appreciation. "But your camera's on the bottom of the lake. I'm so sorry that happened."

"And it's not your fault," he said. "Not in any way. I was just clumsy. I must've leaned too far over. Although . . ." He fell silent and shook his head.

"Although what?"

"I've been kayaking for a very long time, in every kind of weather, on bodies of water with rapids and tides and huge waves, not to mention crocodiles," he said. "I won't say I'm an expert but . . . okay, yes. I'm an expert."

We shared a chuckle.

"But today—you saw it—this lake was like glass," he went on. "There's not a whisper of wind out there, not so much as a ripple on the surface. I can hardly believe I went over. It almost felt like"—he turned his head to look back out toward the water—"like something big came at me from underneath."

A cold wave passed through me.

"Once, I was kayaking in Puget Sound and a solitary gray whale came up to the surface underneath me," he said. "I didn't go over that time, I got out of the way, but I could feel this huge presence under the kayak. It was sort of like that, in a way. But it couldn't have been, could it? There are no whales in Lake Superior."

"No," I said. "There's nothing like that. No sea life. We've got big fish. Beavers and otters, too, but nothing that could possibly capsize a kayak."

"No Loch Ness monster?" He grinned.

"Well, you never know about that." I smiled back at him and raised my eyebrows. "Lake Superior is deep and old and mysterious. Lots of myths exist about it being a living thing, the lake itself. You may well have encountered the great spirit of Gitche Gumee out there today. I know some locals who would swear you did."

"If I did, he didn't like me much," he said, rubbing his neck.

"Or he just wanted your camera," I said, wincing again when I said the words. "Do you have another?"

"Oh, I come prepared, Norrie Harper," he said, giving me a wink.

I noticed him shiver and felt the cold running through me as well. "You should go back to your suite and take a hot shower. I'm going to do the same. Just leave your wet clothes in the bathroom—I'll send somebody up later to deal with them."

I watched him go and wondered what, exactly, had just happened.

~

After a long, hot shower, I settled in to read some application letters, but I didn't see any of the other fellows for the rest of the afternoon. Even Henry, who had been positioned in the gardens, was nowhere to be found. That was good, I thought to myself. All was calm. At least for the moment. Even so, I felt like I had been on high alert for most of the day. Doom, it seemed to me, was floating in the air. I tried to read, but my ears were perked, listening for a cry, a moan, or worse, a scream. The expression *waiting for the other shoe to drop* went through my mind over and over as I scanned the house and grounds from my chaise. It was quiet, but something was coming. I could feel it.

Now, it was nearing dinnertime. I stood in front of the mirror, giving my hair one last brush, rehearsing what I was going to say to the group. No matter the words I put together, they all sounded ridiculous. But Diana and I had come up with a plan, and I intended to at least try to go through with it. I set my brush down on the vanity with an air of finality. "Okay," I said to my reflection, "let's do this."

I marched downstairs to find Richard had beaten me to the drawing room. He stood at the sideboard, pouring himself a glass of Scotch. When I entered the room, he turned and smiled.

"After what happened today, I was a little anxious for a snort," he admitted, the particular twinkle back in his dark eyes.

"I will second that," I said, reaching for the Chardonnay bottle that was perched in the ice bucket.

"I notice Harriet has put the gin out for Miss Particular," he said out of the side of his mouth, his voice low. "But you just know she's not going to want it tonight, now that it's there. She'll ask for something else."

I grinned at him. "It sounds like you've got experience with her type."

"Seven long years of it, yes," he said, taking a sip of his Scotch. "Once, if you looked up *daft* in the dictionary, you'd find my picture there. Thankfully, in *Webster's* new edition, that's been changed for more than a decade now." He raised his glass.

So, Richard had been married before. Or at least, coupled. That twang of jealousy sizzled through me again. But why? Who was this man to me?

"You seem to have warmed up after your dip in the lake earlier," I said, smiling at him. "Any ill effects?"

"A hot shower was just what I needed," he said. "But I'm still upset with myself about the camera. I can't believe I let it go."

"And I'm still upset with myself for not talking to all of you about the dangers here," I said. "Cliffside will replace your camera, Richard. It's only right. I'll speak to our accountant about it in the morning."

He smiled and cocked his head to the side. "You don't have to do that," he said. "I was the fool who went headfirst into the lake."

"I insist," I said. "Please. I really do feel badly about it."

"In that case, I thank you for your generosity, Miss Harper," he said.

I took a sip of my wine and let myself look into his face. I had avoided too much eye contact with him, but now, somehow, something made me want to simply languish there in his gaze.

We stood, close enough to touch, just simply looking at each other, neither, apparently, wanting to be the first to break free of whatever web had suddenly woven itself around us.

He was taller than me but not by much. His dark hair was thick and unruly, curling around his ears and standing straight up in spots on the top of his head. He had a scar on his strong jawline, and it made me wonder what sort of escapade he'd been on when he got it. He wore a hint of cologne, so slight that it almost wasn't there at all.

I can't explain what it was or why, but something was happening between us, right there, in the drawing room. Neither of us could look away. It was as though I was memorizing his face, and he was memorizing mine. There was an energy, a sense of magic that vibrated in the air around us, my body vibrating with it. My peripheral vision blurred as though the room had fallen away, disintegrated into dust, and there was nothing in the whole world except Richard Banks's dancing eyes.

"Eleanor Harper," he whispered.

"Good evening, you two!" Henry chirped. And just like that, the spell was broken.

I snapped my head around and saw him entering the room, Brynn on his arm. She was smiling one of those strange, faux smiles you see on women who are competing in pageants, a smile with a tempest going on behind her eyes.

"Hello!" I managed, a little too loudly, I thought. I cleared my throat and tried again. "Henry, you were getting some great work done in the gardens earlier. Did it continue?"

"Oh yes, oh my, yes," he said, winding Brynn's arm out of his own and plucking a microbrew out of the ice bucket. "If every day is like today, I'll have a whole series by the time our session here ends."

"Wonderful!" I said. But oddly, his words hit me hard. Their time would end. Soon these people would be gone and a new group would come. Of course, that was the whole idea of this place, and of course, it was no surprise to me. And yet, it felt wrong, somehow. As though us being together at Cliffside was the way it should be. I remembered Miss Penny had warned me about getting too close to any of the fellows—maybe this was why.

Richard's voice muffled those thoughts. "What can I get you, my dear?" he asked Brynn. "I'm on bar duty tonight."

She squinted at the display on the sideboard and shrugged her shoulders. "I guess I'll have a white wine."

Richard caught my eye for the briefest of seconds and winked as he was pouring her Chardonnay. I didn't even try to stifle my grin.

Soon, Cassandra and Diana had joined us. The fellows began chatting about their days, who had made what sort of progress on their projects, and Richard's untimely dip in the lake. I stood off to the side, letting them talk among themselves, while I planned what to say to the group.

Diana and I exchanged a glance, and I knew it was time to bring up the subject at hand.

I cleared my throat. "I want to talk with you all about something tonight."

"Is it about the heat in our rooms?" Brynn piped up. "Because mine's ice cold. It has been, all day. I could barely work."

A wave of annoyance washed through me. "No, Brynn," I said. "It's not about that. But I'll mention it to Mr. Baines after dinner."

She huffed.

"Let's all sit down," I said, gesturing to the sofa and chairs. "I'm hoping we can do a little brainstorming together."

They did as I asked, taking seats here and there. Richard sat next to me and crossed his legs, draping an arm on the back of the sofa.

"What's this all about, Eleanor?" he asked.

I took a sip of my wine and tried to gather my thoughts. Everything I had practiced in my head that afternoon had flown away, and now I was at a loss.

Thankfully, Diana jumped in. "Eleanor and I were talking about what happened to Brynn's journal last night," she began.

But Brynn cut her off. "I know exactly what happened," she said. "One of you"—she looked pointedly at Cassandra—"is jealous."

Cassandra looked from side to side. "What, me?" She let out a strained laugh. "You think I destroyed your journal?"

"I've been thinking about it all day," she said, squinting at Cassandra. "Here you are, writing your fancy history about this place. You've done years of research, and yet you had no idea what really happened here. You were as surprised to find out about it as all of these people were." She gestured around the room. "If that's not a motive, I don't know what is."

She crossed her legs and leaned against the back of her chair, triumphant.

"But I thought I was your culprit," Richard said, a slight grin on his lips.

"I changed my mind."

Cassandra shot me a look and rolled her eyes before turning back to Brynn. "For your information, my book isn't going to include innuendo and gossip. I deal in facts. That's why my genre is called *non*fiction."

Her arrow had hit its mark, the sting evident on Brynn's face. If she wasn't so annoying, I might have felt sorry for her. I wouldn't relish being on the wrong side of an argument with Cassandra. But, as it was, I just wanted to steer the conversation back on course before it derailed.

"Listen, everyone," I said, addressing the room but looking at Brynn. "I need your help here. We all do. As I said, I'm hoping we can work out, together, why we're all here at Cliffside at the same time. Every one of us, including me, was invited to come to Cliffside for this particular session at the last minute."

"Except me," Diana said.

"Yes, except Diana, but I think we're going to find our way around that."

Richard shook his head. "What are you getting at, Norrie?"

I took a deep breath. "Okay," I began. "Penelope Dare went to great pains to make sure all of us were together at Cliffside during this session."

Cassandra was nodding. "You know how it happened for me," she said to me, "but the rest of you don't. I've been applying for seven years to come here. And suddenly, out of the blue, I get a call from Penelope Dare saying I've been accepted for this session."

Brynn huffed. "Well, that's not how it happened for me," she said. "Miss Dare saw the description of my work and thought it was special. That's why I'm here."

"Oh, Christ," Cassandra said under her breath. She pushed herself out of her seat and went over to the sideboard to refill her drink.

I let it go. Brynn was obviously going to be of no help, and it was best not to engage her at the moment.

"It was Henry's story that really got me thinking," I went on, turning to him. "Do you feel comfortable telling everyone? Or should we leave it between us?"

"Not at all!" he said, holding his glass aloft. "I'll have you all know that I was conceived right here at Cliffside."

This brought the room to a standstill.

Cassandra slid in next to him. "Well, you little devil," she said, patting him on the shoulder. "When were you going to let us in on this secret?"

"Oh, it's no secret," he said. "My mother was a nurse here, back in the day. I didn't mention it last night—that was Brynn's story. But I know for a fact that it's one of the reasons why I was accepted to come here. Penelope Dare called me personally."

Cassandra, Henry, and Richard were all nodding, exchanging knowing glances. They were seeing the outline of something begin to fill in, just like I was.

"So, you all are beginning to understand that we're here together at Miss Penny's bidding," I said. "She gathered us here, personally. But we don't know why. That's what I hoped we could brainstorm about together."

Henry rubbed his chin. "You said it was my story that got you thinking. Why?"

"You've got a prior connection to Cliffside," I said, first looking at him and then around the room. "I thought—maybe we all do, too. I was here twenty years ago, as was Richard. Brynn's grandmother was here as a patient. Cassandra and Diana, that leaves the two of you. Do you have prior connections to this place?"

Diana shook her head. "As I said this morning, I'm the odd girl out," she said. "As far as I know, I don't have any connections to Cliffside."

Cassandra was sipping on her drink. "As for me, I thought you knew," she said, slowly. "My grandfather was a patient when it was a sanatorium. He had TB. It's funny—it's like I can feel his presence here, even though I never knew him."

"But he survived?" I asked.

"No," she said. "He was the last patient to die at Cliffside."

# CHAPTER 24

Harriet had come in at some point in the discussion to let us know it was time for dinner. Her scowl had also let me know she was none too happy with the line of conversation, but that didn't matter to me, not really. I felt like we were on to something, and I wanted to continue with it.

"Okay," I said, after we had all settled in at the dining room table and Harriet and the girls had brought in the big bowls of stir fry and chicken fried rice, "so, it's true, then. We all"—I shot a look to Diana—"well, most of us have a prior connection to Cliffside. So what?"

"What do you mean, so what?" Brynn sniffed.

I let out a sigh. "It's a question to get people thinking, Brynn," I said. "So, what? What does it matter that we all have a connection and we're all here together now?"

Everyone was looking at each other across the table, puzzled.

"Maybe she only accepted people with prior connections to Cliffside," Richard offered. "I mean, not just us, but everyone."

I shook my head. "That's not right," I said. "I've been reading the application letters of the entire next year's worth of fellows."

"And none . . . ?" he ventured.

I shook my head. "None that I could see, not yet, anyway. And Diana can't put her finger on a prior connection, either."

I looked around the table. People were turning their attentions to their dinners, trying not to meet my gaze. They were losing steam for this idea, I could see that. Mysteries had been my life, but not everyone was as intrigued as I was. I caught Diana's eye, and she shrugged. She felt it, too. I decided to let the subject drop, for now. It was pointless to keep pushing. Maybe I was the only one really invested in finding the answers.

"I'm just asking you all to let me know if anything comes to mind," I said, finally. And the conversation turned to other things—progress on people's work, the house and the grounds, items in the news.

After everyone finished eating, they all went their separate ways. I stayed at the table for a while, letting ideas and possibilities drift through my mind. But my thoughts were like so many phantoms, ethereal and wispy, without any real substance.

Richard poked his head around the archway. "I'm going out for a walk," he said. "It's a beautiful evening. Care to join me?"

Given what had begun to happen between us earlier, I knew I shouldn't accept. I had already decided to be every inch the proper director of Cliffside. Miss Penny didn't go off walking in the twilight with male fellows, I told myself. But despite all of that, I pushed my chair back from the table and smiled at him.

"I'd love to," I said. Caution, meet wind.

He was right—it was a beautiful night. It was after eight o'clock, but there was still plenty of light in the sky. A slight breeze whispered around us, carrying the scent of lilac on the wind, reminding me of other times, my childhood, and, it seemed as I walked with Richard Banks, something earlier than that.

I steered us toward the path down to the water, thinking the shoreline at dusk might be safer than one of the trails through the woods. Animals crept out of their lairs at night, stealing through the forest, doing whatever it was they did when the light of day wasn't shining on them. I had no wish to encounter a bear or worse. So we scrambled down the path on the cliff until we reached the bottom.

The shoreline stretched for miles in front of us, and we strolled lazily along the water's edge as the lake gently caressed the sand and the rocks, polished by years of such activity. It was a hypnotic, soothing sound, and I could feel my breathing begin to keep time with it. That's just what it seemed like, this great lake's respiration, its breathing soft and steady, as though it, too, were winding down after a long day.

Richard had a camera slung over his shoulder, and as we walked, he began snapping photos. We didn't say much at first. I was content to listen to the lake's breath and watch him capture the beauty of the landscape around us.

"I think we're going to get quite a lovely sunset," he said, finally.

"You've seen sunsets all over the world," I said. "How do you think this one will compare?"

He smiled at me. "Oh, I think it will stack up against the best of them."

We walked a bit farther, when something struck me. "Your application, what I have of it, says you retired," I began. "But you're a little young to retire, aren't you? Either that or you're extremely well preserved."

"I prefer to think I'm both of those, thank you," he said, grinning. "But you're right. I'm not exactly retirement age."

I wanted to know why he had given up his career of traveling to exotic locales, camera in hand, but I didn't ask the follow-up question. What some people called curious, others called nosy. I waited for him to continue, if he so chose.

"I got tired of the constant travel," he said, shrugging. "It's a young man's game, that. Hopping from continent to continent."

"Oh, the tedium of it all," I teased him.

He smiled. "Don't misunderstand, I'm grateful for everything I've been able to do," he said. "I've seen, with my own eyes, up close and personal, what most people only see in pictures."

"In your pictures."

"Well, yes," he said. "But, speaking of tedium. People think it's exciting, photographing animals in the wild, and it is. But glamorous it is not. Those dramatic shots don't just happen in an instant. Sometimes it takes hours or even days. So, there's a lot of waiting and watching through the lens. And crouching. And hiding."

"And bugs."

"Ach, yes, the bugs," he said, wrinkling his nose. "And weather extremes. I'd be on the African plains stalking elephants one week and in the Arctic following a polar bear family the next."

"From a safe distance, I assume."

He smiled. "Sometimes not so safe. I took my share of chances."

"Is that why you stopped? The danger?"

"An angry mother bear had something to do with it, yes." He raised his eyebrows. "Like I said, it's a young man's game. When I got out of hospital—"

I broke in. "Hospital?"

"Indeed," he said, lifting his shirt to show me a long scar across his abdomen. "She got me. I started thinking maybe it was time for a change."

"That's when you opened your gallery?"

"I did," he said. "In Saint Ives. I started yearning for a quieter sort of life, one without all of that travel and danger. It was as though I was settling down. The only problem was, I didn't have anyone to settle down with."

And there it was again, the electricity charging the air. It was shimmering around us, as though the very molecules in the air were vibrating and humming. An image floated through my mind and filled up my vision—I could see us lying there together, in the sand, faces close, his hand stroking my cheek. But it wasn't this beach, it was someplace else, a different shoreline, a different time. I could smell the salt air and taste it on my tongue.

"And, what about you, Norrie Harper?" he said, his voice breaking my vision. "You're living here at Cliffside on your own. But is there anyone in your life I should be concerned about?"

Our eyes locked in the same mesmerizing gaze we had begun in the drawing room hours before, a gaze that seemed to reach deeply into my past, as though there were nothing about me this man couldn't see. "Why would you be concerned?" I managed to say.

"Because," he said, his voice almost a whisper. Before I knew it, he pulled me close, wrapping his arms around my waist, our faces nearly touching. "Because I've wanted to do this since the moment I laid eyes on you." And he kissed me then, the tenderest, gentlest kiss I've ever felt. My legs were shaking as I put my arms around his neck and drew him closer, wanting him closer still, until reason got the better of me. I pulled away and cleared my throat.

"Why, Mr. Banks, I do believe you're making a pass at me," I said, my voice wavering as I tried to lighten the mood.

"You picked up on that?" he said with a grin.

He turned the camera on me, then, and began snapping. I laughed and put out a hand toward the lens. "I must look a fright."

"Not a bit," he said. "You look lovely." He kept snapping frames as my face heated up.

"Come on, then," he said, still pointing the camera at me, "give me your best fashion model pout. This is for the cover of *Vogue*."

I struck a pose and smiled at him. He snapped a few more frames, but then he gasped and lowered the camera, looking just over my shoulder.

"That bad?" I winced.

"No," he said, quickly. "Not at all. It was just . . ." He was still staring behind me, his mouth open. I turned to look, but there was nothing but sand and rocks and water.

"Richard, what is it?"

He shook his head. "Damned if I know," he said. "I could've sworn someone was standing behind you just now. I thought I saw it through the lens. But . . ."

A shiver ran through me.

"Through the looking glass," I said, raising my eyebrows. "It's our world, but not quite."

His scowl, directed toward whatever it was he thought he saw, told me this wasn't a joke to him. He let his camera dangle from its strap around his shoulder and put a hand on my back. "Come on," he said. "I think it's time we get back."

I looked up to the west and saw a dark, gray bank of clouds had moved in—I had been so entranced with our conversation, and that kiss, I hadn't noticed the weather building.

"Good idea," I said, pointing up at the cloud and thinking of Nate and how we had been caught out in a storm. "It looks like a storm is coming."

He squinted at the sky. "That kicked up quickly, didn't it?"

"It happens like that here," I said. "Before you know it, the weather will change. It's one reason why boating on Lake Superior is so dangerous. You never know when the wind will change and bad weather will roll in."

We walked together back the way we had come, a bit faster now, his hand on my back all the while. I made no move away from him. It felt good and right to have him steering and protecting me.

Night was falling when we reached the path that snaked its way up the cliff.

A loud rumble of thunder rolled as a huge bolt of lightning lit up the sky and drops of rain began to fall.

"I think Mother Nature has something against us today." He smiled. We scrambled up the path, but not fast enough. The sky opened up and it began to pour, soaking us to the skin as we hurried across the lawn toward the house. Just then, a pang of guilt zipped through me. I had done the same thing with Nate not so long ago.

# CHAPTER 25

"This is the second time in one day that we've been drenched while fully dressed," Richard said as we opened the veranda doors and made our way into the house. "That's got to be some kind of—"

His words trailed off when we both realized the lights were out in the house. Some, albeit murky, light from the windows was illuminating the area just inside the veranda doors, but beyond that, it was inky blackness. I wasn't sure if I could find my way to the stairs without tripping over something.

"Oh, great," I said, trying to adjust my eyes to the darkness. "There must be a power outage."

"Do you know where the fuse box is?" Richard asked. "I could probably muddle my way through throwing the proper switches."

I groaned. "I really have no idea," I said. "I'm still getting used to this place. But I'm sure—"

I cut off my own thought when I heard footsteps scurrying across the marble floors. Harriet emerged from the darkness carrying two flashlights.

"I thought you two could use these on your way upstairs," she said, flipping each one on in turn and illuminating herself with an eerie glow. "You're going to catch your death if you don't get out of those wet things."

All at once I felt like a kid skipping school caught by the headmistress.

I handed a flashlight to Richard and took one myself. "Thank you, Harriet," I said, trying to sound as dignified as possible. "Can I assume Mr. Baines is handling the fuse box?"

She shook her head. "We haven't blown a fuse," she said. "It's an electrical outage. Mr. Baines heard from a friend in town—a transformer was hit by lightning a short while ago, and half the county is dark."

That was probably the huge bolt of lightning we had seen.

"Ah," I said. "So the lights just recently went out, then?"

"Yes, ma'am," she said. "Within the last few minutes."

Only then did I think about the fellows. It was my job to see to their needs, and when the place had been plunged into darkness, I was nowhere to be found. For the second time in one day I was chagrined at myself. Some director I was turning out to be.

"Have you checked on any of the fellows?" I asked her.

"No, Miss Harper," she said, giving me a stern look. "That will be up to you."

Zing. Why did I always feel like I was a schoolgirl and Harriet was grading my performance?

She reached into her apron and pulled out a plastic bag containing several boxes of wooden matches. "All of the fellows have flashlights in their desk drawers, candles in their rooms, and fireplaces, of course. There are extra candles in the linen closet on the second floor, across from the director's study. And here are some extra matches"—she held the bag out to me—"just to make sure they have what they need. There's no telling how long the power will be out, and there's no use wasting flashlight batteries if they don't need to."

I took the bag from her. "Right," I said. "I'll go upstairs now and check on everyone."

Richard took me by the arm and directed his flashlight ahead of us. "We'll go together," he said to me and then turned to Harriet. "Thank you, Mrs. Baines," he said, flashing her a smile. "I'll make sure Miss Harper gets upstairs safely."

And we walked off into the darkness as Harriet muttered something under her breath.

Upstairs, we found everyone out of their rooms, clustered together in the hallway. Henry and Cassandra had found their flashlights and were illuminating the dark, casting monstrous shadows that seemed to dance and sway on the walls.

"Swimming, at this hour?" Henry asked, grinning at us.

"It's getting to be a habit," Richard said, patting him on the arm as they shared a laugh.

"I see you found your flashlights," I said to Henry and Cassandra. "For you others, they're in the top drawer of your desks."

"How long is the power going to be out?" Brynn asked, shivering. "I was planning to work tonight, and I only have a few hours of battery life left on my laptop."

"According to the all-knowing, all-seeing Harriet, a transformer in town was hit by lightning," I said. "Half the county is dark, she told me. So it might be awhile."

Groans all around.

"Listen, everyone," Richard said. "I'm going to get out of these sodden clothes, but then I'll come to each of your rooms and light a fire in your fireplaces."

"Good idea," I said, smiling at him. "And you've all got candles in your rooms and here"—I reached into the plastic bag and began handing out the boxes of matches—"in case you're running low. We have extra candles, too, so if you need some, just let me know."

"Don't worry about me," Cassandra said. "I've got a fire and some candles already lit, so I'm good to go." She broke into a conspiratorial smile. "And I took the cognac from the sideboard when I went upstairs after dinner," she admitted. "Who wants a brandy by candlelight?"

The other fellows gave me questioning looks. Was this allowed? I was sure Miss Penny wouldn't have approved. But, I reminded myself, I was the director of Cliffside now.

I grinned. "Sounds good to me," I said, shivering a bit in my wet clothes. "Give me a few minutes to change, and I'll join you. Anybody else?"

"Delightful!" Henry said.

"I'm in, too," Diana chimed in.

Richard caught my eye and winked. "What better thing to do on a stormy night than to chat with fellow artists around a roaring fire," he said. "It's almost like you planned this, Miss Harper."

"We do what we can." I grinned at him. And then I turned to Brynn. "How about you? I know you said you wanted to get some work done, but won't you join us for a bit?"

She crossed her arms and leaned back against the wall. "I don't think so."

"Nonsense," Henry said. "You can't sit by yourself in the dark."

"I don't like brandy," she sniffed.

Henry rolled his eyes. "Oh, for goodness' sake. I've got one of these." He shone his flashlight into her face, causing her to blink and squint at him. "We can simply go downstairs and get whatever you'd like to drink." He took her by the hand. "Now come on, my hothouse flower." He turned over his shoulder to the rest of us. "We'll be back in two shakes."

"Right," Cassandra said. "I'll deploy the brandy, you all bring glasses from your rooms."

She and Diana walked together to her room then, and Richard gave me a smile as he opened his door. "I'll see you in a few minutes," he said. "Unless you'd like to join me now."

I gave him a mock scowl, my pulse racing a bit at the suggestion. "Thank you for offering to light fires for everyone."

"We do what we can," he said, repeating my words, and then disappeared into his room.

I hurried into mine, closing and locking the door behind me. I peeled off my wet clothes and dropped them down the laundry chute—Harriet's staff doing the laundry once a week was one of the perks of being here at Cliffside. I thought of simply throwing on a pair of jeans, but instead I quickly lit some candles in the bathroom and hopped into the shower for a quick step-in-step-out. I was chilly to the core. As I stood under the warm stream of water, the steam rising and condensing on the glass shower door, my mind ran in several directions at once.

What had just happened with Richard? I didn't normally run around kissing men I had recently met, but somehow, down there on the lakeshore, it had just felt . . . right. As though I had known him my whole life. But of course, I hadn't. Our paths had never crossed before, had they? I had spent my adult life working on crime cases and chasing bad guys right here, and he had spent his on every continent on this planet taking some of the most stunning nature photographs I had ever seen.

I put my face under the stream. I was in trouble, and I knew it. It was plainly obvious, even to me—and I tended to deny such things—that I was attracted to this man, and I had to admit that it felt great. But what good would this newfound attraction do me? He was leaving when this session was over. He lived an ocean away. *Way to set yourself up for heartbreak, Norrie.*

I wondered if I should just nip this thing in the bud, or . . . I let my mind wander. Maybe I could just enjoy it for what it was—a flirtation that would end when he left Cliffside. Would that be so bad? Or . . . maybe I could convince him to stay.

Although, I thought, what of Nate? There hadn't exactly been fireworks between us, not like when I was alone with Richard, but I had to admit it—I had feelings for him, too. He was so easy to talk to. Our senses of humor meshed perfectly. I smiled to myself, remembering our banter the other night. And when I thought about it, I realized I trusted him and valued his opinion. That's exactly the kind of friendship that could grow into true and lasting love—or so magazine articles had told me.

All at once, Miss Penny swirled into my mind. Her deeply lined face, her ramrod straight posture. I could see her, in her formal slacks and sensible black shoes, greeting fellows with a curt nod of the head as they arrived, a clipboard clasped between her hands, almost like I was right there with her. She would never have entertained a flirtation with one of them. *It would be the height of unprofessionalism,* I could almost hear her saying to me. *That's not how a director should behave. What would Father think? Scandalous!*

But, as I toweled off, I shook her voice out of my mind. I gazed into the mirror as I combed my hair and dabbed some moisturizer on my face—I was still a young woman. Well. Young-ish. And, despite the fact that I had agreed to be the director of Cliffside, I had no intention of living alone, devoting my life to this place like Miss Penny had. That had not been a part of the job description. I could step into Miss Penny's shoes, but I didn't have to follow in her footsteps, running Cliffside alone for decades.

I had been so busy for so long with my all-consuming career, I had left no room for love. But now? My whole life had changed when I'd lost my job and taken on this position. Maybe it was time my love life changed, too.

I hopped into leggings and a comfortable black tunic top and slid my feet into flats. Not perfect, but it would have to do. I grabbed a glass from my bedside table, scooped up my flashlight, and headed to Cassandra's room to join the others. I was sure, as I closed my door behind me, that Miss Penny had never done any such thing, and I could feel her nagging at me, somewhere deep inside, to follow her lead. But there were five interesting, vibrant people in the next room, and I wanted to join in the fun on this dark and stormy night. No matter what she thought of it.

# CHAPTER 26

When I knocked on Cassandra's door, pushed it open, and poked my head around it, I found all the fellows already there. The fire blazing in the fireplace and candles flickering around the room bathed everything in a yellowish glow, softening their faces, blurring the lines.

I stood there for a moment and took it all in—Cassandra was perched on the edge of her bed, Diana curled into a wing chair next to the fire. Henry was pulling one of the chairs from the study into the main room, and Brynn was already settled into the other, which had been moved near the bed. Richard had arranged some of the throw pillows on the floor next to the fireplace and was stretched out there, leaning on one elbow, his hair wet and slicked back.

All at once I was reminded of summer camp when I was a child, sneaking off with newfound friends to sit around a fire and tell ghost stories when we should have been snug in our beds. I hoped these people didn't think of me as the type of stern camp counselor I remembered. No, that was Harriet's role, not mine.

Cassandra patted a spot on the bed next to her. "There's room here." She smiled. "I've already poured you a brandy."

I settled in next to her and took the glass in her outstretched hand.

"We found a connection," Henry announced. He was beaming, as though he had just aced a school paper.

"Us and Cliffside?" I asked, raising my eyebrows and taking a sip of my drink. "Do tell."

"Well," he said, crossing his legs and leaning toward me, "when darling Brynn and I were making our way through the gloom to the liquor cabinet, I asked her when her grandmother was here as a patient."

"It was 1952," Brynn piped up. "I know it for sure, because she dated every journal entry."

"For the good of the group, I'm going to have to admit—though I'm loath to do it—that 1952 was the same year my mother left Cliffside," Henry went on. "I was born the following year. And now you know how old I am, damn it all. I tell people I'm ten years younger."

I smiled at him. He was right, I had thought he was about fifty.

"It's just a number, chap," Richard chimed in. "You're in better shape than many people I know who are twenty years younger."

"Sixty is the new forty, that's what everyone is saying now," I said, leaning over to squeeze Henry's arm.

"Don't say the number out loud," he huffed. "I've been fifty for more than a decade. I don't see why that should change."

As we were talking, Cassandra slid off the bed and padded over to her study, where she put on a pair of glasses and held her flashlight over a manila file of notes, squinting at them. She ruffled through the papers until she found the particular one she was looking for.

"I thought so," she said with a triumphant air, and turned back to the group. "My grandfather died here in 1952. That was also the year Cliffside Sanatorium closed."

"And the year Temperance Dare died," Brynn added. "Or was murdered."

"An eventful year," I said, my mind whirring through what I knew about that time. "So, 1952. Miss Penny told me that she and her sister Chamomile moved into Cliffside as their family home when the patients left, so it must have been that same year. They were just kids then, probably about ten years old or so."

Richard sat up and brushed a lock of wet hair out of his eyes. "There's your connection, Eleanor: 1952 at Cliffside was significant for Henry, Cassandra, and Brynn. And for Penelope Dare, too, by the sound of it."

"I think you're right, but why?" I said. "Yes, her sister died that year. Is that all there is to it? It's maddening. And, also, Richard, what of you and me? We don't have any connection to Cliffside back then. Ours is more recent."

"And I'm the wild card, as usual," Diana said. "I still can't think of a single thing tying me to this place."

Henry took a sip of his brandy and gazed into the fire. "It really is strange, don't you think, that Cassandra's grandfather, Brynn's grandmother, and my mother were all here at Cliffside at the same time," he said. "I'm sure Mama knew both of them. She would have known all the patients."

"Did she ever mention my grandfather's name?" Cassandra asked him. "Archie Abbott?"

Henry squinted, as though he was looking back through his memories. "Not that I recall," he said. "But she talked a lot about Cliffside. She really did love working here and clearly idolized Chester Dare."

"What did she say it was like here back then?" Cassandra asked. "These are the questions I intended to ask Penelope Dare but never got the chance. I'd appreciate hearing your insights."

Henry swirled the ice around in his glass. "It was by turns horrible and wonderful," he began. "She worked here for nearly five years, before she left to have me. The suffering these poor people endured. Weakness, night sweats, fever. And of course, the coughing. TB, by another name, was consumption, because it was like the disease consumed its patients. She said some days there was so much death, so much coughing, blood everywhere, so many people wasting away that she and the other nurses would have to get out for a while, walk in the forest or go for a boat ride, just to clear their heads and steel their resolve to keep doing the job."

I shivered. I could just imagine it.

"But it was important work they were doing," Henry went on. "Saving lives. For my mother, it was a calling. The patients were here for so long—many months, even a year for some—that the staff really got to know them. They became very close, like family. Mama loved her patients, most of them, anyway. The children, especially. She could hardly stand the thought of them being away from their homes and their parents. She became like a substitute mother to many of them."

"It must have been terrible for her when one of them didn't make it," Cassandra said. "I can't imagine how hard that was."

Henry shook his head. "She said it took a little piece of her, every time. Day after day, not knowing who would be next. It would be like watching your family die all around you, every day."

I took a sip of my brandy.

"But when someone would be cleared to go home, it was a true celebration, and it buoyed her," Henry went on. "She had helped save the life of someone she loved. That gave her the will to get through the bad days."

"Even people who were making progress toward getting better sometimes would take a turn and die," Cassandra said. "I know—that's what happened to my grandfather, Archie Abbott. He was set to go home, he had already told my grandmother, and then he suddenly dropped dead."

It was as if I heard the whole room sigh.

"That's a harsh blow," Richard said.

"My grandmother never got over it," Cassandra said. "She was left with two small children—my dad and my aunt. It was doubly strange because Archie always believed he didn't have TB at all. We've still got the letters he wrote to my grandma. He'd tell her about sneaking around at night with another couple of men when they were all supposed to be in bed. They'd raid the refrigerator or break into the liquor cabinet they weren't supposed to know was there. They'd go out on the lawn and play catch or run down to the lakeshore. They were sick of being cooped up all day, forced to lie around quietly. They were bored out of their minds."

Henry chuckled at this. "You won't believe this, but my mother actually told me a story about a gang of men who were troublemakers. Never doing what they were told. Never staying in bed. It gave the other nurses fits, but she secretly liked it and cheered them on. They might have been breaking the rules, but at least they weren't lying on their backs gasping for their last breath like so many others, she'd say. I wonder if that's who she was talking about."

Cassandra's eyes lit up. "I'll bet it was," she said, smiling broadly. "And that's the thing—it was such a shock for my grandma to get the word that he had just up and died so suddenly. She was expecting him home in a few days."

As they were speaking, I was imagining Cliffside back then, how it must have been. I could see the people lying on chaises set up on the veranda, the old couches in the drawing room, the game room where people, clad in their pajamas and robes, played cards or checkers. Just like in my dream a few nights previous. It was so real, so vivid that I could almost smell the antiseptic. All at once, a flash of anger sizzled through me, and I didn't want to hear any more about Henry's sainted mother or Cassandra's insubordinate grandfather. I was about to say so, when I caught myself. What was I thinking?

I took a sip of my drink and then another. Something seemed to be gripping at me, almost as though I had been infected with negativity. I wondered if places had auras, or energy, like people did. If so, what that old man in the boathouse, Pete, had said about Death himself being at Cliffside might not be too crazy after all. There had been so much death and suffering here. Had it lingered long after the last patient had died? Was it affecting me somehow?

Just then, a great gust of cold wind blew through the room, taking the breath from all of us. The fire extinguished itself as though it had been doused with a bucket of water, smoke filling the air, and the candles all went out in a whoosh. All was dark.

Somebody screamed—Brynn, I thought. Another couple of people coughed from the smoke. An ice-cold shudder passed through me as I fumbled for my flashlight.

"Well, that was dramatic," Henry said, out of the darkness.

Richard shone his flashlight beam around the room. "Is everyone okay?"

"I'm fine," Diana said, coughing into her sleeve. "But—what just happened?"

Cassandra, still standing at her desk in the study, began relighting the candles one by one. "What could have caused it, do you think?" she asked, looking at me. "A downdraft from the fireplace?"

"I have no idea," I said, slipping off the bed and making my way over to it. I shone my flashlight into the charred remains of the logs—not a single ember smoldered there, despite the fact that it had been a crackling fire just a moment earlier.

My stomach tightened. *How does a thing like that just happen?*

But as I turned back to the group, I noticed nobody else was particularly shaken, nobody but Diana. She caught my eye.

"'By the pricking of my thumbs, something wicked this way comes,'" she said to me, her eyes wide, her voice almost a whisper. I wondered if anyone else heard it.

I knew the quote. It was from *Macbeth*, a play about witches inciting dark, evil acts. At that moment, I didn't appreciate the reference.

A loud knock at the door startled us all. Cassandra, staring at the door, held her match suspended above one of the candles until it burned her fingers. Brynn flew from her chair and knelt down next to Henry, who put a hand on her shoulder. Diana gave me a stern look.

"It's probably Harriet," I said, sliding off the bed and making my way across the room.

Richard pushed himself to his feet. "Wait," he said, putting one hand on my back and grasping the doorknob with the other. "Let me." He opened the door. But nobody was there. Richard looked back at me and shook his head, confused.

I poked my head around the door and peered out into the dark hallway. "Hello?" I said, my voice cracking. "Harriet? Is anybody there?"

Richard and I shone our flashlight beams up and down the corridor. It was empty. I listened for footsteps coming from beyond the range of our beams but heard only silence.

"I'll go that way," Richard said, pointing in the direction of the third-floor staircase. "You stay here."

"No," I said. "Two flashlights are better than one. I'll come with you."

I turned to the group. "You all stay put. We'll be right back."

Richard and I set off down the inky hallway, shining the beams back and forth as we went. I reached for his arm.

He opened each door along the way, sweeping the room with the light until he was satisfied nobody was lurking inside.

"Did you ever play hide and seek in the dark?" he whispered.

"No," I said.

"That's what this feels like."

But it didn't feel like a child's game to me. I could feel my pulse quicken.

When we got to the third-floor stairway at the end of the hall, I stopped him. "We can't go up there," I said, clutching his arm tighter.

He turned to me and furrowed his brow. "Why not?"

Miss Penny's room and that strange childhood shrine of a playroom floated through my mind, and I knew I couldn't face it, not right then, not in the dark with a storm raging outside. It was bad enough in the light of day.

"We just can't," I said, shaking my head. "Richard, you're a very practical person and I get the sense that you don't believe in anything you can't see, but I'm telling you, there's something up there."

He squinted at me and then turned his gaze to the stairs. "What kind of 'something' are you talking about?"

"Something that would probably cause me to die of fright on a dark night like this."

He stood there looking at me for a moment, his eyes full of kindness. He reached up and tucked a stray tendril of hair behind my ear. "Don't you know by now, Norrie?" he said to me. "I won't let anything happen to you. Besides, I owe you for earlier today." His grin cut the tension I was feeling.

"I suppose you do." I smiled at him.

And so, I found myself climbing the stairs to the third floor behind Richard Banks. We were both holding our flashlights, shining the beams ahead of us. He did a quick sweep of the ward and found nothing. I looked over toward Miss Penny's room and shivered.

"That's where we have to go," I said, and we made our way across the room. I pushed open the door, and we shone our beams up and down throughout the room but saw nothing out of place. It was as tidy as the last time I had seen it.

But then I remembered the little doorway. "There's one more place to check," I whispered.

I led him toward the door, and we both crouched and walked through it.

"Well, this is unusual," Richard whispered after shining his light around the room and seeing all of the toys.

"It's like they hadn't changed it since they were young," I said. "It's some kind of shrine to their childhoods."

He was staring at the shelf of dolls. "God, I hate antique dolls," he murmured. "There's really nothing scarier than that." I couldn't help laughing, in spite of myself.

But my chuckles died down when I shone my light toward the dollhouse. It looked just the same, initially. Or did it? I bent down and looked carefully from room to room, and then I saw it.

In the dollhouse room that depicted the playroom where we were standing, the tea table participants had changed. I remembered distinctly that the tea party guests had been stuffed bears before. Now they were five people. Three women and two men. Just like the fellows. And then I noticed the doll in the director's suite. It wasn't Chester Dare. It was a female, with brown hair like mine. It was me.

I grabbed Richard's hand and just held his gaze—I couldn't get any words out.

"What is it, Norrie?" he asked.

"We have to get out of here," I whispered, my voice barely audible, even to me. "Now."

And then I pushed him toward the door. We crouched through it, hurried through the bedroom, across the ward, and down the stairs to the second floor. I wanted to run right to my room, but he stopped me at the landing.

"What did you see up there, Norrie?" he asked.

"You wouldn't believe me if I told you," I said, "but right now, we need to get everyone safely into their rooms."

We hurried our way back to Cassandra's room. I closed the door and leaned on it, facing the group, my heart beating hard and fast in my chest. "There's nobody out there," I said, finally. "We all heard that knock, right?"

"I heard it, clear as a bell," Henry said.

"Me, too," Brynn said, pulling her legs up underneath her and shuddering.

Cassandra was leaning down to restart the fire in the fireplace, lighting kindling with a match. "I thought I heard a knock," she said, then blew on the glowing piece of bark and tucked it under the logs. "But if nobody was there, that just can't be."

I crossed to Cassandra's study and pressed the intercom on the desk, thinking I'd call Harriet—hoping she had been the one to knock and slip away quickly. But there was no crackling, no buzzing. Of course, when the electricity went out, so did the intercom.

Richard was furrowing his brow. "We all heard a knocking," he said, slowly. "But it might have been something other than someone rapping at the door. Pipes in old houses tend to make loud, knocking noises. It could even have been outside, a tree limb coming down."

It made sense. But the gnarling in my stomach, and what I had just seen on the third floor, told me differently.

"Listen, everyone," I began. But Diana caught my eye. She held my gaze, shaking her head ever so slightly. She put a finger to her lips as if to say, *Shhhh.*

The others hadn't noticed it, but I understood, as clearly as if she had been whispering in my ear. *Don't upset the others and don't try to make sense out of it. And for goodness' sake, stop talking about it.*

It made sense. What would I say? That somebody had been playing with the dollhouse?

Brynn was fishing in her purse for something and pulled out her cell phone. "I know we're not supposed to use these, but . . ." Her words trailed off as she stared at the screen. "I don't have any service." She looked up at me. "I haven't used the phone since I arrived—is there cell service here?"

"There is," I said, my stomach tightening further.

Cassandra had retrieved her phone from her purse and turned it on. "I don't have any service, either. No bars."

My mind ran through several possibilities at once, but then it occurred to me. "I know what happened," I said. "Harriet told me that lightning hit a transformer. I'll bet it hit the cell tower, too."

Richard nodded. "In these remote areas, there's usually only one, or at most, two. It's no wonder you don't get reception."

"It should be repaired within a day or so," I said. Brynn dropped the phone back into her purse and sighed.

All at once, I was exhausted and wanted nothing more than to crawl into my bed and pull the covers up to my chin. I cleared my throat. "I think I've had enough excitement for one night," I said. "If nobody minds, I'm going to hit the hay."

"That's a very good idea," Henry said, standing and stretching. "We should all turn in." He looked to Brynn and held out his hand. "Come, my dear. I'll make sure you get to your room in one piece." She took his hand and unfurled herself from her chair.

"Everyone, keep your flashlights handy," I said, shining mine around the room. "And I think it's best for you all to stay in your rooms, once you get there. And lock and latch your doors behind you. There's no telling how long the power will be out, and I really don't want anyone wandering around in the dark downstairs on their own. Agreed?"

Nods and agreement all around.

"You don't have to worry about me," Brynn said. "I'm locking my door, and I won't be coming out until morning." Henry led her down the hallway toward their rooms, and I watched until they disappeared into the darkness.

I turned to Cassandra, who was firing up her laptop. "Are you going to be okay?" I asked her.

She gave me a smile. "I've got four hours of battery life left in this thing," she said. "I might as well get some work done. You anticipate the power being back up in the morning, right?"

I shrugged. "I'm sure the power company is working through the night to get it restored, but I really have no idea when that might be," I said. "If it's not on tomorrow morning, I'll give them a call and see what's up."

"We can't be without our morning coffee, after all," Richard said with a grin. "We're not barbarians, are we?"

He and I went through the door together, and Cassandra closed and locked it behind us. I heard the click of the latch, as well.

"Quite an eventful day," Richard said, as we stepped down the hallway toward our rooms.

"Quite."

"If you need anything tonight, anything at all, you know where to find me," he said.

I wasn't sure if this was a double entendre or if he was seriously concerned about my well-being. I suspected it was a little of both. "I do," I said to him, as we arrived at his door. "Thanks."

He took my hand and drew it up to his lips, holding my gaze all the while. "You make sure to lock your door behind you, Eleanor Harper," he said. He didn't have to tell me twice.

I headed across the hall to my room, and only then did I see Diana waiting outside my door, a grave expression on her face. I hadn't noticed her leave Cassandra's room, but obviously she had slipped out before I did.

"I heard what you said just before the knock," I whispered to her. "How did you know? Or did you?"

She raised her eyebrows. "I sense things, sometimes."

"What did you sense, exactly?"

She shook her head. "Just like I said. Something wicked this way comes."

I didn't like the sound of it any more than I'd liked it the first time she'd said it. I looked over her shoulder down the dark hallway and shuddered. "What do you mean, wicked? You're scaring me a little, Diana."

"I'm not sure," she said. "The phrase just popped into my head."

I looked into her eyes for a long moment. "What do you make of it—the fire and candles going out and then the knock at the door?"

"That was no downdraft, and that was no knocking water pipe," she said.

"What was it, then?" I asked, not really wanting to hear the answer.

"I think we have to face the fact, Eleanor, that the closer we get to solving this puzzle, the more we're going to awaken the spirits here at Cliffside."

She was right, I could feel it, deep in my bones. But I wanted to hear it from her. "Why do you say that?" I asked her.

"What were we talking about just before it happened?" she asked. "Our connections to this place. Nineteen fifty-two. Temperance. Cassandra's granddad and Henry's mother."

All at once, it was clear as a bell to me. "She's the nurse who gave Temperance that injection," I said, my voice low. "I'll bet anything."

Diana nodded. "I think you're right," she whispered.

"There's more—something you don't know," I said to her. "A couple of days ago, I was looking for something in Penelope Dare's bedroom on the third floor. I noticed a small door on one wall and went through it and found a playroom."

"A child's playroom?"

"Yes," I said. "I'm sure it was the playroom of Penelope and Chamomile when they were children. There's all kinds of antique dolls and toys, and among them is a dollhouse. An exact replica of Cliffside."

A shiver went down my spine as I said it.

"There's a tea table in the dollhouse just like the one in the playroom, and I swear, somebody manipulated the dolls and set three women and two men at the table for tea."

She gave me a long look. "Another juvenile act, don't you think?"

"I don't know. I really don't. Part of me thinks we should all get out of here. But part of me is compelled to stay and see this through."

She nodded. "All sorts of fears and ideas and scenarios much wilder than the one we just lived through can swirl around in our minds when it's dark and stormy and we feel vulnerable," she said. "Let's wait to sort this out by the light of day. Everything looks different when the sun is shining, don't you agree?"

She didn't wait for me to respond. Instead she set off down the hall toward her room. I shone my flashlight beam to guide her way. When she was at her door, she looked back and we nodded to each other. "Goodnight!" I called to her, and then we both opened our doors, slipped inside, and locked them behind us.

# CHAPTER 27

I lit several candles around my room, changed into my pajamas, and slipped into bed with a book and my flashlight, snuggling down into the pillows and pulling the covers up as far as they could go. I had only read a few pages when I heard a soft knocking at my door. My heart jumped into my throat.

"Norrie," Richard said, quickly. "It's me."

I hopped out of bed and let him in, shutting and locking the door behind him. "You scared me half to death with that knock," I said, managing a laugh.

"I know," he said. "And I'm sorry. I thought of waiting until morning to show you this, but I really don't know what to make of it, and considering what happened tonight . . ." He let the rest of his thought hang in midair as he sank down into one of the chairs, a strange look of confusion on his face. Only then did I notice he was carrying his camera.

"What is it?" I asked him.

He shook his head. "I went around to everyone's room to make sure they had been able to get fires lit in their fireplaces"—he glanced at mine—"I'll do yours in a second if you'd like me to. Anyway, I got back to my room and started going through the images I took tonight during our walk."

I was quiet, waiting for him to go on, not really wanting to hear what he was going to say to me.

“Remember when I was shooting some shots of you on the beach, and I thought there was someone standing behind you?” he asked.

I nodded.

He picked up the camera, clicked a button or two, and held it out for me to look at the screen on the back of it. “Take a look at this.”

I sank down to the floor on my knees next to his chair and leaned my head close to the camera, peering at the lighted square that contained the image. All I saw was me, smiling rather shyly but looking happier than I had felt in a long time. I couldn’t help but smile, remembering that moment.

“I usually don’t like photos of me, but this one’s nice,” I said, looking up at him. “But, you didn’t come in here to show me a shot of myself. What else am I supposed to be seeing here?”

“Just wait,” he said and clicked the advance button. Another image popped onto the screen, and when I saw it, I gasped aloud.

It was nearly the same shot, me grinning straight into the camera lens. But behind me, the frame was filled with people. Well, not people exactly, not people with faces, but shapes and forms, as though the shadows of a dozen people were cast on some unseen wall behind me. Within those shadows, one stood out—taller than the rest, ramrod straight posture. I knew exactly who it was. And, at that realization, it felt like ice water shot through my veins.

I stood up and backed away a few steps. “What is that, Richard?”

He shook his head. “I’ll be damned if I know,” he said. “But I know what it isn’t. It’s not a double exposure, and it’s not some fault in the camera. I thought I saw that behind you, just for an instant when I was looking through the lens, when I was taking the shot. But when I lowered the camera to get a better look, it was gone.”

My heart was pounding, and my mind was racing a mile a minute. My flight instinct had kicked into high gear. I had had enough, and this creepy photo seemed like the last straw. All I wanted to do was run from this place. But to where? It was storming outside, there was no electricity anywhere in the county, and town was several miles away. I couldn't leave the fellows here to fend for themselves, and I couldn't lead them on a dangerous expedition away from here in the middle of a rainy night. Nobody would go with me, even if I asked. I was sure they were all tucked into their beds at this point.

"You know, earlier, you said you thought I wouldn't believe something until I saw it?" he asked.

I nodded.

"Well, now I've seen it."

I looked at him, not knowing quite what to say. He was the one who was supposed to offer rational explanations.

I had been shrugging off everything that had happened since I'd arrived at Cliffside: the coughing I heard in empty corners, the laughter, the children's footsteps, the visions I had seen—or whatever they were. The strange old man at the boathouse. Brynn's journal getting ripped apart. The disembodied knock at the door. The weird negativity that seemed to hang in the air. The dollhouse. And now this.

"Would you light that fire now?" I asked, finally, my voice wavering. I blinked several times to ward off the tears that were stinging at the back of my eyes.

While he was getting the fire going, I hurried across the room and slipped back into bed, pulling my covers up around me and wrapping my arms around my knees to keep them from knocking. He had to use several matches, but the kindling finally caught fire, and soon the room was filled with a soft glow as the flames danced.

I wished I had never taken this job. I wished I had never laid eyes on Cliffside. And I wished, more than anything, that I was anywhere other than in this house of horrors. What had I gotten myself into? I tried to keep the tears at bay, but they came, and I put my face into my knees, my shoulders shaking.

Richard sat down beside me and put an arm around my back. "Shhh," he said, his voice soft and gentle. "It's okay, Norrie."

But it wasn't. I turned to him, and he put both arms around me and let me cry into his chest as he rubbed my back and said soft, soothing words. Finally, I pulled back and grabbed a couple of Kleenex from my nightstand.

"I'm sorry," I said between gasps, my words as thin as tissue paper. "But I'm just—this is too much."

"I know," he said, his voice gentle and low.

"I'm supposed to be in charge and keep all of you safe and happy while you're here, and after everything that's happened, I have no idea what I should do now," I went on. "This is feeling really strange, Richard, and frankly, you and the others getting some time here to focus on your art seems insignificant and unimportant when you weigh it against the risks."

He shook his head. "What risks are you talking about?"

"What risks?" My voice shot up an octave. "It should be painfully obvious by now to even the most practical and level-headed among us that Cliffside is haunted. And not by Casper the Friendly Ghost."

He tried to suppress a grin but it escaped, and the edges of his mouth curled up as his eyes danced. "Does that make you Wendy?"

"I'm serious, Richard," I said. "Everybody thinks I'm making too much of this. I don't get it, I really don't."

But then it dawned on me. Only Diana knew that the messages scrawled on those pages were written in Miss Penny's hand. The others had no idea, and most suspected Brynn had written that message herself. Well, that would end now. I needed to confide in Richard. I needed him to know it all.

I slipped out of bed and marched into my study. I fumbled in the dark to find the two pieces of paper I had put in my desk drawer, finally found them, and took them back to show Richard.

"You don't know this," I said, holding the suicide note out to him. "Nobody but Diana does. The world thinks Penelope Dare died of natural causes. But she didn't."

He took the letter, and I shone my flashlight beam onto the page while he read.

He looked up at me. "Suicide?"

"Yes," I said. "She was clutching the suicide note that I gave to the police. I found this in an envelope under the covers of my bed on my first night here, after she died. She put it there before I even arrived. She planned this, down to the smallest detail. Read the whole thing."

After a moment, he looked up from the page and held my gaze, the light from the fireplace casting his face in a yellowish glow. "So that's why you've been so interested in finding the connections between us," he said. "You're trying to unlock whatever mystery she left you to solve."

"That's right," I said, nodding.

He glanced back down to the letter and shook his head. "But this last line, the bit about your nightmare beginning. That's a threat if I ever heard one. You found this on your first night at Cliffside?"

"I did."

"It's a wonder you didn't pack up and leave right then," he said. "I know what this says about you being financially responsible, but that's a load of rubbish and would never stand up in court. Why didn't you go?"

I let out a breath I didn't realize I was holding. "Harriet and Mr. Baines convinced me not to make too much of the ramblings of an old lady who was about to kill herself. And, also, I'm only the third director in its history." I swallowed, hard. "All of the people employed here. All of the fellows who are scheduled to come. They're all depending on me. I couldn't very well just leave."

"You felt a responsibility."

"I did," I said. "But now I wish to God I had packed up and left that first night. I don't know what I'd be doing right now, but I can guarantee you that I wouldn't be huddled in my bed, terrified of every little noise."

Richard took my hand. "Oh, Norrie."

I went on. "The ominous words Penelope Dare wrote to me in that letter are coming true. I do feel like I'm living a nightmare. And why? Why, Richard? What did I ever do to her that she would want me to be caught up in a nightmare?"

"Listen," he said. "I'll grant you that letter is terrifying. But maybe Harriet was right. Maybe it was nothing more than the ramblings of a demented old lady in the moments before she killed herself."

"For one thing, she wasn't demented," I said. "She was as sane as you or me. She trained me, for goodness' sake. I spent most of that day with her. She was calm, cool, and collected, and gave no hint that anything was wrong, that she was about to go upstairs to her room and swallow a bottle of pills."

He nodded, a sadness coming over his face. "Unfortunately, I have some experience with suicide, and from what I've been told, oftentimes, when people decide to do it and create a plan of action, they are very calm, and even happy, in the hours or days before."

I wondered who in his life had taken that ultimate step, but I didn't ask him, not right then. If it was someone close to him, that pain would never go away, and I didn't want to dredge it up any more than I already had.

"There's something else I wanted to show you," I said, laying the page from Brynn's journal on the bed next to the suicide note. "Do you notice anything?"

Richard looked from one to the other and then up at me. "The handwriting is the same," he said in a whisper, his eyes widening. Even in the soft light of the fireplace and the candles, I could see his face blanch.

I nodded. "Now you know. I told Diana, but the others have no idea."

"But," he drew out the word into several syllables, "Brynn's journal was defaced long after Penelope Dare died."

I just nodded and looked into his eyes. He leaned back against the headboard and ran a hand through his hair.

"That photo you showed me just now," I said. "One of those shadows, or shapes, or whatever they are—one of them is her. I recognize her."

He shook his head, seemingly trying to take this all in.

"And you don't know the half of it," I said, talking faster now. "Before you all got here, I was walking in the woods and ran into this creepy old man, who told me that Death himself lived at Cliffside. And after what Diana said about the dead not leaving here . . ."

Richard and I just looked at each other for what seemed like forever. "I've never been one to put any stock in the paranormal," he said, finally. "But this . . ."

"I know."

"Nobody could have knocked on that door tonight and gotten away without us seeing them," he said. "It's just not possible."

"I know."

"And those shapes or whatever the hell they are in the photo . . ."

"I know. And the dollhouse."

"What about it?"

"When I first saw it, the dolls were arranged differently. Somebody put us, all of us, around that tea table."

He winced. "I hate dolls," he said. At that moment, I hated them, too.

"Maybe we should just bloody well get out of here," he said. He got up from the bed and walked over to the window, pushed aside the curtains, and peered outside. Rain was still falling in sheets and thunder roared through the sky.

"I have a car," he said. "We could just march out there right now and go."

I shook my head. "No, driving on that road tonight would be more dangerous than staying here, I think," I said, my voice wavering. "That's where Chester and Chamomile Dare plunged to their deaths."

"Then, we'll go tomorrow," he said. "I'll help you convince the others." He let out a sigh. "I'll go back to my room, then," he said. "Not that I'll be getting much sleep."

All at once, I didn't want him to go. Everything that had happened to me since I had arrived at Cliffside was swirling around in my brain, and I felt like every cell in my body was trembling.

"Please stay," I said. "I can't stand the thought of spending all of these hours alone until morning. I'll admit it, I'm terrified right now."

His face softened. "We can't have you terrified," he said. "Of course I'll stay. I'll just stretch out by the fire."

"You won't be comfortable on the hard floor," I said, scooting over a bit toward the edge of the bed. "You can sleep up here with me."

He squinted at me. "And just like that, the evening takes a happy turn."

I couldn't help grinning. "Just sleep," I said. "Don't get any ideas, mister."

He hopped up on the bed and turned on his side to face me. "Oh, I've already had ideas, Norrie Harper. For days now. Make no mistake about that."

I leaned over and gave him a kiss on the cheek, and I began to wish we were anywhere but in this house of horrors so our evening could indeed take a happy turn. But as it was, I pulled back. "Good night, Mr. Banks."

I blew out the candles on my bedside table and snuggled down on my side, facing away from him. He put an arm around my waist, and I could feel the full length of his body against mine.

"You sleep tight," he said, soft and low in my ear. "No ghost, not even the ghost of Penelope Dare herself, is going to bother you tonight while I'm here to protect you."

I lay there, savoring the feeling of being next to him, until my breathing slowed and my thoughts began to swim. I drifted off to sleep knowing that, when morning dawned, we would be finished with this nightmare once and for all.

# CHAPTER 28

I awoke to find Richard standing by the window, gazing out into the fog. I lay still for a moment and watched him. It was so strange to wake up and have somebody else in my room. I couldn't remember the last time it had happened. I felt a twinge of misgiving—my head told me that having this man I barely knew remain in my room until the light of day wasn't the wisest thing to do, but at the same time, my heart told me it felt right and normal, as though he should have been here all the time. Usually, I went with my head in such matters, and I had to admit that, given the state of my love life in recent years, it hadn't been serving me too well. I supposed it was high time the heart won and I took a risk.

When he heard me rustling, he turned to me and smiled. "Good morning, Miss Harper," he said.

"Good morning to you, Mr. Banks." I sat up and stretched, hoping I didn't look as disheveled as I felt. "I didn't hear you get up. Have you been awake long?"

"A while," he said. "I just saw the driver take the car out of the garage and pull away, only to come back a few moments later." He turned his gaze back to the window and scowled. "I wonder why he did that. The fog?"

I remembered the foggy drive on the precarious, winding road on the cliff the day I arrived, and my stomach dropped. "I don't think that would've stopped him," I said. "He told me he could drive that road blind if he needed to."

I slipped out of bed, padded over to my closet, and grabbed a change of clothes. "I'm going to throw this on, and then we should go downstairs," I said, stepping into the bathroom and leaning against the doorframe. "Are you still convinced we should all get out of here today?"

"It seems a little hysterical in the light of day, doesn't it?"

I winced. "I'm not sure. I was terrified last night, that's all I know." A pang of guilt sizzled through me. "Okay, say we leave this morning," I began. "What will happen to Cliffside? The program, I mean. The fellows who have already been scheduled are all counting on coming."

He furrowed his brow and a flash of anger crossed his face. "After everything that woman has put you through, I have to ask, Norrie, do you really care?"

I realized just then that I did care, much more than I thought I did. If I left, would Cliffside fall apart, everything Chester Dare had done with his life, ruined? Yes, there were other applicants for the job I could hire before leaving, but for some reason, I didn't want to do that. I had the inexplicable sense that I belonged at Cliffside, perhaps more than I've belonged anywhere. I was finally and truly home. I'd never felt that way before about any of the places I'd lived, certainly not any of the foster homes, even with the Harpers, whom I loved deeply.

And yet, another part of me wanted to run very fast and far away from here and never return.

"Give me two minutes to change, and we'll go find the others and see what they have to say," I said.

"I'm going to pop across the hall for a quick change as well," he said. "I'll knock on your door in two minutes."

All at once, I changed my mind. "No," I said. "I'll come down in a bit. On second thought, I'm going to hop into the shower."

"Right," he said. "I'll meet you downstairs, then."

I followed him to the door and shut it behind him.

~

Down in the winter garden, I found Diana, Cassandra, and Henry chatting with Richard over coffee and croissants.

"I don't know how Harriet made the coffee without electricity but, frankly, I don't care," Henry said, taking a long sip. "And we've got yesterday's croissants, but again, I don't care." He sunk his knife into a pat of butter and spread it on the flaky roll before tearing a piece off and popping it into his mouth.

"Did you all sleep okay?" I asked, making my way to the sideboard and pouring a cup of coffee, sensing the first salvos of a headache.

"I must confess to being a little spooked," Cassandra admitted. "I'm not usually bothered by things that go bump in the night, but things that knock loudly on my door? That's another story."

I took a seat next to her. "I was scared, too," I said, shooting a glance toward Richard. He nodded to me, as if to say, *Go on.* So I did. "Listen, I was thinking. Considering everything that's happened, should we cut our losses and leave?"

Richard jumped in. "This is starting to feel dangerous, for Eleanor especially."

Diana, Henry, and Cassandra exchanged glances.

"Oh, dear," Diana sighed.

Why was she the one who was always making this more difficult? She knew it all, more than anyone other than Richard and me.

"But—you all were there last night and heard that knocking, the same as I did," I said. "And there's more—"

But I didn't get to finish that statement. Diana held up a hand to cut me off. "I know what you're going to say, and you've got very valid points." She turned to the others. "If you haven't got the drift by now, Cliffside is haunted."

Henry and Cassandra exchanged scowls.

"No, no, scoff if you want to, but I knew it the very first minute I stepped on this property," Diana went on. "And, if last night and the display involving Brynn's journal is any indication, the spirits have not exactly rolled out the welcome mat for us."

Cassandra set her cup on the table with a clatter. "Are you seriously suggesting that we all just pack up and leave?" she asked. "We just got here! I'm getting great work done. And my return flight isn't for more than three weeks. The penalties for making any changes are exorbitant, and I can't afford to stay in a hotel all of that time."

"Nor can I," Henry said, taking another sip and crossing his legs. "Yes, last night was a bit eerie, I'll grant you that, but—leaving? Don't you think that's a little extreme?"

He took in my expression and chuckled. "Darlin', I'm from the South. There are ghosts everywhere. A little knocking on any given night isn't going to drive me away. Believe me, I've heard of a lot worse."

"The fact of the matter is, leaving isn't going to do you any good," Diana said. "I've told you before, Eleanor, you can get away from Cliffside, but that doesn't mean you're going to get away from the spirit, or spirits, who are doing this. They're ghosts, for goodness' sake. They can follow you anywhere."

That hadn't occurred to me. I pulled a chair out from the table and sank into it. *What now?* I didn't have long to ponder that question, because Harriet came scuffling into the room.

"Miss Harper, may I have a word?" she asked.

"Of course," I said, pushing myself to my feet. She turned on her heel and walked out of the room, and I followed.

"What is it?" I asked when we had reached the kitchen.

"I wanted to give you the news," she said. "They anticipate the electricity being back up soon. It might be another several hours, but they're hoping to get it restored before nightfall."

"Oh, great!" I said.

"It's the road that's our main concern right now."

And just like that, my heart sank.

She nodded. "Yes, the road out to the main highway. We got so much rain last night, parts of it have eroded, slipped right down the cliff. Nobody can get in or out until it's repaired."

So that explained the driver's short journey that morning. We couldn't leave, even if we wanted to. I let out a long sigh. Why did I feel like Miss Penny had arranged this, too?

"When are they going to fix the road?"

"Mr. Baines spoke to the road crew this morning," she said, crossing her arms. "They've got a few other washouts to take care of first, but it shouldn't be too long. A few days, at most. Mr. Baines has his men out there right now taking a look to see if they can cut a makeshift path, so we can get a car through if necessary."

"Do we have everything we need here until the road is fixed?" I asked.

She gave me a quick nod. "We do, for the most part."

"Well, that's it then," I said. "We'll be fine. Thank you, Harriet."

She was about to leave when something occurred to me. "How were you able to call the road crew? I thought the phones were out along with the electricity."

"No, ma'am. The land lines work just fine."

That was good news, anyway. With a working phone, we wouldn't be completely cut off from the outside world. And I had one in the director's study, just in case.

As I was coming through the archway of the winter garden, I heard Henry say, "Where the devil is Brynn?"

Cassandra shrugged and took a sip of her coffee. "Sleeping late?"

Henry shook his head. "I don't think so. She asked me to escort her down to breakfast every morning, saying she didn't like to make an appearance in a room full of people on her own. We agreed that she would knock on my door at quarter past eight each day."

"And today she didn't," I said.

"That's right," he said. "When she didn't come, I went to her door, but she didn't answer. I expected to see her here, in the breakfast room, but she was nowhere to be found. And now—it's very odd that she hasn't come down."

"She might have gone for an early morning walk," Richard offered.

"Brynn?" Henry snorted. "Please."

Cassandra pushed her chair away from the table and took a last sip of her coffee. "Wherever she is, I really don't care," she said. "I've got work to do, and I'm going to get to it."

Henry dabbed the corners of his mouth with his napkin. "I'll join you," he said. "Now that the rain has let up, I'm going to gather my things and head out to the cliff. I think I'll start on a shoreline scene today."

"And now," Diana said, "I'll take my leave as well. After last night, I'll spend the day pondering the meaning of eternity."

After she had left the room, I turned to Richard. "So much for our grand plans to leave," I said. "The road from Cliffside to the main road to town is washed out at the cliff. Harriet told me this morning."

He let out a sigh. "That's it, then."

We both got up from the table and made our way together through the house. As we walked, I filled him in about what else Harriet had said, the phone being up and the crew coming to do road repair soon.

"And the electricity?"

"It should be up by the end of the day."

We reached the stairway, and he turned to me. "What are you going to do today?"

I hadn't thought about it. After last night, I assumed we'd all be packing up and leaving. Now I was at loose ends. I shrugged. "No idea. What about you?"

"After what I saw through the lens yesterday, I don't feel much like photographing the grounds of Cliffside for posterity, I can tell you that much," he said. "How about we delve into this mystery of yours?"

That was an interesting idea. "What did you have in mind?"

"I thought you'd never ask," he said, taking my arm and leading me up the stairs. "You believe the key to this whole thing is solving the riddle of why Penelope Dare wanted all of us here at the same time, right?"

"Right," I said, running my hand along the smooth banister as we climbed.

"And we've already figured out that at least some of us are directly related to people who were here in 1952 with Temperance."

"Right."

"And you also said Penelope Dare was a meticulous record-keeper," he went on.

"Right again. Everything is laid out in triplicate, except for your letters of application, it seems."

"I'll bet she kept them, or at least some record, somewhere, of why she was so intent on selecting this group of fellows," he said. "Why don't we see if we can find it? I'm up for a little treasure hunting today if you are." He raised his eyebrows and grinned like a little boy with a new game. I couldn't help grinning back.

And all at once, it hit me. Miss Penny's office! Of course. With everything that had happened since the fellows had arrived, and all the time we had spent brainstorming about our shared connections to Cliffside, it hadn't even occurred to me that the answers might be right under my nose in that office.

"I know just where to look," I said.

A few moments later, we were in the director's study with the door closed behind us. I flipped on the overhead light without thinking, and then opened the blinds to give us as much light as possible. As I took a first look around, I realized that I hadn't been in this office for days.

I wondered if there was any mail or other paperwork I was supposed to be getting to, in addition to reading the applications of prospective fellows. I should have been checking it every morning after breakfast. Another gold star for job performance, I thought with a wince.

I glanced at the inbox on my desk—it was full of mail. I'd get to it, but I had other fish to fry at the moment.

Richard turned in a circle, looking around the room. "I'll take those," he said, pointing to the gray file cabinet that stood under one window, "if you want to start in the desk."

"Let's do it," I said, pulling out the desk chair and plunking myself down in it.

We both dove into our respective assignments, rifling through file after file, drawer after drawer.

After a bit, Richard broke the silence between us. "I think I found something," he said, pulling a file folder out of the cabinet where he was searching. "Take a look at this."

He opened the file in front of me on the desk, and I saw that it was stuffed full of newspaper clippings. I rifled through them for a moment, thinking maybe something in those articles would shine some light on things. Only then did I notice the bylines. I quickly ruffled through the rest of the pile.

I looked up at Richard. "These are all written by me," I said.

"Apparently, Miss Penny was either a devoted fan of your work or she was keeping tabs on you," Richard said.

"But what for?" I said, shaking my head. "What could possibly be the purpose of that?"

He shrugged. "It's one more piece of the puzzle," he said. "But it could have something to do with why she chose you to succeed her here at Cliffside."

I stared at the clippings, not knowing what to think.

I went back to my search, and Richard went back to his. After a while I glanced up at him. "It's got to be about noon," I said. "What do you say we break for lunch? I don't think we're going to find anything here."

But as I said it, I noticed he was holding another fat manila file and grinning. "This might shine some light on things," he said.

"What is it?"

"A record of Cliffside's expenses from 1952."

I stared at him for a moment, my mouth agape. "You're kidding."

He shook his head. "No!" he said, gesturing to the opened file drawer. "These bottom three drawers are filled with nothing but folders containing the yearly expenses here. All the way back to 1935."

All at once, the overhead light flickered on and off and then shone brightly.

"And let there be light," Richard said. "I guess they got the electricity back on."

"Well, thank goodness for that, anyway," I said. "If you want to start going through the file you just found, I'll pop across the hall and grab my laptop."

"What do you need the laptop for?"

I swung my chair around and faced him. "Could it be as simple as Googling *Cliffside, 1952*?"

He smiled. "That would be very simple indeed," he said. "Of course, it would take all the fun out of our search. But, I suppose"—he raised his eyebrows—"we could make our own fun."

I crumpled up a piece of paper on the desk and threw it at him. "You're terrible," I said, grinning.

"That's not what I've heard," he called after me as I made my way across the hall.

In my room, I grabbed my laptop and its charger. I was about to go back to the study, but I decided to take a minute to freshen up, brushing my teeth and hair and dabbing on a bit of makeup. I squinted at my reflection in the mirror—my eyes looked like I hadn't slept in weeks. I shrugged at myself. It was as good as it was going to get, for now.

Just then, as I was staring at my own reflection, another face swam into view in the mirror, superimposed over mine. A hideous, clownish face with garish red lipstick and dark circles around the eyes. I let out a gasp and took a few steps backward, but when I looked again, the vision, or whatever it was, was gone. The slightest hint of pain slithered up my spine and took hold at the base of my skull.

That was when I noticed the doll.

# CHAPTER 29

It was sitting on the windowsill in my room—a doll from Miss Penny's dollhouse. I couldn't be sure, but it looked like one of the dolls that had been seated at the tea table.

How had it gotten there? I picked it up and put it in my pocket and hurried back to my study, my computer under my arm.

Richard had positioned himself on the opposite side of the desk, where he was poring over the expense reports.

"Guess how much a gallon of milk cost in 1952?" he asked, looking up at me. "Ninety-six cents. That's more than a gallon of petrol cost! Twenty cents for a gallon of American *gas*. If I'm remembering right, that's the same year our dear queen took the throne. Although I would wager—"

He stopped. "What's the matter?" he asked.

I set the computer on my desk and fished the doll out of my pocket. I held it out to him.

"I found this in my room."

He took it from my palm. "It's from that bloody dollhouse."

"What do you think it means?" I asked him, sinking down into my chair. "Who would have put it there?"

"Damned if I know," he said. "Somebody, or some *thing*, is trying to scare you, that's clear."

"It worked," I said, shivering deep in my core.

"I think the sooner we solve this puzzle, the better," he said. "Once we know what, exactly, we're dealing with—"

"We'll be armed," I finished his thought. I agreed with him. I wanted to know, once and for all, what Miss Penny intended to do by gathering us all here. Kill us? Scare us to death? Torment us?

I plugged in the charger, opened the laptop, and waited a moment as it whirred to life. I was about to call up my search engine when I had a better idea. I picked up the phone's heavy, black handset and dialed my old newsroom. Richard looked up from his file and squinted at me. I held up a finger as if to say, *Just wait.*

"Hey Meg," I said, when I heard her familiar voice. "It's me."

"Norrie!" she said. "How are you doing? I've been wondering how you've been getting along since Penelope Dare's death."

I'll bet she had.

"Just fine, thanks," I said, "but listen, Meg. I gave you the information I had the day of her death, and now I'm calling for a favor from you in return."

"Oh?" I could hear her tapping at the keyboard in the background. "What's that?"

"I need your password to access the paper's online archives," I said. "I assume mine has already been deleted, and I need to get into those files."

She was silent for a moment. "Why?"

I took a deep breath. "I just want to do some research into Cliffside's history, to find whatever old articles the paper might have published in the past," I said. "Two of the fellows here this session are doing projects involving Cliffside's past, and they've run into a brick wall. I said I'd help them out, and when I couldn't come up with anything in the files here, I thought of the paper's archives."

I winced at the white lie, but Richard nodded his head in approval. It wasn't exactly the truth, but I had no intention of telling her what I was really up to. Because I was using her password, or hoped to, she'd be able to access my search after I logged off, and the story about helping the fellows with research would likely be enough to put her off the scent.

"You know we're not supposed to give out our passwords," she said.

"I'm not going to steal your identity, for goodness' sake, I'm just going to spend an afternoon looking through really old newspaper articles. Please? Can't you help me out?"

She let out a great sigh. "I suppose," she said, and rattled off her password, which I jotted down. "But you've got one day. I'm going to change my password tomorrow morning so you can't get into the files anytime you feel like it."

*By all means,* I thought to myself with a huff, *do all you can to prevent the heinous crime of somebody reading old newspaper clippings willy-nilly.*

"Thanks, Meg," I said to her. "I owe you one."

"I'll remember that," she said, just before I hung up the phone.

"You're very crafty," Richard said. "Good thought, that."

"We'll see," I said, calling up the newspaper archive's website and punching in Meg's password. "It might turn out to be nothing."

"Or everything," he said, pulling his chair around the desk to sit beside me. "Let's find out."

I punched *Cliffside Manor, 1952* into the archive's search engine and watched as a long list of hits came up. A sizzle of anticipation flashed through me. Maybe we'd find what we were looking for after all.

"That's . . ."—Richard did a quick count as I scrolled through the list—"twenty-seven stories your newspaper did about Cliffside that year. That's quite a bit of coverage on one institution, right?"

I nodded. "This search engine finds any story that has all the specific keywords in it, in our case *Cliffside Manor* and *1952*, so some of these might be stories about other things that merely mention it. But you're right. It seems to have been a banner year for Cliffside."

Rather than reading them all, one by one, on the archive website, I clicked on each of the stories and downloaded them to my laptop. That way, I didn't have to worry about Meg changing her password. I'd have these stories safe and sound on my own computer whenever I wanted to read them.

"What else should I search for?" I asked him. "We might as well cover our bases."

"Penelope Dare," he said. "Temperance Dare. And what was the sister's name? Oolong?"

I let out a snort. "Chamomile, you goofball."

"Who the hell names their child after a tea?" Richard said, his eyes twinkling. "This is my daughter, Orange Pekoe. And her brother, Earl Grey."

That was it. Despite everything, the laughter bubbled up from somewhere inside of me and took over, my shoulders shaking with the force of it. Catching my breath and dabbing at my eyes, I said, "I haven't laughed that hard in a long time."

"You're a very easy girl to laugh with, Norrie Harper," he said. "But I shouldn't make fun of her name," he went on, wiping the tears from his eyes. "I met her once."

I turned to him. "Who?"

"Chamomile Dare," he said.

"When?" I asked. "Twenty years ago when you were here the first time?"

He nodded. "I was talking to Chester, and she came over and introduced herself. At first, I thought she was a nice lady, but then she got kind of creepy, to tell you the truth. The way she looked at me made me really uncomfortable. If she didn't have a good thirty years on me, I would've thought she was coming on to me."

I grimaced. "You're kidding."

"No," he said. "I couldn't wait to get away from her. But when I was walking the grounds scouting for good locations to shoot, I noticed she was following me around. Trying to hide so I wouldn't see. Every time I'd turn around I'd see her disappearing behind the odd bush."

"Sounds like she took a shine to you. Maybe she wanted a boy toy." I raised my eyebrows.

He shook his head and laughed. "Whatever she was selling, I wasn't buying. It was really odd, though. I heard them arguing. He said something about 'not again' and 'unseemly' and shortly thereafter, he asked me to leave."

That set my mind alight. Richard's visit to Cliffside, Chamomile's crush, the accident, and then my visit to Cliffside. My gut told me there was a connection, but I couldn't put my finger on what it might have been.

I turned back to the screen, punching in names and downloading the articles as fast as they appeared. Soon the desktop screen of my computer was loaded with articles about Cliffside.

"It looks like we've got some reading to do," he said.

I nodded. "Indeed we do," I said, glancing at the clock on my computer screen and then looking back up at Richard. "Wow, it's two o'clock already. Are you hungry at all?"

"I am, at that," he said, pushing his chair away from the desk. "Let's go see what Harriet has rustled up. Then we can get back to this."

It sounded good to me. We closed the study door behind us and I locked it. Not that I was worried anyone would get in—not much, anyway—but my laptop was inside and I wanted to protect the treasure trove of information that was on it. We were rounding the corner to the main staircase when we met Henry on his way up.

"Hey there, sir!" I said, giving him a big smile and intending to invite him to join us for a bite if he hadn't already eaten, but the look on his face stopped me short.

"What's wrong?" I asked him. "You look worried."

He leaned against the banister and let out a sigh. "It's probably nothing," he said. "I do tend to make mountains out of molehills."

"What is it?" I pressed. "I'll help if I can."

"I know you will, dear," he said, giving me a weak smile. "And as I said, it's probably nothing, but—have either of you seen Brynn at all today?"

Richard and I exchanged a glance. "She still hasn't turned up?"

"No," Henry said. "Not only did she stand me up for breakfast, but last night we made plans to take a picnic lunch to the cliff today if we both were at a stopping point in our work. We were supposed to meet in the winter garden at one o'clock. But she didn't show up."

I was beginning to get a very bad feeling in the pit of my stomach. There were all manner of dangers here on the property—Richard knew that firsthand—and I immediately began to think she might have wandered off outside and ended up at the bottom of the cliff or lost her way in the woods. But, not wanting to alarm Henry, I asked the obvious question first. "She tends to get caught up in her work, from what I understand," I said. "You went to her room looking for her, I take it?"

"I did," he said. "I knocked but she didn't answer, so I tried the door. It was open, but she wasn't there. I thought maybe we missed each other somehow—it's such a big house—so I traipsed back downstairs, but she was nowhere to be found. Harriet said she hadn't seen her, either."

"It could be she just went off someplace," Richard said. "Outside. Maybe she took a walk."

Henry shook his head. "She wouldn't go walking in the woods alone. She told me she had no intention of exploring the forest. She's not the outdoorsy type. And I've already looked in the gardens."

"I hate to even mention this, but—did you look in the pool?" I winced, picturing her tripping and hitting her head, and floating facedown.

Henry took my hand. "I know. I thought the same thing. The pool, the bottom of the cliff. I looked. Oh, I know she can be a bit of a diva with all of that bluster of hers, but she really is a dear girl, underneath it all."

I squeezed back. He cared about her, that was plain to see. Shades of his mother's compassion. "We'll find her, Henry. She can't have gone far."

"And the others?" Richard piped up. "Have you seen them?"

He nodded. "I ran into Cassandra while she was having lunch, and Diana helped me look for Brynn outside." Henry looked from Richard to me and then back again. "Neither had seen her all day, either. I'm starting to get worried. I'm not one to go in for all of this paranormal mumbo jumbo, but . . . it just has me spooked."

Richard put a hand on Henry's arm. "Let's go to her room right now," he said. "I know you already looked there, but as you say, it's a big house and she could have gone back without you seeing her. We'll start there."

He turned and walked down the hallway toward the suites with Henry and me close behind. We reached her door and Richard knocked loudly. "Brynn?" he called out. No answer. He knocked again, but the silence on the other side of the door was tangible. He tried the knob and pushed open the door, and the three of us stepped inside.

"Brynn?" I said, but I knew she wasn't going to answer me.

Richard opened the closet. "Her clothes are still here," he said. "I was thinking she might have gotten fed up and left without telling anyone, after everything that's happened."

I shook my head. "She couldn't have left," I said. "The road is out, remember?"

Henry was on his knees, peering under the bed, and at this, he popped his head up. "What road?"

All at once it occurred to me that I hadn't told the rest of the fellows that news. "It's nothing to worry about," I said, quickly. "In all the rain last night, part of the road leading to the main highway to town washed out. Mr. Baines said a crew is going to get to it as soon as they can, but in the meantime he and his guys are going to cut a makeshift path through the woods so we can drive around that spot and get out to town. It could be done now, for all I know, but if not, there's no way Brynn could've left Cliffside."

"So, she's still here somewhere," Henry said.

"Who's still here?" It was Cassandra, poking her head into the room.

"Brynn," I said. "You haven't seen her at all today, I hear?"

"That's right," she said, nodding her head toward Henry. "It's a big place. She's probably holed up in some quiet corner working."

I cast an eye toward the study and noticed Brynn's computer and the journal on her desk. "She could be holed up someplace, but she's not working," I said, crossing the room to the study and buzzing the intercom.

Harriet's voice crackled, "Yes, Miss Kendrick?"

"Harriet, it's me, Eleanor," I said. "I understand you haven't seen Brynn today?"

"That's right, Miss Harper. She didn't come down for breakfast or lunch, and I haven't seen her in passing."

"It's probably nothing, and I hate to bother you with this, but since nobody has seen her at all today, would you mind terribly asking the staff to go through the house looking for her?"

"Absolutely, Miss Harper," she said. "I'll have Mr. Baines set the outdoor crew on the search as well."

"We'll look through the rooms up here on the second floor," I said to her, glancing from Richard to Henry to Cassandra, and getting nods all around.

"Very good, ma'am," she said, and the intercom went silent.

And so the four of us fanned out, knocking on doors and searching the rooms, but to no avail. The emptiness was evident as soon as I opened the doors, but I checked the closets, bathrooms, and under the beds anyway. I knew the others were doing the same.

I made my way down to Diana's room and rapped on the door. She opened it a moment later, a worried look on her face.

"It's about Brynn, isn't it?" she said. "She hasn't turned up."

"How did you know that?" I asked her.

She shook her head and sighed. "Henry asked me to help him look for her out in the gardens, and I got a very bad feeling about it. When we didn't find her out there, it got worse. I've been in my room ever since, meditating and trying to get a read on where she might be."

Meditating. That was one way to handle the situation. I preferred action, though.

"Would you mind helping us look for her?" I asked, trying to hide my annoyance. "I know it's cutting into your work time—"

She put up her hand. "Not at all," she said. "But I don't think we're going to find her anytime soon."

I didn't like the sound of that. "Why?"

"I'm not sure," Diana said, rubbing her temples. "It's just that I'm not getting any sort of reading on her. It's like she's disappeared."

More of her psychic stuff. I suppressed the urge to roll my eyes. "Well, that may be, but I need to search the entire house and grounds anyway," I said. "She could have fallen ill somewhere—or just fallen—and needs our help. Or maybe she lost her way outside." At this, a dark thought occurred to me. "May I come in and use your intercom for a moment?" I asked.

Diana opened her door wide. I made my way through the clutter and piles of clothing to her study and buzzed Harriet.

"Harriet, it's me again," I said. "Will you make sure Mr. Baines and his crew go down to the old boathouse? I want to make sure she hasn't run into—what's his name? Pete?"

The thought of that threatening old man getting his hands on Brynn, or just scaring her so badly with that ridiculous *Death himself* business that she lost her way as she hurried away from him, made me shiver.

"Already done, ma'am," she said. "One of the boys is on the way down there right now, and two others are checking the woods. I've got my people combing the first floor and the basement."

I let out a sigh. Thank goodness she was on full alert. I felt more calm knowing the crew was already on the job both in and out of the house.

I thanked Harriet and rang off, then turned back to Diana. I was just about to ask her to come with me and help with the search when Henry, Cassandra, and Richard appeared in her doorway.

"Any sign of her?" I asked them.

Henry shook his head. "We've been in every room on this floor," he said. "She's not here."

"Harriet has her people searching on the first floor and Mr. Baines has a crew looking outside," I said.

I caught Richard's eye, and my stomach dropped when I realized what he was going to say. There was one place we hadn't yet looked. I fingered the doll in my pocket and, all at once, I felt ice cold.

As if he could read my thoughts, he said, "You know we have to go up there."

Henry frowned, looking from Richard to me and then back again. "Up where?"

I rubbed my arms with the opposite hands, trying to get warm. "The third floor," I said.

"I didn't know there was a third floor," Henry said.

"Oh, yes," Cassandra piped up. "That's where the children's ward was when this was a TB clinic. I've been meaning to ask you if I could explore it."

I took a deep breath and let it out again. "It's also where Penelope Dare's bedroom is," I said.

Cassandra raised her eyebrows. "Really? I didn't know that."

I nodded, and a vision of my last visit to that bedroom swam through my mind. "I've been up there," I said, the foreboding wrapping around me like a cloak. "I don't mind telling you . . ." I couldn't finish my thought.

"What?" Henry said, taking a step closer to me, his voice dropping to a whisper.

"It's just . . ." I began. All eyes were on me. "It's really creepy," I said, finally.

What else was there to say? They'd be seeing it for themselves in a moment. I knew Richard was right—we had to search that floor. But somehow, I couldn't make my feet move from where they were planted.

"We'll all go," Henry said.

And so, I began to move, one foot and then the other, and before I knew it, we were at the staircase. "Okay," I said, breathing deeply to try to find some resolve. "Let's get this done."

We quickly ascended the stairs, and I flipped on the light as we walked into the main room. There it was again—the coolness, the dread, hanging in the air like fog. So I hadn't imagined it the first time I was on this floor.

"The children's ward," Cassandra mused, her voice thin and papery.

Henry rubbed his arms. "Does anyone else feel that?"

"The cold?" Richard asked.

Henry nodded slowly. "It has to be twenty degrees colder up here than it was on the second floor. It's almost like there's a draft coming from somewhere."

I knew it was no draft.

"I don't like this," Cassandra said, a discernable shiver going through her. "It's almost like you can feel the suffering and death that happened right here in this room. But that's silly. Isn't it?"

Her words just drifted away. Nobody responded. I think we were all thinking, *It isn't silly at all.*

"I can't see Brynn coming up here on her own," Henry said. "I know I wouldn't."

As we stood huddled together at the top of the stairs, I scanned the nearly empty room. I gasped when I caught sight of the toy chest in the corner. It was upended, and toys were strewn everywhere. Old metal tops, their paint peeling, a small rocking horse, several balls. An ancient telephone. A red wagon, now faded, its handle bent and worn.

I wasn't about to tell the others that the toys had been neatly stored in the toy box the last time I saw it, but I grabbed for Richard's hand and caught his eye. He was thinking the same thing.

Only then did I notice Diana was not with us. I wondered why.

Richard cleared his throat. "Okay," he said, turning to Henry and Cassandra. "We can see she's not here in the main room. You two check the bathrooms over there"—he pointed across the room—"and Eleanor and I will check the bedroom. And then we can get the hell out of here."

Henry nodded and took Cassandra's arm. "Let's go, my dear," he said. "The sooner we do this, the sooner we can get back downstairs and march straight to the liquor cabinet." And they set off across the floor. Richard gave me a soft nudge on the back and I started to move, too, toward Miss Penny's room.

After what felt like an eternity, we reached her door. I pushed it open, flipped on the light switch, and peered inside. I was wholly unprepared for what I saw.

The room, which had been neat and tidy when I last left it, was in utter disarray. Both of the beds were rumpled, as though they had been slept in, their pillows thrown here and there. Dolls sat on the window seat, books propped up in front of them. Clothes were strewn on the floor, children's clothes, as though they had been worn and discarded.

Through the archway to the study, I saw the desks had been shoved out of the way to make room for the papers that were littered all over the floor, crayons, pencils, and boxes of paints beside them. It was as though children had been playing there, making a mess of the tidy room. My breath flew out of my body when I thought—the Dare children.

And then I felt it, a presence, more than one, hovering in front of me, beside me, and around me. We were not alone.

"Eleanor Harper," I heard, in a child's singsong voice. "Why won't you play with us?"

I clutched Richard's arm. "Did you hear that?" I whispered. He shook his head, almost imperceptibly, his eyes wide, taking in the room for the first time.

I followed his gaze across to the playroom door. We both crouched down and crept through it. And that's when I began to scream.

# CHAPTER 30

It was Brynn.

She was sitting in a tiny chair at the tiny table in the corner of the playroom, the tea set in front of her, places set for three. Two ancient and worn antique dolls were positioned in the other chairs as her companions.

Brynn's face was painted, made up in garish, smeared red lipstick, heavy eyeliner and eye shadow and bright rouge, as though a child had gotten into her mother's makeup kit and gone to town with it. Her eyes were open, staring straight ahead, and her head was lolled to the side, a portion of her hair curled haphazardly into ringlets. Her mouth was contorted into a horrible smile. I saw Miss Penny's grotesque death expression in my mind and wanted to run from the room, but I was frozen to the spot.

Richard was at her side in an instant. "Brynn!" he shouted. "Brynn, can you hear me?" He shook her by the shoulders, and she slid off the chair, crumpling to the floor like a rag doll.

"Is she dead?" I squeaked out.

"I don't think so," Richard said, kneeling next to her and putting two fingers to her neck.

I heard footsteps thundering across the room and, in a moment, Henry and Cassandra were in the doorway.

Henry cried out and flew to Brynn's side. He put his head to her chest and listened. And then he put his cheek down near her lips.

"Does she need CPR?" I asked him, recovering my senses. "I'm trained. I can do it."

Henry looked up at me, his eyes wide. "I don't think so." He turned to Richard. "She's breathing steadily. Her heart is beating. She's got a pulse."

"What in the name of God is wrong with her?" Cassandra said.

*Drugs?* I mouthed to her.

Richard took Brynn by the shoulders and gently shook her. "Brynn!" he said, his voice loud and commanding. "Brynn! Can you hear me?"

But her head just flopped around like a rag doll's, her eyes fixed and staring straight ahead, her mouth still smiling that terrifying smile.

"We need to call an ambulance," Richard said.

And then the realization hit me. "We can't," I said. "The road's washed out. An ambulance can't get here."

Richard just stared at me for a moment. "Of course!" he said, his voice harsh. "Of bloody course the bloody road is im-bloody-passible when we need an ambulance."

All at once, I thought of Nate. "We don't need an ambulance," I said. "We've got a doctor who lives on the grounds! And I'm sure he's not at work because the road is washed out."

"Call him," Henry said, staring at Brynn, his eyes wet with tears. "Right now. Please."

*Damn it,* I thought. "I don't have his number," I said. "But his house is just across the back lawn. You three get Brynn out of this horror chamber and down to her room and put her on her bed. I'm going to run and get Nate."

One of them said something, but I didn't stop to listen. I flew across that accursed ballroom and pounded down the stairs, only to be met by Diana, who was standing outside her door. "Tell them to bring her in here," she said, gesturing to her room. I took a quick glance inside and saw candlelight and smelled incense. How did she know? Whatever she was up to, I didn't have time for that nonsense.

"Tell them yourself," I said to her and kept running down the hallway toward the stairs, but then I stopped short and turned back to her. "Buzz Harriet and tell her we found Brynn," I yelled down the hall.

"Will do!" I heard her say, and then I was off, hurrying down the stairs to the main floor. I didn't see anyone—*they must all still be on the search for Brynn,* I thought—but I didn't concern myself with that. All I knew was I needed to get to Nate.

I pushed open the main doors and tore across the driveway. I kept running across the lawn and over the hill until I saw Nate's house, standing in the distance.

Just as I reached the edge of his lawn, Nate burst through the doors and hurried down the porch steps toward me.

"You have to come, right away," I said, bending over at the waist and breathing heavily. "It's one of the fellows. She—"

He put up a hand to stop my words. "Tell me on the way. I'll grab my bag."

He hurried up the steps to the house and emerged a moment later with a black, old-fashioned doctor's bag. The look on my face must've betrayed what I was thinking, because he said, "It was my dad's. I like tradition."

We set off together, hurrying back across the lawn toward the house. On the way, I told him about Brynn's disappearance and where and how we found her.

"It sounds like a catatonic state," he said. "Do you know if she's on drugs of any kind?"

I had no idea, but when we reached the driveway, I stopped and took his arm.

"Nate," I began, not really wanting to ask the question but knowing I had to, and now, while we were out of earshot of the others. "Can something like this be caused by fear?"

"In extreme cases," he said, nodding. "Fear and trauma can cause a psychotic break."

"I think that might be what we're dealing with here," I said.

We stood and looked deeply into each other's eyes for a moment, just a quick flash of time, but it seemed to last forever, and somehow, his eyes told me that he knew exactly what I was talking about, and who had caused that fear.

"Let's go," he said. And we rushed through the doors.

# CHAPTER 31

We found Brynn laid out on the bed in Diana's room, her eyes still open, her mouth still contorted into that ghastly smile. Someone had washed the garish, clownish makeup off her face, thank goodness, but they couldn't wash away the dread all of us were feeling.

Diana had obviously set the stage for something—what, I didn't know. The room was aglow with the flickering light of dozens of candles, and a fire was crackling in the fireplace. Incense wafted through the air, and all of the mirrors, I noticed, were shrouded with towels. A Ouija board was set on her bedside table.

Everyone was gathered there, concerned looks on their faces, when Nate and I hurried in.

"Everybody, this is Doctor Davidson," I said. "He lives here on the Cliffside grounds."

Nate perched on the bed next to Brynn.

"Can you get the bottle of smelling salts out of my bag?" he asked me.

I opened the bag, fished around, and handed him the bottle.

He waved it back and forth under her nose. No response. He tried again. Nothing.

I turned over my shoulder to the group. "Has she said anything?"

"Not a word," Henry said, his voice crumbling. He dabbed at his eyes. "We carried her down here and put her on the bed, and Cassandra and I used some towelettes to get that horrible paint job off her face." He took a deep breath in. "She's just not there." He was barely able to say the words.

Nate shook his head and stood up, turning to face everyone. "She should be in the hospital," he said.

"What's wrong with her?" I asked him.

"You were right, before," he said to me. "This is a catatonic state. We don't know precisely what causes it, but there are many possibilities."

"Such as?" Richard asked.

"Drugs," Nate said. "Previous psychotic breaks. Various neurological issues."

"Well, it's not drugs, I can tell you that," Henry piped up.

"How do you know?" Nate asked him.

"I was taking my blood pressure pills the other morning and she went on a rant about me taking them," Henry said, looking from one to the other. "You were there, Diana, I think."

She nodded. "Now that I think about it, yes. She was going on and on about not putting anything like that into her body."

I turned to Nate. "You said fear and trauma could also cause this."

He nodded. "Very possible," he said. "Whatever the cause, we need to get in touch with her next of kin. Eleanor, I'm assuming you have that information?"

My heart sank. I had no idea. I had not seen anything in their files about a next of kin, and truthfully, it had not even occurred to me to ask. I must've looked like a deer in headlights. My eyes darted to Nate. *Please help.*

He sensed what I was asking without me asking it. "I believe Miss Penny kept next-of-kin info with the fellows' applications," he said.

"I'll get it," Richard piped up. "Eleanor—the keys to your study."

I dug them out of my pocket and tossed them to him. "Thanks," I said, sharing a quick smile.

I turned back to Nate. "We won't be able to get an ambulance here tonight," I said. "The road hasn't been repaired."

"Well, that's it, then," Nate said. "I'll sit here with her and monitor her vitals."

He opened his bag and fished out a hypodermic needle and a vial. "In the meantime, I'll give her something to help her sleep," he said, drawing liquid from the vial into the hypo and injecting it into her arm.

We all stood in silence for a few moments, until Brynn's eyes fluttered closed. I think the whole group of us exhaled simultaneously.

"We should move her to her own room," I said, catching Diana's eye. "You need somewhere to sleep, too."

She pursed her lips and shook her head. "What I set up here for her has not served its purpose," she said. "She can't be moved now."

I felt a pang of annoyance at her continued mumbo jumbo. But Nate piped up, stopping my thoughts in their tracks. "I agree with her," he said. "Not about the setting"—he gave me a quick wink—"but as long as she's on the bed here and resting comfortably, we shouldn't jostle her around. Let's let her be."

Diana opened one of her drawers and retrieved a nightgown. "I can sleep in her room," she said. "It's not a problem."

I shrugged. Where she rested her head for the night was the least of my worries. I had a feeling none of us were going to be getting much sleep, anyway.

"We'll get you some clean—" I started, when Richard stopped my words by walking back into the room carrying a file.

"I couldn't find any information about Brynn's next of kin," he said, looking from one to the other of us. "Or any of ours." He put the file down, along with a spiral notebook, on the desk in Diana's study. "Before anybody leaves this room, write down your emergency contacts and next-of-kin information. I'll do the same. I'm not saying anything else is going to happen, but we can't be at loose ends if it does."

Nods all around. But once again, I realized what a poor job I was doing as director. I should have made sure all of that was in place when they got here.

"I'm sorry, everyone," I began, but Henry put up his hand to stop me.

"Don't even say it," Henry said, his eyes flashing. "You've been nothing but wonderful since the minute we stepped onto the grounds. And you've been dealing with such extraordinary, horrible circumstances."

"Hear, hear," Cassandra said, crossing the room and taking my hands into hers. "If anything illustrates a trial by fire, this is it. And you've handled it all with grace and good humor. It's not your fault our next-of-kin information isn't in the files. It's Penelope Dare's."

Her words stopped me short. Was it Miss Penny's fault? And if so, did she omit that information simply to put an obstacle in my path? What else had she done to make sure I wasn't successful?

But I let that thought go, too. "Please, let's just get our info written down, and we'll leave Brynn to the doctor."

They did as I asked, and I tore the sheet of paper out of the notebook and put it into the folder. Then we all filed out of the room but lingered in the hallway outside the door.

"What in the name of God happened to her?" Henry whispered. "I've never seen anything like that in my life."

Richard and I exchanged glances. "I don't know for sure," I said, "but I really don't think any of us should be alone tonight. It felt dangerous before, but now it *is* dangerous. There's safety in numbers."

"Agreed," Henry said. "What do you say we all head into my room and watch a movie? Something light and airy."

"That's a great idea," I said, smiling at him and squeezing his arm. "I'll join you in a few minutes."

Richard gave me a scowl. "This, from the one who just said we shouldn't be alone?"

I took a deep breath and decided to fill everybody in. "I want to take some time to read all of that info we found today," I said, turning to the others. "I've dug up a bunch of articles about what was happening here in 1952. If we know what we're up against, we'll be better armed."

"I'll go with you," he said.

I shook my head. "You go with the others and I'll be there as soon as I can."

With that, I turned on my heel and made my way down the hall to my study just in time to see Harriet at the top of the stairs, a worried look on her face.

"How's the girl?" she asked.

"Brynn's resting right now," I told her. "But . . . it's not good, Harriet. The doctor—Nate—is tending to her, monitoring her vital signs for any change."

She nodded. "He's the best there is."

I didn't know quite what to say. We looked at each other, both understanding the gravity of this situation. I wondered just how much Harriet knew.

"The dinner is all prepared," she said, finally. "Shepherd's pie. It's warming in the oven."

She left me then, going back the way she had come, and I opened the door to my office, hoping I'd find the key to this whole mess in those files I had downloaded.

# CHAPTER 32

I flipped open my laptop and waited as it whirred to life. And then I clicked on the first article.

### Dare Daughter, Temperance, Dies of TB

Temperance Dare, age seven, the youngest daughter of local businessman and philanthropist Chester Dare, died yesterday at the Cliffside Sanatorium in Wharton.

"What a tragedy," said the san's resident physician, Nathan Davidson. "The man built this place to take care of tuberculosis patients, and his own daughter winds up succumbing to this horrible disease. We did everything we could to save the child, but it was not to be. It's one more sad example that TB knows no class, no age, and no sex. Everyone is vulnerable to this plague."

Chester Dare and his older daughters are said to be grieving in seclusion.

I clicked on the next article. Nothing pertinent. And the next, and the next, until something relevant caught my eye.

## Newsman Archie Abbott Dies at Cliffside Sanatorium

*Cassandra's grandfather,* I thought. I read on.

> Famed Chicago newsman Archie Abbott died yesterday at Cliffside Sanatorium in Wharton.
> He had been treated for tuberculosis for several months and was reportedly recovering when he died suddenly.
> "It's a shame," said Edward R. Murrow, using more colorful language than this reporter can relay. "Abby was one of the greats."

I checked the dates. The very day Temperance died. I read on. The next article stopped me short.

## Sanatorium Doctor, Dead at Age 42

> Doctor Nathan Davidson, the renowned physician at Cliffside Sanatorium and in Wharton at large, has died at age 42 in his home on the sanatorium grounds. The cause of death has not yet been determined, but it is initially thought that it is not related to TB.

I read it again, and then again, shaking my head. This just didn't make sense. Nate told me his father had practiced well into old age before turning over his practice to Nate.

And then I looked at the picture, and gasped at what I saw. I knew those eyes. I knew that grin. He was even wearing the same white coat, with the same name stitched above the breast pocket, that I had seen Nate wearing. He was a dead ringer for his dad. Or . . . but that couldn't be.

I shook my head, trying to shake those ridiculous thoughts away. Nate had told me he liked tradition. He was using his dad's doctor bag. He probably wore the same type of white coat, too.

But . . . if his father died in 1952, which he did, according to this article, then that would make Nate more than sixty years old. And that simply wasn't possible. The timelines just didn't add up.

I stared at the photo on the screen, trying to gather my thoughts. He had told me that his *father* had been the doctor at Cliffside when it was a sanatorium, right? Not his grandfather? Because that would make more sense. That had to be it. This article had to be about his grandfather.

But he had told me he was Nathan Davidson *Junior*. Hadn't he?

I had to clear this up. The man was right down the hall, for goodness' sake. I pushed my chair back from my desk, intending to go ask Nate about this, when I heard a quick knock on my door. I opened it and found Richard there, a grave look on his face.

"What's the matter?" I asked him.

"Cassandra has disappeared," he said.

"What?" I asked him. "How? Everyone was together, I thought. It's only been, what, twenty minutes since I came in here?"

He cocked his head to the side and gave me a strange look. "Eleanor, you've been in your study for a good four hours. I was tempted to come and see what you were doing, but you made it clear you wanted to be alone. It's nearly ten o'clock."

Another ice-cold wave washed over me. I turned to the clock on the desk and realized he was right. Four hours had indeed passed. The light that had been streaming in from the windows had faded, and darkness had taken its place. I hadn't even noticed. But . . . how? I had only just powered up my computer, hadn't I?

And there, sitting on the shelf behind my desk—another doll. Richard saw it the same time I did.

"How did that thing get in here?" he asked.

I just shook my head. "I have no idea," I said. "I didn't notice it when I came in. Did you lock the door after you were in here looking for our contact info?"

He closed his eyes and shook his head. "I didn't," he said. "I'm so sorry."

I reached out and put my hand on his arm. "Richard, I don't like this," I said.

"Neither do I," he said.

"How did she go missing? I thought you were all together?" I asked.

"After we all watched a movie in Henry's room, Cassandra went downstairs to get a bite of dinner, and nobody has seen her since. I can't believe I let her go down there alone." He ran a hand through his hair.

My stomach seized up, and the room began to sway. I put a hand on the doorframe to steady myself. I knew just where we had to look for her, but I couldn't make myself say the words. So I just looked at Richard with wide eyes and hoped he would understand.

He nodded, his expression grave. "I thought the same thing. The third floor."

My heart sank. "We should get the others and—"

A shout cut off my comment. We both hurried into the hallway and found Henry carrying Cassandra toward Diana's room. We followed.

Nate, who had been sitting in an armchair across from the bed, shot to his feet and gasped. "Oh no," he said.

That's when I saw she had the same garish makeup painted onto her face. The same ghastly smile. How she would hate that, the woman who never had so much as one hair out of place. A tear escaped my eye and ran down my cheek as I hurried to the bathroom and plucked several of Diana's makeup-removing cloths from their case. Then I sat on the bed next to Cassandra and began wiping that horrid paint from her lips and eyes, my own wet with tears. She didn't react, her eyes staring into space as though she was still looking at the last thing she'd seen before retreating to wherever she was now.

Nate bent over Cassandra and took her pulse. "She's in the same state as Brynn." He reached into his bag and fished out another hypodermic, filled it with liquid from the same vial he had used before, expelled a bit from the tip of the needle. He caught my eye. "I really shouldn't be giving either of them a sedative without knowing their medical histories, but I don't see any other choice."

"You're working with the information you have right now," I said. "That's all you can do."

He nodded and plunged the needle into Cassandra's arm.

I smoothed her hair behind her ears and watched as her eyes fluttered closed. Whoever—whatever—had done this to these women was a monster.

Nate ran a hand through his hair, clearly exasperated. "They both need IV fluids," he said. "But there's none of that equipment on hand anymore. This place used to be a hospital, for chrissake. What I wouldn't give for two bags of saline."

Henry leaned against the wall, exhaling a deep breath. "Does anybody else want a brandy?"

"Where was she?" Richard asked Henry. "I mean to say . . ." We all knew what he was getting at.

"The same way," Henry said, a visible shudder going through him. "At the tea party. Somehow I just knew she'd be there."

"You shouldn't have gone up there alone," Richard said. "You should have had me go with you. You could have run into whoever, whatever, is doing this."

Henry sighed. "I know. I just acted without thinking."

Nate turned to face all of us. "Okay," he said, "I'd like for all of you fellows to stay together tonight. In one room, as Eleanor suggested before. Nobody goes anywhere without company."

There were nods all around.

Nate continued. "Let's just let this night pass and get daylight on the situation, and we'll take some action."

"What are we going to do?" I asked him.

"We need to get these two to the hospital," Nate said. "And then I think it's time that everyone pack up and leave here. We—all of us—know now that what happened to Brynn wasn't an isolated incident. It's not a stretch to say you're all in danger." He turned to me. "Our first priority when the sun comes up is getting everyone off the property safely."

Richard squinted at him, a look of suspicion in his eyes. "Eleanor is leaving, too," he said. "I won't go without her."

Nate returned his stare. "I'm just as committed to getting Eleanor out of this safely as you are," he said. "Make no mistake about that."

*Oh, Lord,* I thought. *Male egos.* Now was not the time.

"Listen," I said to the group. "I think Doctor Davidson is right. You all go into Henry's room. I'll bring some extra bedding. Everybody's sleeping there tonight."

"Including you?" Richard asked, eyeing me and then giving Nate a look.

"Including her," Nate answered.

"I just need to ask the doctor something," I said, speaking primarily to Richard. "In private. I'll follow in a few minutes, I promise."

"I don't think—" Richard started, but Nate held up a hand.

"I'll make sure she gets back to you safely," Nate said.

"See that you do," Richard said. Then he turned to me. "If you're not there in ten minutes, I'm coming to get you."

"While Norrie is talking to the doctor, let's, the three of us, make our way downstairs and get some water for us all, and anything we'd like to eat," Diana suggested. "That is, if anybody feels like eating."

She turned to Nate. "Are you hungry? You've been tending to them for hours."

He smiled at her. "I could do with a little something," he said. "That's very kind."

They filed out then, leaving Nate and me alone with the unconscious bodies of Brynn and Cassandra. It was an eerie sight, the two of them laid out like that, candles blazing all around them, the smell of incense hanging in the air.

I pushed the door closed and turned to him. "I have a question to ask you that is going to sound sort of strange."

He smiled up at me, that same impish smile I had seen so many times over the past several days. "Well, that sounds interesting," he said. "What is it?"

"How old are you?"

He chuckled. "Why? Do my boyish good looks contrast too sharply with my deep wealth of medical experience and knowledge? If so, I've been told that before."

"Well, there's that, sure," I said, giving him a weak smile, not quite knowing how to ask what I really wanted to ask. "The thing is, I just read an article online that didn't make sense to me, and I wanted to clear it up with you."

"Ah, the Internet. It's the root of all evil, you know. Don't believe everything you read, Norrie."

I pressed on. "It said that Nathan Davidson, the doctor at the Cliffside Sanatorium, died in 1952."

He raised his eyebrows. "Is that what it said?"

"Yes. But you said your dad was the doctor back then."

"Yes, that's what I said."

"But that can't be right," I said, leaning against the closed door. "If the man who died here in 1952 was your dad, then you would have been born before then or shortly thereafter, I suppose. And that would make you a whole lot older than you are, by, like, two decades. Plus, you told me that your dad practiced well into old age before you took over."

"Yup, that's what I told you."

He wasn't really answering my questions. And his demeanor was so calm. So unruffled. He seemed completely unconcerned that I had just caught him in a lie. I started to get a very bad feeling in the pit of my stomach, and I couldn't explain why—I really liked this man—but I was very glad I was so near the door. I put my hand on the knob.

"So, it was your grandfather they were talking about in the article, right? He was the Nathan Davidson who died here in 1952?"

I thought for a minute before adding, "And your dad took over when he died. But that doesn't make any sense either because you told me he was the doctor at the sanatorium, but it closed right around that time. There were no patients for him to be the doctor to."

He just sat there, next to two unconscious bodies, smiling at me. As though I were asking him about the weather. "I guess I'm not sure what you're getting at," he said, finally.

"What I'm getting at is, I'm confused," I said. "Can you please explain to me how the doctor who died in 1952 at Cliffside Sanatorium could have possibly been your dad, when you look to be no older than forty?"

Nate rose from where he was sitting, crossed the room toward me, and took my hands in his. "Norrie," he said, his voice soft and soothing. "Can we please drop this subject? Whatever you're thinking, please let it go."

I didn't get it. What was he saying to me, exactly?

"So you don't have an explanation for that?" I said, a bit louder than I intended. "I mean, I could just chalk it up to a misunderstanding, but we've got two people lying near death, here. And your story doesn't add up. You told me one thing, but it's clearly not true. And now that I think about it, nobody knows what you were doing when these two poor women were nearly frightened to death. If this was a police investigation that I was covering, you'd be a 'person of interest' right now."

He sighed. "Then I guess we can be very glad the police aren't here."

Something changed in the room between us. I couldn't quite put my finger on what it was. I was looking into the face of a man I had become very fond of, but all at once I realized I didn't know him at all, not really.

My mind raced in several directions.

Could it be? Was he the monster who did this? Did he nearly frighten these poor women to death, paint their faces, and pose them like toy dolls? Now that I thought about it, he had access to drugs—he might have drugged them into the state they were in. He was so nice, so affable, it didn't seem possible, but, I thought, so was Ted Bundy. At this thought, a sense of dread engulfed me, and I tried to pull away, but he squeezed my hands tighter.

"It's you," I said to him, my voice a whisper. "Why are you doing this? What have any of us done to you? Am I going to end up like them now?"

Tears stung at the back of my eyes and began to fall. He raised a hand and wiped a tear off my cheek, and I took that moment to break free of him and run to the other side of the room.

"I'm going to start screaming if you don't let me out of here," I hissed at him, but I wasn't sure I could make the sound. And conveniently, he had sent everyone down the hall to Henry's room. I doubted they'd hear me even if I was able to scream. My legs began shaking so violently that I thought I might fall. I steadied myself on the back of a chair.

He put his hands up, his palms facing me. "No, you're wrong," he said. "I can see you're terrified, Norrie, and my God I can't stand to have you looking at me like that. It's not me. I promise you that, Norrie. I swear on my mother's grave. I am not the monster who did this."

I wasn't buying it. "Well, who are you then? Because you sure as hell aren't who you said you are."

He looked into my eyes with an intensity I'd never felt from him before. "Yes, I am. Eleanor, I am Nathan Davidson. I'll swear that on my mother's grave, too."

I shook my head. "How? How is that even remotely possible? Tell me."

He let out a long sigh and ran a hand through his hair. "I've handled this very badly, I see that now."

"Handled what?"

"I'm just going to be straight with you," he said, crossing the room toward me and sinking down into the armchair. "I shouldn't have told you that stupid story about my dad, but I didn't see any other way. And now you've caught me in that lie and don't trust me. I've made a mess of this thing, and I can't think of a way to untangle it other than to just tell you the truth."

"Which is?"

He took a deep breath. "I am Doctor Nathan Davidson, Norrie," he said, holding my gaze with those clear, blue eyes. "The only Doctor Nathan Davidson. My dad's name was James. And he wasn't a doctor. He ran a general store."

I squinted at him. "I don't follow you. Nathan Davidson died in 1952. I have the article open on my computer right now if you want to see it."

He shrugged and smiled a weak smile. "I don't have to see it. You're right."

"But . . ." I started, but all at once, what he was saying to me sunk in. I remembered the photo that had run with the article. It wasn't just a great likeness of Nate. It was Nate. My legs couldn't hold me any longer, and I slumped to the floor and put my head into my hands, hoping that when I looked up again, he would be gone.

He slipped down from the chair and joined me, taking my hands into his and looking deeply into my eyes. "Now you see why I told you the story about my dad being the doctor here," he said. "I couldn't exactly tell you the truth. It was the only way to explain my presence."

"You're telling me that you're the Doctor Nathan Davidson who died here in 1952?" I whispered. "You're . . . dead?"

"It sounds sort of dramatic when you say it like that," he said, smiling.

"But that can't be," I said, searching his eyes for any other explanation.

"It's really not a big deal," he said. "We're around you every day and you don't know it. You would not believe the amount of dead people you encounter on the street or on the bus every single day. Don't even get me started about the subway."

Diana had said the same thing to me days before, and I shuddered at the thought of it. "But," I started and reached out to touch his arm, then his chest, then his face. He felt so . . . solid.

He chuckled at this. "What, you thought you'd put your hand right through me or something?"

I squinted at him. "Well . . . yes. I don't get it. Are you messing with me? I've seen you eat. You drank a beer! Several beers if memory serves. Dead people don't do that."

"Who says?"

"Charles Dickens, for one."

He smiled. "Oh, come on. The Ghost of Christmas Present was a glutton."

I shook my head, still not quite believing what he was saying to me.

"You don't have to believe me, and that's okay, but you did see the photo that ran with the article about my demise, right?"

"But, that's crazy," I said, shaking my head.

"I see you're a girl who needs proof," he said, and then he slowly faded from view until he was gone. He reappeared a moment later on the other side of the room. "It's one of the perks of the condition," he said.

I just sat there, dazed by what I had just seen with my own two eyes.

"Don't think too much about this," he said. "I'm still the same guy you've known for the past two weeks."

He helped me to my feet and sat me down in the chair. He crossed the room and poured a glass of water and handed it to me.

"Drink this," he said. "You look like you've seen a ghost, Miss Harper."

I brought the glass to my lips with shaking hands and took a sip. "That's not funny."

"Oh, I think it was," he said, grinning. "And I can't believe you thought I was the bad guy. Don't you know me better than that by now?"

I eyed him over the rim of my glass. "Apparently not."

He kneeled down next to me so we were face to face. "So, now you know. Are you afraid of me?"

I thought of our fun banter back and forth, his wit, his easy laugh. I gave him a weak grin. "Why are you here? Shouldn't you *go to the light* or something?"

"Meh." He shrugged. "Heaven is overrated."

This did produce a chuckle. "I can imagine eternal paradise gets boring," I said, my hands still shaking.

He smiled and tucked a tendril of hair behind my ear. "Thank God I didn't lose you," he said. "When you first brought this up and I knew I had to be straight with you, I thought you were going to run screaming out of here."

"There's still time."

"Seriously, Norrie, you weren't afraid of me ten minutes ago. You don't have to be afraid now. I'm the same guy I was then."

I eyed him, my heart still pounding in my chest.

"What happened to you? The article said you were forty-two when you, you know. Died."

He sighed. "It's a long story that I'll tell you another time."

"But it was 1952. The same year Temperance died. The same year the sanatorium closed. The same year Cassandra's grandfather died here, the same year Brynn's grandmother wrote that journal here. The same year Henry was conceived here."

He nodded. "Right on all counts."

"So, what's going on? Why are we all here together? Why are we being terrorized like this? What was the mystery Miss Penny wanted me to solve about our shared connections here?"

"I think I know, but I can't tell you right now."

"Why not? Let's just end this once and for all. Tell me what you know. At least then we'll all know what we're up against."

He shook his head. "You freaked out at my 'big news.' Hearing what I suspect is going on will definitely put you in bed with Cassandra and Brynn."

I shivered. "That bad?"

"Yeah," he said. "Trust me on that."

And then, something occurred to me. "You're not alone here, are you?" I asked. "You're not the only, um, dead guy at Cliffside."

He shook his head. "I told you the last time we talked that this is a very strange and mysterious place," he said. "Things happen here that don't happen anywhere else. Me still being here, for example. We're tied here, every one of us who died on this property."

I grimaced and sank farther back into the chair. "So that explains everything I've been hearing and seeing since I got here."

"Yeah," he said. "The kids are the worst."

I thought of the dark images on the photos Richard took of me. "So, Miss Penny is still here, too? And Chamomile?"

He nodded. "And many others."

I took a quick breath in. "We've got to get everybody out of this freak show," I said, casting a glance toward the window. "I wish we could leave right now."

"So do I," he said. "But venturing out into the woods at night isn't wise, and not just because of the animals. If you do that, we could well have five more dead people tied here to Cliffside."

I tried again to get him to tell me what he knew. "Who did this to Brynn and Cassandra, and why?"

"Like I said, trust me on this," he said. He took a deep breath and continued. "It's the reason I'm here, and the reason that I sought you out on the veranda that night. When Miss Penny died, I suspected that something was put into motion, and now I'm sure of it. Something very dark and very twisted is going on in this house. More dark and twisted than even legions of naughty ghosts trying to scare you by making things go bump in the night and knocking on doors—I'll speak to those little brats, by the way."

So I hadn't been imagining it.

"What you're saying is scaring me," I said, my voice dropping to a whisper. "It sounds like you're telling me there really is such a thing as supernatural evil. Like, demons or the devil. Is that what you're saying?"

He put his hands on my arms and squeezed. "Yes. And before the night is through, I'm afraid we're going to come face to face with it. But I'll promise you something. You—Eleanor Harper—will get out of this alive and unscathed. I am in this house now, and I'm not going anywhere. There's nothing in heaven or, more precisely, hell that will harm you while I am here. I would lay down my life to protect you." His eyes twinkled. "Of course, that's sort of an empty statement, considering."

I managed a smile. "The thought's nice, anyway."

"And now, I think it's time to take you back to the others," he said. "They'll be wondering. I'd advise you to not tell them any of this."

"I don't know what I'd say," I said, pushing myself out of my chair. "'Hey, everyone. Just FYI, the doctor is a ghost and there's a demon on the property. Sleep tight!'"

He laughed, and I stepped closer to him. "There's just one more thing," I said, wrapping my arms around him. "Thank you."

We looked into each other's eyes for a moment, and before I thought about what I was doing, I planted a kiss on his mouth. He pulled away.

"What are you doing, Miss Harper?" he asked, his voice husky.

"I wanted to know what it felt like to kiss a ghost."

He smiled a broad smile, our faces still close. "If you want to do further research on that, I'll be happy to oblige." He raised his eyebrows. "I can make the earth move for you. Literally."

"Every man says that." I smiled at him.

"Dammit," he said. "You just saw through my best line."

He drew me closer.

"As long as we're being honest, I'm going to admit something else," he said, his voice low. "I wish I could really be with you, Eleanor. I fell hard for you the first time I met you, that night out on the veranda. And even before that, when you first came to Cliffside. I watched you arrive. I've been watching you this whole time."

"Not in the bath, I hope." I smiled.

"I may be dead, but I'm still a gentleman," he said. "Seriously, though, I've had to remind myself over and over again that you are among the living and I'm not. I can't believe I finally found the woman of my dreams and I can't even try to win your heart. It wouldn't be fair to you."

But he had won it, at least a piece of it. I truly didn't know who I'd choose if it came down to it, but now I didn't have to make that decision. I turned my face up to his and felt his lips on mine, an ethereal, soft touch that quickly grew in intensity into something I wouldn't be strong enough to deny, despite what I felt for Richard. My legs started to tremble for the second time that night.

"I told you I'd make the earth move," he said, raising his eyebrows. "But you've got a guy down the hall who is just as crazy about you as I am. And he's alive, that lucky bastard."

Just then, as if the mention had summoned him, Richard opened the door. He stared at us for a moment as I drew back from Nate.

"I was just coming to check on you," he said. "I can see there was no need." With that, he turned and left the room, his anger lingering in the air.

"Go after him," Nate said. "You can make this right, and if you can't, I'll tell him the truth myself."

I stared into Nate's eyes for a long moment before hurrying out of the room and down the hallway, catching Richard just before Henry's door.

"That wasn't what it looked like," I said.

"It seemed pretty clear to me," he said, his eyes flashing with anger. "When I asked you, Eleanor, if there was anyone else on the horizon, I thought you might have a guy in your life. Why wouldn't you? You're bloody amazing. But I had no idea he was right here on the property."

I took his hands. "Nate and I aren't involved," I said. "I really like him. We're friends. I'll admit there was a little flirtation between us, but that's all it is. It would never work between us, I promise you."

He squinted at me. "Does he know that? Because I saw how he felt about you the first second I met him. I won't be part of a triangle. I don't do that, Norrie."

"He knows, believe me," I said. "There is no triangle." But as I said the words, I realized there had been, in my mind, anyway, before I knew the truth. Early on, I had been conflicted about which man to choose. I liked both of them. But all at once, I knew it had been Richard all along. What had I been doing flirting with both of them? Kissing Nate just now? It was so unlike me. I could've messed up the best thing to have walked into my life in a long time.

He pressed on. "I don't just date around. When I fancy someone—" He stopped mid-sentence and looked away.

A wave of relief washed through me. Maybe I hadn't messed it up after all. "Do you fancy me, Richard?"

His whole face softened, and he exhaled. "It's really not the best time to blurt that out, but I thought it was completely obvious. I think I could fall in love with you, Eleanor."

We just stood there for a moment, looking into each other's eyes. "I feel the same way about you," I whispered. "But you're right, it's not the best time. When all of this is over, when we're out of here and safe, let's have this conversation again."

He stroked my cheek. "You can count on it."

# CHAPTER 33

Henry's room was warm and cheery. He had fires lit in both the main room and his study, and several candles flickered here and there.

"What were you talking about with the good doctor?" Henry said.

If he only knew. "I just wanted to hear his prognosis about Cassandra and Brynn." I felt bad lying to him, to all of them, but the truth just wasn't possible.

"And?" Diana piped up.

Now I had to outright make something up. "He thinks it was likely caused by fear or trauma, and he wants to get them to the hospital in the morning," I said. "He also reiterated that we all need to leave as well." I looked around the room at these people who I had only met recently but who had come to feel like family. "I'm so sorry that your time here at Cliffside has turned into such a nightmare," I said. "But we're all going to get out of here. We're going to be okay."

"Hear, hear," Henry said, lifting his glass of brandy in salute. "This hasn't exactly been the time of quiet reflection and creativity that I had expected, but I will say it is a time I'll never forget."

I gave him a half smile. What a dear man he was.

While I was talking with Nate, they had been downstairs raiding the kitchen, and I saw a plate of shepherd's pie on the desk in Henry's study, along with cheeses, crackers, and a few apples. Despite everything, I found myself a little hungry, so I excused myself and went to make a plate. Richard followed.

"I thought you might have been asking the doctor about our theory," he said, his voice low. "About 1952."

I nodded and turned my back to the others. "I did," I said, my voice almost a whisper. "I don't want to alarm anybody, but we were right, it is the key to everything."

*Dammit,* I thought to myself. *Temperance.* That was the one thing I hadn't thought to ask Nate. All at once, it made a strange kind of sense. Miss Penny had set this all in motion, and Nate was here to stop it.

"We know Brynn and Cassandra have strong ties to Cliffside from 1952 and they were the first victims," he said. "Henry's ties are strong, too. Even stronger than theirs." Richard dropped his voice even lower. "If anybody's next, it's him."

I turned and glanced across the room at Henry, sitting in his armchair, sipping his brandy. "I think the nurse who gave Temperance the injection was his mother," I whispered. And, I swallowed hard, was Nate his father? I searched Henry's face for any resemblance but found none. I did, though, see a little of Miss Penny around the eyes.

Richard brought me out of my imaginings. "Do you think somebody, or some *thing*, is exacting revenge for the murder of that little girl all those years ago? Is it as simple as that?"

I nodded. That's exactly what I thought. We knew Brynn's grandmother had been here, witnessing everything. And I suspected that Cassandra's grandfather had been part of it as well.

As I was taking a forkful of the shepherd's pie, I heard the phone ringing. So did everyone else—we were all startled by it. But it wasn't Henry's phone.

"Where's that coming from?" Diana asked.

"I'll bet it's your office, Norrie," Richard said. "It's just across the hall." He and I exchanged glances. "We better answer it," he said. "I'll go with you."

Something about it felt wrong to me, as though I really didn't want to answer that phone, but I shook it off. Not everything was going to be dark and evil, I told myself. Sometimes a phone call was just a phone call. And he was right, it could be the crew letting us know the road was passable. If so, we could get Brynn and Cassandra to a hospital.

"You two stay here," I said to Henry and Diana. "And lock the door behind us. We won't be a minute."

Richard and I hurried across the hall to my office and, sure enough, that's the phone that was ringing. I picked up the receiver.

"Hello?" I said. "This is Cliffside."

As I listened, a rush of ice-cold air blew through me. "What?" I managed to squeak out. My eyes grew wide, and I reached for Richard's arm.

I quickly hung up the phone, my mind reeling. First Nate and now this.

"You're trembling," Richard said, a look of concern on his face. "What is it?"

"That was Diana Cooper's husband," I said. "He was calling to let me know Diana is in a hospital in Madison."

He furrowed his brow. "What are you talking about?"

"She was in a car accident the day she was to arrive at Cliffside," I said. "She's been in the hospital ever since."

"So who's that?" Richard flailed his arm in the direction of Henry's room.

"I don't know, but it's not Diana Cooper."

Whoever that was, she was alone with Henry. The thought hit both of us at the same time, and we tore out of my study and were pounding on his door in an instant.

We heard the bolt click, and a worried Henry opened the door. "What is it?" he said.

Richard pushed past him, and we both saw Diana sitting on the bed with a glass of wine, just as she had been before. "Is everything okay?" she asked.

"Oh, it will be," Richard said, his voice deep and threatening. "As soon as you tell me who in the hell you are and what you're doing here."

She furrowed her brow, confused. "I don't know what you're talking about."

"Diana Cooper's husband just rang," Richard said. "That was him on the phone, to tell us that Diana is in hospital after a car accident."

"That's impossible," she said. "I didn't have an accident."

"Who was that on the phone, then?" Richard demanded.

"I have no idea," she said, reaching down for her purse. "But I can prove I am who I say I am." She pulled out her wallet and plucked several cards from their sleeves and threw them on the bed. "There. My driver's license, my university staff ID card, my insurance card, my credit cards. And if that isn't enough to convince you, go onto the university website, where you'll find my staff picture."

Richard picked up each one of the cards and studied them. Then he looked at me, utterly confused. "She's telling the truth," he said. "What in the hell was that, then?"

I just shook my head, which, by this time, was starting to pound. It was all too much. I wished Nate could give me some of the sedative he had given Cassandra and Brynn.

The room started to spin. I felt tired, bone tired.

"I need to lie down," I said, rubbing my forehead. "I'm going to my room."

"I don't think that's a good idea," Richard said. "You can lie down right here."

"No, I think I'm getting a migraine. You three stay here together. I'll be fine." I turned and left, Richard on my heels.

As I collapsed onto my bed, he thoroughly checked out the room, looking under the bed and in the closets, in the bathroom and even out the windows.

"I'm going to stay here with you," he said.

I wanted him to stay, to lie down with me and hold me close. But when I spoke, the words surprised me.

"No," I told him. "You stay with Henry. I don't want him alone with Diana or whoever the hell she is. I'm afraid for him, I really am."

He nodded. "I am, too."

"I don't know what that phone call was all about, and at this point, I don't really care," I said. "All I care about is passing these last cursed hours here in this cursed place before we can all get out of here once and for all."

He bent down and kissed my forehead. "Amen to that, Norrie. I'll get you out of this nightmare safely. I promise you that. Now, lock the door behind me. I'll come check on you soon."

I heaved myself up to my feet and put a hand on his arm before he went. "Thank you," I said.

He kissed my cheek. "Tomorrow, after we leave here for good, I'm going to take you somewhere and sweep you off your feet," he said. "We'll get as far away from here as humanly possible, and before you know it, you're going to forget that Cliffside even exists."

It sounded good to me. I locked the door and sank down onto my bed, feeling safe and protected by the two warriors I had in my corner.

# CHAPTER 34

The next thing I knew, I was sitting at the desk in my room. All was dark, save for the greenish glow of the desk lamp. I glanced at the clock. Two fifteen. It was several hours after I had lain down with a headache. I didn't feel any trace of it anymore. I must've conked out right away after Richard had left and slept right through.

But, how did I get here, to the desk? I searched my memory but could not bring it to mind. It was like there was a vast area of blackness where that memory should have been. Had I been sleepwalking? I had never done it before, but anything was possible in this crazy place.

It was then I noticed a book was open in front of me. What was this? I looked down and noticed writing on the page. It was a diary. It looked rather old, but it wasn't Brynn's grandmother's journal, I could see that right away. I began to read.

*Soon, it will all be over. It won't be long now. What was that old saying, the sins of the father? To that, I would add the mother and the grandparents. They had no idea, poor, misguided souls that they are. Death is my old friend.*

*Richard is just as I remembered, even better, if that's possible. What a lovely man he is. Soon we will be together, here at Cliffside, as it should be. As it should have been long ago. I just need to take care of some housekeeping first.*

I just sat there, staring at the page, not quite understanding what I was reading. I flipped back several pages.

*She is arriving today. My choice, the next in line, is on her way to Cliffside at this moment! It's always an exciting time, the succession. I've grown to love it over the years. Everything feels new, at least for a while. A new face. New hair to style. It's almost like having a doll, isn't it? I've always loved dolls. And I've been in one place for so long. I just couldn't find the right one. But when she finally did turn up, I recognized her right away. Imagine, it took me this long to put this plan in motion, but it is finally happening. Finally. Everyone will be on their way shortly. I do love killing two birds with one stone. Two? That makes me laugh a little bit. Many. I've always heard that revenge is a dish best served cold, and you know, it's quite true. There is a certain satisfaction in knowing that none of these people has any idea what's coming. That, because of the sins of their fathers, they are doomed to languish here at Cliffside forever, for as long as I remain. But more than that, the ones who tried to harm me will have the joy of seeing their own loved ones tortured. Ah, this was a long time coming. I do so love my role.*

I shook my head. I had no idea what this meant. It sounded like whoever had written this journal was referring to all of us, the people at Cliffside now. And then it hit me. This had to be Miss Penny's journal. And she, for whatever reason, had assembled us all here to avenge her sister Temperance's death. It made a kind of sense, and it was what Richard and I had talked about earlier—I remembered that clearly enough—but this bit about succession? What was that? It sort of sounded like she was writing about me and the succession of directorship at Cliffside. But she made it sound like it had happened several times, and I knew it hadn't. I was only the third director in Cliffside's history.

And what she wrote about dolls was just weird. Although poor Cassandra and Brynn had been made up like dolls and sat at their tea party table. And the dolls I found today from the dollhouse, harbingers of what was to come. I shivered as I thought—*Is this it? Is Miss Penny's ghost really responsible for this? Did she kill herself specifically to terrify us from beyond the grave?*

I looked again at the writing and my stomach flipped over. This was the same spidery scrawl of Miss Penny's suicide note and the message on Brynn's journal, I was certain. I didn't even have to compare them.

I was going to pick up the diary and take it to Nate and the others, but something stopped me. Something didn't feel quite right. I turned again to the page that had been opened when I first came to.

She mentioned being together with Richard at Cliffside. I thought back to what he had said about Chamomile having a crush on him. The words in the diary sounded like a child's fantasy, having a crush on a guy and imagining ending up with him.

But . . . the sister who'd had the crush was Chamomile, not Miss Penny. And either way, both of them were dead. So, how could either one of them have written this passage in the diary, and, for that matter, how could they have wound up with Richard here at Cliffside? I couldn't make sense of it. Was this Chamomile's journal, or Miss Penny's?

And that's when I noticed the pen in my own hand.

# CHAPTER 35

I dropped it as though it were on fire. What sort of strange and twisted game was this? I couldn't possibly have written those words. Not only would I never say those things, but it wasn't even remotely like my own penmanship.

Still. Everything inside of me was screaming the opposite. I picked up the pen and, with shaking hands, put it to paper.

> *You still haven't figured this out, you stupid girl. I thought more of you.*

I hadn't intended to write that. Not in the least. I was just going to write my name. I dropped the pen and scooped up the diary, standing up so fast my chair toppled backward. I raced through the room, turning on every light as I went, and got to the door. It was unlocked. I knew I had bolted it and closed the latch after Richard left—so who had unlocked it?

I didn't have time to wonder. I needed to get to Nate, and fast. I threw open the door and pounded down the hallway toward Diana's room. I saw the glow of light coming from its open door and I hurried inside. I was wholly unprepared for what I saw there.

The carpet had been taken up, the bed shoved to the side. On the floor, there was a huge pentagram drawn in black ink with candles burning all around it. A white, powdery substance was strewn in a circle around the outside of the star. And in the center, an armchair, where Diana was dozing. Nate was leaning against the wall, his arms folded.

"Hello, Norrie," he said, smiling at me.

"What's going on here?" I said, a little too loudly.

Diana's eyes fluttered open. "Oh, good," she said, stretching. "You're here."

"What is all this, Diana?" I said, flailing an arm toward the pentagram. "Is that permanent ink you put on the floor? I've had patience with your psychic stuff up until now, but this? Harriet is going to have a fit when she sees this. What will the next group of fellows think?"

"I thought you were leaving with us in the morning," she said, calmly. "Now there's going to be a new group of fellows?"

I shook my head, confused. She was right. I don't know why I said that. I don't know why I cared one bit about the floor at Cliffside or what Harriet would think of it. But I looked at that symbol on the floor and all I could think of was what a disgusting abomination it was.

I looked at Nate, hoping he could explain what was happening. His eyes were so kind, so sad.

"What have you got in your hand?" he asked me.

I held it out to him. "I found this just now," I said. "It's a diary."

He took it. "You found it just now, you said?"

"Yes."

"What happened when you found it?"

I looked from one to the other of them. "Wouldn't you like to know?"

I gasped, and my hand flew to my mouth. I hadn't intended to say anything of the kind. "I'm sorry," I said quickly.

"I know," he said. Then he turned to Diana. "Get the others. It's time."

She nodded and hurried out of the room.

"Time for what?" I asked him. "Nate, you're scaring me."

"Sit in the chair in the middle of the circle, Norrie," he said.

I felt cold all of a sudden. And very small. As though I wasn't part of my own body, not really. It felt like I was somewhere inside, but crowded. Cramped. Like I was shoved into a corner within my own skin.

"Hurry," he said, grabbing my hand and pulling me into the circle. As I stepped across the line, my whole body sizzled with pain.

"No!" I growled at him.

"It will protect you," he said, pushing me down into the seat. "Remember what I said to you, Eleanor. You are going to come out of this alive. So help me God." He looked upward. "And I do mean that literally."

"What is all this?" I asked him again.

"What happened when you found the diary?" he asked me again.

Something inside of me, something big, was fighting my every word, as though telling Nate what really happened in my room just now would put me in danger. But at the same time, I knew he was only there to help me. I trusted him. I was going to get those words out if it killed me.

"I came to," I said, finally. "I had been sleeping, but the next thing I knew, I was sitting at my desk. I had no idea how I got there. The diary was open on the desk in front of me. So I started to read it. It didn't make any sense. But then I recognized the handwriting. It was Miss Penny's."

Nate nodded. "And then?"

"And then I noticed I was holding the pen," I said, my words wavering. Tears began to well up in my eyes.

"Do you remember writing anything?" he asked.

"No," I squeaked out. "But something inside of me told me to write something in the book. So I did. You can see for yourself on the last entry page."

He opened the diary and flipped through the pages until he got there. He read for a moment and then turned his eyes back to me. "You must've been terrified," he said.

"I ran straight here," I said.

"Good girl," he said. "That was the right thing to do."

"What's happening to me? What is all this?"

Nate sighed and sank down to the floor just in front of my chair. "I have a story to tell you, Norrie. Now is the time. But you have to promise me something."

"What's that?"

"At no time are you to leave this chair," he said. "Once things are put in motion, if you go outside of this circle, you will be in real danger."

I just nodded, not knowing what else to do. But I knew one thing. I was not moving from that chair.

"You asked me, earlier tonight, if there was real evil in the world, remember?"

I nodded.

"And I said yes, and that we'd likely come face to face with it tonight?"

I nodded again.

"Well, now the time for that has come," Nate said.

I went ice cold. He didn't have to worry about me moving from the chair—I didn't think my limbs were operational at that point. My legs wouldn't have held me, even if I'd tried to stand. I was frozen to the spot.

"I have to warn you that this is going to get worse before it gets better," he went on.

"You're scaring me," I said, my voice trembling.

"I know," he said. "I'm scared, too. But I'm also mad as hell you have to go through this. And I promise you, Eleanor Harper. It *is* going to get better. You *are* going to get out of this unscathed. We are going to go through what we have to go through right now, and when the sun comes up you will leave Cliffside with everyone else and go on to live the happy, wonderful life you deserve." His voice broke and he choked back a sob.

"If we do this right, all of you, even these two"—Nate glanced over at Cassandra and Brynn, still laid out in the same positions—"will get out of here. Remember that, when everything inside you is telling you differently. Can you do that for me?"

"I will," I said. Then I thought of Richard and Henry. "Where are the men? Are they the ones Diana is getting? You said, 'get the others.'" My words were coming slowly now, slurred, as though I was having trouble controlling my own tongue.

He shook his head. "There's no reason they have to endure any of this."

"I still don't know what 'this' is," I said, weakly, as though the words themselves were a struggle. And all at once, I felt it again. That same bone tiredness I felt earlier, and had, off and on, since coming to Cliffside. And there was the headache again.

"Stay with me, Norrie," he said, loudly. "Don't go." He shook me by the shoulders and I felt my head flop back and forth like a rag doll's. At this, something in me smiled.

"I like dolls," I said, my head still at an odd angle. "And I like you, Doctor Davidson. I always liked you. So handsome. I was going to be your wife. All of the nurses had crushes on you. I killed one of them. The one you liked. Did you know that?"

My hand flew to my mouth. What in the name of God was I saying? I stared at Nate, wide-eyed.

Just then, Diana came back into the room with Harriet and Mr. Baines in tow.

"Harriet, look at this floor," I said to her, my head still flopping to the side, my voice high and singsongy, like a child's. I pointed at Diana. "She did it. I'm not going to take the blame."

Nate turned to Harriet. "It's in full swing right now. We're just in time."

"We're going to take care of it this time, by God," said Mr. Baines. "She's not going to get the best of us again."

"Yes, we are," Nate said. "Norrie knows she's not to leave that chair, under any circumstances. Right, Norrie?"

"Right, Norrie?" I parroted.

My vision was hazy and blurred, as though I was having trouble seeing out of my eyes. And—how can I describe what I was feeling? Like before, I felt crowded in my own body, as though someone else was in there with me. I felt diminished, as though whatever it was was pushing me farther and farther away. I could not easily say what I wanted to say, and my thoughts weren't my own.

"Can you hear me, Norrie?" Nate said, his voice loud and commanding.

It took every ounce of strength I had, but I nodded my head. "Yes, Nate," I squeaked out.

"Now I'm going to tell you the story I promised," he said, drawing another chair into the circle and sinking down into it. "Give me your hands. That will ensure we stay connected through this whole thing." I moved my hands toward him, and it was like I was moving thousand-pound weights. "I'm not going to let go, no matter what. Do you understand?"

I forced my head to nod.

"You stay with me," he said. "Promise me."

But I couldn't nod again. That took too much effort. So I blinked a couple of times. He got the message.

And then he began to speak.

# CHAPTER 36

"In the year 1945, a little girl was born right here at Cliffside," Nate said. "I delivered her myself. Mr. Dare hadn't intended for his wife to deliver their baby here at the sanatorium, but the baby had other plans, and came prematurely while Mrs. Dare was visiting her husband during his lunchtime.

"As soon as she came into this world, as soon as she breathed her first breath of life, she took the life of her mother," he said. "I have no other explanation than that. Mrs. Dare was fine one minute and dead the next."

Harriet dabbed at her eyes.

Nate went on. "We saw right away that something was wrong with the child. Not in terms of her health, which seemed fine to me, but it was her demeanor. There was a look in this child's eyes that I had not seen before. It scared me, to tell you the honest truth. But, that wasn't for me to judge, was it? I was simply the doctor. We took care of her here at the san for a time, until Mr. Dare and the girls had come out of the worst of their mourning, and then they took Temperance home."

He took a sip of water and glanced at Harriet. She nodded for him to continue.

"As she grew, odd things began to happen. People would fall ill and die after seeing her. Strange accidents took place, not only at their property in town, but here at Cliffside as well. And further, she was a sullen, strange little girl who, frankly, scared people with her gaze. It was as though she was boring into your very soul with those soulless eyes."

Every fiber of my being wanted to lash out at this, to leap from my chair and start scratching at him. But I held firm to my promise. It took all of my strength, but I would not leave that chair if it killed me. And I had the feeling it just might.

"What we didn't know then, but know all too well now, is that Mrs. Dare had given birth to what can only be described as a demon," he went on. "You told me that Pete at the boathouse, the man you thought was crazy, said that Death himself lived at Cliffside."

I tried to nod. I did remember that, somewhere deep inside.

"He was nearly right. Death herself lived here, ever since that morning in 1945. And still does. Until today. It all is going to end today."

"So you say," I said to him, smiling broadly.

He went on as though he hadn't heard me. "Years passed. All of us who worked at Cliffside, and many who didn't, understood that Temperance was a very disturbed little girl, but we didn't realize how much until one day, Chester Dare came to me and told me, in confidence, he had to get Temperance away from his other daughters, Penny and Milly. She seemed to get pleasure out of their pain, accidents were happening daily, and he was afraid she was going to hurt them, badly."

At this, I laughed.

"So he brought her here, under the guise that she had TB," he said. "I knew, in short order, that she didn't. I didn't know it then, but I think he hoped she would contract it and pass away, God help him. He did it to save his other two girls."

"Daddy would never do that," I spat.

"But she didn't get sick," he continued. "Just the opposite. She would lead the children on nightly raids. They were forever stirring up trouble. It became a madhouse. If it had just been a group of unruly children, that would have been one thing. But patients were dying left and right, much more than before."

At this, Nate shuddered.

"A few of the patients caught on before I did. The look in her eyes—it was terrifying to people. The other patients were afraid of her. Many requested isolation and even threatened to leave if I couldn't keep her away from them. But I was a man of science, and she was just a little girl—a strange, troubled little girl, but a little girl nonetheless."

*So Brynn's grandmother was correct,* I thought. Mine was now a small voice, somewhere deep inside. But it was still there.

"It took me a while to put two and two together, but finally I saw that people would die after an interaction with Temperance, especially if she didn't like them. And it wasn't just patients. Animals, too. It was the day I saw her playing out in the garden with a group of squirrels that convinced me. I remember looking at her through the window as she fed them. They'd come to her, one after another for a peanut or whatever she had. It was such a nice sight, I thought. Maybe this little girl wasn't so bad after all. But later, after my rounds, I saw she was still there in the garden, but the squirrels were all dead. She was playing with them as though they were stuffed animals."

"Ashes, ashes, they all fall down," I sang, a gurgle of laughter rising up.

"That's just what she was singing when I saw her with the squirrels that day," Nate said. "I pleaded with Chester to take her out of Cliffside. But he refused, finally confiding his fears. The girl was pure evil, he told me, and God help us, we had to do something."

He took a deep breath and continued. "But, I fear that in the doing, we set something even more dark and evil in motion, unleashing . . ." He stopped to gather himself, his eyes brimming with tears.

"You did what you thought was best at the time," Mr. Baines piped up. "We all did. None of us knew."

This jolted me back into myself for a moment. "You were here back then, Mr. Baines?" I asked him.

He returned that query with a smile. "Yes, Miss Harper, I was," he said. "And if I may say, it's good to hear from you right about now."

The timeline didn't quite make sense to me, considering his age, but I didn't bother to even wonder about it. Nothing at Cliffside made sense; that was one thing I knew.

"You're going to tell me about the nurse giving her the injection," I said, but at the last word, my voice broke, and I couldn't continue.

Nate nodded and cleared his throat. "The year was 1952. Poor Brynn's grandmother had it about right. But not exactly. I decided—"

"We all decided," Harriet interjected.

"We all decided," Nate repeated, and he stopped to smile at her.

"You know what we decided, Norrie," he went on. "Temperance had to be taken care of."

I felt that same fury bubbling up inside of me, willing me out of that chair. But I battled it and held tight to the armrests. I would not move, not if I could help it.

"And so I filled a hypo full of morphine, and gave it to my most trusted nurse, Sarah Dalton," he said.

I opened my eyes wide, hoping he would catch on to my question.

He did. "Yes. Henry's mother. And no, to answer your next question, I'm not his father." He glanced up at Harriet, and she nodded.

"When I learned about the pregnancy," Harriet said, clucking, "I knew full well who the father was. It was our chef at the time. Henri Bertrand. Married. Sarah left here without telling him about the baby. Despite the fact that she loved him very much, she didn't want to break up his marriage."

Somewhere deep inside, I hoped I could tell Henry he was named after a French chef. I thought he'd enjoy knowing that.

"The reason I had Sarah do it instead of just doing it myself? I knew Temperance would see me coming—she began to suspect me early on—but she probably wouldn't suspect my nurse. So she gave her the injection."

"Sir, if I can break in?" Mr. Baines interjected, clearing his throat.

"Please," Nate said.

"That's when I got involved," Mr. Baines said. "We had a patient here who was nearly ready to go home, Archie Abbott. We gave him the keys to the Bentley and had him standing by to take Sarah to the train station. After doing what she did, we knew she wouldn't be safe, if it didn't take hold, so to speak. So we got her out of here right away. Mrs. Baines knew about the pregnancy—Sarah couldn't have stayed on anyway—and insisted. She had her bags packed for her, and as soon as she gave that infernal injection, Archie was there to spirit Sarah away. She was off the property and on the train before Temperance actually died."

Nate nodded. "It probably saved her life. And enabled Henry's. But now we come to the part of the story that takes an even darker turn."

# CHAPTER 37

“Temperance died,” Nate said. “But the strangeness, the sickness, the terror she carried in her wake didn’t die with her.”

A chortle of laughter bubbled up inside of me and spewed forth, as much as I tried to contain it.

Nate went on as though he hadn’t even heard it. “Chester Dare made a good show of mourning, but he privately expressed his gratitude and relief that it was all over. But we soon learned it wasn’t over. It continued, long after that evil little girl was buried in the ground. None of us could figure it out, until Chamomile came to visit me one summer afternoon.

“I was surprised to see her at my door. I hadn’t seen her since the day Temperance died—she and her sister happened to be on the san grounds on a rare visit to their father that day. But in any case, a few weeks had passed since the death, and there Chamomile was on my doorstep. I was delighted to see her. She was always such a sunny child. I let her in.

“‘And what can I do for you, my good Miss Dare?’ I said to her. She took my hand in hers and, quick as a flash, I felt something cut my palm. She kissed the abrasion and looked into my eyes, smiling a broad smile.

“‘You can die, Doctor Davidson,’ she said.

"That's when I looked into her inky, soulless eyes and realized it was not the sweet Chamomile I had come to know and love standing before me. It was Temperance. I had no idea how, but it was Temperance.

"She turned on her heel and flounced away, and that was that. I fell to the ground, and after a few spasms—quite painful, I'll have you know—I was floating above my own body. As quickly as that. At that moment, I felt astonishment, regret, and above all, anger. This horrid little girl had won.

"I drifted out of my house and was completely bowled over to find scores of souls, like me, just meandering around the grounds. I spotted Archie Abbott. He had died shortly after returning from the train station that awful day. Just fell to the ground as soon as he stepped out of the car.

"He was surprised and dismayed to see me. 'Oh, Doc,' he said, shaking his head. 'Not you, too.'

"'What's going on here, Arch?' I asked him. 'Am I dead?'

"'I'm sorry to be the one to break it to you, Doc, but welcome to the great beyond,' he told me. 'Only for us, this is all there is. She keeps us here somehow.'

"'Who?' I asked him.

"'You know.' He nodded. 'Everyone who has died on this property since she was born is still here,' he told me. 'I don't know what she is, but she is not of this earth. And until she's gone, none of us is going anywhere.'

"'But I don't get it,' I said to him. 'I filled the vial that killed her. Her body is in the ground. Shouldn't she be floating around here just like us?'

"He shook his head. 'That's only for those of us with souls. Word on the street is that this little girl was born Death incarnate. Spawned by the property itself, on account of all the dying that's been done here. That's what people are saying. You've gotta admit, we've seen our share of death here at Cliffside. Look at all of us. And that's just in the years since this demon was born. I guess it decided to take up residence, permanent-like.'

"He continued, 'What happened to you, Doc? How did you end up here?'

"'Chamomile,' I told him. 'But when she came into the house, it was like I was looking at Temperance. As though that sweet little girl wasn't there at all.'

"He nodded. 'She wasn't,' he said. 'Temperance has taken her place.'

"'Taken her place?' I parroted. 'I don't get it. Whose place?'

"'Chamomile's,' he said, lowering his voice and shifting his eyes back and forth.

"'In her body, you mean? Temperance is inside Chamomile?'

"He shrugged his shoulders. 'That's what people are saying.'

"'How is that even possible?' I asked him.

"'That, I can't tell you,' he said. 'But what I've heard is, it's a jump.'"

At this something deep in my core jolted. I stood up from the chair and moved toward Nate. But the four of them—Nate, Diana, Harriet, and Mr. Baines—were all on me in a second, pushing me back into my chair.

"Do you think we should tie her down?" Mr. Baines asked Nate.

He shook his head. "I'd hate to do that. Let's give her one more chance." He turned to me. "Norrie, remember what I said. No matter what happens, do not get out of that chair."

I sneered at him, despite my best efforts to smile.

"Where was I?" he said. "Oh yes. The jump." He turned to Diana. "I think this is where you come in."

Diana cleared her throat and crept toward me, kneeling in front of my chair and taking my hands in hers. "This is going to scare you," she said. "But we're all here. Remember that."

I managed a nod.

"I am Diana Cooper," she said. "I know that was in doubt a few hours ago, but I think that was Temperance trying to have me thrown out of here."

"Aren't you clever," I said. "Of course there was nobody on the phone. Terror is so easy."

She went on, as though I hadn't spoken. "Something you don't know about me, that few people know, is that in addition to being a poet, I'm also a demonologist."

I raised my eyebrows.

"Call it a hobby," she said, smiling at my reaction. "It's a little dramatic, I know. But hearing everything I've heard from Nate, I'm convinced that Miss Penny—somewhere deep inside, the real Miss Penny—set up this session when I was going to be here, because she knew what was going down. We'll talk more about this in a bit, but I'm here now, and I'm going to help make sense of this, and then make it go away. We're telling all of this to you, Norrie, because we need you to be strong and present to fight.

"Nate was talking about this 'jump' just a moment ago," she went on. "I'm sure you're curious about that, and now I'd like to explain it to you. It's what happens when a soul, or a spirit, in this case a very evil one, migrates into another body at the point of death."

My insides were roiling. I wanted nothing more than to fly out of my chair and set on these idiots. I hated them at that point. But I kept my place.

"You can't ask the questions I know you want to ask, so I'll take the liberty of explaining them to you," she went on. "What happens to the soul, and the consciousness of that body, when another consciousness jumps into it? The answer is, it gets squashed to the side. Almost like a vessel that is half full of sand gets a whole lot more sand poured into it. There's not a lot more room in the vessel."

I managed a nod.

"It starts little by little at first, the new consciousness taking over. There are periods of blackouts. Followed by periods of complete lucidity. Headaches. Dreams. Oftentimes, the new host body has no idea what's occurring until it's too late."

I went cold. It sounded just like what had been happening to me. I wanted to tell her that, but instead, I shook my head, violently. Host body? I struggled mightily to get the words out, to ask the question I absolutely needed to ask.

"Is this thing inside of me?"

Nate came back into the circle then and took my hands. His face was filled with kindness and compassion.

"Yes," he said. "And what we're doing here, is getting it out."

That same fury raged up from within me. "Who are you to do this? How dare you?"

"I speak only to Norrie," he said. "And we have more of the story to tell her."

"I don't care about your story."

"I know that only too well," he said. "But Norrie does. And she's going to hear it."

I struggled to the surface. "But why now?" I asked him. "Why didn't you tell me this when I first arrived, to prevent all of this from happening?"

"It was too late," he said. "And also, when I saw that Diana was here and could sense what she was, I saw an opportunity for myself and the others. I saw the people who were assembled for this session, and I knew we had a unique opportunity to rid ourselves, and this world, of this monster."

I blinked, unable to respond.

"I suspected immediately when Miss Penny died, but I knew for sure when you came asking for olives," Harriet said. "They were Temperance's favorite food."

"Back to it, then," Nate said, turning to Harriet. "Where was I? Chamomile?" She nodded.

He smiled at me and went on, still keeping hold of my hands. "So now, here we all were, stuck at Cliffside, knowing that somehow, this demon was inside Chamomile. Nobody could do anything about it."

"But to be fair, for many years, nothing much happened," Harriet piped up. "TB was cured, the patients went home, and the Dare family came to live here on the property. All was well, for a time."

"For years, in fact," Nate said. "It was as though Chamomile's spirit was so strong, Temperance's evil couldn't really take over, not completely. We started to hope it was over, and yet, we were still tied here. But slowly, death started to seep in."

Harriet nodded her head. "It did, that. She couldn't help herself. I think Miss Penny suspected something, but what was she to do? Chamomile was her sister."

Harriet continued. "Poor Mr. Dare had no idea that this monster he had tried to rid us all of was living inside his other, sweet daughter, so, oblivious, he turned his attention to the arts. It had been his wife's greatest joy."

Mr. Baines coughed. "It was Chamomile who convinced him to turn this place into a refuge for artists and writers," he said. "We're being honest here. Let's be honest about that, too. We all know she wanted a steady stream of humanity coming to Cliffside. Not quite as much as in the old days, but people nonetheless. She had to prey on somebody."

Harriet and Nate exchanged a look, and then Nate spoke. "He's right," he said. "It's not like there were murders at every session, but a good deal of people died after coming here. It's almost like Temperance would attach part of herself to these poor fellows and go home with them, festering into an illness until they died, shortly after returning home."

I shuddered.

"But when Richard Banks came, all of that changed," Harriet piped up. "It was apparent to anyone with eyes that Chamomile wanted him for herself."

I struggled to speak. "He was sure she had a crush on him," I said, finally.

"He was the catalyst, to be sure," Harriet said. "She followed him all around the property like a puppy. I had never before seen her do anything like that."

"I was nearby when Chester Dare realized his daughter had feelings for this young man," Nate said. "He became furious and told her it was unseemly. She had had many inappropriate . . . affairs, let's just say, over the years that he'd had to cover up for the sake of propriety."

"Even a baby out of wedlock when she was much younger," Harriet piped up. "She had no interest in raising it, of course, so Mr. Dare asked me to take it to the orphanage. It nearly killed him to do it, his own grandchild, but he knew that child had no chance at life if it stayed at Cliffside."

"Back to Richard Banks," Nate said. "Chamomile was decades older than he was, and that was the last straw for Chester. He told her in no uncertain terms that she was to stay away from the poor boy. She reared up—I had never seen anything like it. Her face was like that of a devil. I can't even describe it. A horrible, disgusting thing, and Chester Dare was frozen to the spot, nearly dead himself. He knew he had to tell Richard to leave.

"They all said their goodbyes, and Richard drove off," Nate told me. "I watched as Chamomile stomped off, and Chester hurried into the house. After what he had seen, I knew that he knew then what was inside of his daughter. The next morning they were both dead."

"Chamomile engineered it," Mr. Baines added. "I saw the whole thing. I have no idea how she got him into the car, but she somehow forced him to drive the two of them right off the cliff. It was no accident."

I somehow summoned the strength to speak. "Chamomile died there."

Diana nodded. "She did. At the point of death, the demon jumped to Miss Penny."

My look of confusion must have caught her eye. "These kinds of spirits, Eleanor, don't have bodies," she said. "They jump from one to the other, muscling the residing soul out of the way. In extreme cases, the host soul gets swallowed up."

I knew they were all speaking the truth. I could feel it inside of me, roiling, full of hate, trying to take control. But I was determined not to let it. Nate said I was going to come out of this alive, and if I had anything to say about it, I'd prove him right. As much as it tried to muscle me out of the way, I shoved back.

"I knew Miss Penny was up to something," Harriet went on. "I heard the calls she made to Richard Banks, trying to lure him back to Cliffside. But I couldn't figure out why. Miss Penny's body had aged into that of an old woman. She could never have hoped to attract him to her. But then, she got an idea. It wasn't until I heard her on the telephone, calling your boss at the newspaper and demanding he fire you, that I began to suspect what was going on.

"I knew she had had her eyes on you for years," Harriet said. "She kept tabs on you, read all of your articles. She had me clip them out of the newspaper. Temperance, within Miss Penny, chose you, Miss Harper, and made sure you were available when the time came to succeed her. She knew you'd be drawn in when you heard she was retiring."

I nodded, remembering finding the file of my clippings. Had it really been just earlier today? It felt like years had passed since then.

"But why?" I said, struggling to force the words out.

Harriet looked from Mr. Baines to Nate and then back again. Nate nodded.

"You were the one she chose to carry on the Dare family legacy because she believed you belonged at Cliffside," Harriet said. "And she was right about that. You, Eleanor, are the baby I brought to the orphanage. Chamomile Dare was your mother."

# CHAPTER 38

Somewhere deep inside, I was trembling. *Me, a Dare daughter?* That couldn't be true.

"How could you possibly know that?" I asked her.

"I knew the first minute I laid eyes on you, and so did Penelope," Harriet said. "I think she started hatching this plan way back then. It took her this long to put the pieces together, but through that connection, she was able to pull you here."

I thought about what she was saying. It was true that I had long felt a kinship to Cliffside even before being here twenty years earlier. And I had idolized the Dare sisters growing up. I had thought about the place often, dreamed about it. Could it be that Temperance was pulling me back, all of that time? Could Harriet possibly be right?

Harriet answered my unspoken question. "She created this mystery for you and the others to solve, something that would terrify you all, doling it out in small doses. She wanted revenge on the others, but she wanted Richard Banks here to be with you—a rightful Dare—until it was time for her to jump to the next in line, likely after you had both grown old and Richard had died."

I could feel it then, bubbling up inside of me. Who were they to try to ruin the plan I had so painstakingly put into place? It was going so beautifully, every step of the way! Richard was falling for me just as I knew he would. He had said so.

It was then, in that moment, sitting in the chair in front of Nate, Mr. Baines, Harriet, and Diana, that I knew. They were right. I remembered it all.

My first day at Cliffside, a short while after Miss Penny had left me to unpack, I had curled up before the fireplace and stared into the flames when the phone in my room rang.

"Eleanor, dear," she said, her voice slurred and slow, "will you come up to my room, please? Right now? It's on the third floor."

"Of course," I told her. "I'll be there right away."

As I put the receiver down, I was wrapped in that same, familiar fear that had been plaguing me for months, as if something was coming, something bad, but I didn't know what it was. It was as if a tendril of evil was reaching out to me and tickling, just a bit.

I pushed it out of my mind, left my room, and headed to the third floor to find Miss Penny. She sounded out of sorts. I hoped nothing was wrong. I climbed the stairs and found myself in the empty ballroom, her bedroom door to one side. *Creepy,* I thought. As I stepped into the room, I noticed how chilly it was, but I couldn't really concern myself with that at the moment. I just put my head down and hurried across the room to Miss Penny's door.

I pushed it open to find her on her bed, her eyes nearly closed. "Come here, dear," she said. "Come here."

I moved to her bedside and knelt down as she extended a hand to me. I clasped it.

"Should I get you a doctor, Miss Penny?" I asked. "Are you ill?"

"No," she said, her voice thin and papery. "It is how it should be."

With that, she smiled a broad, unnerving smile and opened her eyes wide, squeezing my hand with what seemed to be all of her might.

The next thing I knew, I was standing above her, making up her face. It wouldn't do to have her looking like death warmed over. A little lipstick. A little eyeliner. There! All better. Then I slipped an envelope into her hands. I simply turned and walked away, humming a little tune. In the ballroom, I paused before crossing the empty floor to the toy box, running my hand along its lid.

And then I walked down the stairs, back to my room, and closed the door behind me. I was moving, it seemed, in slow motion, as though I couldn't quite get used to my limbs and arms, like an astronaut in a space suit, in zero gravity for the first time.

I sat at my desk, pulled out a sheet of paper, and began to write. Finished with that missive, I folded it up, put it in an envelope, and slipped it under the covers of my bed. And then I sat down and waited. I knew it wouldn't be long before Eleanor took over again. It sometimes took days for me to be fully in control, and Penelope had put up quite a struggle. I was glad to be rid of her once and for all.

I loved this young, new body and couldn't get enough of using it, stretching my new legs, being active, walking in the woods.

The next thing I remembered, I was using my key to enter Brynn's room. That twit. And the book she was writing! Scandalous! Father had nothing to do with it. I wouldn't have her bringing Cliffside down, its reputation in tatters. She'd be my first victim, but in the meantime, I tore up the journal and wrote my message on the pages, a giggle escaping my lips. This would terrify them.

Then the scene shifted. I was slipping out of my room and padding down the hall to Brynn's. I knocked softly at the door.

She opened it a crack. "Oh," she said. "It's you."

I smiled at her. "Will you come with me for a minute?" I asked her. "I need your help with something upstairs."

She sighed and folded her arms. "I was just about to head down to breakfast."

"It'll only take a minute," I said. "I have something to show you that I just know you're going to love."

I led her upstairs, singing a little tune to myself. When we got to the top of the stairs and took a step into the ballroom, she stopped.

"This is creepy," she said, looking back and forth. She had no idea.

"Nonsense," I said, my mouth curling up into a broad grin. "Come on. It's over here."

I took her by the hand. It was so easy, really. When we got to the bedroom door, I ushered her inside and shut it, my back to her.

"Ew," I heard her say. "What is this?"

"Your worst nightmare, my dear." And it was then I turned around, showing her my true self. The very face of death, filled with the pain and suffering of all that I had taken, my eyes, black as night, jagged peaks where teeth might have been.

She was frozen in terror, but as I rushed toward her she tried to let out a scream—she was so terrified, she didn't make a sound—and fell to the ground. I gave her a few kicks. Nothing. Her eyes were open, her mouth contorted into what looked like a smile. She was still breathing. I hadn't scared her to death as I had planned—maybe I was a little off my game—but I could use this, nonetheless.

"I'd like some tea, how about you?" I said to her. And I dragged her over to the tea table and settled her on a chair. I scowled at her. "This won't do," I said. "You look like a dead fish. But you're as pretty as a doll."

I crossed the room and opened a dresser drawer, fishing out a makeup kit. "There," I said, after painting her lips and her eyes. "Much better. Now, how about that tea?"

I poured for her—you always serve guests first—and was just taking my first sip when it occurred to me that I should really get downstairs. Richard, my beloved Richard, would be wondering where I was. I couldn't let him find me like this. So I shook off the mask of death I had shown to poor Brynn and slipped out of the room and down the stairs.

The scene shifted again, and after a little play with the dolls—I do so love terrifying people—I saw myself walking through the house toward the kitchen. It was there I found Cassandra.

"I was just trying to rustle up something to eat," she said. "Hungry?" She had no idea.

"I'm glad I ran into you," I said to her. "I think I figured out the key to this whole thing. I don't want to tell the others yet, but I've got something to show you."

"Oh?" she asked, clearly intrigued.

"Come on," I told her. "We have to hurry."

I led her up the backstairs to the third floor.

"You're kidding," she said. "I'm not crazy about this."

"Don't worry," I said, talking quickly. I might lose her. She wasn't dim-witted like Brynn. "Listen, I found a link to your grandfather."

"Really?"

"Yes," I said, leading her across the floor toward the room. "You know that he was a patient here in 1952, but you don't know that he actually drove the nurse—who was Henry's mother, by the way—away from the property after she killed poor Temperance."

"The nurse was Henry's mother?" she said. "Whoa."

Indeed. I shut the door to the bedroom behind her.

It was then that troublesome Archie Abbott appeared. I'd known he was here somewhere, of course, but hadn't seen him in a long while. I'd had a feeling he'd materialize when his granddaughter arrived on the property, and I was right.

Cassandra's eyes grew wide.

"You're not going to hurt her, Temperance," he growled at me.

"Oh, but I think I am," I said, and he flew back across the room and through the door. What a dolt, confronting me alone.

"What just happened?" Cassandra said, her voice shaking. "Who was that?"

"The thirst for revenge is a powerful thing, Cassandra," I said to her. "It can live inside you for years. Decades, even. But when it comes time to enact that revenge, the wait makes it all the sweeter. Don't you agree?" I raised my voice. "Archie, don't you agree? Payback time."

He materialized between me and his granddaughter. "You'll have to go through me first, you old witch," he said. "Cassie, run. Now. Get everybody out of here."

Cassandra flew to the door and opened it. She might have gotten through it and away from me, blowing my whole plan to smithereens. But I just said her name. She turned around and made the mistake of looking at me. "Norrie, why are you doing this?"

"This is why," I said, showing my true face again.

She didn't scream. She just slumped to the floor. At first I wondered if she'd had a heart attack, but no. She was in the same state as the first one. The others were so terrified by my little tea party setup, I decided to try it again. I dragged her back into the bedroom and then through the little door. And so that's how I left her, before making my way back down to my office.

And the others were none the wiser. They were such dolts. This was going to be easier than I had thought.

"Are you remembering?" Harriet asked, bringing me back into the present, back into the room with her and the others. "Can you remember what you did while she was in control?"

I nodded.

"And you're still there, Norrie," Nate said, his voice loud and commanding. "You haven't left us?"

I nodded again.

"Okay, then," Diana said, clearing her throat. "That's very good news. It's time we get this done."

# CHAPTER 39

They all gathered around me in a circle then, Nate, Mr. Baines, and Harriet with Diana facing me.

That's when I noticed she was holding a large sprig of burning sage in one hand.

"You know that's a ridiculous waste of time," something inside me said. "Sage. It's ghost-busting for dummies. That never works."

She steeled her eyes. "Oh, yes, it does. And I'm here to call you by your true name, your first name, Temperance Dare, and to send you back to whatever realm of suffering and despair spawned you before you take another life."

"Good luck with that," I sneered at her.

"It's not only us who are joining forces," she said. "It is the granddaughter of Alice Kendrick, who initially called you out in her journal. It is the granddaughter of Archie Abbott, who worked with Doctor Davidson to rid the world of you."

"They're not very lively right now," I said. "I don't think they'll be of much help."

And then, I—she—unleashed it, the face of death. I could feel it overtaking my own face, erupting from my every pore. Nate, Harriet, and Mr. Baines stood firm, but Diana jumped back, just for a second.

"I know what you are," she hissed at me. "I am not afraid of you, and you will not win this."

"Oh, but you're wrong," I said, a smile creeping onto my face. "You force me out of this one, I'll just jump into the next one. Maybe you. Maybe a man this time. That would be interesting."

"You won't be able to do that," Diana said. "Because your host body isn't going to die."

I stared at Nate, wide-eyed. He nodded at me. "She's got that right."

"How are you so sure the host body needs to die for me to jump?" I hissed back at her.

"Because I've spent my life learning about *things* like you," Diana said. "Knowledge is power, and I've got it, right now. Your sister, Penelope Dare, somewhere deep inside of that body, knew it, and set up this session to rid the world of you. It was her last act. She was a true heroine."

Inside, I fought as hard as I could, and I could feel the internal struggle of good against evil, of my soul against the demon that had taken up residence within me. I prayed with every ounce of strength I had for help, for a legion of warriors who would help me break free of this thing.

Diana, seemingly sensing what I was doing, opened her arms wide and called out, "It is time. We need the help of all who are trapped here."

It took a moment, but then I saw a shape appear, and then another, and then another, and then the room was filled with spirits, some well-defined, others shadowy. But I could clearly make out Miss Penny and Chamomile standing next to an older man—Chester Dare. Soon they were as clear and solid as Nate was. I saw another man, obviously Cassandra's grandfather, standing next to her and stroking her hair.

The Dare family stepped forward, hand in hand.

"We have waited many long years for this day," Chester said, extending his hand. And then I noticed another woman coming into view. She must be Temperance's mother.

"I knew, deep inside, where my soul still clung on, cowering in a corner, that you would be the one to help us," Penelope said to me.

"And you," she said, turning to Diana. "When you applied, I knew it was finally time to stop fighting her plan. I knew letting it come to fruition would be the end of her."

"When I got one inkling of what was going on here, I knew it, too," Diana said. "I'm going to do everything I can to make that happen."

I could see her clasping hands with Nate and Harriet. She cleared her throat and began.

"We stand together here as one," Diana shouted, "a force for good, to banish the evil that is Temperance Dare from this world. Every soul you have wronged is here, standing against you."

I could feel it inside, bubbling and churning, pacing as if it was hitting back and forth against my insides.

Everyone in the room seemed to speak as one, a chorus. "We now call upon the legion of all that's holy to join with us to banish this evil, forever."

All at once, the room filled with a blinding light. I screamed—the pain seared through me like a hot knife, slicing away at me, inside. I writhed against it. "Help me, Nate!" I called out. "If you love me, make it stop!"

But he did nothing. I lunged from the chair and tried to fly at him, but the circle—whatever it was on the outside of it—stopped me as though I had hit a brick wall. I reeled back, a shriek of frustration and despair coming from my lips.

And the pain went on, inside. The room began to shake, books fell from their shelves, lamps toppled, and still the pain went on, as though it was eating away at my very soul.

Diana was shouting: "Now with the power of love from the past and the present surrounding Eleanor Harper, and all the souls you have wronged in the past in attendance and speaking as one, we, buoyed by our shared conviction, command you to leave this woman, leave this place, and leave this earth. In the name of God and all that's holy, I banish you and command that you leave."

Plaster began to fall from the ceiling. Windows cracked. Long fissures snaked their way through the walls, as though they were aging and crumbling right in front of my eyes. I heard great cracks and booms from inside the house.

I was growling and hissing, but then I saw Henry, and then Richard, burst into the room.

"What in the name of Jesus—" Richard started but then fell silent at the sight of me, there in the chair, and at the sight of everyone in the room.

"What have you done to her, man?" he bellowed at Nate, lunging for him. Nate simply put up a hand and stopped Richard in his tracks.

"I thought the sedative I gave both of you would have kept you asleep so you didn't have to see this."

"See what? That you've got some sick and twisted group ritual going on?" Richard said, gesturing toward the crowd. "Who are these people?"

"Stop him, my love," I hissed, from somewhere inside of me. "He's hurting me."

But Richard just stared at me. And then turned back to Nate.

Diana broke in, addressing both Richard and Henry. "I'm glad both of you are here," she said. "Norrie is going to need your help to get through this."

"Through what?" Henry squeaked out. "What in God's name is going on here?"

Diana looked at him square in the eye. "Whatever has been haunting Cliffside is now inside of Eleanor," she said. "We have assembled to get it out."

"Who has assembled?" Richard broke in, his eyes scanning the room.

Nate said, "All of those who have been hurt by this evil in the past. We can count you as one of our number now." His eyes shifted to Henry's. "And you, too. We need you to join with us now."

Richard's eyes grew wide as he saw Miss Penny and Chamomile.

"Yes," Chamomile said. "It's us. We have never formally met you, Richard. But please stand with us now."

Henry grabbed Richard's hand. He extended the other to Miss Penny. Richard did the same. Everyone, one by one, clasped hands. My head whirled around, and I noticed I was surrounded by a ring of people—or spirits—all holding hands. Intertwined into one.

Diana cleared her throat and repeated her refrain. "Now with the power of love from the past and the present surrounding Eleanor Harper, and all the souls you have wronged in the past in attendance and speaking as one, we, buoyed by our shared conviction, command you to leave this woman, leave this place, and leave this earth. In the name of God and all that's holy, I cast you out and command that you leave."

The tempest was raging inside of me, like a caged animal.

Diana looked around the room. "Everyone, say it with me." And the entire room of souls, living and departed, spoke as one. "We command you to leave this woman, leave this place, and leave this earth. In the name of God and all that's holy, we cast you out!"

I let out one last great roar of pain, and then it was over. I opened my eyes and looked around the room.

"Norrie?" Richard said to me. "Are you all right?"

"I think so," I said. "I think it's gone. I can't feel it anymore."

It was then I noticed the curtain on the other side of the room was on fire.

"Where's a fire extinguisher?" Richard shouted at Nate.

But Nate just shook his head. "We need to get the living out of here right away," he said. "We can't waste time trying to save this place. Let it burn."

Richard moved toward me, but Nate grabbed his arm, casting an eye toward Henry. "You get these two out of here," he said, gesturing to Brynn and Cassandra, who were still out cold on the bed.

"On our own?" Henry said. "I don't know if I can—"

But Archie Abbott stopped his words. "Don't worry, mate. This one's mine. It's personal." And he picked up Cassandra, as easily as if she were a feather, and walked through the door.

Richard was on me in a second, taking my hands and pulling me up from my chair. My legs were like limp noodles. I wanted only to put my arms around him, but Nate intervened.

"No," he said to Richard. "You need to get Brynn out of here. I'll take care of Eleanor."

Richard scowled at him, but when Nate scooped me up into his arms, Richard did as he asked.

As the house crumbled and shattered and burned all around us, Nate ran, with me in his arms, down the hallway, down the grand staircase, into the foyer, and finally, thankfully, out the door.

We stopped on the lawn—rapt by the sight before us. As Cliffside burned, a bright light was beaming down over the calm, glassy lake. Stars shone in the sky, but this light was brighter, more beautiful, illuminating the dark water with a shaft of shimmering light. Nate set me down near the others—Harriet and her husband, the Dares, and all the fellows.

I watched as, one after another, the souls captured here at Cliffside, doomed to wander this property until Death itself had left, moved toward that light. It was proof that Temperance was truly gone. One by one, they disappeared into the brightness.

"Unbelievable," Diana murmured. "It's so beautiful."

And it was. Richard's eyes were brimming with tears; Henry was staring, open-mouthed. We all knew we needed to get Brynn and Cassandra to the hospital, but we couldn't tear ourselves away, not just yet.

Chester Dare was standing near Nate and Diana, and put a hand on each of their backs. "It seems that she's gone, for good this time," he said. "The words *thank you* are insufficient, yet they're all that I have."

Nate smiled. "We've been fighting this fight for years, my friend," he said. "Now our work is done. It took a few strong women to help us pull it off."

"It was my pleasure," Diana said, beaming.

And then Chamomile was standing before me. She wrapped her arms around me and pulled me close. "There is a whole lifetime of things I want to say to you, Eleanor," she said, her voice soft in my ear. "Had circumstances been different, we would have had that lifetime together. Temperance took that from both of us." She pulled back to look into my face. "I am so very proud of the woman you have become. And I'll be watching out for you."

I couldn't speak. So it was true, then. I was Chamomile Dare's daughter.

Chester turned to his wife and daughters, who, like all of us, were rapt by the light above the lake. "Well, girls," he said. "This chapter has finally, thankfully come to a close. Who knows what the next one will bring?"

"I think we're about to find out, Father," Penelope said to him, a wide grin on her face. "Goodbye, Eleanor. And thank you."

And the four of them held hands and disappeared.

I turned to Harriet and Mr. Baines, wondering what would become of them now that Cliffside was in flames, but their expressions stopped the question I was about to ask. They were beaming at each other.

"Is it time we get going, too, Mr. Baines?" Harriet said to her husband.

"Long since time, Mrs. Baines. Long since time."

She turned to me. "I'll be watching, too," she said. "You went through hell to set us all free. All of us, make no mistake, are grateful to you. I wish you all the best in whatever life has in store for you, darling girl. Live it well. Make the most of every day."

Mr. Baines extended his arm to her and she took it, and I watched in wonder as they floated off toward the light together.

I noticed Archie Abbott, still holding Cassandra. He shook his head in answer to the question I didn't pose. "I'm not going anywhere until she's taken care of," he said. "I'll get her to the hospital myself, now that I can leave the property. After that, we'll see."

I felt an ache in my heart as I turned to Nate. "Are you going, too?"

He encircled me in a hug. "Despite all of this madness, I'm so grateful I got the chance to meet you," he said, his eyes brimming with tears. "I wish so badly it had been under different circumstances, that all of this hadn't happened to you. I wish we could have sat together on my front porch, laughing and having cocktails for years to come while you ran Cliffside. More than that, I wish we had lived in the same time. But it wasn't to be. I know that."

"All that you've done for me, I can't ever—"

He touched my lips and shook his head. "I'd do it all again, and more, to get you away from that monster. I love you, Eleanor, and I always will."

I looked up at him through tear-soaked eyes, my heart breaking. "This can't be the end. I can't not see you again. You mean too much to me."

He ran a hand through my hair. "I'd love to stay and do everything in my power to muscle that other guy out of your life," he said. "But that wouldn't be fair to you, Norrie. We both know it. And there's someplace else I'm supposed to be." He flashed that impish grin of his, one last time. "But you never know. If you hear something go bump in the night, it just might be me."

Just then, I saw an enormous black-and-white dog bounding across the lawn toward us. Nate bent down to ruffle his thick fur. "Ranger," he murmured, his eyes glistening. "I haven't seen you in years, boy."

He looked back at me. "I think my escort has arrived," he said, smiling brighter than I had ever seen him smile. "I'll be seeing you, Norrie Harper." With the dog leading the way, I watched Nate vanish into the light, waving to me. I watched until the light, too, vanished, leaving only the night sky, full of stars.

# CHAPTER 40

A scream jolted me awake. Richard was there, holding me in an instant, and I realized I had been the one screaming. "Another bad dream?" he asked.

I coughed and looked around. We were in a room I recognized, sharing a queen-sized bed. The walls were plaster, painted a soft yellow. Several windows were letting the morning sun shine through.

I yawned and stretched and slowly came back to myself. Oh, yes. We were in Richard's house in Cornwall, England. We had come here together after that last ghastly, yet beautiful, night at Cliffside. I couldn't remember all of it, not then. It was like my brain was shutting out what was too painful for me to endure, allowing me to only remember the good stuff, the happy times. But bits and pieces had been haunting my dreams for months.

We had settled into life together now, but early on, it wasn't an easy road for us. I questioned everything. I missed Nate terribly, and I wasn't sure if I, Norrie, really loved Richard, or if Temperance had been the one loving him all along. I knew it was silly, and I knew it could never be, but I began to suspect I was in love with a ghost. I entertained thoughts of leaving, of setting up a life of my own and simply waiting to join Nate when the time came. But something Harriet had said to me lingered in my mind—live life to the fullest. I knew I couldn't simply wait to die like so many had at Cliffside. I had to embrace the here and now.

And so, over the first weeks and months we were in Cornwall, Richard's love for me pulled me along. He was so patient, so kind. We really got to know each other there, in his house on the edge of the sea. Each day something new about him tugged at my heartstrings. Each day, he made me laugh. It didn't take long for me to truly know the feelings I had for him were real. I still don't know which of them I would've chosen, had I a choice to make. But I knew I loved Richard Banks now. And he loved me back.

Later that morning, we were in the kitchen drinking coffee when there was a knock at the door.

Richard opened it to find Diana standing there. "What are you doing here?" he asked her. "I thought I told you to stay away."

"I don't care what you told me," she said, pushing past him. "I'm here for Norrie."

"Diana?" I said, standing up from my chair.

She nodded. "That's right, Eleanor," she said to me. "I'm here to see how you are."

Against Richard's loud protests and better judgment, I spent the rest of the day with Diana, learning. As we walked along Cornwall's windswept coastline, we talked of our time at Cliffside, and slowly, the memories began to return.

She told me what happened to the others, after we all fled the property that horrible night, making our way through the woods to the road that led to town.

Both Brynn and Cassandra spent weeks in the hospital and longer than that in therapy after they were released, but both recovered. Neither remembered what happened to them—what Temperance did to them. Only time would tell how complete their recoveries would be. Henry went back to his home down south and continued his painting. And Diana herself had given up her position as a professor of poetry and begun teaching a course in demonology, wanting to pass on her knowledge.

It seemed like everyone was getting along just fine. Except for me. But I suppose that was to be expected. They had all gone through a trauma, but I was at the epicenter of it all.

A few days have passed since Diana's visit. I don't know if I'll ever fully move past what happened to me during those few weeks at Cliffside. You just don't forget an evil that strong, residing inside you. But I'll do all I can with what I have, and I'm determined to follow Harriet's advice. Life is for the living, and I'll grab every ounce of joy I can.

As for Nate, he has not visited me, not yet anyway. I often wonder if he stays away because he sees how happy I am with Richard. But I ache to see him again, to hear his laughter, to look into his eyes. His last words to me were *I'll be seeing you, Norrie Harper.* I hope, with every part of my being, that he will. If not in this world, then in the next.

And Cliffside itself? It burned to the ground that night. Diana told me that people in the area say the property has a malevolence about it, a residue of the evil that took hold of that beautiful and rugged coastline when Temperance was born. Parents caution their children to keep away from there, but they don't have to be warned. They can feel it.

And so, we are at the end of my strange tale. I don't think I'll speak of it ever again. I want to get on with my future with Richard and bury the memory of Temperance Dare in the past forever.

But I will leave you with a word of warning. If ever a feeling of dread or foreboding overcomes you, and if ever you feel pulled to a place, inexplicably, the way I did, take heed. It may be trying to tell you—something wicked your way comes.

# ACKNOWLEDGMENTS

I was inspired to write this story by tales I've heard about a real TB sanatorium that was located on a cliff overlooking Lake Superior in Bayfield, Wisconsin. It was called Pureair Sanatorium, aptly named for the crisp, pure, Lake Superior air that swirls through the forests there. My grandfather was a patient at Pureair back in the day and recovered. My great-aunt, however, died there as a girl. They really were called "waiting rooms for death," because there was little doctors could do to treat tuberculosis. Confined to a sanatorium and isolated from the population at large, people with TB just waited to either get better or . . . not.

The sanatorium is long since gone—one of the best restaurants in the area arose in its place decades later on what's still called Old San Road—but many institutions like it have been repurposed into golf clubs and other types of recreational retreats throughout the country.

When I was just beginning to formulate the idea for this book, I was giving a talk at a high school near Bayfield and one of the teachers asked what I was currently working on. I told her I was thinking of setting a tale at the Pureair Sanatorium, imagining it had not been torn down but instead repurposed into a retreat for artists and writers. Her eyes lit up. "I grew up here and used to babysit for the family that lived in the former doctor's house on the san grounds," she said to me. "This was before the san itself was torn down. I was always terrified. Parents in this area used to get their kids to behave by threatening to drop them off at the old, abandoned san. Everyone who grew up here was scared to death of the place."

A tingle went up my spine and I knew I had the right setting for this rather dark and twisted tale.

As always, I have several people to thank for the help they gave me as I brought this story to life. My friend David Hileman's father was in a TB sanatorium when he was a young man. He used to tell Dave stories about leading nightly forays out of the san and getting into mischief with the other patients. I believe chickens were involved at some point. Thank you, Dave, for sharing those stories with me. Archie Abbott is based on your dad. I can just hear your mom and dad clinking glasses and toasting that one.

To my friend and agent Jennifer Weltz, you are a treasure. Not only do you make me laugh every time I talk to you, but you are my greatest supporter and champion. I don't know where I'd be without you and your stellar team at the Jean V. Naggar Literary Agency but I certainly wouldn't be putting the finishing touches on my fourth book and starting my fifth.

To Faith Black Ross and Danielle Marshall, thank you both for loving this story and for all of the work you did to make Temperance's terrifying tale the best it could be.

To all of the bookstore owners and booksellers who have placed my books into customers' hands over the years—you have made my career. I am truly grateful for your support and your friendship and I will do everything I can to bring readers into your stores for events, should you be kind enough to ask me back.

To Pamela Klinger-Horn, one of the strongest champions of authors in the Twin Cities (I like to call her the warrior princess of books), I hope you know how much each and every author whose life you have touched appreciates your hard work and dedication. We are truly lucky to have you in our collective corner. Now you must take a picture of this book with your dog and post it online.

And to you, the reader holding this book in your hands right now. I've met many of you on my book tours, and I want you to know that I really do write with you in mind and I'm so grateful you've read my books. Thank you from the bottom of my heart.

I sincerely hope you enjoyed this tale. I'll have another one for you very soon.

# ABOUT THE AUTHOR

*Photo 2010 © Steve Burmeister,*

Wendy Webb knew from the minute she read *A Wrinkle in Time* at age eleven that she was destined to be a writer. After two decades as a journalist, writing for varied publications including *USA Today*, the *Huffington Post*, the *Star Tribune*, *Midwest Living*, and others, Wendy wrote her first novel, *The Tale of Halcyon Crane*. When it won the 2011 Minnesota Book Award for genre fiction, she started writing fiction full-time. Her second and third novels, *The Fate of Mercy Alban* and *The Vanishing*, established her as a leading suspense novelist, who reviewers are calling the Queen of the Northern Gothic. She lives in Minneapolis with her part-time dog, Zeus, and is at work on her next novel. Visit her online at www.wendykwebb.com and on Facebook and Instagram as wendywebbauthor.